Celestial Convergence

T.A. McEvoy

DRAGONS OF ACARI

T McEvoy

Copyright Registration Number: Copyright © 2025 T.A. McEvoy. All rights reserved. U.S. Copyright registration pending.

Library of Congress Control Number: 2025920186

Book Cover by: NovelStormDesigns.etsy.com

Map by: Rob Donovan (Snikt5 on Fiverr.com)

First Edition: 2025

Printed in the United States of America

9781964250199

Imprint: T.McEvoy

A Word Before You Begin

Welcome to The Dragons of Vacari series!

You're in the right place if you love high-stakes adventure, legendary dragons, and a richly crafted world steeped in magic, mystery, and danger. The Dragons of Vacari is a sweeping fantasy saga filled with intense dragon battles, deep friendships, ancient secrets, and the ever-present struggle between light and darkness. Whether you're here for the action, the emotional journeys, or the evolving lore, this world was built to draw you in—and keep you coming back for more.

Planned as a nine-book epic, The Dragons of Vacari will unfold gradually, with each volume expanding the world and deepening the story. While the series is connected, every installment can be enjoyed as a stand-alone adventure. For those who read or listen in order, however, you'll uncover layered mysteries, character arcs, and long-building revelations that reward the journey book by book.

From noble dragonriders and treacherous alliances to awakening powers and ancient threats rising from the shadows, this is a tale meant to challenge heroes—and readers alike.

While you await the next release, you can explore more of Vacari through exclusive content on my YouTube channel. Just search for "Theresa McEvoy" for behind-the-scenes lore, worldbuilding, and character insights. You can also find me on TikTok under T.A. McEvoy.

https://www.youtube.com/@theresamcevoy612

Your patience and support mean the world to me as I bring each chapter of this story to life. Thank you for joining me on this adventure—I hope you enjoy the twists, turns, and surprises that await!

— T.A. McEvoy

A Note from the Keeper of Dragons

The Living Dragons of Vacari

I have always loved dragons.

In the world of Vacari, they are far more than beasts or background legends. Here, dragons are living, thinking, feeling beings with their own choices to make, burdens to bear, and destinies to forge.

My dragons are characters, with voices, emotions, and personalities as complex as any hero or villain. Some are fierce protectors, others cunning schemers—and a few... well, a few might just surprise you along the way.

I know this approach may not resonate with every reader. But for me, it is part of what makes Vacari truly alive.

Dragons are not merely part of the world—they *are* the world, woven into its very breath and heartbeat.

Thank you for stepping into their story.

I hope you enjoy meeting the dragons of *Vacari* as much as I have loved bringing them to life.

World Map

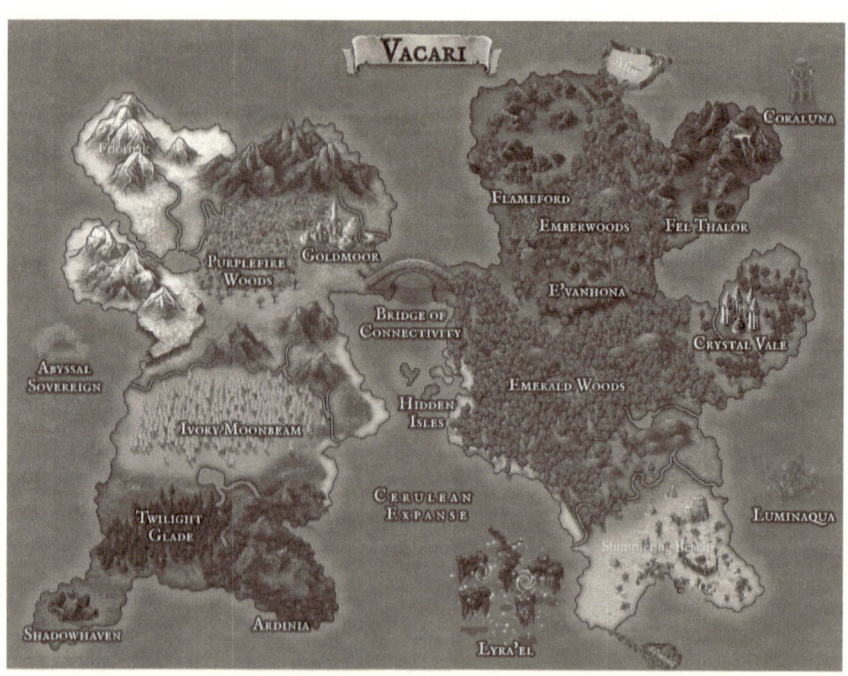

Vacari – The Living Realm

Dragons of Acari

To One Who Walks Among the Stars

Robert Otto
Beloved husband of my cherished friend, Caroline.
Your spirit ascends beyond mortal shores,
woven now among the constellations,
a sentinel of light and memory.
Your laughter, bright as dawn,
and the warmth of your humor
echo in every heart you touched
treasures the eternal cannot take.
Though you walk the halls of the eternal,
your legacy endures
a star that shall never fall.
(April 26, 2025)

DRAGONS OF VACARI

Dedication

Tom Vick

To my wonderful boyfriend, Tom—
thank you for reading every draft of this book, even when they were
barely stitched together.

Since we met, my life has grown brighter in more ways than I can express.

Your steady encouragement, fierce loyalty, and endless belief in me mean
more than words can say.

Special thanks, too, for fending off the marketers—though I think you
scared them off for good!

You are my anchor, my champion, and the reason I keep moving forward.

Roots of an ancient tree

Thomas E. Vick, Sr.

Beloved father of Tom Vick

Like the roots of an ancient tree,

your presence anchored generations.

Though the branches now stretch without you,

they carry your strength,

your laughter,

your love.

Your legacy stands unbroken—

a shelter for all who follow.

(August 19, 2025)

Contents

Prologue
Shadows in Lyra'el

The chamber was silent, lit only by the slow pulse of violet flame each hiss a secret breathed into the dark. At its heart, Rhys stood before the brazier that never needed tending. The air around him shimmered, thin as breath yet heavy as judgment. Blackened stone walls, seared by ancient magic, drank the firelight instead of reflecting it, their runes buried beneath layers of soot.

From the shadows came a voice that was smooth, ageless, and calm. It carried no gender, no origin, only a weight too deliberate to be anything but power.

"You know what you must do."

The violet glow painted Rhys's skin like war paint. His eyes burned like molten lava beneath the hood of his shadow-dark hair. He inclined his head, graceful, precise.

"Of course," he said, voice a low thrum of restrained might. "The Order will follow me. They already whisper."

The shadows shifted not with movement, but with intent.

"And if Radiantus returns?"

The air contracted, colder, as though the name itself were a wound reopened. It was not merely spoken; it was invoked, carrying the chill of prophecy and the sting of unfinished war.

Rhys did not blink.

"Then I will be ready. I will know the instant the Platinum Dragon sets foot in Lyra'el. And if others come..." A shard of crimson flared in his gaze. "I will know their names before they draw breath in this realm."

He did not voice the rest, though the thought lingered like ash in the air. If she came, the one whose light had fractured the Abyss and shattered Vuarus's final gambit, he would be ready for her as well. Her survival had cost them both Vuarus and Phoenix everything. It had denied him not only victory, but destiny itself.

"You will not act unless commanded."

"Understood." Rhys placed a hand over his chest. It was not loyalty, but strategy. "Your faith honors me. I will not fail."

The silence that followed pressed close, heavy as a vow sealed in fire. The violet glow dimmed. The voice withdrew. The presence was gone.

Rhys did not move. His face betrayed nothing, yet within, his mind sharpened like a blade drawn across stone. Every promise he had spoken was another step toward something greater. The Order was only a piece of the game. He aimed for the board itself.

Deep inside him, ambition stirred cold, patient, ravenous. Part of him almost wished for Radiantus return. It would make the victory sweeter.

For now, he would obey.

But when the moment came, it would not be obedience that decided Lyra'el's fate.

It would be him.

Chapter 1
The Echoes of Chains

The grove lay silent, the air steeped in ash and dew.

To Valeon, it was too quiet, unnaturally so, as though even the grove itself held its breath after the storm.

Sunlight filtered through the canopy in fractured golden strands, but even that radiance seemed hesitant. Emberwings drifted like wandering memories, small guardians of fire and remembrance. Their wings shimmered with cinders that glowed but did not burn, each spark no more than the flicker of a candle at a grave.

Beneath the scorched branches of an ancient flame tree, its bark blackened by spells and steel, yet stubbornly clinging to life, Valeon stood before the brazier that never needed tending. The air around him wavered, thin as breath, heavy as judgment. Gnarled roots curled through the earth like veins that refused to wither. The tree endured. He was less sure of himself. His own resolve felt brittle, threatening to break beneath the weight of truths left unspoken.

He fixed his gaze on the sky, where the first stars pierced the veil of dusk. He did not look at the city below. He could not.

Aurelia lay silent, still mending. Keisha moved with a new stiffness, graceful, yet a shadow clung to every step. Both had suffered because of him. Because of what he had not said. Because of what he could not.

The words had never belonged to him.

The lie had never been his to speak.

His jaw tightened.

Why, Father? Why did you bind us to Maelgrim?

Memory pressed in like cold iron. His father's voice, calm and assured, had spoken of legacy and loyalty in the same breath as sacrifice. Promises made in desperation, bartered with a figure Valeon had known only by whispers and dread: Maelgrim Shadowwalker.

A pact. Sealed in shadow.

Whatever power, protection, or favor it had once granted had died with his father.

All that remained was the chain.

He had not agreed to it.

He had not even known.

But that did not matter. Not to Maelgrim. Not to fate.

The burden had passed to him, silent and inescapable.

"I didn't choose this," he whispered, voice brittle. "I never chose any of it."

An Emberwing drifted down, its light falling like a benediction. It perched on a blackened root, wings flickering gold, its glow steady and unjudging.

"I never wanted to deceive them," he said, still staring at the horizon. "I only wanted to protect them. But it wasn't my truth to speak only the weight I carried in silence."

The Emberwing gave no answer. It only lingered, a fragile ember in a grove steeped in regret.

But something deeper stirred.

A spark of defiance.

Small. Fierce.

Unextinguished.

He exhaled sharply.

Gailen.

The memory rasped with shadow-magic, cold and hungry: The prince could be eliminated before his training begins. One less variable. One less threat.

And his answer, trembling yet unyielding: No.

That had been the first choice he had made for himself, the one line he refused to cross. If nothing else, he could hold onto that.

Had he faltered, Gailen might never have lived to ride a dragon. Never discovered who he truly was. Never stood as a beacon of hope for a realm on the edge of ruin.

Valeon closed his eyes.

I saved him.

And yet... was it enough?

The question coiled in his chest, corrosive, unresolved.

Would it have been better to confess then, before the bloodshed, before the revelations, before bonds were tested and broken? Had his silence ever protected them... or only delayed the inevitable?

"I should have told them when this began," he murmured. "Told Gailen. Told Keisha. Warned them before the cracks spread."

But fear had sealed his lips. Shame had nailed them shut.

His father had welcomed Maelgrim's shadow into their bloodline, reaped its power, and left only ashes for the rest.

None of us gained anything, Valeon thought bitterly. Only Father.

If not for his mother's desperate courage, he might have been consumed by that legacy before he had the chance to resist. He remembered her trembling hands pressing a flame-carved pendant into his palm.

So, you remember your fire, she had whispered, even if the world tries to bury it.

The Emberwing circled once around his shoulders, scattering sparks, before retreating to the branch. Its glow flared, brighter than before, as though it had heard him.

Valeon lifted his gaze again to the stars. This time, he did not look away. Fear pressed at his ribs, but shame no longer held him.

If they hated him for what he had hidden, so be it.

He would carry that weight.

But he would no longer carry the lie.

They deserved more.

His shoulders squared. He stepped toward the waiting city, Crystal Vale's lanterns flickering in the twilight, its spires veiled in fading smoke.

This was not a rebellion.

This was reclamation.

He aimed not for a piece of the game.

He aimed for the board itself.

Chapter 2
The Weight of Truth

The palace doors opened with a soft creak, golden light spilling across the polished floor like a path waiting to be followed. Yet the air beyond felt heavier than it should, as though the stone itself braced for what was coming.

Valeon paused at the threshold. His heart beat too quickly, too loudly.

Guards dipped their heads. Servants bowed in passing. Their greetings blurred into a dull hum, drowned beneath the weight of the request he was about to make... and the consequences it might unleash.

At the antechamber to the throne hall, a scribe looked up from a scroll, eyes widening faintly.

"I would like to see King Manard," Valeon said, his voice measured, almost quiet.

The scribe gave a crisp nod and slipped into the adjoining room. Moments later, the door opened, and King Manard emerged, his robes trailing like morning mist. The king's watchful gaze warmed at the sight of his visitor.

"Valeon," he greeted, smiling. "You need not stand on ceremony. You are always welcome here."

Valeon bowed his head, though the gesture felt weighted, reluctant.

"Thank you, Your Majesty." His gaze lifted, faltered, then fell once more. "I... would ask something further of you."

Manard stepped closer, his smile softening into concern. "Of course."

Valeon drew in a steadying breath. Beneath his words, tension coiled tight. Memory intruded—his mother's hurried whispers, her hands pressing him toward safety, away from promises he had never made. His father's shadowed legacy pressed hard against his chest, but he forced the words free.

"Could you gather a few people for me? Prince Gailen, Thalorian, Kaelorn, Keisha... and Ong." He hesitated. "And I would ask you to be there as well. In one of the private chambers, if possible." His voice dropped lower. "There is something I must tell you all."

The king's brows lifted, but he did not question. His gaze sharpened instead, reading the tautness in Valeon's shoulders, the flicker of doubt in his eyes, the fingers clenched against the stone.

"Of course," Manard said softly. He gestured to a steward, who bowed and vanished without a word.

Valeon inclined his head again, the knot in his chest drawing tighter as he turned away. He followed the passage toward the conference rooms reserved for strategy and secrets. Tapestries lined the walls, councils of kings and dragons woven in threads of firelit gold, their ancient colors glowing in the hush of enchanted lanterns.

When he entered, the chamber was dim and still. A long table stretched the length of the room, flanked by high-backed chairs of dark wood. A wide window looked out upon the horizon, where twilight had deepened into full night.

He did not sit. Instead, he braced both hands on the stone sill, gazing down at Crystal Vale shimmering in the starlight.

Will they ask me to leave?

The thought cut deep.

Or worse?

His reflection stared back from the glass, haunted, uncertain, heavy with truths left unspoken.

Footsteps echoed down the corridor. Valeon knew their rhythm steady, certain.

King Manard entered first, with Gailen at his side.

"There you are," Gailen said, grinning. "Stare out a window long enough and you'll start to look like some brooding noble from a tragic play. Don't tell me sulking has become a hobby?"

Valeon offered a faint smile, but no words.

The grin slipped from Gailen's face. He studied his friend more closely the rigid set of shoulders, the restless hand, the unease buried behind his silence.

"You all right?" he asked.

Before Valeon could answer, Manard placed a steadying hand on his son's shoulder and guided him farther inside. "Let's wait until the others arrive."

They moved toward the polished table beneath the lantern glow. The air itself seemed to hold its breath, weighted and expectant. Even the flames in their sconces bent low, as though wary of the tension that clung to Valeon.

The door creaked again. Thalorian entered, his stride measured, eyes narrowing as they flicked from Gailen to Valeon. His jaw tightened.

"Did I interrupt something?"

"Not yet," Gailen said with a shrug.

Thalorian folded his arms and took up his place against the wall, silent, watchful.

A moment later, Keisha appeared, her step calm yet purposeful, Ong beside her like a shadow at her shoulder. Behind them came Kaelorn, relaxed in carriage but intent in his gaze, eyes lingering on Valeon as if reading the weight that pressed against him.

No one spoke.

The chamber, built for strategy and counsel, now brimmed with silence. Tension thickened like winter mist, curling in every corner.

Valeon stood at the window, hands braced on the cold stone sill. Torchlight flickered in the glass, gilding his reflection. Beyond, Crystal Vale shimmered beneath the stars.

His reflection stared back haunted, uncertain, burdened by truths unsaid.

King Manard's voice finally broke the silence, warm yet edged with command.

"Valeon. Everyone is here, as you asked. What troubles you?"

Valeon turned slowly. His gaze swept the room: Gailen's concern, Thalorian's guarded stillness, Kaelorn's quiet scrutiny, Keisha's steady encouragement. Last, Ong, his eyes unreadable, his presence unshaken.

Valeon's throat tightened. Words threatened, then died. He closed his eyes.

You can no longer run from this.

When he lifted his head again, his expression had changed. Still uncertain, yet no longer wavering.

I... I do not know where to begin," he said, his voice rough. "But there is something I must tell you. All of you. And I do not know how you will take it."

His gaze flicked to King Manard. "But I cannot keep it to myself any longer."

Silence stretched a heartbeat too long.

Then Keisha stepped forward, her voice calm, gentle. "Take your time, Valeon."

He looked at her, really looked, and found no judgment in her eyes. Only patience. Steadiness. As always.

He nodded once, drew a breath.

"Perhaps... it is best to start at the beginning."

The hush deepened. Gailen straightened. Thalorian's eyes narrowed. Even Pumpkin, resting near the door, lifted her head. The weight of his words cracked the stillness, just enough to let the storm seep in.

"I was born outside Fel Thalor," Valeon said. "My mother sent me to Etharyon, seeking safety for me. But for the first twelve years of my life... my home was outside Fel Thalor."

The ripple of surprise was subtle—no gasps, no outcry, only shifting posture: Thalorian's brow lifting, Gailen leaning forward, Kaelorn's fingers tightening against his arm.

I lived in Etharyon until I was old enough to train as a warrior," Ong said, his frown softening. "My mother, Seraphina, sent me to Crystal Vale to study under King Manard..." He paused, the title catching in his throat before he corrected himself, softer but certain. "...my father." His voice carried both hesitation and a quiet pride, the weight of truth still new upon him. "Leaving her behind was the hardest thing I've ever done. Etharyon stood alone then, cut off after the attack on the king. For a time, we had to make do without aid from the rest of Vacari. Still... it always felt apart."

Thalorian's gaze cut toward him, precise and cold. "Etharyon was once veiled, hidden in distance and shadow. But those days are past. Trade now flows with Vacari's cities, and Etharyon stands openly among them once more."

Valeon lowered his gaze, fixing it on the far wall as if the memory had carved itself into the stone.

"My mother... she knew something was wrong. She never spoke it, but she knew what my father had done—what he had promised. What kind of legacy did he leave us?"

His hands flexed against the sill.

"She had little, barely enough to live. But she scraped together what she could and paid someone to smuggle me out. She said it was for my safety that if I stayed, I'd be dragged into something I could never escape."

His voice dropped, weighted with memory. "She was not wrong."

The lanterns crackled faintly. Outside, the wind pressed against the windows, reminding him that the world still turned while his truth unraveled here.

"She gave me her last coin," he whispered. "Sent me to Etharyon. I knew no one. I barely understood their tongue at first."

A faint smile tugged at his lips. "But I survived. Odd jobs, mostly... though I had a knack for mixing drinks. So, I worked the cantinas."

He glanced at Gailen, touched with wistful humor.

"That's where I was when we met."

Gailen tilted his head, glancing at Ong before looking back. "So... that cantina where Thalorian, Kaelorn, and I found you was your place of work?"

Valeon nodded. For a moment, amusement cracked the tension.

"Yes. And the Druchii you saw? He accused me of cheating him over a rare vintage. I told him if he wanted to rob someone, he should at least learn what a clean glass looked like."

A ghost of a smirk touched his mouth, quickly fading. A ripple of chuckles stirred the chamber, even coaxing a brief, sharp exhale from Thalorian that might have been a laugh.

But the mirth died as swiftly as it had come. Shadows reclaimed Valeon's face as he turned back toward the window.

"That is not what I came to tell you."

His voice was low now. Steady. Heavy.

You need to know... my father served Maelgrim Shadowwalker."

The room shifted.

No one spoke. Yet the silence roared louder than any cry of shock.

Valeon kept his gaze on the night beyond the window.

"He was given power enough to sway courts, to bend men and lords to his will. But it was not free. In return, he pledged our family. Not just himself. All of us. Blood and name."

His hand curled against the stone sill, its chill biting into his palm.

"My mother and I gained nothing from that bargain. No protection. No honor. Only scorn. Whispers. Trouble."

He stopped.

Keisha's gaze flicked toward Ong, who met it with narrowed eyes and a tense brow, but said nothing. Kaelorn stood with his arms crossed, his face unreadable in the lantern light. Thalorian straightened, his watchfulness sharpening into something more complex.

And Gailen... Gailen looked at Valeon as though he were hearing a story only to realize, too late, that he had been written into its final page.

At last, Valeon turned from the window. His eyes passed over each of them until they came to rest on Ong.

His voice was quieter now, no longer brittle, no longer trembling.

Only honest.

"I vowed never to return home."

The words lingered in the air like smoke.

"But then I heard whispers. That a warrior had risen fierce, unstoppable. One who struck down Maelgrim's son."

He let the name hang there.

"Ong Swifthammer."

His gaze locked on Ong's. There was no challenge in his eyes, no plea. Only truth.

"So when Gailen spoke of returning to Crystal Vale, I thought... perhaps it was safe. Perhaps the shadow on my family had finally lifted."

He shook his head slowly.

"I was wrong."

Again, silence fell. The lanterns hissed in their sconces. Outside, the wind whispered against the glass.

Kaelorn broke the stillness, his voice low, cautious. "How were you wrong, Valeon? What happened?"

Valeon nodded once. "A few weeks after we reached Crystal Vale... I was summoned."

The word seemed to darken the chamber.

"I did not wish to go. I fought it. But some power greater than my own will—dragged me under."

His hand lifted, faltered, then dropped heavily to his side.

"I remember no path, only that I stood within Fel Thalor."

The name rippled through the room. Even Thalorian's expression shifted, his eyes sharpening like a blade unsheathed.

"I stood before a presence immense, ancient, cold. Familiar, yet veiled. I never saw their face. They never stepped into the light. But their power..." He shook his head. "It was stronger than anything I have ever felt."

His voice caught.

Ong stirred, but Keisha's hand came to rest on his shoulder—not to restrain, but to steady. Her gaze urged patience.

Ong nodded once, jaw tight, eyes fixed on Valeon.

The moment hung, charged like the hush before a storm.

Valeon looked at Ong the warrior who had unknowingly given him hope then at Gailen, then at King Manard.

This may be the end of everything. But they deserve the truth.

"The figure told me I was still bound by obligation," he said, voice low but unwavering. "Even though the Shadowwalkers are gone, the pact holds."

He did not look away.

"I argued. I told them I had never sworn it. That I had never received their gift. But..."

His eyes closed briefly.

"Their power was too great. It crushed the air around me. Burned through my mind."

A breath, sharp and trembling.

"And at last reluctantly I yielded."

The room shifted again. Still silent. Yet no longer still.

Valeon opened his eyes and fixed them on Gailen.

"The first command they gave me... was to kill you."

The words dragged from his throat like stone tearing across flesh. He braced against the window, jaw set, gaze falling before he forced it upward again. Meeting his friend's eyes cost him more than he cared to admit. Silence snapped into place, taut and cutting.

"They wanted me to stop you from bonding with Aurelia. To end your training. They spoke of the Crystal Dragon's legacy—of the Crystalbow. They knew things... ancient things. But I did not care."

He shook his head, slow and deliberate. "I refused."

His voice steadied, no longer trembling, no longer hiding.

"They said if I disobeyed, they would kill me. And I told them..." He drew in a breath, eyes flicking between Gailen and Manard. "I told them to go ahead."

Silence.

"And they did not," he whispered. "They let me live. Instead... they changed the order. They commanded me to describe Gailen. Enough for them to send an Obsidian Dragon to strike at him in the first battle."

He faltered, voice sinking into the hush. That was all.

He stood unmoving, breath shallow, awaiting judgment, fury, banishment, perhaps worse.

Gailen's stare held steady, unreadable. But it was King Manard whose face shifted most. The warmth had gone from his eyes, replaced by something colder, heavier. His silence weighed more than condemnation.

Valeon's shoulders drew taut. He lifted one hand slightly, his voice hoarse.

"Please... let me finish before you speak. Before you cast judgment. Or worse."

Neither moved. The silence stretched, drawn tight as a bowstring.

"I was summoned again," he said, forcing the words out. "Not just once. Several times."

He glanced at Keisha, then at Ong, before letting his gaze pass over the others.

"I tried to twist their commands. To give them shadows instead of truths. But..." His voice broke to a rasp. "I failed. I revealed things I should never have spoken."

Shame clung to him like frost.

"And the last time..." His breath caught.

"It was after you, Gailen, asked me to tend the wounded."

His eyes lifted to his friend's raw, unguarded.

"I was summoned again. They told me an attack was coming."

The silence deepened, heavy as the air before a storm.

"I did not warn you."

The final word tore from him.

"If I had... Aurelia would never have been wounded."

He turned then, slowly, to Keisha.

"You would never have been wounded."

His voice cracked. He bowed his head, shoulders collapsing under the weight of it. Not dramatized. Not a plea. Only the raw confession of a man who had hidden too long, now waiting for judgment to fall.

The lanterns flickered overhead. The chamber held its breath.

Valeon did not lift his head.

He waited.

The silence was shattered.

"You what?!"

Ong's voice cracked through the chamber like a war hammer against stone. The lanterns flared, casting shadows that slashed across the walls.

Kaelorn winced at the force. Thalorian's head snapped toward him. Keisha flinched. Gailen stepped back, eyes wide.

Ong surged forward, fists clenched, fury rolling from him in waves.

"You knew they were going to attack and said nothing?" he roared. "Keisha nearly died! She could barely stand, and you" his voice broke, ragged with rage "you let it happen?!"

Valeon did not lift his head.

"If anything had happened to her, if she hadn't pulled through—"

"Enough!"

King Manard's voice thundered, cutting through the storm.

Ong froze, chest heaving, but his eyes still burned. The king stepped forward, regal composure stripped away, raw fury kindling in its place.

"You endangered my son," Manard said, each word cold as steel. "You endangered my people my kingdom. Do you understand what you have done?"

Valeon flinched but did not answer.

"And worse," Manard pressed, his voice rising, "you knew. You knew something would happen, and you let it unfold, like a coward watching from the shadows!"

"You lied to me!"

Gailen's voice cracked like a whip, his fists clenched white.

Valeon finally lifted his head—and Gailen's face, raw with betrayal, nearly undid him.

"You stood beside *me*. Fought with me. Ate with me. Laughed with me." Gailen's voice trembled. "And all the while, you gave them enough to strike? Aurelia was wounded because of you!"

The air itself seemed to pulse with their anger.

Then Keisha stepped forward, her voice calm yet edged like tempered steel.

"If you three are finished shouting... may I ask something?"

The silence that followed was different. This one listened.

All eyes turned to her, Ong still seething, Gailen taut with betrayal, Manard cold with fury. No one spoke. They yielded the space to her.

Keisha faced Valeon, her expression composed, unreadable.

"While they are right to be angry," she said steadily, "I have two questions."

Valeon met her gaze, uncertain.

"First—why now? Why tell us this at all?"

He hesitated, then let the words fall, stripped of pretense.

"Because I could not live with the lie any longer. Not after everything. Not after... all of you."

His gaze swept the room. "I knew you cared. And that made it worse. Every day I kept silent, it coiled tighter. I could not carry it anymore."

Keisha inclined her head, her face shadowed with pain. Not forgiveness reckoning. Memory flickered in her eyes: dragonfire's burn, the helplessness she had sworn never to feel again.

Her voice cut cleanly through the stillness.

"Second... how did this figure claim any right over you? Because from what I know, what my people have safeguarded, not even Maelgrim, not even Phoenix, could bind blood and legacy beyond death."

She folded her arms, gaze unwavering. "I will confirm with my father. But that pact should have died with yours."

Valeon's brow furrowed. He stepped from the window, careful, deliberate.

"I do not know. They said the binding remained, that it lived in me. As if it were carved into my blood."

His eyes searched hers. "What did you mean, that not even the Shadowwalkers could enforce it?"

Keisha's gaze deepened, her silence weighted with knowledge not yet spoken.

"That," she said, "is what I intend to discover."

Kaelorn exhaled, the sound quiet but heavy. He glanced around the chamber: Gailen's fists still clenched white, Ong's fury simmering, Manard's doubt flickering sharp across his face. Then he looked back at Valeon.

"I do not approve of what you did," Kaelorn said evenly. "You should have told us sooner."

Valeon's shoulders tightened. He did not argue.

But..." Kaelorn said at last, "I have seen how power twists. How fear cages. I understand why you did not come to us when it began. That does not make it right." He gave a faint shrug. "It only makes you human. Or whatever lofty word you'd choose while brooding into your books."

A fragile attempt at levity, but it eased the weight, if only slightly.

Thalorian's voice followed, cooler, yet not unkind.

"Valeon is no warrior. We all know it. He was not raised for battle, nor trained to withstand the kind of pressure he describes." His gaze flicked to Gailen, then to Manard.

"That does not absolve him. But perhaps it means we do not hang him yet."

Valeon bowed his head lower. Every word cut and yet, in its way, comforted.

Keisha straightened. This was more than betrayal. It was legacy oaths, bloodlines, and protections older than any crown. An ancient weight lent steel to her bearing.

She turned to King Manard, her tone calm but firm.

"Allow me to summon my father, Lord Karrenen. And ask him to bring Lysander, God of the Sea, and Kadona, Goddess of Light, defender of the Eladrin."

The chamber stilled.

"If this binding is what I believe it to be," she continued, "the gods will bring it before the Council. And the shadow will lose its hold on Valeon."

Her gaze softened as it met his.

"After that... we will decide how to proceed."

Manard gave a slow nod. "Do what you must. I trust your judgment."

Valeon lifted his head enough to meet her eyes. "Thank you," he whispered. Not relief, only the raw weight of a kindness he had not expected.

Keisha's smile was faint, but knowing. She turned to Gailen and Ong.

"I think you two need a walk."

Valeon blinked, her words falling like a gentle note after thunder. His chest rose in a slow, uneven breath. The knot behind his ribs loosened not absolution, but recognition. Mercy had come before judgment was finished.

He watched her with something close to awe. Or perhaps fear that he did not deserve it.

Ong's fists were still clenched, his jaw grinding like steel on stone, but he did not argue. Gailen looked as though he might protest, yet Keisha's lifted brow silenced him.

The silence between them stretched taut, betrayal straining against restraint.

"Go," she said. "Walk off the fire."

Then, softer: "Pumpkin."

From the hallway, the sleek black panther padded forward, emerald eyes gleaming. She brushed against Ong's leg before circling to Keisha.

Valeon watched her with quiet recognition. He had met her before, but now her presence felt different—as though she, too, had judged... and chosen not to turn away.

Keisha bent low, resting her brow to Pumpkin's.

"Keep them out of trouble," she whispered.

Pumpkin gave a low chuff, then padded after Gailen and Ong, her tail flicking once like punctuation.

As the door closed, Kaelorn exhaled and gestured to the table.

"Well. We may as well sit. No sense in pacing until the gods arrive."

Thalorian inclined his head and lowered himself into a chair. Keisha followed after a moment's pause.

Valeon lingered, uncertain. At last, he drew out a chair and sank into it, his fingers brushing the worn armrest. For a breath, he let himself feel the weight of the gesture being allowed to sit among them again.

Disbelief flickered through him. And with it, a quiet, aching hope he had not dared in years.

The storm had passed—

For now.

Chapter 3
Wings of Arrival

The trees of Emerald Woods swayed gently in the afternoon breeze, emerald leaves scattering light like jeweled canopies. A faint warmth lingered in the air, edged with the scent of lightning-kissed pine. Then the birds fell silent, and the wind shifted—carrying something more: a presence.

Lord Karrenen paused at the clearing's edge, his gaze lifting skyward.

Beside him, Lysander's trident shimmered with a sea-blue glow, sensing the divine before sight confirmed it. Kadona's golden cloak caught the wind as she tilted her head, already smiling faintly.

A vast shadow swept across the treetops.

Moments later, a dragon descended with majestic grace, wings folding like silken banners of starlight. Platinum scales gleamed like forged moonlight as his massive form touched down beyond the trees, the earth quivering softly beneath his weight.

Radiantus had returned.

Kadona drew a quiet breath, her eyes flicking to Lysander and Karrenen. Even for them, the moment held weight. Radiantus did not descend lightly.

"Well now," she said with a warm laugh, stepping forward. "We do not often see you beyond the heavens."

Radiantus inclined his head, voice resonant yet calm. "I arrived only recently. When I sensed your presence, yours, Lysander's, and Lord Karrenen's, I came to see why you traveled toward Crystal Vale."

Karrenen bowed slightly. "My daughter, Keisha, sent for us. She says there is a matter requiring divine attention—something unusual. Possibly dangerous."

Kadona's gaze lingered on Radiantus, thoughtful. "Then perhaps you should join us. If Keisha calls upon the gods, you may well be needed."

Radiantus studied her for a long moment, starlight flickering in his eyes. "I agree." His wings lifted slightly, scattering platinum light. "If the matter is urgent, climb onto my back. I will carry us faster than magic or foot."

Lysander arched a brow. "Then do not let us fall, Radiantus."

A low rumble echoed from the dragon's chest, a rare chuckle. "You have my word."

One by one, the god, the goddess, and the elven lord climbed onto his back. With a single, mighty beat, Radiantus rose, Emerald Woods shrinking into a jeweled sea beneath them.

Far to the east, an emerald dragon tilted her head mid-flight. The light across the canopy shimmered strangely, and the wind carried something ancient. Then she saw him: a dragon, platinum as moonlit steel, soaring with three figures upon his back.

Verdantia's eyes widened. *Radiantus.*

She veered south, green scales flashing as she raced toward the forest's heart. He had once mentored her through her first flight into battle.

Their bond was more than respect; it was a legacy. She had to tell the others.

High above Crystal Vale, Radiantus descended with reverence, wings folding as he touched down near the inner grove. The land still bore scars of battle—charred roots, torn soil, trees blackened by shadow. Kadona's smile dimmed, resolve hardening. Renewal pulsed here, but so did loss.

Radiantus turned toward the grove where Aurelia lay.

Her crystalline body, once radiant with prismatic light, dimmed with exhaustion. Struggling, she tried to rise. Radiantus lowered his head, his voice warm, kind.

"No, Aurelia. Rest."

Her eyes met his. She huffed softly, then eased back down.

He remembered her in war, shielding his flank at High Aramoor, her wings bearing the strike meant for him. Seeing her now stirred a vow deep within him: she would rise again. He would see to it.

The wind shifted once more.

Verdantia descended, regal and radiant, her emerald presence carrying the scent of renewal. She dipped her head.

"Welcome home, Radiantus. Vacari is brighter for your return."

Radiantus bowed, solemn. "I have been gone too long."

Karrenen knelt beside Aurelia, pressing a hand to her scales. Gentle light pulsed from his palm. "She is healing. The wounds no longer worsen. But no battles. No flights. The damage runs deep."

Aurelia blinked slowly in gratitude.

Radiantus turned to the others. "Do you know what Keisha asks of us?"

"No," Aurelia murmured, her voice faint as crystal chimes.

"She sent only urgency," Verdantia added.

Radiantus inclined his head. "Then rest, Aurelia. You have given enough."

Verdantia spread her wings. "I must return to Emerald Woods. Call if danger rises." She lifted skyward, vanishing in emerald light.

Kadona turned to Radiantus with a sly smile. "If you walk with us through the city, perhaps appear smaller unless you wish to clear rooftops as you go."

Radiantus laughed, a deep, thunderous sound. "Very well."

He hesitated, reverent, then closed his eyes. Light shimmered, scales dissolving into threads of brilliance, until a tall figure stood where the dragon had been a man of sun-warmed bronze, robed in silver, his hair gleaming platinum, his eyes ageless with starlight.
"Would this be better?"

Kadona laughed. Lysander clapped his shoulder. Even Karrenen's lips twitched.

"Well," Lysander said, "you will turn heads, certainly."

And turn heads he did.

As the divine quartet entered Crystal Vale, whispers spread like wildfire. Work stilled. People bowed. Eyes widened as Radiantus walked among them in mortal guise, flanked by gods and an elven lord.

The gods had come.
And with them, change walked beside the wind.

Radiantus glanced skyward, as though reading a name written in fate. The winds of destiny had stirred before—but now, they carried choices. Consequences.

He walked on, knowing the next storm would not wait long.

Chapter 4

An Unexpected Arrival

The palace gates loomed ahead, gold and emerald carvings flashing beneath the midday sun. Etched with the crests of Vacari's noble houses and the ancient sigils of Elvenkind, they stood as much a symbol of power as of protection.

The guards posted there were usually unshakable and trained to recognize kings, nobles, and dignitaries from across the realms.

But today?

Today they stared.

Hands hovered near hilts, posture stiffening at the sight of the approaching company: two gods, a high elven lord... and a stranger whose very presence thrummed with contained power.

Radiantus, veiled in his human form, walked with effortless grace beside Kadona and Lysander. His hair shimmered like molten platinum beneath the sun, starlight threading through his aura as though a dream had taken flesh.

The guards exchanged uneasy glances. One shifted his stance, caught between duty and awe. Another opened his mouth, faltered, then quickly bowed as his eyes moved from Karrenen's serene composure to the overwhelming weight of Radiantus's presence.

Kadona stepped forward, her voice cutting through the hesitation like sunlight through mist.

"We have been summoned by Lady Keisha and by King Manard himself."

At the king's name, the guards straightened at once.

"Of course!" one stammered, bowing low. "This way, my lady, my lords ah... sir."

Flustered by the unfamiliar figure, he stumbled over the title. Radiantus only offered a faint, knowing smile, a kindness wrapped in mystery.

As they were escorted through the gates, Lysander let out a low chuckle, drawing a sidelong glance from Kadona.

"They will be speaking of this for weeks," he murmured, his amusement rich. "Poor lads likely believe a star-spirit has wandered into the palace."

Kadona smirked but did not correct him. Karrenen, ever composed, said nothing, though the faintest twitch of his lips betrayed his agreement.

Their footsteps echoed along the main corridor. Nobles and servants slowed mid-stride, gawking openly as whispers rose in their wake like leaves caught on a divine wind:

"That is a god two, no, three wait, who is that?"

"Look at his eyes..."

"Is that... starlight?"

At last, they reached the double doors of the council chamber. The lead guard hesitated, gathered his nerve, then pushed them wide and bowed deeply.

"Your guests have arrived, my king."

Radiantus, Kadona, Lysander, and Lord Karrenen stepped inside. The murmurs of the hall died as the doors swung shut with a muted thud—sealing the chamber in a hush, like the air before a storm.

Radiantus's gaze swept across the gathered faces, not cold, but weighted with attentive gravity. His eyes lingered on Valeon a heartbeat longer. Not judgment. Not warmth. Observation measuring the heart of one about to confess.

At the far end of the table, Ong turned toward the door, half-ready with a dry remark.

"You're a bit la—"

The words broke off.

His eyes fixed not on Kadona or Karrenen, but on the tall, radiant figure beside them—platinum-haired, robed in silver, each movement steeped in something not quite mortal.

Ong blinked, then looked to Gailen. To Manard.

Both only shrugged.

Off to the side, Keisha hid a smile behind her hand. Laughter had not yet broken, but it hovered, waiting.

She stepped forward, as graceful as ever, and inclined her head with quiet warmth.

"Welcome home, Radiantus. Though I must say... seeing you in this form is unusual."

Radiantus pressed a hand to his chest in mock offense, his eyes widening theatrically.

"Keisha! How dare you spoil the surprise? I rehearsed this entrance every step."

That was enough.

Even Thalorian, stoic, unflinching Thalorian, let out a short, startled laugh. The sound cracked through the tension like stone giving way, as though the foundations of the universe had tilted for a heartbeat.

Kadona only raised a brow, lips twitching at the corners, amusement restrained. Yet her eyes betrayed the truth: she, more than any of them, remembered why the gods had come and that this fragile levity would not last.

Keisha glanced toward Kaelorn. His arms were folded, his expression calm, but the faintest glimmer of a smirk lit his eyes.

Ong squinted at Radiantus, frowning hard.

"All right," he said, waving vaguely toward the too-perfect stranger. "Who is this? And do not just give me a name."

The laughter broke like a wave.

Kadona braced a hand against a chair, shoulders shaking. Lysander chuckled openly, tossing his hair back in careless amusement. Even King Manard, the image of composure, struggled not to smile, his lips twitching as his poise slipped.

By the window, Valeon looked utterly lost, his brow furrowed as his eyes darted from face to face, searching for context he did not possess.

Gailen leaned toward Ong, stage-whispering, "Are we meant to know him? Or did we all collectively forget a visiting king?"

Ong did not so much as smirk. He crossed his arms with a grunt, unimpressed.

If this was some royal jest, some private game between gods and kings, he wanted no part of it.

He shook his head. "Forget it. I do not want to know."

At last, Keisha caught her breath, still smiling despite herself.

"Meet Radiantus," she said softly, warmth in her voice. "The Platinum Dragon."

Silence.

Four sets of eyes, Ong, Gailen, Manard, and Valeon stared at the radiant figure.

Then, as though orchestrated by the gods themselves, their jaws dropped in perfect unison.

Ong's scowl deepened. He shot Keisha a look edged with betrayal, then jabbed a thumb toward Radiantus.

"How do you know that? That is a man, not a dragon."

At that, even Thalorian stoic, unflinching Thalorian broke. A bark of laughter tore free, raw and startled. He stumbled into a chair, shoulders shaking, eyes wide with disbelief.

Radiantus only arched a brow in quiet amusement, a subtle gleam in his gaze betraying delight at the chaos.

Keisha gave up all pretense of composure. Her grin was irrepressible.

Lord Karrenen turned toward Ong, his tone dry as desert stone.

"You have lived in E'vahona for years, surrounded by Silver Dragons in their human forms. And still you ask this?"

Ong opened his mouth, closed it again, and muttered darkly, "That is different."

Laughter rippled louder through the chamber.

Keisha drew in a breath, forcing her voice back to steadiness.

"Most metallic dragons can shift forms, Ong. Radiantus is no different. He is... more radiant about it."

A flicker of eye contact passed between her and Kadona, brief but heavy. The goddess's smile had already faded, shadowed by an unspoken weight. Keisha saw it, and though her lips curved in humor, the light behind them dimmed.

She gestured toward Radiantus. "Think for a moment. If he had walked through Crystal Vale in his true form..."

She let the thought hang.

"This palace would be rubble before sunset."

King Manard finally chuckled, low and reluctant. "Then we should be grateful for restraint."

Radiantus pressed his hand to his chest with mock dignity. "I tread very carefully, I will have you know."

Keisha's laugh rang once more, quick and bright, before she turned toward the long table.

"All right. Let us sit." Her tone softened, though steel-edged it again. "Take your breath. We have matters of weight to discuss."

Chairs scraped against polished stone as the laughter ebbed, leaving only anticipation in its wake.

The mirth was gone.

But the storm still waited on the horizon.

Keisha turned to King Manard, her gaze thoughtful, though a faint glimmer of humor lingered in her eyes.

"Perhaps we should order emerald punch and crystal berries before we begin. Give everyone a moment to... recover."

Manard gave a dry chuckle and rang a silver bell. Within moments, an attendant appeared, accepted his order, and slipped out.

The silence that followed was not empty; it breathed.

Chairs creaked. Sleeves whispered. Armor gave a faint clink. Even Pumpkin, lounging at Ong's side, flicked her tail in slow, steady arcs, each thump a quiet metronome of waiting.

Beneath it all, tension coiled tighter.

Invisible. Unrelenting.

Valeon sat rigid, fists flexing against his knees.

Are they humoring me? Waiting until the gods have eaten? Will judgment fall when the last bite is gone?

He stared down at the polished wood before him, faces shimmering faintly in its reflection—half-familiar, half-feared.

The door creaked open. He flinched.

The attendant returned with trays of emerald punch, crystal berries glistening like dew, and sugar-dusted pastries. Sweetness drifted into the air, softening the tension but only on the surface.

Valeon swallowed hard. Fear clung to his tongue, bitter, unmoved by sugar.

Lysander set down his untouched glass and gave Manard a quiet nod.

The king straightened. His voice was steady, but iron lay beneath it.

"We are gathered. And though there is much we might speak of, I will allow Keisha to explain why we are truly here."

Every gaze shifted.

Keisha did not answer at once. She turned to Valeon instead, calm, steady, though her eyes carried the full weight of truth.

"You may tell them," she said gently. "Or I can."

Valeon looked down at his hands. Fists. Palms. Fists again. Slowly, he rose, as though lifting himself from beneath a stone that refused to shift.

"I will."

The gods. The king. The warriors.

Every eye was fixed on him.

And he spoke.

He told them of the first summons that had dragged him into Fel Thalor, of the figure cloaked in shadow who bent his will, how he had refused to kill Gailen, only to be forced into revealing enough for an Obsidian Dragon to strike. How he had been summoned repeatedly, dodging, deflecting, but always betraying more than he meant.

And how he had failed to warn them.

Of the ambush. Of the wounds. Of Aurelia. Of Keisha.

He gave them everything.

No one interrupted. No one looked away.

When at last the words were done, silence fell not disbelief, not outrage, but the solemn stillness that comes only after truth is laid bare.

Lord Karrenen turned to Keisha. His voice was low. "It is a grave matter. But why summon us?"

Keisha met his gaze, unflinching, her eyes clear with resolve.

"Because you needed the history before I revealed what has not yet been spoken."

Her gaze shifted first to Valeon, then to Kadona. The weight in the chamber climbed higher.

Even Pumpkin stilled, ears pricked, emerald eyes sharp.

The air thickened, every breath drawn tight.

For a heartbeat, the world itself seemed to pause.

The moment before the storm breaks.

Chapter 5
The Deeper Chains

The last echoes of laughter had long since faded.

Only a heavy, watchful silence remained.

Kadona leaned forward, her hands resting on the polished table. Her bright, discerning gaze locked on Keisha.

"What have you or Valeon not told us," She asked evenly, "that required summoning gods and your father?"

A subtle shift rippled through the chamber. Lysander stilled, his expression unreadable. Gailen's fingers curled tight against the table's edge.

There was no accusation in Kadona's tone, only certainty. She knew Keisha too well to think she would call upon the divine for something trivial.

Keisha inclined her head, her voice steady yet weighted with more than grief.

"You are right. If this were only about Valeon's betrayal, I would not have asked for your presence."

She paused, letting the words gather like storm clouds.

"It goes deeper than that."

The quiet sharpened. Every ear strained for what would come next.

Keisha lifted her chin, her gaze passing from Lysander to Kadona, then to King Manard, then to Lord Karrenen.

"What we face is not bound to one man's guilt. It is larger. Older. Something that reaches far beyond what we were prepared to confront."

The words themselves were simple. The weight behind them was not.

Unease stirred the chamber. The shadow of what drew them here had only begun to take shape.

Radiantus, silent until now, shifted. Starlight clung faintly to his human form, his eyes sharpening—ancient, piercing—as he studied Keisha.

"What is it, Keisha?" His voice was low, commanding. "I sense more than betrayal in this room."

His gaze flicked to Valeon—measuring. Weighing.

"Though 'simple' is not the word I would choose," he added dryly. "Still... considering we were summoned—and that you are not in chains, Valeon, something greater must be at stake."

The air seemed to hold its breath.

Keisha nodded, her expression somber.

"You are right."

She turned fully toward Valeon, her voice firm yet not unkind.

"Valeon. Explain to them why you did what you did. And" she pressed the word gently, yet with unmistakable clarity, "explained what the figure told you when you tried to refuse. When you said this should not involve you."

At the mention of the figure, tension rippled through the chamber like a drawn bowstring.

Thalorian's hand twitched near his hilt. Ong's shoulders squared. Even Lysander and Kadona, usually serene, grew taut, their divine senses sharpening like blades.

All eyes turned to Valeon. Waiting.

He rose slowly, knees stiff not from weariness, but from the weight bearing down on him. Centuries of power and memory stared through him. A faint itch crawled up his spine, the echo of old fear. He drew a steadying breath, glanced at Keisha, then fixed his gaze on the others.

Their eyes pressed against him heavily, expectant, wary.

But he met them anyway.

"The mysterious figure..." His voice was low, but steady. "They summoned me to Fel Thalor. Dragged me there against my will."

The chill of memory sank into his bones.

"When I arrived, they told me I was still bound to them—by the pact my father made with Maelgrim Shadowwalker."

A more resounding ripple shivered through the room.

Valeon gripped the back of his chair, nails biting wood.

"I argued. I told them the pact should have ended with my father's death. I remember clenching my fists until the skin on my knuckles broke. Years of rage poured out of me. I swore whatever promises he made should have died with him."

He lifted his head, voice taut.

"But they insisted. The binding remained. It did not matter who swore it—or why."

A grim smile touched his lips. "And when I refused, when I said I wanted no part of it..."

He hesitated.

"They nearly killed me."

The words fell like stones into water.

No one moved.

No one spoke.

Only the sound of breathing filled the chamber—slow, strained—as though the world itself had grown less safe.

Lysander leaned forward, calm yet implacable.

"Explain the agreement, Valeon. Everything you know. What was gained... and what was lost? Especially what you and your mother received or did not."

Valeon nodded once, standing rigid, anchored against the weight of his own confession.

"My father made the pact during the Druchii conflict, when war threatened the Flameford borders. He swore a blood oath to Maelgrim, gaining power, political favor, and protection. And not just for himself. He pledged our entire family line."

Disgust twisted his features.

"He gained standing almost overnight. Doors opened. Alliances bent. He was untouchable. But my mother? She received nothing. No wealth. No protection. He never returned. She scraped to survive while he played the noble."

Valeon's hands tightened. "My mother lived in poverty while he hoarded his power."

At last, he met their eyes, no longer flinching.

"That is the truth."

Radiantus studied him, starlight flickering in his gaze.

"How old were you when the pact was forged? And have you lived in Vacari since?"

Valeon exhaled, shoulders stiff.

"I was barely four, perhaps five. My mother knew it was not safe. When I turned twelve, she paid to smuggle me into Etharyon, a hidden refuge within Vacari. with only a handful of coins and a warning never to look back."

His fists clenched again, then slowly eased.

"She told me I was no fighter. That surviving there by wit and speed was my only chance."

Radiantus's gaze deepened, the weight of ancient knowledge stirring behind his eyes.

"So, you were never meant for war."

A low rumble stirred in his chest, not judgment, but contemplation.

Lord Karrenen folded his hands upon the table, his voice calm yet firm.

"From what we know, this figure has no right to enforce the pact. Even if Phoenix Shadowwalker still lived, the claim would have ended with Valeon's father. Blood oaths pass only if all bound parties consent or receive the bargainer's favor. Valeon did not. His mother did not. The line was never sealed. In such cases, the bond dies with the one who forged it."

His gaze swept the chamber. "The figure may know of the pact. But they cannot enforce it. Not Phoenix. Not Maelgrim. Not whatever shadow lingers now."

Radiantus inclined his head slowly. "Agreed."

Valeon stood stunned. His brow furrowed as the words sank in. He opened his mouth, closed it again. Fear did not vanish in an instant... but something small, fragile, began to loosen in his chest.

Around the table, silence held.

Gailen's jaw clenched, betrayal still raw.

Ong's fingers tapped restlessly against his hilt.

Kadona's gaze remained steady, unreadable.

Lysander narrowed his eyes, listening to echoes no one else could hear.

Then Kaelorn leaned forward, catching the flicker in Valeon's expression. He turned to the gods.

"Why would this figure claim Valeon was still bound?"

Lysander inclined his head. His voice was calm, cutting.

"They knew Valeon was not forged for defiance. They preyed upon fear. Manipulation thrives in cracks left by doubt."

Valeon flinched, but Lysander's tone anchored him.

"But they also found something they did not expect," the sea god continued. "Valeon refused certain orders. Refused, even in fear. That is strength."

The gods exchanged a glance, silent agreement sparking like a current.

Lysander's voice sharpened. "Steps must be taken to ensure this shadow never touches Valeon again. I propose that Radiantus, Kadona, and I convene with the Council of the Gods. We will deliver a warning."

A faint sea-blue shimmer flared around him.

"They will be told: cross this line again... and face the wrath of the heavens."

Radiantus inclined his head, his voice like closing gates.

"I agree. The time has come."

He turned to Keisha, his gaze warm.

"You were right to summon us. This was never for mortal judgment alone. It required the hand of the divine."

Keisha bowed her head, a breath of relief slipping free. The weight she had carried—calling Radiantus down from the heavens eased, though not completely.

Then Radiantus looked to Valeon, platinum eyes fixing him in place. Valeon's breath caught—not with fear, but with the crushing weight of being seen fully. Not as a pawn. Not as a suspicion. As a soul laid bare.

"For now," Radiantus said, his voice steady as stone, "we will deal with the one who dares reach beyond their rightful grasp."

Then his tone hardened.

"As for you, Valeon, you must still face those you have wounded. Apologize if you have not. More than that, listen."

His gaze swept to King Manard, Gailen, Ong, Keisha, and Thalorian.

"It is theirs to decide what place, if any, you still hold among them."

A tremor passed through Valeon. Not fear something quieter. The weight of a second chance.

He bowed his head low.

"I will. And... thank you."

Radiantus inclined his head, offering neither pardon nor condemnation. Only truth.

Around the table, the tension eased, just enough to breathe.

But the road ahead for Valeon, and for Vacari remained unwritten.

Chapter 6
The Reckoning

The air still carried the weight of divine presence as the gods rose from their seats.

Radiantus stood first, his expression thoughtful, unreadable. Without a word, he inclined his head once to King Manard and Keisha, then turned toward the door.

Kadona and Lysander followed silently, their radiance fading like sunlight slipping behind clouds.

Lord Karrenen lingered a heartbeat longer. He laid a gentle hand upon Keisha's shoulder as he passed, then turned his gaze upon Valeon, not in judgment, but with the calm of long-earned wisdom. Then he, too, was gone, borne back to E'vahona on silent magic.

The chamber seemed to exhale. The faint hum of divinity withdrew, leaving only polished cedar, cold stone, and the muted glow of stained glass.

Stillness settled.

No gods. No echo of ancient power.

Only the truth and those left to face it.

Valeon felt it pressing down. Not crushing, but inescapable. Relief and dread tangled within his chest. No more hiding. Not now.

King Manard turned to him.

"Sit," he said.

Valeon hesitated, then obeyed, folding his hands tightly in his lap to still their tremor.

The king remained standing, his voice firm but not cruel.

"We are going to speak of what you have done."

His gaze swept the table: Gailen, Ong, Kaelorn, Thalorian, Keisha.

"But before we begin," he continued, "remember the words of the gods. And recall what Thalorian has already said: Valeon is no warrior. He was not raised for this. That does not excuse his silence or his choices, but it matters."

Afternoon light fractured through the tall panes of stained glass, casting ribbons of gold and blue across the marble floor.

No one spoke.

Not yet.

The reckoning had begun.

King Manard clasped his hands behind his back and turned his gaze on his sons.

Gailen sat rigid, jaw clenched, eyes hard as stone. Ong's arms were crossed, his frame wound tight, as though holding himself from breaking apart or breaking something else.

The king exhaled through his nose, then shifted his attention to Keisha, Kaelorn, and Thalorian, whose faces remained thoughtful, composed, unreadable.

At last, he nodded to Keisha.

Would you like to guide this discussion? It may go better coming from you."

Keisha did not answer at once. She turned toward Kaelorn, calm and thoughtful.

"No," she said at last. "I could, but I believe it would be better if the words came from Kaelorn. Or from Thalorian. Perhaps both."

Her tone held no hesitation. Only trust.

Manard studied her for a moment, then gave a single, approving nod. "Very well."

Kaelorn leaned forward, fingers laced atop the table. Beside him, Thalorian inclined his head, his expression grave but unwavering.

Kaelorn's gaze swept the chamber before he spoke.

"Thalorian and I will guide this conversation. But that means every voice must be heard before it ends."

His eyes rested briefly on Ong and Gailen, not in challenge, but in expectation.

"You may be angry. You may feel betrayed. That is fair. But no one storms out. No one casts blame without offering a path forward."

Thalorian's voice followed, quiet yet firm.

"We are not here to condemn him." We are here to decide what comes next."

Valeon sat motionless, eyes lowered, absorbing every word. The air was quieter now, not sharpened by rage, but steadied by intent.

Ong and Gailen turned toward one another at the exact moment, their mirrored expressions a tangle of restrained frustration and unspoken challenge.

Keisha exhaled softly, glancing at Manard with a faint, wry smile.

"If ever there was doubt, they are brothers," she murmured, "just look at them now."

The tension cracked. Laughter rippled through the chamber.

Valeon blinked. The sound felt distant, unreal. The corner of his mouth twitched, as if he were ready to answer, but the weight in his chest held him still. Part of him longed to join them, to let the warmth in. Another part braced—uncertain whether the laughter was meant to welcome him... or to remind him of his place outside it.

So, he said nothing, letting the sound wash over him like sunlight through a window he had not dared open. Not loud, but real. Even Thalorian released a quiet breath that might have been a chuckle, and Kaelorn's lips curved, faint but genuine.

King Manard smiled at Keisha, his shoulders easing slightly.

"You always did know how to speak what we were all thinking."

Only Valeon remained silent. His head bowed, hands folded tight, his gaze flickered but did not rise.

Kaelorn's expression sobered once more, steady and severe.

"We need to know when this began," he said evenly. "Why did you not come to one of us at once? Why remain silent?"

The laughter faded into stillness. Every gaze returned to Valeon.

He hesitated, then lifted his eyes to Kaelorn before letting them drift across the table.

"I was afraid," he admitted quietly. His tone was not defensive, only raw. Honest.

"I did not know if you would believe me. Or if you would think I was only trying to hide something worse."

His gaze fell again to the polished wood.

"I did not know who I could trust. I did not even trust myself."

The sharp crack of flesh striking stone shattered the silence.

Ong's hand slammed against the table, the sound reverberating like a war drum through the chamber. Valeon flinched, jolting in his seat as the ache in his chest twisted with the echo.

"I might have understood that at the beginning," Ong snapped.

The air froze.

"But why not later?" His voice shook with restrained fury. "Before Aurelia was wounded. Before Keisha—"

His words fractured, breaking for the briefest heartbeat.

Memory surged: Keisha's bloodied body crumpled on the stone. The metallic tang of blood. The thunder of his own heart. The silence that had stretched into weeks, heavy with fear that never left him.

"That," he finished, voice raw, "I do not understand."

Keisha touched his arm, gentle but firm.

"Patience," she murmured. "Your anger will not help."

His jaw worked, scowl tight, but after a long moment, he gave a short, stiff nod and leaned back—still coiled like a drawn bowstring.

Thalorian's gaze shifted to Valeon, his tone cool yet edged.

"You said you could not even trust yourself."

He folded his arms.

"Why?"

The question hung heavier than the rest.

This was no longer about guilt. Or betrayal.

It was about the truth that Valeon had yet to speak.

And now... he had to.

Valeon lifted his head slowly, his eyes meeting Thalorian's across the table.

"I have always relied on my wits," he said, voice rough but steady. "My charm. Talking my way out of trouble. That is how I survived."

His fists curled against the table.

"But this time... it was not enough. I could not talk my way through it. I did not know how to fight it. I did not even know how to face it."

A ragged breath left him.

"And somewhere along the way... I began to believe they were right."

He looked down, then back up, locking eyes with Thalorian.

"That no one would think I was worth fighting for, that my friends would not listen. Would not believe me."

Valeon's mouth twisted, bitter with self-loathing.

"You were important." Dragonriders. Mages. Warriors. And me? Nothing. I could not and still cannot do anything to help."

The words hung raw, bleeding into silence. Even the torchlight seemed to falter, shadows stretching long across the polished floor. For a heartbeat, Valeon was back in the grove, throat tight, wishing someone might see past the walls he had built.

Kaelorn shifted, his face unreadable. No one else spoke. They only listened.

Ong leaned forward, ready to snap, but Keisha's hand found his arm. Her green eyes were calm, piercing.

"Remember what I was like," she said softly, "after the Battle for Vacari."

The words struck harder than any rebuke. Ong froze, his mouth snapping shut.

The memory came swiftly and sharply: Keisha after the battle, her spirit shadowed by memories she had buried too deep. Her recovery had been slow, her steps uncertain, her gaze always somewhere far away. Ong remembered, and the anger caught in his throat."

He swallowed hard, then gave a reluctant nod. Turning to Valeon, his voice came rough, though steadier.

"I think I understand what you were feeling."

A fleeting glance of apology flickered toward Keisha before his tone sharpened once more.

"But I still cannot understand why you stayed silent after. Why did you not come to us when everything began to unravel?"

Before Valeon could shape an answer, Gailen's voice broke through quieter than Ong's, steeped not in fury, but in hurt.

"What I cannot understand," he said, eyes fixed on Valeon, "is why you did not come to me afterwards."

His hands clenched against the table, knuckles white.

"After you refused to kill me. After you chose not to. Why not tell me then?"

He remembered the look on Valeon's face that day, torn, as though wrestling an enemy only he could see. He had hoped Valeon would come to him after. That whatever was broken might still be mended.

But no words came.

And now the silence echoed twice as loud.

The chamber stilled once more, heavy with betrayal, confusion, and something more fragile, more dangerous to admit.

Hope.

Or something close.

Valeon's gaze moved between Ong and Gailen, then flicked briefly to King Manard. The king's expression remained unreadable, but intent burned in his eyes.

Valeon's voice was quieter now, stripped of all defenses.

"By then... I was already too deep." His eyes returned to Gailen. "I no longer knew what you would believe."

He swallowed hard, then gave voice to the guilt he had buried even in the grove.

"It was my description of you, Gailen."

The memory struck like a blade, black wings tearing through storm-gray skies, the Obsidian Dragon wheeling above the tower, its shriek splitting stone and air. The moment he realized the shadow had fallen upon Gailen, his heart froze and has never truly thawed.

"That is how the Obsidian Dragon knew whom to strike in the first battle. When you and Ong stood upon the tower."

Gailen's jaw tightened. He did not speak.

Valeon's voice shook. "They told me you would not be harmed, that they only meant to delay the bond, to slow the legacy. But you were targeted. You were wounded."

He dragged a hand through his hair, then clenched it into a fist against the table, wood creaking beneath his knuckles.

"After that... I did not know how to come back. Everything was spiraling, and I—"

He broke off. There was nothing else he could say that would undo it. Only truth. Only silence.

Thalorian leaned forward, gaze locked on him, not in anger, but with the cold intensity of a soldier who knew when words weighed more than steel.

"Perhaps," he said slowly, "we can accept that you were afraid. That you felt trapped."

His voice was calm. Too calm.

"But why did you not at least try to warn us before the last battle?"

His eyes never left Valeon's.

"Did you know Nocturna was commanded to kill Aurelia and Prince Gailen?"

Valeon froze.

Thalorian's tone dropped, sharp as a blade.

"And Verdantia? Keisha? Did you know they were marked as well?"

The chamber fell utterly still. Even the whisper of wind against the spires seemed to die. The lantern flames flickered once, then steadied, as though the room itself waited.

Valeon met Thalorian's gaze and said nothing. Not yet. Some truths were heavier than betrayal, soaked too deeply in blood.

But silence could not hold forever. He shifted beneath their eyes, then forced the words out, rough but clear.

"I was not certain. I only knew they despised the noble dragons. That much was plain."

His gaze flicked toward Keisha, guilt hardening his features.

"But I was never told why. I learned that from you."

A slow, unsteady breath.

"When I pressed further, when I asked why, they silenced me. Told me it was not my concern."

His hands curled into fists again before he willed them open.

"And then…" His voice dropped, strained. "I overheard a dark elf woman telling a male that the black dragons could kill Keisha. Because she was… a threat."

The room tensed, but Valeon pressed on.

"At the same time, I was hiding things from them as well. I did not tell them about the reinforcements in Crystal Vale. Or in Emerald Woods."

The words dropped heavy, carrying the weight of treason to some, of protection to others.

Silence stretched until Kaelorn arched a brow, a wry smile tugging at the corners of his mouth.

"You mean," he said dryly, "you withheld that information?"

A ripple of startled laughter broke through the tension. Even Ong smirked, and Keisha's lips curved in reluctant amusement.

Kaelorn chuckled under his breath. "Oh, boy…"

The laughter faded quickly, yet something had shifted. Not forgiveness. Not yet. But perhaps it's the beginning of it.

Manard leaned forward, his voice calm but probing.

"Why take that risk? They could have discovered the truth and killed you."

Valeon's gaze steadied. "Because it was then I realized you were my friends."

He looked around the table, Gailen, Ong, Keisha, Thalorian, Kaelorn, and a faint smile ghosted across his lips.

"That you cared about me. Even when I had no magic. No dragon. No title."

His eyes lingered on Gailen, warmth flickering beneath the weight of memory.

"And when you asked me to tend the wounded… You told me we each have our gifts."

The smile strengthened, faint but real.

"And the figure did find out. After the battle, they summoned me back furious. Accused me of sabotage."

He lifted one shoulder in a weary shrug, a flash of old mischief breaking through.

"So I told them... 'You win some, you lose some.'"

He braced for silence. For judgment.

Instead, the chamber erupted in laughter. Valeon's eyes widened. The sound was like sunlight breaking through storm clouds, sudden, warming, almost disorienting after so much shadow.

For a moment, he did not know how to respond. Then, slowly, his shoulders loosened, and he let the warmth wash over him.

"And then?" Kaelorn prompted.

Valeon spread his hands. "And then they stormed out."

This time, Ong's bark of laughter rang so loud it startled even him. Gailen tried to smother his grin, but failed, collapsing against his brother until both were doubled over, laughing helplessly on the floor.

The rest chuckled more softly, the warmth spreading. Even Manard allowed himself a smile.

For the first time since Valeon had stepped into the chamber, hope flickered. Fragile, trembling—but there.

Thalorian arched a brow as the brothers righted themselves, still chuckling. A rare glint of humor touched his eyes.

"Well," he said dryly, "it seems you have some promise after all."

Gentle laughter rippled again.

Manard's smile warmed as he turned to Valeon.

"We understand more now. But you will still need to earn back our trust."

He folded his hands behind his back.

"You will not be exiled. You will not be cast into the dungeons. But perhaps... it is time you learned to be useful."

"Besides eating and sleeping?" Gailen cut in with a wide grin.

The laughter returned, brighter this time, free of strain. Even Valeon smiled, ducking his head.

When the mirth at last quieted, he lifted his gaze, hesitant but unguarded.

"I have been thinking," he said slowly. "I know I am no fighter. I may never be. But... do you think I could become a healer? Even without magic?"

The question hung in the air, fragile as glass.

Keisha leaned forward, her voice gentle yet firm.

"You have already shown you have the heart for it. Now we will see if you have the discipline."

Valeon's expression faltered, hope dimming until she smiled.

"That does not mean impossible. Healing begins not with spells, but with herbs and remedies. They are overlooked, but vital. And you notice what others miss. That is where it starts."

Her words carried the weight of E'vahona's oldest traditions, rooted in healing as sacred as any magic.

"It will not be easy," she finished softly. "But you could do it."

Valeon stared at her, uncertain he had heard aright.

Manard's gaze shifted to Keisha, quiet approval in his eyes.

"Excellent. Then his training begins at once."

The finality of the words broke something loose inside him. His throat tightened, tears spilling before he could stop them.

"Thank you," he whispered. "I thought... I thought—"

Kaelorn cut him off with a dry grin.

"Yes, yes, we know what you thought. But now? You are getting to work. Training begins soon, healer."

Laughter rose again, soft, unforced, warm.

Valeon exhaled, as if he had been holding his breath for years.

Perhaps this was what healing felt like. Messy. Slow. Real.

And for the first time in a long while, Valeon smiled through his tears.

DRAGONS OF ACARI

Chapter 7
The Halls of Judgment

T he skies above the mortal world gave way to brilliance.

No sun. No moon. Only light shifting, unbound, pure.

Radiantus soared upward, wings thundering into eternity, platinum, and starlight trailing behind him like falling constellations.

Kadona sat tall upon his back, sunlight tangled in her hair. Lysander gripped a ridge of platinum scale, his sea cloak snapping in the wind, his jaw set with resolve. Together they pierced the veils between realms, rising into a place untouched by time.

The Realm of the Gods unfolded—vast, still, impossible. Light dwelled in the air itself, pressing softly against the skin like velvet. Courtyards of crystal spiraled in defiance of gravity; rivers of silver light whispered as they flowed. Temples shifted from columns into wings, as if the stone remembered flight. At the realm's heart stood the Sanctum of Accord, carved from rock older than dawn.

Radiantus circled once, reverent, before descending.

"Prepare yourselves," he rumbled, voice echoing in twin tones. "The Council does not suffer the twisting of mortal will. If this shadow dares appear... they will regret it."

"They were arrogant enough to claim Valeon as property," Lysander said grimly.

Kadona's eyes narrowed. "Then let them be burned by truth."

Radiantus landed in a wash of molten starlight. The Messenger of the Gods emerged, silver and opal robes gleaming, voice calm.

"I will announce your return to the Council—"

"No."

The single word cracked the marble beneath Radiantus's claws.

"You will not speak of my return. This council is not about me."

The Messenger faltered, then bowed low. "As you wish." He lifted his hand, releasing a golden wisp into the heavens. Its ringing ascent was a summons no one could ignore.

Until the Council gathered, they waited beside the Lake of Echoes. Its waters shimmered with memory, reflecting not only faces but the weight of past vows: Lysander's first storm, Kadona's first dawn, Radiantus's long-forgotten oath of balance.

They stood in silence as the lake hummed with the echoes of every promise ever spoken. Even gods required stillness before war.

At last, Radiantus broke the silence, his gaze fixed on the rippling surface.

"This figure is the one who dares to claim Valeon. Who are they? Why does no one truly see them?"

Kadona's expression remained serene, but her voice carried the weight of memory.

"We encountered them only once when a charge was brought against Lysander."

Lysander's eyes darkened, sea-light rippling faintly across his features.

"The accusation: that I had overstepped my place by bringing the noble dragons to Vacari's defense. When Kimras and Amara rose against Phoenix and Vuarus to save Keisha."

A low growl reverberated in Radiantus's chest, his wings twitching.

"And this shadow dared speak against you?"

"Yes," Lysander said. "Their voice was veiled in echoes, shadow layered on shadow. The Council allowed their words, but never their face."

Kadona's tone dropped soft, but unyielding.

"When I spoke of your possible return, Radiantus, the Council scowled. Yet they dismissed the charge. Still, the shadow left us with a warning: not to forget our place."

Radiantus's eyes flared, burning like captured stars.

"Then they should remember who defines that place."

His tail swept slowly across the stone.

"And now they strike at the noble dragons repeatedly. First, Kimras and Amara. Then Aurelia and Verdantia."

Kadona's jaw tightened. "They want the noble line broken."

"They have failed," Radiantus said, voice like closing gates. "But they will not stop."

The Lake of Echoes pulsed, rings of golden light spiraling outward. A voice resonated from the very air itself:

"The Council has been summoned. The assembly will convene at first light."

Radiantus exhaled, starlit vapor curling from his nostrils. "So be it."

Within, a vow burned. This time, he would not falter.

Lysander gave a terse nod. Kadona's gaze lingered on the shimmering lake, her expression calm yet heavy with dread.

Above them, the constellations did not simply pause.

They dimmed.

Waiting.

Chapter 8

Divine Veils

D awn in the Realm of the Gods was unlike any morning in the mortal world.

It did not rise with light; it awakened with intention.

The Sanctum of Accord shimmered awake, its spires glowing as runes pulsed with golden awareness. No birdsong broke the silence, only the harmonic hum of magic aligning with the will of the day. Corridors unfurled like living petals, revealing the vast hall where judgment would soon unfold.

But the Council was not yet assembled.

In the hushed stillness before the summons, three figures crept through the outer passageways.

Lysander led, his storm-blue cloak trailing as he whispered a spell that bent the air around them. Kadona walked beside a cloaked presence, no cloth, only layers of divine concealment. Radiantus.

His platinum brilliance had dulled to silver, starlight muted into a faint shimmer, yet the power beneath it could not be hidden. Every step, every breath carried the weight of memory and the fury of a vow long deferred. He had not returned for the spectacle. He had returned for justice.

"Technically," Lysander murmured, "we are not sneaking. We are staging."

"Staging a thunderstorm in a wine cellar," Kadona said dryly.

Radiantus rumbled low, amusement edged with steel. "Then see that the barrier holds. I would rather not give anyone a heart attack. Not yet."

They guided him into a secluded arch where forgotten relics lay beneath dust and the faint perfume of incense. Kadona lifted her hand, weaving golden and silver threads into a shimmering veil that wrapped him from sight.

"Hidden," she whispered.

"Listening," Radiantus answered.

"Perfect," Lysander said. "Now we wait."

They slipped back into the chamber as the first pulse of summons rippled along the spires.

One by one, gods arrived. Some descended in columns of light; others stepped through mirrored gates, bringing with them storms, fire, and starlight. With each arrival, the air shifted heavier, as if the chamber itself strained to hold their combined presence.

And then—

The final figure crossed the threshold. Shadows clung to them like armor, veils that drank the light. Where they passed, the runes dimmed, shrinking back as if unwilling to touch. No face, no form, only a voice that echoed in layered distortion, like words carried from the depths of a cavern carved from shadow.

The chamber darkened.

The gods turned.

A hush fell, as deep as the breath before a thunderstorm.

"The Council is now in session," declared the High Arbiter, his voice a chord of ancient law. "Called at the request of Kadona, Goddess of

Light, and Lysander, God of the Sea. We are told a grave accusation awaits us."

Every gaze turned upon them.

Lysander stepped forward, calm as the sea before a storm.

"We thank the Council for convening. Everything will be revealed... as this meeting progresses."

He did not elaborate.

Instead, his gaze slid slowly, deliberately toward the shrouded alcove where the shadowed figure waited.

The silence deepened, taut as the moment before lightning strikes.

Across the hall, the veiled figure remained silent. But the air thickened, every breath dragged through shadow. Darkness coiled tighter around them, answering Lysander's look with cold defiance.

Lysander inclined his head once and took a step back.

Kadona moved forward, light pooling about her like a mantle of dawn against the encroaching dark. Her voice rang out, sharp as crystal.

"Certain allegations have been brought before us, accusations of grave impropriety, made by one who may have overstepped their bounds in the affairs of mortals."

The words fell like blades into still water.

Several gods inhaled sharply. The weight of such a charge could shatter even divine standing if proven true.

Only the shadowed figure remained unmoved. Their head tilted, a smirk curving beneath the veil.

"What accusation?" The voice slithered through the chamber, echoing from nowhere. "And who dares to bring such claims?"

The shadows tightened, cloaking their form, as if drawing strength from the confrontation.

Kadona's light did not falter. She offered no answer because she did not need to. Not yet.

Lysander's eyes cut toward the figure, though his words were for the assembly. His tone was measured, deliberate.

"The source is Keisha, the Eladrin."

A murmur rippled through the hall, storm, flame, forest, star, every divine domain whispering the same name.

"I doubt," Lysander continued, his voice rising with the weight of certainty, "that any here would claim an Eladrin speaks lightly. And never without proof."

The silence held a heartbeat too long. Then his gaze returned to the veiled figure.

"Even if doubt remained..." His sea-blue eyes narrowed. "...the charges were easily verified."

The words fell like anchors into deep water.

The smirk vanished. The shadows recoiled, curling inward. For the first time, the figure gave no reply.

Around the chamber, gods exchanged glances. Some nodded once, slow and deliberate.

The Eladrin were known for clarity. For truth.

And Keisha's name carried weight etched into mortal memory and divine record alike.

No laughter. No protest.

Only silence.

And the tide, turning.

One of the seated gods leaned forward—an ancient being whose domain was memory and vow-binding. Golden threads of oath-light shimmered across the folds of his robe like constellations caught in cloth. His voice was deep, resonant, tinged with unease.

"Kadona," he said, "if such a charge has been brought before us, it must be spoken plainly. What, precisely, does it concern?"

Kadona inclined her head with quiet grace. Her voice rang clear, sharp as crystal.

"It concerns a covenant one forged long ago between Maelgrim Shadowwalker and a mortal who bent the knee."

At the name Maelgrim, a ripple shivered through the hall. Even the marble seemed to tighten, as though remembering the scar of that shadow.

"The man was given power, protection, and influence," Kadona continued. "In return, he pledged his loyalty, his blood, his line."

The words fell into silence, heavy as stones.

"But now," she said, her light sharpening against the gloom, "it has come to us that someone seeks to enforce that covenant upon the man's descendants."

A hush swept the chamber. Chairs shifted. Silk whispered against stone. Divine gazes cut toward the veiled figure.

Kadona's radiance blazed brighter, refusing to yield.

"Such an act is no mere misstep," she said, each syllable precise. "It is a violation of mortal will. And of divine law."

The veiled figure stirred. Shadows coiled tight, serpents winding about their form. A smirk flickered within the darkness.

"You know, Kadona," the voice murmured, layered in echoes, "there are... exceptions. Covenants that do bind bloodlines under certain conditions."

The tone dripped with smug precision, like a scholar delighting in a twisted rule.

Lysander exhaled, the sound sharp as surf breaking on stone.

"Yes," he said, his voice controlled, deliberate. "That is true if the descendants received a benefit. Power. Protection. Guidance. Something equal in measure."

He turned to the assembly, storm-colored eyes sweeping the silent hall.

"But in this case?" His voice hardened, each word striking like a gavel. "The children of that line received nothing. No protection. No power. No voice. Only ruin."

He pivoted back toward the shadow.

"So tell us how you justify enforcing a covenant where one side gained everything, and the other was left only to suffer?"

The chamber froze. Even gods of flame and storm sat in taut silence, their lightning and fire banked low. Lysander's words had stripped the figure's defense to ash.

The veiled one straightened, shadows snapping like banners in a storm. Their voice no longer slithered—it cracked with fury, thunder layered over grinding stone.

"Are you accusing me, Lysander?" The veiled head turned, veils burning with heat. "And you, Kadona, do you dare claim I have broken covenant law?"

The chamber shuddered as a pulse of shadow burst outward. Lightning laced with molten fire seared across the marble floor, leaving black scars where none had marked it for centuries.

"If so," the voice thundered, echoing from every wall, "then name me. Speak my name before this Council if you dare!"

The demand struck like a hammer blow.

Several gods rose, uncertain whether to restrain or watch. The chamber trembled, caught between judgment and eruption.

Lysander's expression did not shift. Slowly, he turned.

Not toward the veiled figure.

But toward the far alcove behind them, where starlight pulsed faintly behind woven threads of concealment.

His voice cut through the silence, calm as the tide, sharp as a blade.

"We will let another answer that."

Kadona lifted her hand. With a single, fluid motion, she unraveled the veil.

The air shattered like crystal beneath a storm. Light burst outward, flooding the sanctum.

Radiantus stepped forward.

Tall. Majestic. A god among dragons. His scales blazed with molten starlight, his vast wings folding like curtains of judgment behind him.

The chamber erupted—not in fear, but in reverence. Gasps rose, voices breaking in awe:

"Radiantus..."

"He has returned..."

"Praise the Balance..."

The echoes rolled through the sanctum like bells rung across eternity.

Only the veiled figure was silent. Shadows convulsed around them, light shriveling as if scorched. A tremor rippled through their form, fear or fury, no one could say. They staggered a step, veils shivering as though their own shadow threatened betrayal.

Radiantus's gaze found them. He did not blink.

He stood tall, wings drawn close, then let one vast span unfurl, radiant fire spilling like sunrise across the chamber. The gathered gods parted before him, bowing their heads in reverent silence.

"I thank you," Radiantus said, his voice echoing like a sky splitting open. "It is good to stand among you again."

He turned, slow and deliberate, until his diamond-like silver eyes locked on the cloaked figure.

"But let us answer your question."

His gaze blazed, sharp as judgment.

"It was you," he thundered. "You sought to bind Valeon, a mortal who has not dwelt in Fel Thalor since he was a child, under a covenant forged by another man's folly."

Celestial fire rippled across his throat and chest, each word burning hotter.

"He and his mother received nothing. No power. No wealth. No protection. Only abandonment."

Another step shook the marble beneath him.

"And yet you dared to claim him. To drag him into chains not his own."

The chamber held its breath.

Radiantus's voice cut sharper, ringing like steel against stone.

"Hear me: you are forbidden from touching him again. Cross this line, and the heavens themselves will answer."

His wings swept wide, casting firelit shadows across the council floor like sentences etched in flame.

"Your day will come. We will know your name. And when the storm breaks..."

His voice fell to a whisper that struck like a blade.

"...you will not stand."

Silence crashed down.

The High Arbiter rose, his words resonant with ancient law.

"Let the record show: the figure who stands accused is forbidden from further interference with the mortal Valeon. Any violation of this decree shall summon divine retribution."

The runes along the sanctum's spires dimmed, folding back into stillness. The Council was dismissed.

Radiantus turned toward the threshold, accompanied by Kadona and Lysander. Yet before stepping through, he looked back once more. His diamond-like silver eyes fixed on the writhing shadow. He spoke no word, yet his silence burned like prophecy.

The warning was clear. Next time, there would be no words.

The gods departed.

Silence claimed the chamber once more until it shattered, jagged and violent.

"Damn that Eladrin," the veiled figure spat, shadows flaring against the marble until black scars marred its flawless floor. "Damn Valeon for confessing."

They paced in a storm of darkness, their movements sharp and erratic. Yet when they spoke again, the fury had cooled, honed into something colder.

"This is not over, Radiantus. Let the Council bask in its false certainty."

The shadows coiled tighter, folding inward until the figure vanished with a hiss of extinguished flame.

"My game," the voice lingered faintly, echoing through the silence, "has only just begun."

Chapter 9
The Weight Lifted

T he skies above Crystal Vale still shimmered with the fading trails of divine presence.

Bands of light rippled where Radiantus's wings had carved the heavens, their glow lingering like the last threads of a dream.

Where battle-scorched earth had blackened the courtyard, healing now stirred. Shoots of green pushed through cracked stone. Golden light slipped between wounded trees, carrying the resin-sweet breath of new growth after fire.

In the palace courtyard, anticipation swelled like a held breath.

Radiantus descended first, vast wings folding inward as his form rippled into the gleam of platinum flesh. A heartbeat later, Kadona stepped through a sunlit veil, radiant as dawn, while Lysander emerged beside her in a wash of sea-spray mist.

Keisha, Ong, Kaelorn, and King Manard were already waiting.

Valeon moved first. His breath caught as the three divine figures approached.

Radiantus's gaze met his without hesitation.

"You have nothing to fear from the one who claimed you," the Platinum Dragon said, his voice steady as stone, vast as thunder. "The Council was unanimous. The decree stands. You are free."

Valeon's knees buckled. For an instant, he thought the ground itself would collapse beneath him—not from terror, but from the sheer shock of release. The burden he had carried for years fell away so suddenly that it left him hollow.

A memory flared chains. Shadows. Silence. His chest seized, breath tearing loose like a snapped tether. And then... nothing. Only freedom.

He dropped to the ground, his palms pressed against the stone, his eyes wide.

"Thank you," he whispered, voice trembling. "Thank you. I—I thought—"

Kadona stepped forward, light settling about her like a mantle. Her words were soft, certain.

"You are free, Valeon."

Lysander's trident pulsed faintly as he reached out a hand.

"Come. No need to kneel. Stand in your own name."

For a moment, Valeon only stared, stunned. Then, with trembling resolve, he took the god's hand and rose. For the first time, he stood not in defiance, nor in survival. He stood in acceptance—like a man glimpsing his first sunrise after years in a cavern.

King Manard's voice broke the silence, warm yet steady.

"Radiantus. Kadona. Lysander. We thank you for settling this. We have already begun preparing Valeon's path."

Radiantus tilted his head, eyes narrowing with interest.

"Arrangements?"

The king's lips curved faintly. "He has chosen to train as a healer. Not with magic, but with skill, herbs, salves, and craft. He will study the plants of Vacari to tend the wounded."

Kadona's smile softened. "A noble path."

Lysander inclined his head, sea-light glimmering along his trident. "One that requires strength of another kind, the kind you already carry."

Valeon swallowed, his gaze shifting between them. For the first time in his life, he did not feel like a liability. He felt as though he belonged. Gratitude welled sharp and hot in his chest. Ong's anger still lingered at the edge of his thoughts, Keisha's wounds, the shadow of what he had caused, but for once, he let himself feel the tiniest spark of hope.

"I... was wondering," he began, rubbing the back of his neck. His voice wavered, shy yet determined. "If I might be allowed into the library. To read the scrolls I never had the chance to. To study. To learn."

King Manard's eyes crinkled with warmth. "The library is open to all who seek wisdom. You are welcome there." His tone shifted, dry but not unkind. "But if you intend to brew anything that smokes, sparks, or bubbles suspiciously... do it outside."

Valeon flushed scarlet.

The group laughed, Ong jabbing him with a grin, while Thalorian allowed the barest of smirks. Kadona tilted her head, lips curving faintly.

"Perhaps," she said lightly, "we can even find you a mentor worthy of your dedication. But patience, Valeon, you will need it."

His throat tightened, words knotting before they could form. Gratitude swelled, fierce and almost unbearable.

And then the air shifted.

A soft gust swept through the courtyard, carrying the scent of sun-warmed metal and the high, crystalline ring of distant chimes.

A shadow passed overhead. Not heavy. Not cold.

But immense. Brilliant.

They all looked up.

Valeon's heart stuttered. Awe rooted him to the stone, silencing every word he might have spoken. Keisha felt it too deeply, an older recognition burning in her blood.

Above them, wings unfurled in radiant arcs. Golds, silvers, and violets blazed like stained glass, scattering prisms across the courtyard floor. The very air shimmered, bending beneath the downstroke of those wings.

This was not mere beauty.

It was legacy reborn.

Radiantus lifted his gaze, reverence softening the steel in his eyes.

"Aurelius," he said, voice low yet resonant. "Ancient among the Celestial Dragons. He and his kin wait at Lyra'el. They have chosen to stand with us."

The great dragon spiraled down, sunlight pouring from every scale. When his talons touched the courtyard stones, sigils of constellations flared briefly beneath his weight, then faded. The air thrummed with music like distant bells carried on a mountain wind.

Aurelius bowed his head to Radiantus with regal ease.

"The Celestial Dragons await you," he said, voice ringing like tempered crystal. "I kept them beyond the city gates, that the people might not meet awe with fear. You should be the one to announce our coming."

Radiantus inclined his head. "Wise as ever."

Keisha stepped forward, her voice low but sure. "Welcome home to Vacari, Aurelius."

The dragon's gaze turned to her, eyes deep with memory and light.

"We are no strangers here. We left when the balance faltered, centuries past. But when Radiantus came to us with news of the threat rising, we knew. We could not remain apart."

Keisha nodded, calm yet resolute. "Then Vacari is honored by your return."

Radiantus's wings flexed once, scattering starlight across the courtyard. His gaze lifted toward the horizon.

"It is time. Aurelius and I will fly to Lyra'el. There is much to prepare."

He glanced back at Valeon, a faint grin touching his lips.

"Do not cause too much trouble with those herbs, healer. I will be checking on your progress."

Laughter rippled through the courtyard, light and unguarded, carrying none of the tension that had weighed them down. Valeon flushed, but his smile held, the warmth of belonging taking deeper root within him.

Then, with a surge of power, Radiantus unfurled his wings. Aurelius mirrored him, gold and platinum rising together, celestial fire blazing like twin suns. Their ascent carved arcs of brilliance across the sky, scattering petals from the palace gardens. The air rang with the sounds of birdsong and the music of light.

For a long moment, the company stood silent, watching the two dragons climb higher and higher until they vanished into the horizon's glow.

For the first time in many years, it felt as though the light was winning.

Beneath the falling prisms, wind curling through his hair, Valeon made a vow—quiet, fierce, unshaken.

He would not waste this chance.

He would prove worthy of their trust.

Keisha's eyes glimmered not with tears, but with resolve. She felt it too.

This was only the beginning.

Chapter 10
Ink, Fire, and Frustration

The library of Crystal Vale breathed in silence.

Ancient shelves groaned like old bones. Parchment whispered against parchment. Shafts of golden light streamed through high-arched windows, turning drifting motes of dust into tiny constellations. The air was thick with the scent of time itself: dry vellum, metallic ink, and faint ghosts of herbs once pressed between pages. Lavender. Sage. A trace of rosemary. Whispers of remedies long gone.

At the center of it all, Valeon was losing a battle.

He sat cross-legged on the floor, encircled by a scatter of unfurled scrolls. One sagged across his knee. Another dangled loosely from his hand. Three more sprawled around him like fallen soldiers. He wasn't sure whether to laugh or curse, so he did neither. He only sighed, staring at the battlefield of parchment.

He squinted at the curling Elvish script until the letters began to blur.

"Why does every healing scroll have to be in Elven?" he muttered, tapping one silver-inked line as though it had mocked him. "I can barely read the alphabet, how am I supposed to know if this is a tea for coughs or something that'll turn a nose green?"

Leaning closer, he sniffed. Rosemary lingered sharp in the ink.

"Is that lavender? Or liverwort? Or fire-salt? No, not fire-salt. Last time was enough smoke for a year—"

"Careful, Valeon."

The smooth voice cut through the quiet. Valeon nearly toppled backward, a scroll sliding from his lap.

Kaelorn stood in the doorway, one brow raised, arms folded over a silver-blue cloak that shimmered like moonlit water.

"I heard muttering," he said, tone dry as parchment. "I assumed either a brewing catastrophe... or that you'd finally lost an argument with parchment."

Valeon groaned. "I've lost several. The scrolls are winning."

Kaelorn crossed the room, the leather of his gloves whispering as he knelt to retrieve a discarded roll. The crackle of old vellum was sharp in the silence.

"Let me guess. Ambitious. Determined. Completely illiterate in high Elvish medical script?"

"Is that what this is?" Valeon flopped onto his back, arms spread wide. "Figures. My mother taught me common sense. Everything else I learned from cantina menus and half-burned trade notes."

Kaelorn's smirk deepened. "Lucky for you, I read this mess fluently."

Valeon pushed himself upright, parchment sliding from his lap. "I'd be grateful. But... could you teach me to read it instead of just telling me? You won't always be here. And if I'm going to do this..." His voice fell, bare and earnest. "...I want to do it properly."

For the first time, Kaelorn's expression shifted from wryness to something softer. Respect, quiet and unexpected, touched his gaze. A memory flickered, ink-stained fingers, nights spent forcing stubborn glyphs into meaning. Seeing the same resolve in Valeon stirred something he hadn't expected.

"That," Kaelorn said, folding the scroll with reverence, "may be the wisest thing you've said since entering this room."

Valeon grinned faintly. "Low bar."

"Still clears it."

A laugh broke from behind the shelves. Both men turned as Thalorian emerged, cedar clinging to him like smoke.

"I wondered how long it would take you to notice the scrolls were in Elven," he said, mouth twitching with rare amusement. "You're not the first to fight them. But Kaelorn is right—if you're serious, you'll need the language."

Valeon blinked. "You've been here the whole time?"

Thalorian shrugged. "Long enough to hear you scold a fire-salt recipe. Worth every moment."

Kaelorn smirked. "You were waiting to see if he'd admit it himself."

"Of course," Thalorian said, a faint grin breaking through. "Far more entertaining that way."

Valeon buried his face in his hands. "I'm never going to live this down, am I?"

"Unlikely," Kaelorn said.

"But," Thalorian added, his tone gentler, "you are making progress. That matters."

Valeon lowered his hands. Despite himself, he smiled. "Then it's settled. I'll learn Elven. Even if it kills me."

Kaelorn passed him another scroll, his voice dry as ever.

"Let's make sure that isn't your first literal translation."

From the doorway, unseen by the others, Keisha leaned against the arch. She didn't speak. She didn't need to.

Soft laughter drifted from within the library, warm as sunlight through leaves, and it washed over her like a balm. Pride bloomed quietly in her chest. Valeon—who once avoided every crowded hall now sat among scrolls and sarcasm, stubbornly determined instead of hiding. She let the sight fill her, a fragile warmth taking root, before she slipped back into the corridor.

Outside, the air smelled of sun-baked stone and fresh herbs from the palace gardens. At the base of the steps, Ong and Gailen hunched over a city map, arguing with the intensity of generals—or perhaps lost travelers.

Keisha arched a brow. "Do I want to know?"

Gailen tucked the map under his arm, grinning. "We're... scouting."

"Highly classified cartographic strategy," Ong said, solemn as a judge.

"Scouting what?" Keisha pressed.

"A place for Valeon to test his potions where he won't burn down the market," Gailen replied.

Ong snorted. "Last time, he burned a hole clear through a fruit cart. The vendor nearly challenged him with a melon."

Keisha laughed until her gaze met Ong's. Mischief flickered in her eyes. "Funny. Remind me how long you struggled to read Elven when you first came to E'vahona?"

Color flooded Ong's face. He scratched at the back of his neck. A year ago, the jab might have cut. Now, it almost felt like belonging. "Keisha..."

Her grin widened. "I still have the letter you tried to write my father. The one where you accidentally proposed to a fountain."

Gailen doubled over, wheezing with laughter, the map nearly slipping from his grasp.

"Please," Ong muttered. "Don't tell Valeon."

Keisha only smiled wickedly and warmly and said nothing.

She watched the brothers walk off, still bickering about "safe explosion zones," her smile lingering as their laughter carried across the courtyard. The world was still scarred. Shadows still loomed. But laughter, unbidden and unguarded, was returning. And that, too, was healing.

Later that day, Valeon found himself surrounded.

Not by scrolls.

By people.

"Where exactly are we going?" he asked, peering over Ong's shoulder as the group herded him along.

"No peeking," Gailen said, grin wide.

"Just trust us," Kaelorn added, tone unreadable but sure.

They kept him in the center as they wound through the city streets, until the bustle faded to birdsong and the hush of wind moving through leaves.

Valeon caught the scents before he saw it: fresh rosemary, warm wood polish, the cool mineral tang of stone.

They stopped.

Keisha stepped ahead, eyes bright. "Look."

Valeon turned and froze.

A modest stone hall rose just beyond the walls, cradled in flame-leaf trees glowing gold and crimson beneath the sun. Vines curled along its foundation, while broad windows spilled soft light across polished steps.

Inside waited rows of shelves: half stacked with translated scrolls, half heavy with curling Elven script. Worktables stood ready, lined with jars of herbs, neat stacks of parchment, and a polished cauldron that gleamed as if eager for flame.

Gailen swept his arm wide. "Your very own mixing hall."

Valeon stared, breath caught, disbelief swelling until it ached. Weeks ago, he had hidden in shadows, bracing for exile. Now... this. A gift. A beginning. A promise.

"I... I don't even know what to say."

Keisha folded her arms, smirking. "Start with: I won't burn it down."

Valeon flushed. "That was one time—"

Laughter burst around him, bright and unrestrained. Even Kaelorn allowed himself to smile.

Valeon shook his head, though his grin was wide and unguarded. "Then I'd better get to work."

He stepped forward, running his hand across the sun-warmed wood of the table. The grain was smooth beneath his fingertips, solid, enduring. His touch lingered on a bundle of dried rosemary tied in twine. The sharp, clean scent rose, grounding him in the present.

The roots he thought were severed were growing again, quietly, steadily, alive.

This wasn't just a room.

It was a chance.

And he would rise to meet it.

Chapter 11

Embers of Wrath

The skies above Flameford churned with bruised clouds, rolling in like a tide of ash eager to smother the city. Sulfur burned in the air, acrid and suffocating, as though the very stones exhaled their anguish. Silence followed, unnatural, heavy as if the world itself dared not speak.

Then the tower doors exploded inward.

The crash rang like thunder against obsidian, and with it came a surge of raw power. Lightning ripped across the vaulted ceiling, gouging jagged scars into black stone before racing down the walls in a web of searing veins. Ozone stung the chamber, sharp and bitter, the scent of things scorched too quickly to burn.

A figure strode through the wreckage, robes snapping in a storm of their own making. Their eyes blazed like molten suns rimmed in shadow, coils of fire and darkness writhing around them, hissing as they struck the floor.

In the far corner, Lyra and Qellaun flinched. She shrank deeper into the gloom, fingers tight around her staff, while he stepped instinctively in front of her. Whatever lay tangled between them, his body remembered: he would always stand between his sister and danger.

The figure paced, fury sparking against the stones. Flames licked their robes as they roared:

"The gods intervened. Radiantus intervened. They dare steal from me, dare to strip me of what was promised. Dominion. Eternity. Mine by right!"

Lightning screamed upward, shattering a brazier and spilling molten fire down the steps in glowing rivulets. The tower shuddered.

When at last the storm ebbed, silence crept in again, tense and waiting. The siblings did not move.

Qellaun's gaze slid toward Lyra. Her breath trembled as she lifted her hands, weaving pale-blue threads of warding light, a fragile barrier against the lingering crackle of power.

Her voice was soft, but the question landed like a stone dropped in still water:

"Then the gods chose him over you?"

The figure's lip curled, flames ghosting beneath their cloak.

"Not just that. Radiantus returned. This means the old scrolls, which were meant to unbind the wards, are now useless. That meddling dragon has tipped the balance."

Their fury cooled into something more dangerous than rage.

"He was supposed to remain absent. Dormant. And now he stirs alliances that should never have rekindled."

The chamber dimmed as their power pulsed outward, no longer wild but sharpened to a lethal edge. Cracks glowed faintly in the stone, as if the tower itself strained beneath their will.

Their gaze snapped to Qellaun.

"You. Prepare for a journey."

Qellaun stiffened, his shoulders tightening before he caught himself. "Where?" His voice was steady, though he would not meet their eyes.

Instinct still drove him to shield Lyra, though every new command tightened the leash around his own throat.

"There is a city. New. Shadowhaven." The figure's mouth curved into something that wasn't quite a smile. "A haven for those who thrive in lawlessness."

They stepped closer, voices a ribbon of silken venom.

"You will go there. Learn what you can. Quietly. We may find allies... or tools."

Qellaun's jaw clenched. "That's across the Ivory Moonbeams."

"I am aware." Fire spat from their sleeve and died in a hiss. "Cross swiftly. Silently. Do not draw the Sylvan Elves' gaze. If they catch you, I will not protect you."

Qellaun's fist tightened at his side. Resentment flickered across his face, quickly buried, but not gone. He lowered his head. He would obey, for now.

In the shadows, Lyra's ward pulsed like a heartbeat. Her eyes narrowed, dread threading her voice.

"Shadowhaven... if even they turn on us, what then?"

The figure's eyes burned hotter, words falling like ash.

"Then we will turn them into what they were always meant to be."

They turned from Qellaun, gaze narrowing on Lyra.

"As for you," they said, voice cold as steel, "forget the scrolls. They are dust now."

Lyra's eyes flickered with unease, but she did not answer.

"I have another task for you that you must not fail."

The air chilled, slicing through the fading heat of lightning. Shadows clung to the figure like a second skin as their voice sharpened.

"You will contact an Umbral Elf named Rhys. Not a request. A command. He will take the mantle of leadership over the Umbral Elves at once."

Lyra's lips parted. "The ones said to be lurking near Lyra'el?"

A slow, cruel smirk. "There are no rumors. They have been watching. Waiting. They will serve—whether they realize it yet or not."

"And you want me to reach him now?"

"Through your magic," the figure replied. "For now. Your presence in Lyra'el must remain hidden until the moment I choose."

Lyra inclined her head, raising her hands. Pale glyphs shimmered into being, silver threads weaving under her trembling fingers. She steadied herself, but not before Qellaun caught the hesitation —the flicker of doubt she had tried to bury.

The figure swept past, cloak snapping like a banner of smoke. They stepped into the open archway, staring out over Flameford's ash-drenched sprawl. The storm muttered low on the horizon.

A cry split the night long, raw, not dragon, not wind. It reverberated through the tower, primal and hungry.

The figure's eyes burned brighter, their smile stretching in the gloom.

"It is time," they whispered. "Let Shadowhaven wake and let the Abyss rise."

Chapter 12
Whispers Beneath the Moonbeams

Qellaun drew the leather straps of his satchel tight, brisk, practiced, almost impatient. The corridor reeked faintly of scorched stone, and the chill of obsidian walls pressed through his cloak as though the tower itself meant to keep him. Inside, vials rattled against folded maps and sigil-etched charms—tools for quiet travel, or, if need be, for flight.

He glanced at his sister, voice low. "I'll admit it, I'm glad to leave. A few days without lightning chewing through the ceiling might do wonders for my nerves."

Lyra offered a faint smile, though it never reached her eyes.

Qellaun exhaled. "But what worries me isn't Shadowhaven. It's getting there."

"The Ivory Moonbeams," Lyra said, folding her arms.

He nodded, jaw tight. "The mysterious one thinks it will be simple for a lone traveler to pass unnoticed. But that forest watches everything. Sometimes you never see the Sylvan Elves... but they always see you. And they don't forgive trespass. Not from anyone who walks out of our lands."

His gaze flicked upward, toward the higher chambers of the tower. "Their temper reminds me of Phoenix."

Lyra's mouth quirked faintly. "True. But a short fuse isn't rare among those who wield too much power. Let magic seep into your bones long enough, and you start to think the world should bend faster to your will."

Qellaun huffed. "And when it doesn't, ceilings start losing pieces."

This time, her smile almost reached her eyes.

Still, as he slung the satchel across his shoulder, hesitation rippled through him. For all his complaints, part of him loathed leaving—not with Lyra trapped here under the shadow of that creature above. The path ahead was treacherous, but what lay behind might be worse. And beyond the Ivory Moonbeams waited Shadowhaven, a name that coiled in his chest like a warning.

Lyra's ward flickered faintly in her hands. She met her brother's gaze. "Shadowhaven... if it turns on us—"

Qellaun cut her off with a rough laugh, pulling her into a sudden, fierce embrace.

"Then it will learn I don't break so easily. And neither do you."

He released her, turned, and vanished into the waiting dark, leaving Flameford behind, stepping toward a forest that never slept, and a city born of shadows.

Lyra stood at the edge of the courtyard, watching until her brother's silhouette dissolved into the folds of mist. A flicker of loneliness stirred in her chest—brief, unspoken, unwelcome. She pressed it down, forcing her features to cool into something unreadable. His absence settled across her shoulders like a weight she refused to name.

Not today.

She turned sharply and slipped back inside. The air was colder here, thick with ash and the sharp tang of stone. Her boots rang against the floor as she gathered a worn satchel, a pouch of raw-cut crystals, and the binding amulet the mysterious one had pressed into her hands weeks ago. The metal throbbed faintly, as though it remembered who owned it.

A sudden flare split the shadows, heat brushing her cheek.

"Where are you going?"

The figure emerged from the stairwell, suspicion coiling in their voice.

Lyra's chin lifted. Frost edged her words. "To Fel Thalor. There is a leyline pool there that is stable enough to reach Rhys directly. More dependable than scrying from here."

Molten eyes narrowed, searching her face as she weighed every unspoken thought. Then, at last, a deliberate nod.

"Fine. But make certain he understands. No delay. No excuses. He takes command of the Umbral Elves now."

"I understand," Lyra said. Her voice was steady, though her fingers faltered over the glyphs. She caught the tremor and forced it still.

The figure turned, cloak snapping like a lash, and vanished into the labyrinth of black stone. No farewell. No trust. Only smoke in their wake.

Lyra moved quickly to the outer chamber, where a jagged arch loomed, veiled in shimmering shadow. She laid her palm against it, and the surface rippled cold, like water sealed beneath ice. For a heartbeat, memory clawed at her another ritual, another silence, a failure that had cut her to the bone.

She drew a long breath. This time, the glyphs thrummed in answer. The darkness curled around her fingers, not pushing her back but pulling her in.

It whispered her name.

Lyra stepped forward, and the gate closed over her like a mouth snapping shut.

Far from the tower's outer halls, past winding corridors where scorched stone drank the torchlight and ancient runes throbbed faintly in the walls, the mysterious figure descended into the heart of a place few knew existed.

At the base of a narrow stairwell waited a sealed chamber, its surface veiled in shadow, obsidian sigils pulsing with dark magic. A sharp gesture, a whispered word, and the runes unraveled, their glow bleeding away. The stone door groaned open.

Inside, the air was colder. Still, saturated not with absence, but with expectancy—like something vast crouched just beyond the dark, waiting to be named.

The figure strode to the center, where jagged crystal spires jutted in a crude ring. Raising a hand, they coaxed each shard alight until the chamber pulsed with fractured, unnatural brilliance.

"Come," they commanded, steel threading their tone, though urgency flickered beneath. "I told you it would soon be time."

The crystals throbbed, light quivering like a heartbeat. A whisper stirred the air, half wind, half voice. Then silence.

The figure's brow tightened. "I need the Shadow Dragons and the Abyssal brood. Both. The veil is thin. The gods stir. And still you delay."

The glow faltered, answering only with a restless hush.

Shadows curled around them as they stepped back, eyes burning with fury reined to a razor's edge. "They should have come already. Flameford waits. Shadowhaven waits. Their hesitation grows... tiresome."

A lash of fire spat from their cloak as they turned, storming from the chamber. The stone door slammed shut with the finality of a tomb.

Far from the tower's sight, deep in the ribs of a lava-forged cavern, two colossal figures stirred.

Zylron rose first, crimson scales dulled by shadow, molten eyes glowing with a hunger that never dimmed. Beside him, Glaciera coiled her frost-edged wings close, each breath spilling ribbons of ice that cracked in the air.

They had not been summoned. But they knew who had.

Their gazes met no words, only the measure of ancient warriors bound by grudges older than kingdoms. Somewhere beyond the horizon, the call to the Shadow Dragons and the Abyssal kin still echoed, waiting for an answer.

Zylron's tail scraped against stone, a low growl rolling from deep in his chest. Glaciera's eyes narrowed—not defiance, not yet... but judgment.

They had heard the summons meant for others.

And still, they remained.

Not loyal.

Not obedient.

And perhaps... not inclined to serve at all.

In the heart of Fel Thalor, where the air tasted like copper and ozone, Lyra stood within a ring of jagged crystal spires, their edges glimmering with fractured light. Ancient runes thrummed beneath her boots, each vibration synchronizing with the rhythm of her breath. When her spell locked into place, the tether of power snapped taut, humming like ice under strain.

A face formed in the veil, half-swallowed by shadow, eyes sharp and watchful. His voice cut the stillness.

"Who are you? Why do you call me?"

Lyra's expression hardened, her words snapping like frost.

"I am Lyra Dreadcrusher of Fel Thalor. I speak by command of the one you will serve. The mysterious one demands you take command of the Umbral Elves—now."

Silence spread, thick as stone.

Rhys shifted, his gaze narrowing. "These things take time. I have been observing—"

Lyra's laugh was cold, edged with venom. "Shall I repeat that for them? 'Rhys requests more time.' Do you think they will be amused?"

His jaw clenched. His breath caught. "No. It will be done. Immediately."

Her smirk sharpened, predatory. Once, she might have lowered her eyes. Not anymore.

"Good."

Rhys hesitated. "Will... you speak to me again?"

Lyra's gaze glimmered with dark amusement that never reached her eyes. "For now, the mysterious one has placed me at your side. But don't mistake me for lenient."

Her magic lashed out. Unseen coils tightened around his throat. He choked, eyes blazing, until she released him with a flick. The threads dissolved into smoke.

"Do you understand?"

"Yes," he rasped.

The shimmer collapsed, leaving only silence.

Lyra exhaled, lips curling with quiet, dangerous satisfaction. Rhys needed the reminder. And she—she had needed the proof. This power was hers, not borrowed.

She shouldered her satchel and turned to the shadow-rimmed gateway. For an instant, she remembered another ritual, another silence, a failure that had cut her to the bone. Her hand hovered, trembling, over the surface. It rippled coldly, like water sealed beneath ice.

Then she stepped through. The shadows surged up to meet her, wrapping her in their chill embrace.

They whispered her name as they closed around her—

Not as a stranger.

But as kin.

Chapter 13

Eyes in the Canopy

The canopy of the Ivory Moonbeams rose like a vaulted hall, sunlight filtering through pale leaves that shimmered like silvered glass. Qellaun placed each step with care, his boots barely brushing the moss-soft earth.

The forest was quiet.

Not the comfort of peace, but the weighted hush of an audience that did not wish to be seen.

He shifted his satchel and swept the underbrush and high, braided limbs with a measured glance. Nothing moved. Nothing stirred. And yet—

"I'm not alone," he breathed.

Far above, in a lattice of moonlit branches, Sylvan Elves crouched in perfect stillness, features veiled in leaf and shadow, eyes glinting like starlight. They did not speak. They did not intervene. They watched.

Qellaun drew his cloak tighter and pressed on. The silence clung too closely, too deliberately, echoing childhood tales that whispered through his mind. The Sylvan Elves were ever-watchful, seen only when they wished.

He paused, glanced back. Nothing but trees and silver light. But he knew.

"They saw me," he murmured. "They always do."

The wind brushed the canopy, soft as breath too soft to be only wind. He shook his head and walked on, pretending not to notice.

When he stepped beyond the edge of their sacred wood, the watchers did not give chase. One slipped soundlessly from a perch and vanished deeper into the trees.

In a hidden glade, beneath the root-spires of an ancient moonwood, the elders gathered. The wind carried news of the trespass.

"He did not disturb the land," one murmured.

"But he entered it," said another.

"And that cannot go unanswered."

An elder with snow-pale braids and eyes like riverstone lifted a hand; moonlight bloomed faintly in her palm.

"A Druchii walks our path, one whose steps have already stirred enough trouble beyond our borders."

A ripple passed through the circle.

"Send word to Lord Karrenen, the Eladrin mage of E'vahona," she said. "He will know what must be done."

By the time Qellaun reached his first clearing, his name was already riding the wind toward E'vahona.

Back in Flameford, the air thickened, carrying the stench of scorched stone—and something older, colder.

A ripple of magic cracked through the volcanic sky as a massive, scaled form descended from the storm, wreathed in tendrils of void-born mist.

Vorathos had arrived.

Her scales gleamed with abyssal sheen, black as the void rimmed in violet fire. Smoke trailed from her wings, not flame, and her obsidian gaze cut through stone and thought alike. Behind her, a host of abyssal kin followed in disciplined silence.

From the balcony tower, the mysterious figure swept down to the Cavern of Ash, ignoring Zylron and Glaciera, where they lurked in silence.

"Vorathos," they called, voice reverent. "We are honored by your arrival."

The dragon's horns curled like void-wrought stone as she tilted her head.

"We felt the pulse," she said, her voice deep and resonant. "The time draws near."

"You may choose any place in Flameford," the figure urged. "Establish your lair where you wish."

Vorathos's eyes gleamed faintly. "This realm is thin. Comfortable enough for connection, not habitation. Our true dwelling remains in the Void."

She glanced past the figure, a smirk curving like a blade.

"So. These are your warriors?"

Her voice dripped with disdain. "No wonder you failed."

The mysterious person's jaw twitched, though they hid the sting.

"These dragons are weak."

Zylron's crimson eyes narrowed at the insult. Heat shimmered beneath his talons, cracking the stone. Glaciera's breath spilled in a plume of frost across the floor, her silence colder than words.

Vorathos did not wait for a reply. "My kind will show you what strength truly is." With a hiss of unraveling magic, she launched skyward, her kin streaming after her in eerie grace. From the northern edge of Flameford, her voice thundered back through the clouds:

"Voraxia and the Shadow Dragons come soon. Then you will have your reckoning."

Silence draped the cavern after she vanished into the storm.

It did not last.

Zylron's growl cracked the air, wings flaring wide. "How dare that abyssal worm dismiss me!" His tail lashed, scattering stone and ash.

From the shadows, Xalzorath unfurled, his voice oozing like oil. "She spoke as if she already ruled this domain."

Zylron's snort was a mix of fire and contempt. "I am Warlord of the Flamebound. I earned it in fire and blood. I remember the Battle of Vacari when I brought down Caelum, the Copper Dragon. I claimed that sky in flame. Let her try to match that."

His lips peeled back, heat curling in his throat. "I have fought more battles for this cause than she ever will."

Glaciera's tail twitched; her eyes glittered with a frostbitten judgment that needed no words. Even Nocturna, still as shadow, gave a slow nod.

"She slighted us all," she murmured.

Zylron's flames flared, then dimmed. "For now, we watch. Let her build. But if the Shadow Dragons dismiss me as she did—"

He left the threat unfinished. The heat rolling from his scales said more than words.

The others bowed their heads in grim accord, wings folding like drawn blades. Something was splintering in the shadows. And it would not take much to shatter it.

Unseen above, the mysterious figure stood cloaked in the upper corridor, eyes narrowing as they listened to every word.

Zylron's fury was no longer a weapon they could wield.

It was becoming a blade pointed at them.

Chapter 14
The Return to Light

The terraces lay pristine, silver-barked trees rising taller than memory, their blossoms spilling soft light into the air. Wind harps strung between crystal branches chimed gently as unseen streams whispered in the distance. Magic hummed here, the old kind, from before the wars and the fractures.

Celestial attendants moved among the grounds in flowing robes, their luminous eyes lifting as he descended. Awe lit their faces; reverence slowed their steps. One bowed low, voice like music.

"Welcome home, Radiantus. We have kept the sanctum ready... for when you returned."

Radiantus inclined his head, his voice gentle thunder. "You have done well. The peace of this place still breathes."

From the far end of the terrace, a woman broke into a run. Sun-touched skin, golden-braided hair catching the light like spun fire, robes of lavender and white streaming behind her. Crystal beads chimed in her hair as she crossed the wide span without hesitation.

"Radiantus!"

Tears glimmered in her eyes as she flung her arms around his massive neck. He froze only a moment before rumbling low—a sound that seemed to vibrate the stone beneath their feet. Lowering his head, he brushed his muzzle gently along her shoulder, scales warm against her skin.

"Tahlira," he said.

She smiled through tears, the kind of smile that carried a lifetime of guarded hope, now burning bright.

"You remember me?"

"I remember your ancestor," Radiantus replied, eyes softening. "He rode beside me through the Burning Skies and the Silence War. His courage saved cities, and he fell with honor. I have not seen his line since."

Her hand pressed to her heart. "I am the fifth generation of his blood. We have trained. We have remembered. I never thought I would see you return."

He studied her quietly. Then, with a gravity that seemed to bend the air itself, he asked:

"Would you consent... to ride with me?"

It was more than a question. It was a bridge across centuries, a soul long alone choosing not to stand apart. Radiantus had resisted bonds for ages. But danger was encroaching, prophecy stirring. He could resist no longer.

Tahlira gasped. "I—yes! I have trained since childhood, dreaming of this moment. I would be honored beyond words."

A low hum escaped him, warm and resonant, like a star exhaling its first light.

"Then it is done," he said. "A bond, reborn from legacy. Let it begin anew."

But already his gaze was distant, weighted with purpose. "More riders will be needed. Your people must be ready—for what is coming, and for what I have brought with me."

Her joy steadied into resolve. She bowed swiftly. "They will come. And when the darkness rises, they will not stand alone."

Radiantus nodded once, sunlight glinting on his platinum scales as he turned toward the open plaza beyond the sanctum, a vast expanse of pale stone ringed by luminous obelisks and silver-arched bridges. At its heart lay the square of Elarion, the living pulse of Lyra'el.

His claws struck the stone like steady drumbeats. Celestials paused mid-task. Children hushed on balconies. Scholars stilled their quills. Some gasped. Others wept.

Radiantus had returned.

Tahlira did not linger. She wove through moonstone bridges and hanging gardens, her voice carrying clear:

"Come! Come to the square! The Platinum Dragon Radiantus has returned, and he brings news!"

The words rippled outward like starlight on still water. Gates opened, windows unlatched, and the square began to fill.

Above, cloaked in stillness, Rhys watched from a high bridge. Crimson eyes followed the gathering throng, envy smoldering beneath a calculating gaze. Radiantus's name rose like a prayer, while his own was spoken only in shadow. That would change.

Below, Radiantus unfurled his wings, his sigh the opening chord of a hymn.

"My people," he said, "I am glad to be home."

Silence fell.

"It has been too long. And for my absence, I owe you an apology. I thought distance would shield you, but in truth, I left you vulnerable. For that, I ask forgiveness."

His gaze swept the elders, the warriors, and the children alike. "The world beyond has not been quiet. The time for our return is overdue. I bring with me the Platinum Dragons, our kin once scattered. They are home now. And not only them... I bring the Celestial Dragons, born of light and wisdom, returned to aid us."

Gasps swept the square. One elder stepped forward, bowing low.

"Their name was never forgotten. They are welcome... as you are."

Radiantus inclined his head. "Then we move forward together. Darkness spreads in Vacari. Shadows once broken now reform. Dragons twisted by the void, and a being hidden who plots against all bonds of light. They seek to consume what we have rebuilt."

The crowd shivered like leaves in the wind.

"But we will not allow it. We will stand. We will protect not only Vacari, but the balance itself."

Strength rose in their voices, no longer whispers but a unified voice. Towers lit with inner glow, bridges gleaming with new resolve.

Yet Radiantus's heart stirred with memory of another crowd, another vow of unity, before fire rained on the Temple of Accord. Not again. This time, he would lead with clarity and caution.

He turned to Tahlira. "Tell them I will return soon. And not alone."

"They'll be ready," she promised.

Radiantus lifted into the sky, platinum fire streaking across the horizon.

And in the ivy-shadowed spire, Rhys slipped away. Glyphs burned faint against his palm, each word a thread of betrayal. His eyes were cold. His mission set.

The Platinum had returned to light.

Rhys would return to the shadows.

Chapter 15
The Flight of Light

The wind swept gently across the high plateau where the
Platinum Dragons gathered—gleaming titans of wisdom and
power, their scales shimmering with the light of ages. Beside them
stood the Celestial Dragons, radiant in their otherworldly grace,
wings folded like veils of molten starlight as they waited in silence.

Then he came.

A trail of platinum brilliance tore through the clouds, each sweep
of his vast wings scattering motes like drifting constellations. Radiantus descended in measured arcs, landing at the heart of the gathering with a soft quake of stone. The wind stilled, as though the very
air bowed in reverence.

He raised his head, his voice strong yet warm.

"It is time. The path is clear. The realm of Lyra'el stands ready. We
return together."

A murmur rippled through the assembly like wind over crystal, like
dawn meeting fire.

Radiantus turned to Aurelius, whose scales shimmered in shifting hues of gold, silver, sapphire, and rose.

"Aurelius," he said, his voice gentling, "some in Lyra'el still remember your kind."

Aurelius blinked, wonder flickering in his ageless eyes.

"After all this time?"

"Vacari never forgets," Radiantus said. His gaze was steady, his tone reverent. "Nor do the Celestials of Lyra'el. Your echoes lived on in song, in story, in spirit."

For a moment, Aurelius could not speak. Then he bowed his head, solemn and moved.

"Then let us return. Not in secrecy. But in light."

Radiantus spread his wings, sunlight blazing across their span.

"To Lyra'el!"

The dragons rose as one Platinum and Celestial together their wing-beats pounding like drums of memory and triumph. The sky ignited with fire and starlight, arcs of gold and silver carving brilliance into the air as they swept toward the horizon.

Ahead lay the cradle of harmony and light. Elarion glimmered in the distance, its lake flashing like molten glass, its towers burning with prismatic glow, its bridges strung in silver arcs. Children and elders alike lifted their eyes, breathless, as the heavens themselves blazed with wings reborn.

But in the highest spire, unseen by the rejoicing multitude, shadows lingered still.

The people of Lyra'el had not been idle during Radiantus's absence. They had labored with quiet devotion, weaving gardens into living ta-pestries of silver and gold, restoring sanctuaries until even the air seemed to sing, rekindling halls that had slept in silence for centuries. Word spread along crystal avenues until thousands filled the terraces, plazas, and hanging gardens to witness the impossible.

The dragons were returning.

The first sign came as a shimmer, faint as a mirage, beyond the silver canopy of the Singing Forest. Then the shapes broke through the horizon: platinum arcs, ribbons of celestial flame, wings like living constellations. Their formation swept in a vast, gliding curve over crystal glades and cascading ridges, the air thrumming with the weight of their power.

Gasps rose like a tide. The young, too young to remember the Age of Harmony except as stories, cried out in awe. Their wings flared silver-blue as they rushed to the plaza, voices tumbling over one another in wonder.

The elders did not move. They only watched, tears carving silver tracks down their cheeks as centuries of silence cracked open. For them, the sight was not only a miracle but also a cherished memory. The dream of return, carried by those long gone, is now fulfilled at last.

"To see them return," one elder whispered, voice breaking, "is to believe in miracles again." Her hands trembled against her chest, and her eyes burned with tears for her sister, Aelira, who had died still dreaming of this day.

Side by side, Radiantus and Aurelius descended—not into the crowded heart of Elarion, but toward the Skyward Sanctums: vast platforms of starstone and quartz suspended along the outer ridges. Waterfalls spilled from their edges, scattering rainbows like blessings across the air.

Claws struck stone with resonant finality. Ancient glyphs flared to life. Blossoms swirled on the wind, catching in wings that gleamed with platinum, gold, and violet fire.

This was no mere return.

It was a renewal.

It was a covenant.

A crystalline bell tolled from the high tower, each note ringing outward like starlight poured into sound. The vow of Lyra'el awakened once more: never again would the realm forget its guardians.

"Radiantus!"

The cry rang bright and familiar. Tahlira approached, robes trailing light, her golden braids glittering in the sun. Pride lit her eyes.

"You've been busy," Radiantus rumbled, warmth threading through his thunder-deep voice.

"As have you," she replied, bowing her head. "But while you gathered the dragons... I gathered their future."

She stepped aside.

Dozens stood ready. Eladrin, Celestial-born, and those of mingled blood. Their stances were steady, their eyes alight with anticipation.

"Dragonriders," Tahlira said. "Chosen. Trained. Ready."

Radiantus's chest tightened. For a heartbeat, the weight of centuries pressed against him—the silence, the losses, the broken vows. And then it lifted, falling away before this living answer.

Aurelius's eyes glimmered, voice hushed with memory. He saw again the starlit peaks, the rush of wind, the laughter of a rider whose absence was still a wound unhealed. To be remembered after so long, it struck deeper than he could bear to admit.

Radiantus stepped forward, voice steady, edged with vow.

"Welcome. Your presence is the promise of tomorrow. Soon you will bond with dragons who will walk with you, fly with you, fight beside you."

His wings lifted, radiant arcs stretching like sunrise across the square.

"The light has returned. And you—" his gaze lingered on Tahlira, her golden braids blazing like sunlight through rain "you are its flame."

The square erupted. Voices rose like a hymn, rolling through terraces and towers, scattering across moonstone bridges. The sound was not a mere celebration. It was a rebirth.

Radiantus let the roar wash over him not as a sovereign receiving worship, but as a guardian receiving a vow. For the first time in centuries, the balance stirred with promise.

Yet above, in the shadowed Highbridge, Rhys lingered. A knot of Umbral Elves waited behind him, cloaked in silence, eyes sharp with old grievance. His crimson gaze burned with envy, though his smile was thin, brittle.

Let them cheer. Let them believe.

The scales would tip soon enough.

And when they did, it would not be toward the light.

Chapter 16

F ar beyond the sanctum, across the realms of Vacari, whispers had already begun. Dragonrider academies—once dismissed as myth, then forgotten as folly were stirring again.

The age of dragons was not merely returning. It was rising.

Yet not every soul was destined to ride. The ancient races, the Eladrin, the Celestial-blooded, the Aquanar Elves, and humankind possessed the strength and balance necessary to form bonds. On Lyra'el, training had never ceased; its people had kept the old disciplines alive through centuries of silence, honing riders without dragons, waiting for the day the skies would blaze anew. When Radiantus and his kin returned, the riders of Lyra'el were ready to answer.

Others could only watch. The fae, too delicate in form, and the merfolk, bound forever to the sea, knew the saddles of dragons were not meant for them.

One fae, perched lightly on a flowering vine, smiled to herself. She could never ride, but her magic had helped weave the healing sanctums that now glowed beneath the dragons. Their return was her triumph too, even if her wings would never share the sky with theirs.

Within the heart of Lyra'el, the echoes of her people's devotion still lingered. For centuries, while dragons slumbered and the rest of the world forgot, the riders of Lyra'el had trained in empty saddles, practicing the bond with nothing but memory and faith. Now, at last, their patience was rewarded. Radiantus, the Platinum Dragon of legend, had chosen.

Tahlira laid a hand on his gleaming jaw, marveling at the warmth that radiated through her palm. From the city below came the chiming of bells, a chorus of disbelief and hope.

"Radiantus," she whispered, lifting her gaze into his molten-gold eyes, "in the sanctum they spoke of others of Crystal Vale, of Goldmoor, of academies I have never seen. Are there truly riders waiting there as well? Could I ever meet them?"

The dragon's massive head dipped until his gaze leveled with hers. The corners of his mouth curved upward in what could only be called a dragon's smile.

"Words are pale shadows, little one," he rumbled, his breath a furnace-warm wind. "Better that you see with your own eyes. But before we cross the world, you must know your own sky. Mount, and I will show you Lyra'el as it was meant to be seen."

Her heart quickened as she placed her foot against a ridge of shining scale and climbed into the saddle. The leather was smooth, yet alive beneath her touch, as though it shared the dragon's pulse. She settled into place, fingers gripping the silver harness.

Radiantus spread his wings. They unfurled like twin banners of light, vast and iridescent, each beat drawing a rush of wind that rippled across the flowering terraces. With a bound, he launched upward, the ground dropping away in a blur.

Lyra'el unfolded beneath them not the labyrinth of narrow streets Tahlira had always known, but a living mosaic: marble towers spiraling like frozen song, bridges strung like harp-strings between floating platforms, waterfalls spilling from the cliffs into mist. From this height, even the grandest spires seemed delicate, as though the city itself were a jewel cradled in the world's palm.

Tahlira pressed a hand to her breast, laughter and tears mingling on her lips. "I never knew it was so beautiful," she whispered, her words carried off on the roaring wind.

"Few who walk the stones ever see it thus," Radiantus replied, his wings bearing them higher still. "This is why the Lyra'el kept faith through the centuries. They remembered the promise of the sky."

Tahlira closed her eyes against the rising sun, letting its brilliance wash over her. For the first time since her father's death, the weight in her chest lifted. She was not only a daughter. She was a rider now and the heavens themselves had opened to her.

Vista One: Goldmoor and the Purplefire Woods

Radiantus's wings beat with measured power as he bore Tahlira toward the golden city. Below, Goldmoor's spires blazed like spears of sunlight thrust into the earth, while the sky above teemed with motion—dragons of gold and amethyst wheeling in disciplined arcs as their riders called commands that rang against the air.

From the highest spire, a dragon rose to meet them, vast, radiant, his scales burning like molten metal. Upon his back sat a young man crowned in gold, armored for war: King Alex of Goldmoor, sovereign of the realm.

Alex guided his mount alongside, awe brightening his eyes. "By the stars," he called, voice carrying against the wind. "Never have I seen one such as you. Tell me, mighty dragon—who are you, that the heavens blaze at your wings?"

Radiantus's laughter rolled like thunder across the sky. "I am Radiantus, first of the noble host, guardian of dawn." He tilted a wing, revealing Tahlira, her golden hair streaming in the wind. "And this is Tahlira of Lyra'el, my chosen rider."

Before Alex could answer, another sound split the heavens. It was deeper than thunder, older than storms—the groan of mountains shifting in their sleep. From the horizon, a dragon even greater than Radiantus descended, wings unfurling in arcs of living gold.

Kimras.

The Ancient Golden fell upon the city like sunrise made flesh, his brilliance dimming even Goldmoor's radiant towers. The assembled riders below stilled, their eyes wide with reverence.

"Brother of dawn," Kimras rumbled, voice thick with timeless fire. "At last, you return."

Radiantus bowed his great head. "Kimras, flame of the ancients. I have long awaited this moment."

The golden titan turned to Tahlira. She felt the very air pause, her breath catching beneath the weight of his gaze.

"And this must be she, the child of Lyra'el," Kimras said. His tone was solemn, but not unkind. "Rare indeed, for one of your kind to be chosen by a noble dragon. My Keisha remains in Crystal Vale, with her warrior-lord. An Eladrin, and yet truer than any I have known."

The name struck Tahlira like a harp string, resonant and bright. To hear Keisha's name spoken by Kimras himself made her feel part of a tapestry older than stars.

Alex's dragon wheeled closer, holding steady against the storm of light. The young king bowed low in his saddle. "Radiantus, your return is a gift to all Vacari. Goldmoor has long held the name of Jewel, but today it is your light that makes the heavens shine brighter. You and your rider are welcome here."

Tahlira's throat tightened. She had expected suspicion. Instead, warmth.

"You would be welcomed in Lyra'el," she said softly. "It remembers its friends."

Kimras's vast shadow cloaked them as he intoned, "So it shall be. The bonds rise anew not for one realm, but for all Vacari."

Radiantus turned eastward, wings catching the sun. With a single sweep, he carried them toward the horizon. Hills unrolled beneath them like waves, fading into deep forest. Ahead, the sky flared violet.

The Purplefire Woods.

An endless expanse shimmered below trees aflame with amethyst light, branches whispering with otherworldly fire. Nymphs darted among the glowing boughs, their laughter falling like silver chimes. Amethyst dragons soared overhead, violet fire trailing from their wings, golden dragons blazing beside them like suns.

"It's... beautiful," Tahlira breathed.

One nymph rose higher, spinning through the air until she hovered before them. Her voice was song and wind entwined.

"Welcome, Rider of Radiantus. These woods are sacred, reborn from ash. Once broken, but through Keisha's courage and the power of those beside her, life has returned. Guard them well. They are hers, and through them the world remembers."

She drifted back into the violet glow. Radiantus's voice rumbled low, his eyes reflecting the firelit canopy.

"The shadow came here once. The forest burned to blackened bone. Yet through her defiance, the Purplefire rose again. What you see, Tahlira, is more than beauty. It is proof that hope cannot be slain."

Tahlira swallowed hard, her chest trembling with wonder. The word "hope" was no longer just a song or a creed. It lived in the light, brushing her skin.

Vista Two: Ivory Moonbeams and Twilight Grove

Radiantus bore them eastward, wings gliding on ribbons of wind. Behind them, the violet glow of the Purplefire faded into a gentler radiance. Ahead stretched a forest of pale boughs, every trunk gleaming like carved ivory, every leaf edged in silver light. Moonbeams spilled through the canopy in liquid streams, casting the land in a dreamlike glow.

"The Ivory Moonbeams," Radiantus murmured, his voice touched with reverence. "Here dwell the Sylvan Elves, keepers of songs older than kings."

Tahlira leaned forward, eyes wide. Among the trees, tall, slender elves moved with unearthly grace, their hair shining like starlight. Their voices rose together in harmony, a hymn so pure it seemed woven into the breath of the forest itself. For a heartbeat, she felt suspended inside a living chord of music.

The forest deepened into twilight. Between the pale boughs rose towers of stone entwined with glowing vines, lanterns burning with soft, eternal flame.

"The Twilight Grove," Radiantus said. "A sanctuary of the Sylvan hidden in shadow and song. Long have they kept their vigil, waiting for the day the skies would awaken."

Tahlira's heart swelled. To know that even here, so far from Lyra'el, others had prepared, guarding the old ways through silence and shadow, filled her with wonder. She was not part of a forgotten tradition. She was part of something vast.

But then, at the forest's edge, darkness loomed. Black towers clawed at the horizon, jagged spires where the light faltered. The air itself thickened, as though unwilling to cross that threshold.

"What is that?" she whispered.

Radiantus's wings stiffened. His voice rumbled low with unease.

"Shadowhaven. Once it was a refuge for wanderers and seafarers, a city of freedom. Now the shadow has claimed it. Pirates rule its streets, and darker masters whisper in its halls. We will not linger."

He banked sharply away, the brilliance of his wings scattering the gloom. Tahlira shivered, casting one last glance at the blackened city. She thought she saw figures upon the ramparts, their eyes lifted to the sky.

A chill clung to her, heavy as iron, until the wind carried her gaze forward once more.

Vista Three: The Shimmering Beach and the Cerulean Expanse.

Then the darkness broke. The land fell away into brilliance, and before them stretched the Shimmering Beach. Sands glittered in hues of silver and gold, as though the shore itself had been forged from starlight.

Beyond, the sea gleamed with iridescent light, its waves rolling like liquid glass.

Tahlira pressed her hand to her chest, breathless. "It's endless," she whispered.

Radiantus's laughter rolled like sunlight over water. "Here, sea and sky embrace. Beyond those waters lies more than you can even dream, little one. Vacari is stirring... and this is only the beginning."

He tilted his wings, sweeping low over the glittering shoreline. The beach shone like spilled constellations, and from the surf came a thunderous roar.

Three immense forms surged from the waves, Bronze Dragons, their scales glinting like storm-polished copper. Water streamed from their wings as they rose, droplets scattering like jewels across the sunlit air. Their cries mingled with the sea's crash, fierce and jubilant.

Tahlira clung tightly, her heart hammering, only to gasp again as her gaze caught sight of the figure astride one of the titans.

His skin shimmered like moonlit water, hair flowing dark as kelp in the wind. Fins traced the curve of his arms like silvered blades, and his eyes gleamed with the fathomless depth of the sea.

"An elf," Tahlira breathed. "But not—"

"Not Sylvan," Radiantus finished, his voice filled with pride. "The Aquanar Elves, children of tide and starlight. Long have they hidden in the Cerulean Expanse, guarding their realm beneath the waves. Few upon the land believed they still endured. Yet they, too, have answered the call. Where the merfolk cannot ride, the Aquanar soar upon bronze wings."

Below, the surf broke in glimmers of green and sapphire as merfolk leapt in joy, their voices rising in song to greet the dragons. The Aquanar rider lifted a hand in salute, droplets of sea-light cascading from his fingers like falling stars.

Tahlira's breath caught once more. She had lived her life among elves but never dreamed of hidden kin who could ride noble dragons. With every beat of Radiantus's wings, the world was widening—revealing wonders she had never imagined.

Her gaze lingered on the sweep of the Shimmering Beach, bronze wings, sea spray, and the Aquanar's shining salute. But beyond the horizon, the waters deepened into a darker blue... where the ocean kissed shadowed land.

Vista Four: Etharyon

Radiantus carried them eastward, wings gliding on ribbons of wind. The glow of the Shimmering Beach faded into silver twilight, until ahead rose forests of pale boughs, their trunks gleaming like carved ivory, every leaf edged with a ghostly sheen. Moonbeams poured through the canopy in liquid streams, bathing the land in dreamlike radiance.

"Silvaraen," Radiantus murmured, reverence threading his thunder-deep voice. "Home of the Moon Elves—guardians of the quiet paths, singers of the night's hymn."

Tahlira leaned forward, wonder swelling in her chest. Among the branches, tall figures moved with unearthly grace, their hair glimmering like strands of starlight. Their voices rose together in harmony so pure it seemed to be drawn from the forest itself. Pale-haired children danced at the roots of the moonwoods, laughter ringing like bells. One tossed a flower-wreath into the air; the wind caught it and carried it upward, spinning weightlessly until it landed in Tahlira's waiting hands.

She held it close, the blossoms glowing faintly as if lit from within. Her throat tightened. This was not a legend. Not memory. This was real.

"They honor what they see," Radiantus rumbled, his tone warming with pride. "The bond between us is not only remembered. It is a herald of hope."

Tahlira pressed the wreath to her chest, tears stinging her eyes. That word again hope. Not as a song sung to children, but as something alive, tangible, breathing.

Radiantus rose higher, and the forest gave way to a vision that stole her breath anew.

Ahead shimmered Aerindral. Towers of sapphire and silver spiraled upward like frozen waves, bridged by threads of crystal light. Waterfalls spilled in luminous veils, scattering droplets that glowed like shards of the moon. Gardens of pale blossoms clung to terraces that seemed to hang between earth and sky. The city itself looked carved from a dream.

"It's..." Tahlira's voice broke into a laugh that trembled with awe. "It's like flying into a song."

Radiantus's golden eyes reflected the crystalline glow. "The soul of Etharyon, reborn. Even here, the riders stir. The song rises, Tahlira. Can you hear it?"

She closed her eyes. And yes, she could, not with her ears, but through the living bond in her chest, a resonance that felt like all Vacari singing at once.

But as they soared higher, her wonder faltered. Beyond Aerindral, jagged peaks tore at the horizon, black stone veined with cold silver, their caverns breathing a deeper shadow.

"Radiantus..." Her voice had softened, wary. "What lies there?"

The Platinum Dragon's wings stiffened, though his flight remained steady.

"Those mountains hold more than stone. The noble dwarves dwell within, keepers of deep fires and forges older than kings. But not all who woke in Etharyon are friends. Dark dragons also coil in those depths. I will not endanger you by drawing closer."

A chill threaded through her awe, but Tahlira only nodded, trusting him.

Radiantus wheeled away, scattering a rain of light across the silver canopy below.

"Come. You have seen enough of what lies in Etharyon. Now we return by another path toward the realm of emerald fire and living strength."

Vista Five: The Crystal Vale and the Emerald Woods.

Radiantus turned them southward, the silver-gold arc of his wings carrying them away from Etharyon's perilous heights. The air grew warmer, rich with the scent of pine and living earth. Ahead, like a sea of emerald fire, the canopy of the Emerald Woods stretched across the horizon.

Verdantia and Thalorian wheeled gracefully beside them, emerald flame twining with Radiantus's argent blaze. Birds darted through the leaves below, their songs blending with the hum of unseen magic.

Then a brighter light stirred. A fairy darted upward on gossamer wings, bearing a wreath of blossoms that glowed with a green fire. With a lilting laugh, she hovered before Tahlira and set the wreath upon her golden hair.

Tahlira's hands flew to her head, startled, but then her lips curved into a radiant smile, her eyes bright with wonder. "Thank you," she whispered, her voice nearly lost to the wind.

The fairy dipped in midair, spiraling down into the trees. As Tahlira's gaze followed, she glimpsed a figure at the forest's edge, A man taller than any Sylvan, with chestnut hair and Glade-Fire eyes a vibrant green kindled with golden sparks, echoing the light of Vacari's sacred glades. Fins traced the curve of his arms, catching the light like silver blades.

Thalorian leaned forward from Verdantia's back, recognition brightening his gaze. "That is Kaelorn, Guardian of the fair folk. Born of fae and man, he bridges their two worlds and watches over the Ivory and Emerald groves."

Tahlira pressed the wreath more firmly to her brow. A half-fae, half-human... and the fair folk followed him with joy. The world was larger, stranger, and far more beautiful than she had ever imagined.

Radiantus lifted higher, sunlight scattering in radiant streams across his wings. "It is time, little one. You have seen much, but now we fly to Crystal Vale. There, destiny waits, and the song grows louder."

The air cooled as they swept eastward. Below, the land rolled in green waves, hills folding into one another until the horizon erupted in brilliance.

Crystal Vale.

Vast cliffs glittered with crystalline growths, shattering sunlight into cascades of color. Waterfalls poured in endless ribbons down faceted rock, spilling into misty pools that turned the valley into a living prism. Bridges of crystal arched between cliffside towers, each glowing as if woven from starlight itself. The city shone as though the world's light had chosen it for its dwelling.

Tahlira pressed her hand to her lips. "Radiantus... how can such a place exist? How could they build it without breaking the world?"

Radiantus's gaze softened. "They did not. The Crystal Dragons themselves guided the first settlers of the Vale. Every stone was shaped in harmony with the land, never against it. That is why it shines."

Her heart swelled with awe until Radiantus angled toward a shadowed alcove carved deep in the cliffs. She frowned, glancing back at the radiant terraces. "Why not the city?"

Radiantus's chest rumbled with sorrow. "Because I must see to one of my own. Aurelia lies within, wounded. She stood against Nocturna, the Obsidian Dragon, and bore the cost."

The joy of discovery dimmed to dread. Tahlira clutched her wreath as they spiraled down into a cradle of crystal and mist. There lay Aurelia, her scales shimmering in prisms of silver and rose, one vast wing scarred and dulled by shadow's bite.

At her side knelt a young man with ash-brown hair, his head bowed in concentration as he pressed a cloth soaked in healing waters against her wound. Across his back rested the Crystalbow, its limbs glowing faintly with his heartbeat. Every motion he made was steady, not from duty, but devotion.

Radiantus lowered his head with reverence. "So, the Crystalbow has awakened for you," he rumbled. "I am proud to meet the rider of Aurelia, and to see you guard the legacy of your line. But take heed, Prince of Crystal Vale. That bow is more than a weapon. Guard it well for the darkness covets what it cannot create."

The young man rose, water dripping from his sleeves, and bowed deeply. "I will. By my life, I will."

Aurelia's luminous eyes softened as they fell on him before turning to Radiantus. "So soon? Twice in as many days? No matter... the sight of you brings strength even to pain."

Radiantus touched his muzzle gently to her brow. "The dawn walks where it is needed."

From the terrace above, a figure appeared with long red hair blazing against the crystalline cliffs. Keisha. Her presence shone as bright as the Vale itself. At the sight of Radiantus, she smiled, and warmth rippled through the bond into Tahlira's chest.

"And this must be your rider," Keisha said, her voice rich with welcome. "Tahlira of Lyra'el, welcome to Crystal Vale."

Tahlira slid from the saddle and bowed, cheeks flushed. To stand before the woman of legend, whose songs she had heard since childhood, was like stepping into a story she had never dreamed she would share.

Beside Keisha stood a tall man with steady eyes and a warrior's bearing. He laid a protective hand on her arm, and she turned to him with a smile that shone like sunlight on crystal.

"This is Ong, my husband," Keisha said warmly.

Tahlira hesitated, then asked shyly, "Are you... a dragonrider as well?"

Before Ong could answer, Radiantus's laughter rolled like thunder, his wings trembling with mirth. "So, it is said. He rides with Amara the Amethyst Dragon, beloved of my brother Kimras, and the most incorrigible of us all. She delights in teasing, though her heart burns fierce and true."

Ong chuckled, inclining his head. "That she does. And I would not trade her for all the crowns in Vacari."

Tahlira found herself smiling, warmed by the easy bond that flowed between them all. These were not just figures of song and legend. They were living guardians, and she was among them.

Vista Six: Afor

Radiantus's gaze swept once more to the horizon, where storm-dark clouds gathered in the east. His voice thrummed with promise. "There are two more places I would have you see, little one. Beyond these cliffs lies Afor. Hold fast, the dawn calls us onward."

With a bound, he leapt skyward, argent wings scattering prisms of light across the crystalline valley as they soared toward the waiting heat.

The shimmer of water gave way to the shimmer of sand. Afor stretched before them an endless desert realm, its dunes rolling like waves of fire beneath a sky blurred by heat-haze.

Tahlira squinted, leaning forward. At the desert's edge, cliffs rose jagged and broken, their faces scarred as though once torn apart and stitched back together by divine hands. "Radiantus... was there once a road there? I think I see a path, but it ends in shadow."

Radiantus's molten eyes narrowed, wings steady against the desert wind. "You see true. Once, a way lay open to all. But after the War of the Ancients, the gods Kadona and Lysander, with the aid of the noble host, sealed it. Now only a hidden path remains, known to few. This realm must be sought, not given. Afor is not entered lightly."

A shiver traced her spine. To wander such a wasteland in search of a secret road... she could almost feel the sun's merciless weight pressing her down.

Then the desert itself roared.

From the blazing dunes, a fortress rose like hammered sunlight, the Brass Bastion, its towers carved into cliffs, banners snapping in the searing wind. From within surged a colossal dragon, scales gleaming like burnished fire.

Aurix, noble Brass, soared upward with a roar that rolled across the desert. His wings beat like bronze shields, scattering sand in spirals of light. His gaze warmed as he leveled beside Radiantus.

"I had heard on the winds that you had returned, brother," Aurix called. "Now I see the truth with my own eyes. And this must be your rider."

Radiantus inclined his shining head. "It is as you say. This is Tahlira of Lyra'el, my chosen."

Aurix's gaze swept over her, fierce yet kind. "Then the dawn rides with us once more. Be welcome, child of men."

Tahlira bowed low in the saddle, her heart swelling with reverence.

They soared on, crossing canyons split by fire and oases glittering like emeralds in the gold. At last, Radiantus slowed, hovering above a jagged scar carved deep into the earth. The air itself felt different here, heavy, trembling, as though the world remembered pain.

Radiantus's chest rumbled, a sound almost like a sigh.

Tahlira touched the silver ridge of his scales. "What is this place?"

For a long moment, he was silent. Then his voice came, low and heavy with memory. "Here, long ago, Phoenix Shadowwalker and Vuarus tore open the Abyss. Here they sought to sacrifice Keisha, to bind her light in shadow."

Tahlira's breath caught. The desert heat suddenly felt cold against her skin. "So... the stories were true," she whispered. "The Eladrin nearly lost one of their own."

Radiantus's golden eyes burned as he gazed down at the scarred earth. "A wound was struck upon Vacari that day. The land remembers... and so do I."

Vista Seven: The Emberwoods

Radiantus veered southward, his argent wings gliding over rolling hills that deepened into shadowed groves. The air shifted warmer now, tinged with spice and resin, alive with the murmur of unseen voices. Ahead stretched a vast forest, its canopy rippling like a living sea in hues of copper and emerald.

"The Emberwoods," Radiantus murmured reverently. "Here dwell the Copper Dragons and their companions, the pixies who flit between leaf and flame. This place guards more than trees, little one. It guards the threshold to realms veiled from most eyes."

Tahlira leaned forward, wide-eyed. She caught fleeting glimpses of tiny figures darting between branches, pixies trailing sparks of living fire, their laughter chiming like bells in the wind.

Suddenly, a dozen of them whirled upward in a spiral of mischief and light. They circled her golden hair, tugging loose strands with giddy delight. Before she could protest, nimble fingers wove blossoms, copper leaves, and glowing embers into a wreath that shimmered as though lit from within.

"Another one?" Tahlira gasped, laughter spilling unbidden as the pixies settled the fiery crown upon her brow.

Radiantus's chest rumbled with amusement. "Pixies adore long hair, little one. Consider it their mark of affection. Few riders pass here without feeling their touch."

The pixies twirled in delight, scattering sparks before vanishing back into the canopy with peals of laughter.

Then the forest itself seemed to stir. A shadow greater than the trees unfurled, wings scattering embers like falling stars. A massive dragon rose, scales burnished copper, his voice rolling like the shifting of earth beneath stone.

Raelithar, the Ancient Copper.

"So it is true," he rumbled, circling once before leveling beside Radiantus. "Dawn returns."

Radiantus dipped his silvered head. "And you, flame of the Emberwoods, still guard the paths entrusted to you."

Raelithar's molten eyes gleamed. "A thousand seasons, and still the maze holds. The pixies weave their wards tighter each year, binding the hidden way."

Tahlira tilted her head. "Maze?"

The copper colossus turned his gaze toward the forest's southern edge, where the trees twisted into a lattice of shadow and flame. For an instant, she thought she glimpsed shifting corridors in the roots themselves, as though the woods reshaped their paths with each breath.

Radiantus's voice deepened, solemn. "Beyond that gate lies Fel Thalor, and beyond it, the path that brushes the veil of Afor. But none may pass save with the pixies' leave, and I will not even trespass without it. The maze was wrought to guard more than land. It shields the realms themselves."

Tahlira's breath caught. She touched the fiery wreath now nestled beside the others, realizing each gift, each welcome was becoming part of her story.

Radiantus's wings lifted them higher, molten gaze lingering on the maze one last time. "E'vahona lies somewhere near, hidden by sacred trust. I could find it if I chose, but I will not. The Eladrin veiled it for reasons even the gods respected, and I honor that trust. Some doors, little one, must remain closed until willing hands open them."

The pixies' laughter trailed after them like sparks as Radiantus climbed above the trees. Raelithar dipped his wings in solemn farewell before vanishing back into copper and flame.

Vista Eight: Firornak

Radiantus slowed, wings spreading wide as he hovered at the edge of the range. He did not draw closer.

Tahlira frowned, leaning forward. "Why do we stop here? What lies beyond?"

The great dragon's molten gaze held fast to the frozen peaks. His voice came low, solemn. "This is Firornak. Here dwells Glaciera, the White Ice Dragon, a queen of frost and shadow. Others of her dark kin also reside in these mountains. One day, perhaps, we will be called to face them. But not today. I will not endanger you, little one."

The weight of his words pressed against her chest. Tahlira shivered, not only from the cold. The jagged white peaks were beautiful yet forbidding, their silence heavy with menace. Somewhere within those glaciers and caverns, unseen wings waited.

"Are there no noble dragons here?" she asked softly.

Radiantus's wings shifted, his silver mane streaming in the icy wind. "Not yet," he said. "But the song of the world is not finished. Noble gems stir in the deep places. When the time is right, they too shall rise to claim their realms. Even Firornak will not remain a kingdom of shadow forever."

Tahlira's eyes stung with cold or perhaps with tears. She pressed herself against his warm scales, arms tightening around the ridge of his great neck. "Then I will wait with you," she whispered.

Radiantus's chest rumbled like distant thunder. He lifted his head toward the heavens, wings beating against the bitter wind. "And together we shall rise," he murmured.

DRAGONS VICARI

Vista Nine: The Return Home

The bitter winds of Firornak still whispered around them as Radiantus wheeled away from the frozen peaks. His wings caught the sunlight, carrying them southward, back toward gentler skies.

"It is time to return home, little one," he said, his voice deep but warm.

Tahlira nodded, her fingers brushing the wreath upon her brow. She felt the weight of the others, too, the pale blossoms of the Moon Elves, the fiery crown of the pixies, the emerald garland of the fair folk. Each had been given in reverence or play, yet together they formed a crown unlike any she had ever worn. Vacari itself had marked her, realm by realm, as its own.

She looked down over all she had seen: the jeweled towers of Crystal Vale, the emerald forests alive with song, the bronze giants rising from the sea, the scar in Afor's heart where shadow had once clawed the world apart. Awe and sorrow tightened her chest, but above them both rose something brighter, steadier.

"I see it now," she whispered into the wind. "I see why we fight. Vacari... our people, our realms, they are worth everything."

Radiantus's chest rumbled, pride and sorrow mingling. "Yes, Tahlira. That is why I carried you across the realms. Others were tempered in academies, forged in discipline and waiting. You were forged in silence, in faith. You did not need to learn the saddle; you needed to learn the sky. This was your trial. And you have not faltered."

His molten gaze softened, then darkened with shadow. "But you must carry this vision back to Lyra'el. Your people must know the truth: even their sanctuary will not remain untouched. The dark dragons stir, and their wings may shadow even your skies."

Tahlira's breath caught. The thought of Lyra'el's home, veiled in darkness, made her heart clench. Yet when she pressed her cheek against Radiantus's warm scales, she felt his strength flow into her.

"I will tell them," she vowed. "And when the shadows come, we will be ready."

Radiantus's wings thundered, driving them higher into the morning light. "Good," he said. Then, with a glimmer in his golden eyes, he added, "For there is still one more you must meet, one who does not yet fly with us. His path is not with dragons, though he has a way of making things... explode."

Tahlira blinked, uncertain whether to laugh at the sudden spark of mirth in his voice. But Radiantus said no more, only turned his argent wings toward the cloud-wreathed spires of Lyra'el.

Behind them, the Snowtip Mountains of Firornak faded into haze. Ahead, the mystic city of her birth rose through the morning light. Yet in her heart lingered both wonder and dread, the knowledge that the dawn had risen, but the storm had not yet broken.

Far beyond the horizon, the Hidden Isles and Ardinia slept beneath their ancient veils of protection. Radiantus's gaze lingered toward that unseen distance, the promise of another journey stirring within his light.

"Another time,"

he murmured, wings catching the dawn's glow.

"When the winds are right."

Chapter 17
Whispers Beneath the Veil

The golden light of Lyra'el did not reach the caverns beneath the Singing Forest—nor was it welcome there. Damp air clung to the stone walls, thick with moss and secrets, while faint veins of glowmoss pulsed like drowned stars. The Umbral Elves moved silently through their shadow-carved halls, every step a whisper, every glance sharp and measuring. None dared question Rhys as he passed. They only bowed their veiled heads and melted from his path.

He descended the winding passage into his private chamber, where the air grew colder still. A shard of mirror-polished glass hovered in the gloom, runes etched across its surface like scars in silver. Drawing it from his cloak, Rhys held it in both hands, his voice a low invocation.

"Lyra."

The air trembled. A breath later, her image shimmered across the glass—pale, perfect, eyes like sharpened frost.

"You're late," she said.

"I observed," Rhys replied smoothly, leaning against the wall as though unconcerned, though tension coiled in his shoulders. "You'll want to hear what I found."

Her silence urged him on.

"They've returned," he said. "Platinum. Celestial. Radiantus leads them. The people greeted him as though he were a god come home."

At that, her eyes flickered with a rare, cold fire. "And what is it you want from me?"

"Direction." His voice sharpened. "Do I keep weaving influence? Take the Council? Or do I move now?"

Her smile curved thin as a knife. "You remember what the mysterious one commanded of you?"

Rhys's jaw tensed. "To lead the Umbral Elves. That has not changed."

"Then push harder," Lyra murmured. "The Council grows restless. Half already look to you. The rest..." Her words lingered like smoke. "They will not follow. Not willingly."

Rhys tilted his head, crimson eyes glinting. "You would have me... remove them?"

"Not with a blade," she said, voice low and silken. "Quietly. Without a trace. A cough at night. A cup of wine that never empties. Results, Rhys, not excuses."

His mask slipped. The cold smile beneath showed its true shape. "No need for another's hand. I know the herbs that tighten the lungs, the roots that turn blood to ice. I will learn more. I will master it."

The shard pulsed once, approval or warning, he could not tell—then went dark, leaving only his fractured reflection.

Alone again, Rhys stood in the oppressive quiet. But the silence here was not stillness. It was waiting. Watching.

"Learn," he muttered. Already, his mind was racing with half-remembered scrolls, recipes whispered in hidden chambers, and gardens where pale blossoms thrived on decay. If his path to power wound through poison and ash, he would walk it without hesitation.

He left his chamber, moving through the labyrinthine halls until he reached a secluded alcove carved beneath an arch of midnight vine. A small stall spilled with bundles of drying herbs, coiled roots, and jars that glowed faintly from within.

Behind the counter, an elder Umbral elf hummed as she sorted leaves the color of withered bronze. Her pale eyes lifted when she noticed him, surprise flickering there before softening into something like pride: Mirelya, keeper of herbs, binder of feasts, whisperer to shadows.

Rhys inclined his head, masking calculation with the humility of an apprentice. "Pardon me, mistress. I've been preparing meals for the others in my hall, but herbs are not my strength. Some add flavor... others," his lips curved faintly, "can be dangerous. I'd rather not make a mistake."

Mirelya studied him, gaze flicking briefly to the satchel at his side, as though weighing his intent. At last, she nodded.

"Good of you to ask. Most would not." She gestured toward the table. "Sit. Learn the difference or risk poisoning yourself."

She lifted a sprig of dark-veined leaves, its edges curled like claws.

"Veinroot Briar. A shred leaves the hands trembling. Too much, and the heart locks in the chest."

Next, a crystalline bloom with glass-clear petals.

"Glassvine Thorn. Harmless to the eye, deadly in wine. It blurs sight, slows the blood. Death wears many masks."

Her fingers brushed a tuft of gray moss, its edges whispering faintly.

"Whispermoss. Clouds the mind, steals focus, loosens memory. Many a Councilor has forgotten his own name after too much."

She split a pale, brittle husk, scattering seeds that shimmered before fading to dust.

"Moonblister Pod. Weakness creeps slowly, like ice in the veins. Hours pass before the body fails."

Last, she revealed a blossom of silver-black petals, sweet fragrance cloying in the air.

"Hollowshade Bloom. Beautiful... and cruel. It does not kill. It unravels the aura, strips magic from the bones. A mage who drinks of it is left hollow."

Rhys listened with rapt attention, every word a weapon, every herb another tool.

"And for flavor?" he asked lightly.

Mirelya smiled. She plucked a sprig of silver-green mint.

"Glowmint. Sharp, clean. Clears the breath."

Next, a star-shaped petal.

"Thistledawn Petal. Gentle, sweet. Healing for small aches."

A twisted copper-brown root.

"Ironfern. Strong and earthy. It gives strength to the weary."

Finally, the faintly glowing leaf she had been bundling earlier.

"Sunberry. Tart, quickening. In measure, it brightens the whole."

Her eyes lingered on him. "You have the curiosity of a cook and the manners of a court-bred boy. Careful. Both can be dangerous. But perhaps... useful."

Rhys bowed his head. "Then perhaps you will make a cook of me yet."

But in his mind, the names of poisons whispered like blades being unsheathed.

He left the stall in silence, satchel heavier than before, not with food, but with possibility. By the time he reached his private chamber, his smirk had given way to something colder.

One by one, he set the herbs upon the stone table, separating the harmless from the fatal, the sweet from the venomous. This was not cookery.

This was war.

A sprig of Veinroot Briar shaved into a dark wine reduction.

A pinch of Moonblister Pod dissolved into broth.

A single flake of Hollowshade Bloom crushed into the glaze of a roasted fig.

Not enough to kill. Not yet. But enough to hollow the Council from within, to plant fear until their voices faltered and their seats grew empty.

On the shelf behind him lay a scroll. Names were written in sharp, deliberate strokes, elders who resisted him, councilors who clung to the past. Beside each name, a vacancy waited.

Rhys's silver gaze lingered on the list. His lips curved slowly, cold, and certain.

"They will ask for strength," he murmured. "And I will give it to them. They will name me what I was always meant to be."

The wards pulsed, shadows stretching long across the stone.

In the silence that followed, his soft laugh carried like a blade being drawn.

Chapter 18
Words Meant to Last

The crystalline spires of the Vale shimmered like frozen moonlight, each tower catching the rising sun in hues of amethyst, silver, and pale jade. Morning mist threaded between the trees, curling around marble arches and lantern flowers whose crystal-blossoms chimed softly in the breeze. The whole forest seemed to breathe, alive with a music older than memory.

Valeon had never liked places that whispered like they were smarter than he was.

He tugged at the collar of his tunic, clean, pressed, and painfully not stolen, and muttered, "A Place like this, even the birds got manners." The grin that followed sat poorly on his face, failing to cover the unease coiling in his gut. Shining cities like this were reminders of everything he wasn't. Jokes were easier than admitting he didn't belong.

He crossed a pale stone bridge, boots barely daring to make a sound. Even the echoes came back softened, as though the city itself was too polite to rebuke him. Lantern flowers turned their crystalline faces as he passed, tilting toward him like watchful eyes.

Kaelorn had called it a "brief pause" in his training.

Thalorian had looked at him like a storm about to break.

And Keisha curse her too-knowing foresight had arranged for someone new to "facilitate a breakthrough." Valeon suspected that meant someone was keeping him from setting another sanctum ablaze.

He rounded a bend and came to a sudden stop.

An Eladrin stood waiting beneath a crystal tree heavy with diamond-like fruit. Tall and slight, robed in green and silver that rippled like starlight on water, they held themselves with unnerving stillness. Copper hair coiled in a flawless twist, and eyes as sharp as emerald glass fixed on him.

Valeon forced levity into his tone. "You must be the lucky soul drafted for babysitting duty."

"I am Lyendris of the Glimmerdeep," they said after a long, measuring beat. "And you must be... Valeon."

He swept a half-bow, far too casual. "In the flesh. Don't worry, I've only accidentally set one person on fire this month. He recovered. Mostly."

A flicker crossed Lyendris's face: disdain, amusement, or both before they replied, voice as smooth as still water. "We will work in the Starbloom Pavilion. There is less flammable material there."

Valeon blinked, then barked a laugh. "Smart. Very smart."

As they walked beneath flowering arches, his gaze strayed to runes glowing faintly along the path. "That one means 'light,' right?"

"It means purity of intent through illumination."

The words struck harder than he expected, not just their meaning, but their weight. Wit had always covered the hollow places inside him, but here, every rune glowed like truth carved in stone. He felt something stir—not the urge to impress, but the quiet ache to understand. To rise.

"Ah. Close," he muttered.

"You were off by approximately seven layers of meaning."

He groaned. "So basically, a typical morning."

They reached the Starbloom Pavilion, a wide circle woven of crystal and vine. Scrolls lay in careful order across low tables, rune-stones set neatly beside them—though Valeon noticed a few blackened edges.

Dropping cross-legged onto a cushion, he picked up a stylus and tapped it against the table. "This one looks familiar. Thalorian had me copy it before the... you know. Incident."

"That word was dawn," Lyendris said. "You wrote desolation."

"One squiggle off! It was humid!"

From the pavilion's edge, a presence stirred. Lord Karrenen stood watching, his green-and-silver cloak lifting in the breeze, expression calm but cautious, no doubt at Keisha's request.

"My lord," Lyendris said, bowing slightly. "You observe from afar. Wise."

"I observe with caution," Karrenen said with a faint smile. His gaze softened as it fell on the young man seated amid scattered scrolls. "And how fares our scholar?"

Valeon twisted around, grin tugging at his lips. "Haven't set anything on fire yet. Progress?"

Karrenen chuckled, warm but vigilant. "We celebrate small victories."

New footsteps echoed along the crystal path, measured, steady, un-mistakable.

Gailen, Keisha, and Ong emerged from the archway.

Ong's grin was already wide, mischief sparking in his eyes like a boy about to throw a stone at still water. "Still struggling with baby runes, Valeon? What's next, drawing dragons in charcoal?"

Valeon groaned, slumping over the scroll. "Glad to see you too, Ong."

Gailen opened his mouth, perhaps to intervene, but Keisha beat him to it. Her red hair caught the light like fire as she arched a brow.

"Do I need to remind you of your first week in E'vahona? When you misread an Elven marker and asked a tree to marry you?"

Ong froze. "That tree winked at me. I still say it wasn't entirely my fault." Then, with sulking grace, he stuck out his tongue.

Valeon couldn't help it, his lips twitched. Their laughter wasn't cruel; it was warm. Fierce, but kind. Maybe that was what a bond looked like in the open, love and loyalty wrapped in jest.

"Well," he said dryly, "at least I've never proposed to shrubbery."

"Yet," Lyendris said without inflection.

Lord Karrenen's laugh carried down the polished path. "Perhaps we should all be grateful the scrolls do not speak back."

Keisha rolled her eyes. Gailen hid a smile behind his hand. Ong spluttered indignantly, which only made Keisha smirk harder.

And yet beneath the teasing, something settled in Valeon's chest. A sense of belonging. A place where even mistakes became part of the song. He touched the glowing wreath the fae had given him, warmth spreading through him like light through crystal.

He shook his head, grinning despite the flush at his neck. "Fine. But one day, I'll write something so impressive you'll all choke on your fancy metaphors."

"Then begin here," Lyendris said, laying out the scrolls with serene finality. Blossoms shifted open around them. "Again. With breath. With thought. With patience."

Valeon exhaled slowly. This time, he didn't force a joke. He let the quiet of the pavilion settle into him. He set the stylus against the page.

"I'm listening," he murmured, not from obligation, but from hope.

Chapter 19

Beneath the Wyrmveil

The chamber lay vast and cold, carved into the blackened roots of the world where no sunlight dared intrude, and even time seemed to hesitate. Mist drifted over obsidian stone like breath that remembered fire. Jagged spires of volcanic glass thrust upward, their veins pulsing faint crimson, echoes of an ancient heart buried deep below. A tremor rolled through the earth, as though the world exhaled in some forgotten rhythm.

Shadows stirred.

And the dragons were waiting.

They perched upon ledges and bone-carved arches, silent as statues wrought from nightmare. Even in stillness, their presence bent the air.

Zylron crouched amid coils of emberlight, crimson eyes smoldering like dying stars.

Glaciera loomed pale as a frozen storm, crystalline wings folded like shards of ice.

Nocturna melted into the blackness, her obsidian scales devouring what little glow remained.

Xalzorath coiled in silence, his vast hide etched with runes that shifted and whispered in tongues no mortal dared name.

And before them, two abyssal shadows:

Voraxia, sinuous and swift, her scales fractured obsidian, edged in violet fire.

Vorathos crouched beside her, veins of molten light glowing faintly beneath her dark hide, each breath a slow sear of smoke.

Footsteps entered the silence. Steady. Unhurried.

The mysterious figure appeared, cloaked in layered silk and veiled power. No light clung to them. No scent marked their presence. Yet every colossal head turned, as though the cavern itself bowed to their arrival.

Vorathos exhaled smoke, her voice a gravelled rumble that crawled across the stone.

"So... this is who commands? You speak of unity, yet send only one. How... optimistic."

The figure did not flinch.

"I did not come to ask for your cooperation, Vorathos."

Her laughter cracked like splitting magma, then died as the chamber shuddered with her growl.

"Careful, little creature. There are flames buried in me that even gods have feared."

The figure raised a gloved hand. Silver rings etched with shifting runes caught the dim glow. One finger pointed at her.

Reality shivered.

Vorathos froze. Not by chain, not by spell, but by will itself. That presence coiled through her, crushing, inevitable. She remembered faintly, unwillingly, an old battle buried in shadow, when another hand had forced her down, when her abyssal fire had guttered like a candle before a storm. The memory burned colder than ice.

She could not move.

Not from weakness. From power.

The figure stepped closer, voice low, cutting silence into shards.

"I remind you, Voraxia. And you, Vorathos. You were summoned not for dominion but for alliance. The world fractures. And those who would shape it must first learn to share the fire."

Voraxia's silver-white gaze flicked toward her sister, measuring the tremor in Vorathos's restraint. Slowly, carefully, she lowered her head. Not in defeat. In calculation. Submission now was not submission forever.

The figure's voice cooled to steel.

"You will work with the others.

You will not devour their allies.

You will not fracture the path we are building."

Their gaze swept across Zylron, Glaciera, Nocturna, and Xalzorath. Not one dared move beneath that unseen weight.

"And you, who lurk in silence—" the voice rang like a chime within the cavern's bones, "this is not the hour for old rivalries. We rise together, or fall separately, scattered, hunted, forgotten. Even you, Xalzorath, cannot unravel prophecy alone."

No answer came.

Only stillness.

Vorathos hissed smoke, fury writhing in her chest, but her jaw stayed clenched. Voraxia's gaze lingered, then returned to the figure, patient as a serpent coiling before the strike.

At last, the figure turned to the abyssal queens.

"You two have a different task."

The chamber stirred. Zylron's wings twitched, rigid with withheld rage. Glaciera's breath frosted the air in a low, disdainful sigh. Even Xalzorath's runes dimmed.

Voraxia leaned forward, her tone sharp as a blade. "A task?"

"Only you two possess what the others cannot," the figure said. "The gift of moving unseen through shadow, through abyss, through fear itself."

"Where?" Voraxia asked.

"Lyra'el."

The name fell like ink into water. Ripples spread through the cavern.

Glaciera hissed. Zylron's tail lashed against stone.

"Radiantus has returned," the figure said. "The Platinum Flight stirs. The Celestial Dragons walk the skies again."

Vorathos's molten veins flared. "Then we strike?"

Voraxia tilted her head. "Or unseen?"

The figure's smile was felt, not seen.

"Let them see you. But do not attack yet. Stretch your shadows across their skies. Let them wonder. Let them fear. Then return and tell me everything."

Vorathos snarled, smoke curling between her teeth. "Why not burn them now?"

The figure turned. Spoke nothing.

But the air bent.

Power pressed down like a mountain. Zylron's flames guttered. Glaciera froze, frost trembling at her maw. Even Nocturna dared not stir. Xalzorath's runes writhed and dimmed.

Vorathos bowed, voice rasping like caged fire. "...As you command."

Voraxia lowered her head as well. Not obedience. Patience.

The figure vanished into shadow, as if the page of the world had been turned backward.

Silence closed over the cavern like water.

Vorathos exhaled smoke, wings restless. "The only reason we share this den is them."

Voraxia's gaze swept the host. "Do not mistake loyalty for weakness. Our claws are sharp. And if that power falters..." She let the words hang sharp like broken glass.

The ancients said nothing.

Vorathos and Voraxia launched together, shadows twining as they vanished into the gloom. Lyra'el awaited, and this time, the skies would darken not with fire, but with fear.

Long after their wings faded, their presence clung like ash that refused to settle.

Zylron's embers flared hotter. "If not for them, I would have ended the sisters myself."

Glaciera's eyes glinted coldly. "They will turn on us the moment it suits them."

Nocturna rumbled her agreement.

Xalzorath's runes twisted into a pattern no one dared name. "Best we keep our distance. Even our thoughts may not be safe."

Zylron's molten gaze lingered on the shadows where the figure had vanished. His wings shifted, restless.

"For now... we wait. We watch. We endure."

His fangs bared in a cruel smile. "But when their fire falters, we strike."

The cavern darkened once more. Its silence no longer still, but simmering.

The alliance held.

But only because fear was bound—

and fear was never eternal.

Chapter 20
When Shadows Meet the Light

The sky above Lyra'el shimmered with ancient enchantments, threads of light weaving between alabaster spires and crystal bridges, a city crowned by song and starlight, guarded once more by dragons born of the heavens.

But far to the north, the brilliance dimmed.

A shadow spread across the horizon.

Voraxia came first, wings veined in violet fire, slicing through the clouds like knives of night. Each beat drew the silence tighter, as if the wind itself dared not resist. Beside her flew Vorathos, abyssal queen of deep flame, her dark hide glowing with veins of molten light that pulsed like a buried sun. The very air around her warped, heavy with heat and pressure.

Neither spoke. They did not need to. Fury bound them, simmering beneath their restraint. Ordered to appear but not strike, their flight tasted of chains. For Voraxia, this was torment. She had not returned to the skies to watch. She had come to be felt, to be feared.

Lyra'el rose before them, its radiance colliding with their advancing dark. Voraxia's snarl split the silence.

"We are death-given form," she hissed. "And yet we are ordered to spectate."

Vorathos rumbled low, smoke curling from her jaws.

"They fear us. That is why we are sent to be seen, but not felt."

Their shadows spilled across the ridgeline, smothering the silver wards overhead. The city shuddered. Sentries froze mid-step, heads craning skyward. Citizens clutched amulets, voices stumbling into old prayers. Even the spire-bells rang sharp, as if bent by the sudden weight pressing upon the sky.

Then light shattered the dark.

A blaze of platinum streaked across the heavens, scattering shadow like glass under a hammer. Two vast forms descended in unison, their wings unfurling in radiant arcs, as divine fire and starborn magic cascaded from their scales. The horizon bowed before them.

Radiantus landed upon the marble arch crowning Lyra'el's eastern pass, argent scales burning with hammered light, diamond-like silver eyes steady and unyielding. Beneath his calm lay an oath forged across centuries: shadow would not claim this realm.

Beside him, Aurelius descended, a living constellation. His wings spilled ribbons of gold and sapphire, scattering starlight with every beat. Power thrummed around him, calm, inexorable, unshakable.

Radiantus's voice rolled like thunder across the sky.

"You do not belong here. Turn back."

Voraxia spread her wings, blotting half the horizon. Her voice slid cold as a blade through the air.

"We were sent to observe. Nothing more. But we will return."

Vorathos's veins flared, fire licking her fangs. One command, one breath, and the city would burn. But Voraxia's silver-white gaze cut to her, sharp and silent: Not yet. They obeyed, for now.

Radiantus's silver gaze did not falter.

"Then return. And find us waiting."

Aurelius stepped forward, light gathering along his wings until the air rang like a temple bell. His voice carried not rage, but grief—an ancient sorrow forged from too many broken pacts.

"Tell your master this: we know you serve another. But shadows thin with every dawn. When that veil falls, judgment will follow."

Vorathos snarled, smoke boiling in her throat, but she bowed her head. The memory of that crushing will still burn against her chest.

Voraxia lingered a breath longer, gaze unreadable. Then she dipped her head in mock acquiescence.

"We will deliver your message."

But inside, her pride seethed raw. This was no triumph, only a leash. The hunger in her bones only sharpened. One day, she would tear it free.

Together, the two queens wheeled upward, wings battering against the light. They vanished into the storm, but their shadows clung to Lyra'el, etched like a scar across the heavens.

Radiantus and Aurelius held their vigil, wings spread, eyes fixed on the horizon as if to bar the night itself. For long moments, silence endured two beacons holding darkness at bay.

High in the drifting stormclouds, Voraxia lingered, her form veiled in magic. Her silver-white eyes narrowed.

"They will not rest until we are gone."

Vorathos's growl seethed low.

"I would rather burn the sky than bow to it."

Voraxia's lips curved, thin and cruel.

"And yet we bow. For now."

She angled her wings to the storm, dragging her sister with her. Vorathos cast one last look at the gleaming city—its towers radiant, its guardians unbroken before vanishing into the clouds.

Slowly, the wards steadied, silver threads weaving whole again. The bells rang accurately, bright, and clear. A breeze slipped through the hanging gardens, carrying the scents of jasmine and rainlit stone.

On the highest balcony of the eastern watchtower, Tahlira lowered her spyglass. Her knuckles were white on the railing, the chill of crystal biting her palms. She had stood from the first glimpse of shadow, every heartbeat measuring against the sweep of Radiantus's wings. She knew he would never draw her into the path of such queens, not yet, but still, she had been ready.

Now, with the darkness gone, her shoulders loosened. Yet the tension in her chest refused to fade. The sky had brightened, but the silence lingered in her bones. They would return. She knew it.

Below, the city exhaled. Markets reopened, children ran across bridges of glass, laughter chasing away prayer. Lyra'el breathed again.

But Tahlira did not move. Her gaze remained fixed on the clouds where the queens had vanished. Her hand tightened on the hilt at her side, the wreath of blossoms still glowing faintly in her hair.

Lyra'el stood radiant, bathed once more in light.

Yet the memory of shadow lingered on the horizon as an unspoken promise.

Lyra'el was safe.

For now.

Chapter 21
Echoes in the Flame

The skies above Flameford rumbled not with thunder, but with wrath.

Twin shadows tore through the storm, wings unfurling wide as they spiraled into the volcanic heart. The ground shuddered at their descent, black stone splitting beneath the crash of the Shadow Dragon Voraxia and the Abyssal Queen Vorathos. Scorched wind howled through the jagged canyons, thick with smoke and fire born from the void.

Steam hissed from vents in the rock. The sky churned like a wounded beast, mirroring their fury.

Voraxia coiled her wings, her body drawn tight as a bowstring.

"They anticipated us."

Vorathos slammed her tail against the stone, molten streaks blazing. Her growl seethed with hunger.

"We should have scorched them. One pass, one breath, and their shining city would already smolder."

Orders had shackled her fire, forced her into silence. To be seen but not felt was humiliation.

A ripple stirred above. From the black ledges carved into the cliffs, silence thickened.

The mysterious figure emerged.

They did not walk but seemed to uncoil from the obsidian itself, cloaked in layered silk and veiled in presence. No light clung to them, no sound dared. Yet every dragon's gaze followed as they descended into the cavern framed by molten falls.

"You returned quickly," the ageless voice said, its tone smooth, sharp, and unreadable.

Voraxia's violet fire caught the stone, her scales gleaming like shattered night. She bowed her head slightly—not in submission, but in controlled agitation.

"We could not enter Lyra'el. Radiantus and Aurelius waited at the pass. As if they knew."

Vorathos prowled forward, molten veins flaring brighter.

"They did more than wait. Aurelius gave a message."

The figure tilted their head, silence tightening like a blade's edge.

Vorathos's growl deepened. "He said they know someone pulls the strings. You. And he said your shadows will not hide you much longer."

The cavern darkened—not from the lava, but from will itself. Pressure cinched the air, suffocating.

Voraxia's silver-white gaze flicked to the figure, then to her sister. "If they watch us this closely... they may already be watching you."

The lava roared louder, as if the mountain itself bristled.

"You revealed yourselves too soon," the figure hissed, words cracking like a whip. "You were meant to observe nothing more."

Vorathos bared her fangs, but Voraxia stepped forward first, wings flaring until violet-shadow cloaked the figure.

"Do not insult us. We obeyed. But Radiantus and Aurelius were already in the sky before we touched the ridge." Her eyes narrowed. "They knew. About us. About you."

The fury in the chamber did not fade; it folded inward, sharp as a blade drawn too close.

From the far side, a rumble like shifting magma.

"You misjudged them."

Zylron stepped from the dark, smoke wreathing his ember-lit form. His tone was grim, unflinching.

"Radiantus and Aurelius are not merely powerful. They are revered. That is a difference you have forgotten. Radiantus is not just a dragon; he is worshiped as Divine."

Crimson eyes burned with memory, not devotion. Zylron despised Radiantus's supremacy but could not deny the weight of it.

The mysterious figure turned toward him. Shadows stretched. The cavern narrowed to two beings: an ancient dragon wreathed in ember and a veiled master swathed in silence.

Zylron did not lower his gaze. Smoke drifted in lazy spirals, defiance smoldering in every line of his massive frame.

The chamber held its breath. Something unspoken passed, a warning, a promise of reckoning.

Then Zylron turned. His colossal wings unfurled, scattering sparks into the lava-lit dark. He launched skyward, each beat louder than any roar.

Voraxia and Vorathos coiled tighter, fury burning in their bones. The figure remained unmoving, shadow wrapped close like a shroud.

But loyalty had shifted. All of them felt it.

The leash was fraying.

Above, the volcanic winds caught Zylron. Waiting on the jagged ledges were Glaciera rimed in frost, Nocturna dissolving into shadow, and Xalzorath, vast coils shimmering with runes that rippled in the haze.

None spoke. The mountains listened.

Nocturna's voice slid free, soft as memory.

"Was that wise?"

Zylron's tail carved black streaks in the rock. His gaze stayed fixed on the horizon where light still lingered.

"Probably not."

The mysterious one would not forget. But for once, he did not care. Something older than fear stirred in him pride, defiance long buried.

"They underestimate Radiantus and Aurelius," he rumbled. "That... is dangerous."

No one argued. Glaciera's wings shivered frost. Nocturna's shadows deepened. Xalzorath's runes rippled faint assent.

One by one, they broke away, leaving Flameford's skies darker still.

Zylron lingered beneath the crimson haze, smoke drifting from his nostrils. He would never love Radiantus, but reverence was a powerful force, and Radiantus commanded it.

Back within the cavern, the mysterious figure faced the two who remained.

"There is a change of plan," they said, voice sharp as fractured glass.

Voraxia tilted her head.

"You will not enter Lyra'el again. Haunt the outer realms. Let them see you. Let them fear. But you will not engage Radiantus or Aurelius."

Vorathos growled but bit back her fire.

Voraxia's wings twitched, violet light rippling, but she gave a slow nod.

Obedience now did not mean forever.

Together, the sisters turned and left, sparks scattering into the volcanic dark.

The figure remained alone, then strode deeper into the spire. In the lower passage, they found Lyra, pale eyes glinting in firelight.

"Contact Rhys," the figure commanded. "It is time. He takes full command of the Umbral Elves now."

Lyra inclined her head. Her voice was calm, smooth. "As you command."

But as she turned, a thought lingered like smoke. Qellaun. Brother. Loyalty. A warning half-spoken. She pressed it down and vanished into shadow.

The figure climbed to the tower's heart.

And there, the silence broke.

A roar split the mountain, raw and unbound. Books were hurled from shelves. Wards shattered. Lava geysered from the floor. The earth itself seemed to recoil.

Beneath the fury lay more than anger at Radiantus's return. It was a memory. Defiance long past. Radiantus had risen once before and undone everything. Now he had returned a wound reopened, a truth too vast for shadow to bury.

Cracks split the obsidian floor, glowing with sullen fire. The tower groaned as if the world itself wished to scream.

Then the fury folded inward. The voice that followed was cold steel.

"The leash will hold. Until I choose to break it."

Outside, the air was thick with heat, but Lyra's skin prickled with a chill not born of Flameford's winds.

She had her orders: Rhys must lead. Yet with every step towards Fel Thalor, a thought gnawed at her silence.

Do I warn him?

Her jaw tightened. She sank deeper into shadow, vanishing into the volcanic haze.

But her brother's warning followed her still like a shadow she could not shake.

Chapter 22

Of Seeds and Sky

Valeon squinted at the curling script on the parchment before him. The Eladrin letters shimmered faintly, shifting just enough to make him question his eyesight or his sanity.

"Is that an r or a... fork?"

Across the table, Lyendris arched a brow. "That is the glyph for saelenthra. Not a fork."

Valeon blinked. "Right. Of course. Saelenthra. Different from thalenthra, which makes your teeth fall out."

"You're learning," Lyendris said, folding his hands behind his back. "Though ideally, without losing body parts."

Valeon offered a sheepish grin, then reached for two sprigs: one pale blue-green with silvery edges, the other a violet blossom veined with gold. He crushed them together in the mortar.

The mixture hissed.

Then it hummed.

Then the air itself warped, a low whine filling the chamber as glowing veins spidered across the stone table.

"Oh no."

Lyendris did not flinch. He pressed his palm over the mixture, whispering a sharp phrase in Eladrin. The glow guttered out, though not before every crystal jar rattled violently. A few toppled, shattering in a spray of light.

Valeon stared at the mess. "That was supposed to be a focus draught."

Lyendris regarded him for a beat, then said evenly, "You mixed storm-root with dreamshade blossom. That combination erases memory. In larger doses, it is reserved for funerary rites. A sip more, and you might have forgotten your own name."

Valeon sagged onto the bench, rubbing his neck. The acrid-sweet scent lingered, heavy with more than smoke. Not just the danger of the potion, but the temptation of its effect. To forget. To lose the names and failures that haunted him. Some nights, the idea felt almost like mercy.

Lyendris watched him quietly, wry detachment softened by something gentler. "Do you know why the Eladrin keep to the old ways?"

"Because they work?" Valeon guessed.

"Because they last." Lyendris crouched, brushing shards of crystal from the floor. "Your world rushes to mend what it breaks. We wait. We listen. We act when the rhythm is right."

Valeon exhaled, gaze drifting to the glowing runes on the wall. "I'm trying. I swear I am. But sometimes it feels like everything here was built for people with starlight in their blood. Not for someone who grew up sleeping on the floor of a tavern's storage closet."

Lyendris rose, holding a whole jar in his hands as if it were precious. His copper hair gleamed like woven flame. "The seed does not know it is a tree," he said softly. "It grows anyway."

Valeon blinked. The words landed deeper than expected, threading into the hollow places inside him. Maybe they weren't just about Eladrin patience. Maybe they were about him. Hope slipped in like sunlight through a cracked door.

"...Is that Eladrin poetry, or are you just trying to make me feel better?"

A flicker, almost a smile, touched Lyendris's lips. "Both."

The audience chamber of Crystal Vale shimmered with refracted light. Sunlight scattered rainbows across the polished floor, beauty veined with gravity.

Valeon stood awkwardly at the center, trying not to fidget beneath King Manard's gaze. Ong stood tall beside him, nervous but proud. Gailen leaned against a crystal column, while Lyendris lingered near the rear, calm and unreadable.

Manard stepped down from the dais, cloak shimmering faintly.

"You've made progress. Lyendris has spoken well of your diligence."

Valeon cleared his throat. "I've... tried, Your Majesty. I'm still not sure what half the herbs do, and my Elven script looks like a drunk spider fell in ink—"

Ong snorted a laugh.

Valeon winced. "Sorry. I mean—thank you."

Manard did not smile, but his eyes softened. "Honesty is rare. And valued."

He glanced at Lyendris. "How much further can his training go here?"

"The foundation is set," Lyendris said. "What he lacks now is not knowledge, but application. He must see what he studies alive, in motion."

Manard nodded, then turned to Valeon.

"You are going to Lyra'el."

The chamber stilled.

Valeon forgot how to breathe. The words fell on him like a cloak he hadn't known was waiting. Excitement tangled with fear.

"I—what?"

"There is wisdom among the Celestial Flight," Manard continued. "You will learn from them, especially those who serve dragons. They will show you how herbs, healing, and flame align."

"But—" Valeon floundered. "Dragons? I've read about them and once talked to one. She judged me."

"You'll get used to it," Gailen murmured.

Valeon shot him a look. "Easy for you to say. You belong here. I'm just a scrappy human who can mix a headache draught and mostly not light himself on fire."

Manard raised his hand, silencing him. "You will not go alone."

From behind a crystalline arch, Keisha stepped forward.

"You will accompany him," Manard said. "Not to lead. Not to protect. To guide. Your presence will steady him and remind the Celestials that our strength is not divided."

Valeon gaped. "Wait, you're coming with me?"

Keisha folded her arms. "You say that like it's a bad thing."

"No! No, I mean—it's great. Just... unexpected."

Gailen chuckled. "You'll need it. Celestial dragons don't suffer fools... or fainting apprentices."

Valeon groaned. "Perfect. That's exactly the kind of supportive imagery I needed."

Ong stepped forward, laying a hand on Valeon's shoulder. "You'll be fine. You always find a way."

Quiet, unwavering, his words steadied Valeon more than any decree.

"And I'll stay here," Ong added, glancing toward Gailen. "It's time I got to know my brother. And... maybe let the king be a father, too."

Manard's eyes flickered, something old and aching behind them. "It would please me."

The crystalline terrace overlooked the Pegasus stables. Their wings shimmered in hues of pearl and moonlight, their bodies larger than Valeon expected.

He froze. "They're... bigger than I expected."

Keisha adjusted her satchel. "You've met dragons."

"Yes, but dragons expect you to be afraid. These creatures look disappointed in advance."

One tossed its head with a sharp snort.

Valeon edged closer. "Easy. I'm not food."

Most ignored him. But one silver-dappled, violet-eyed broke away. She stepped toward him.

"Oh no," he muttered. "She's looking at me. Why is she looking at me?"

"Maybe she likes you," Keisha said.

"That's worse."

Pegasus nuzzled his ear, pressing her head against his shoulder. Valeon yelped, half-laughing, half-panicked. "Okay. That's... fuzzy. And ticklish."

Slowly, he lifted his hand and brushed her mane.

"Looks like she picked you," Keisha murmured.

Valeon blinked. "Why would she do that?"

"Because she sees something in you that you're too busy doubting."

Before he could argue, Pegasus bent her legs. Valeon swallowed, then clambered awkwardly into the saddle.

"Okay," he said, gripping the reins too tightly. "But no flips. And no judging if I scream."

The Pegasus flicked her ears, amused.

"Ready?" Keisha asked.

"No. Let's do it anyway."

Wind roared past as the Pegasus leapt skyward, scattering light like shards of starlight.

At the overlook, Ong stood in silence. Manard stepped beside him.

"They'll be fine," Ong said, with more hope than certainty.

"I could tell you not to worry," Manard replied, "but I know better."

Ong's voice was low. "Keisha is giving us time. To get to know each other."

"She probably knows you need it," Manard said.

Gratitude flickered in Ong's chest. Keisha always seemed to know. But letting her go stirred old instincts, the memory of nearly losing her once before.

"Part of me still wonders if letting her go alone was the right idea."

Gailen joined them, his presence steady. "They'll be all right. If Valeon doesn't try to make tea mid-flight."

Ong let out a rough laugh despite himself.

The three of them stood shoulder to shoulder, watching until the Pegasi dwindled into specks of light.

The silence that followed was not empty. It was heavy with beginnings, fragile, uncertain, but real.

Yet even as hope stirred, the winds carried darker whispers across the realms. Shadows had risen. And peace, in Vacari, was never meant to linger.

Chapter 23
The Radiant Threshold

The sky around Lyra'el shimmered not with heat, but with light. It draped itself across the ridgelines like living silk, shifting in a slow celestial dance. Mountains rose in a half-circle of luminous stone, jagged backs forming an eternal watch. From their cliffs poured crystalline streams, cascading in rose-gold and starlight blue, braiding into silver rivers that wound through the forested lowlands.

Valeon leaned forward in the Pegasus saddle, eyes wide. Something stirred inside him a pull, fierce and unfamiliar, as though a long-quiet part of his chest had suddenly remembered how to breathe. The Pegasus beneath him coasted effortlessly, unbothered by his restless fidgeting.

"Is this still the outside?" he asked, blinking at a spiraled tower of braided moonstone, its crown circled by lanterns that never seemed to burn out.

Keisha's smile was faint, fond. "Only the beginning. The true city lies beyond the inner ridge. Few beyond the Lyra'el ever see even this much."

"Could we—" Valeon hesitated, then pointed toward a ridge where white-blooming trees ringed a floating platform. His voice softened. "Could we circle the outskirts first? ... This is the most beautiful place I've ever seen."

"Of course." Keisha's Pegasus angled toward his, their cloaks streaming as the wind carried them into a graceful arc.

She named landmarks as if reciting memories. "Those are the Aetherboughs, their blossoms never fall; they fade into light. And there, half veiled in mist, that arch is the Gate of Velaurien. It marks the edge of the old territory, where the first of the Celestial Flight once walked."

"It looks like the stars carved it," Valeon whispered. "Even the air feels different."

"It is," Keisha murmured. "This land breathes magic. You can feel it if you let it."

Valeon closed his eyes. The wind carried no pine, no frost, but something brighter like memory warmed by morning. His heart swelled with a word he did not yet have.

"I get why the dragons chose this place."

For a heartbeat, something flickered in Keisha's eyes, pride, shadowed by sorrow. Then it was gone. She guided her Pegasus higher, silver mane streaming in the light. Below, mist coiled around glowing lakes where Celestial elk grazed among translucent ferns. Small towers crowned distant hills, pulsing faintly like patient stars.

"But the heart of Lyra'el waits higher still," she said at last, lifting her chin toward a second veil of radiant cloud. "Unseen. Watching."

Valeon pointed toward a lonely outcrop suspended above them, no larger than a village green. Its jagged surface was plated in black stone, thorned brush clinging stubbornly to its edges. The air around it shimmered with hostile currents, as though the world itself rejected its weight.

"What's that?" he asked.

"The Circle of Naming," Keisha replied. "Here, the Celestial dragons bring their young for the rites. Each rune carved there is more than a letter; it is a song, bound into the stars. Only those with the Sight can hear them in full."

Valeon shook his head slowly. "This place is insane."

"Sacred," she corrected, though her voice carried a wistful edge. "Even to those who no longer believe."

The Pegasi caught a rising current, and for an instant, Valeon's silver-dappled mount soared higher than Keisha's. He let out a startled laugh, gripping the reins as her amused glance flicked his way. The moment felt light, unbound—until it ended.

Because ahead, above the drifting veils, another shape waited.

A shard of land hung suspended in the sky, but not like the others. This one was jagged, dark, its edges bristling with thorn-spined ridges. A patch of shadow clung to it, drinking the light, making the air itself tremble.

Keisha's gaze flicked to it, measuring. Too exposed. Too unstable. If forced to land, she would sooner trust open air than that waiting snare.

"We should head for the gate," she said, her tone calm but clipped. "The Celestials will be expecting us."

Valeon nodded, reluctant but obedient, as their Pegasi angled toward the pale spires of the Velaurien arch. The runes carved along its surface glowed faintly, thrumming like a heartbeat.

High above the thermals, half-hidden against a fractured ledge of black stone, Voraxia crouched. Her scales drank the light and returned it as a venomous violet sheen. Beside her, coiled in the seam between rock and cloud, lay Vorathos—molten veins dimmed to a slow, seething glow.

"You've stared at that elf long enough," Vorathos rumbled, smoke coiling between her teeth. "Planning to eat her?"

Voraxia did not answer at once. Her gaze was fixed not on the nervous human clinging to the Pegasus below.

But on Keisha.

"She doesn't move like the others," Voraxia murmured, voice low, edged like obsidian. "Even in the air, the wind bends to her."

Vorathos gave a rasping snort. "You're waxing poetic. Dangerous."

Voraxia's eyes narrowed, violet fire threading her silver sheen. "She's Eladrin."

Silence followed—heavy, broken only by the hiss of Vorathos's molten breath. Her head lifted, embers burning brighter beneath her hide. "Certain?"

"I am now," Voraxia said. "She hides it well, but I can taste it in the rhythm of her magic, in the way she listens to the land instead of bending it. The blood of the ancients sings in her veins."

Vorathos's tail lashed, carving a glowing scar into the stone. "The master spoke of an Eladrin meddler. If this is the one…" Her voice thickened, almost reverent in its hunger. "…then imagine what it would mean to silence her. To offer triumph, not defiance."

Voraxia's lips peeled back, fangs glimmering in the fractured light. "Remove her, and the master would rejoice. Perhaps then, the rebukes would cease. Then, we would not be reminded of leashes."

Vorathos's molten wings twitched open. "Orders were to observe," she growled, though conviction wavered in her tone.

Voraxia's gaze lingered on Keisha measured, merciless, certain. "We will be seen," she whispered. Shadow curled around her words like flame around oil. "But we will decide where the seeing cuts deepest."

Below, Keisha laughed at something Valeon said, her voice bright as silver chimes, unaware of the weight coiling above her. Her Pegasus drifted in a steady glide, wings spread wide, sunlight sliding across her armor like liquid fire.

"It's time," she called, steady as dawn. "Back to the gate."

They banked toward the shining arch.

But high above, the shadows moved.

Voraxia and Vorathos rose in unison, obsidian and abyss, wings folding tight before snapping wide into a dive. The air thinned. The wind twisted. The sky itself seemed to shudder with warning.

Keisha's head snapped upward. Her heart lurched. "Valeon—go!"

For one heartbeat, he froze—caught between instinct and memory, between his urge to stay and the raw terror of loss he had felt once before.

Then the Pegasus beneath him screamed and surged forward, hooves skimming the light, and he kicked hard, driving it faster.

Keisha wheeled her Pegasus into the path of the oncoming storm. Radiance and shadow collided in the air around her, light flaring, darkness folding in. She yanked the reins, plunging into a desperate dive, then climbed hard, dragging the hunt away from Valeon and the gate.

"Come on, girl," she breathed through clenched teeth, stroking the Pegasus's silver mane. "Not today."

The sky cracked.

A suffocating weight slammed into her chest, Voraxia's shadow-forged will, sharp and merciless. Pain lanced through her ribs like molten iron driven into bone. Her cry tore free, vision sparking white at the edges. Still, she held the reins, refusing to yield.

"She endures," Voraxia hissed, voice like a blade drawn in darkness, banking to strike again.

Behind her, Vorathos laughed a grinding sound like stone in fire. "Protecting a Pegasus? Bleeding for a beast of feathers?" Her molten veins blazed brighter, abyssal fire coiling up her throat. "Sentiment kills."

The second strike fell like a hammer of frost and flame. It slammed into Keisha's shoulder, and agony lit the joint, then turned it numb. Her fingers slipped, caught, slipped again, only stubborn will anchoring her to the saddle. The Pegasus shrieked, feathers scattering like sparks, but the blow had struck her alone. She had twisted her body, shielding the creature with her own.

The world narrowed into blinding light and choking shadow. Through the haze, Keisha glimpsed the jagged shard of sky-island she and Valeon had passed earlier, closer now, its thorned ridges looming. The air currents tore around it like claws, unstable, lethal. To land there would be to die.

She gritted her teeth, forcing her Pegasus higher, clinging to the open sky. Better the storm than the snare.

The mount's wings strained, tearing through the wind with hooves flashing light.

Valeon clung tight, the gale ripping the breath from his chest, panic pounding harder than the wingbeats beneath him. The gleaming arch of Lyra'el rose ahead, its runes blazing like a shield of stars.

The Pegasus stumbled as it struck the terrace stone, skidding across the plaza. Valeon nearly toppled, catching himself on the saddle's edge before leaping down, legs shaking, chest heaving.

He didn't wait. He staggered toward the gathering in the courtyard. Crystal armor gleamed in the morning sun, sentinels bracing, hands on blades. Among them stood Radiantus, Aurelius at his side, their vast wings half-furled from patrol.

"Keisha—" Valeon choked, voice cracking on her name. "She—she stayed behind. The sky—shadows—two of them! She's not with Kimras, she's on a Pegasus—she sent me ahead—"

The words tumbled out in fragments, but they were enough.

Radiantus's head snapped toward the horizon, his argent mane flaring with light. For the first time since his return, his calm fractured. A thunderous roar rolled from his chest, shaking every crystal terrace.

"She faces them alone." His wings unfurled, scattering shards of brilliance across the plaza. The air vibrated with his fury, every spire ringing in answer.

Aurelius's luminous white eyes narrowed, golden-silver light sharpening to a blade. "Voraxia. Vorathos."

Radiantus's voice thundered, low and fierce. "Then they will not face her alone for long."

With a single earth-shaking bound, the Platinum Dragon launched skyward, the terraces trembling in his wake. Aurelius followed, his vast wings igniting the clouds with celestial fire as the two noble giants surged eastward, toward the storm-wracked horizon.

"Just a little longer," Keisha whispered, steering the Pegasus toward the Velaurien arch toward the veil, toward hope.

The heavens tore in light.

Radiantus and Aurelius burst through the higher veil, platinum wings flaring brilliance across the cloud-tops. Below them, a Pegasus faltered, one wing trembling, its rider slumped in the saddle, hands still clenched on the reins.

"There," Aurelius said, awe softening his voice. "She still protects it."

"That's Keisha," Radiantus growled, silver eyes narrowing. "She would die before abandoning any creature in her care."

Crimson droplets trailed in the wind, terrible proof. Radiantus's voice sharpened to command. "Get to her. Free the mount. She won't release it on her own."

"And you?" Aurelius asked.

"I'll deal with them."

Aurelius fell like a comet. Radiantus leveled into the oncoming dark.

The Celestial Dragon drew alongside Keisha, matching the failing rhythm of Pegasus's wingbeats with impossible grace.

"Release the reins," he called, low and certain, extending a foreclaw. "Let him go. He'll be caught at the gate."

Keisha lifted her head, pale and sweat-slick, eyes blown wide with pain. She nodded once, fingers clumsy but deliberate as she unbuckled the strap and slid the line free. The Pegasus shuddered, confused, unwilling.

"Go," Aurelius told it, his voice deep as a bell. "The wardens will meet you."

Then, with infinite care, he curved one talon inward, forming a cradle of argent scale and light. He gathered Keisha against his chest, small and fragile within his vast hold. She groaned, but her hands found the ridge of his scales, clinging as if that touch alone tethered her.

"Take me to the city," she whispered and then, stronger: "Do not let him face them alone."

Aurelius sighed, half exasperation, half respect. "Elves." He tilted into a climb and drew level with Radiantus.

Ahead, Voraxia and Vorathos checked their dive, circling back to measure the blaze of light.

"He came," Voraxia said, unreadable.

"And brought another," Vorathos muttered.

Radiantus's voice rang like a blade across the sky. "Leave now or suffer the wrath of the Platinum Flight."

Even the wind stilled.

Voraxia's eyes flickered once, calculating, before she said flatly, "We leave. The master forbade engagement."

Vorathos hissed, fire trembling at her fangs, but swallowed it. Together, they peeled away, vanishing into mist and shadow, their absence sharp as an unspoken threat.

Radiantus watched until the last ripple smoothed from the sky. Then he turned. "Let's get her in."

The Velaurien Gate brightened to meet them, runes singing in layered chords. Wardens and healers raced across the terrace of white stone, flowering vines shivering with urgency.

Aurelius descended in a slow spiral, vast wings breaking the air until he touched the crystal platform as softly as drifting snow. Only then did he lower his foreleg, angling his talons with impossible precision.

"Gently," he rumbled.

The healers stepped forward, fearless before the Celestial's claws, and lifted Keisha from the cradle of argent scale. She was barely conscious, face colorless, lips bloodied, her hand slipping weakly from Aurelius's grip as they carried her into the chamber of soft light.

The doors closed with a resonant chime.

Her blood gleamed against the crystal floor like fallen rubies.

Valeon paced the archway, knuckles white, eyes fixed on the door as if he could will it open. "Should I contact Ong?" he blurted, turning to Radiantus, who stood nearby, wings half-folded, gaze fixed on the peaks.

Radiantus considered. "Not yet. Panic serves no one when we don't yet know the extent of her injuries." His head tipped, a glint of grim steel in his silver gaze. "And I doubt Kimras will wait for a message. He will feel this. I almost pity the fools who struck his rider."

Aurelius exhaled, some of the light leaving his shoulders. "This wasn't a mistake. They knew exactly what they were doing."

Valeon froze, the words cutting deeper than he expected. His throat went dry. "What do you mean, knew?"

Radiantus's gaze lowered to him, heavy as the weight of dawn. "You saw it too. They came for her. Not you. Not the Pegasus. Her. The one who bears the Eladrin flame." His wings shifted, scattering a harsh gleam across the terrace. "Do not fool yourself, Valeon. The shadows did not stumble into her path. The hand that commands them remembers her. Perhaps it even desired her gone."

Shock rippled through Valeon, colder than the mountain winds. He thought of Keisha's laughter, her voice steadying him when doubt gnawed, the way she had shielded him without hesitation. His stomach knotted. "Then it's my fault. If I hadn't—"

Radiantus's voice cut across him, sharp and unyielding. "No. The fault is theirs. The master's hatred is older than your years, and it hunts what it cannot corrupt. You are not the cause, Valeon—you are the witness. Remember what you saw today and let it steel you. For the day will come when neither she nor I can shield you, and you must choose to stand."

Valeon swallowed hard, protest dying on his tongue. For the first time, he understood his place among them was not chance, nor mistake. It was a summons.

The doors to the healing chamber remained closed, the glow behind them steady. Outside, the ward-lanterns brightened as night crept toward Lyra'el.

The storm had passed.

But the war had already begun.

Chapter 24

Embers Beneath Stone

The volcanic winds howled outside Flameford, but within the central cavern the air was still—tainted with smoke, thick with brimstone, heavy with the weight of rivalries left unsaid.

Voraxia landed first, wings folding sleek against her frame as molten light ran along the fractured edges of her scales. Each step rang deliberately against soot-stained stone. Controlled. Calculated.

Vorathos followed, her vast coils grinding across the cavern floor with a hiss like splitting obsidian. Together, they claimed the center. Waiting.

Toward the rear, Zylron stood rooted in silence. His posture was taut and unreadable, but his crimson eyes burned with a steady suspicion fixed not on Vorathos, but on Voraxia.

And he was not alone.

Glaciera loomed rimed in frost, settling just behind his flank. Nocturna's dissolving shadow stretched across the stone beside her. Xalzorath coiled to complete the arc, runes flickering faintly along his vast hide. Their formation curved around Zylron, not apart.

In dragon-language, it was no accident.

Voraxia's tail flicked once. Her gaze tracked the arc, narrowing as she weighed angles and intent. It was a declaration. Warning. And though her jaw tightened, the flash of irritation cooled quickly to calculation. She never forgot alignments. She never forgave them.

Shadows shifted at the cavern's mouth.

The mysterious figure entered.

Black-cloaked, they drank the molten glow without reflecting it, their presence bending the silence itself. They halted at the center. The lava's light trembled as though reluctant to touch them.

When they spoke, the voice was smooth, calm yet honed like a blade's edge.

"Before we begin, remember one thing."

Their gaze swept the gathered host, one by one. Shadows stirred tighter, betraying the temper barely veiled.

"I am the one in command."

The words fell like ash clinging, inescapable.

"I expect loyalty. No hesitation. Not factions. Not whispers. What we are building is greater than the pride of any single one of you. And if any of you have forgotten—" their tone curved sharp, steel drawn taut, "—you will not be warned again."

A low growl rippled from the cavern's edge. Whether defiance or assent, it went unanswered.

Zylron did not move. His crimson eyes lingered on the cloaked figure a heartbeat longer than wisdom allowed. Measuring. Remembering.

The mysterious one turned at last, fixing their gaze on the abyssal sisters.

"Well? Give your report."

Voraxia lifted her head, the lava painting her scales in fractured violet. When she spoke, her tone was smooth, measured, each word chosen with care.

"We ensured we were seen—circling the outer territories as instruct-ed. It was then that we observed two figures crossing Lyra'el's border upon Pegasi."

Her tail flicked, too precise to be idle.

"One was human. Young. Nervous. Inexperienced."

The mysterious figure tilted their veiled head. "And the other?"

Voraxia paused not long, but long enough for the silence to deepen. "A female. Eladrin."

The word left her throat like shattered glass. For an instant, some-thing shifted through her—satisfaction, honed with unease. That face had not been expected to return. Not there. Not riding beneath starlit wings.

The syllables lingered in the cavern like a coin still spinning on stone.

Zylron's crimson eyes narrowed, lifting.

Voraxia's voice remained even. "The male was granted passage. The dragons allowed him within Lyra'el."

The mysterious figure's reply came in a quieter, colder tone. "And the Eladrin?"

Voraxia did not blink. "She flew beneath me during a descent. I veered, but the air was tight. There was... turbulence."

She let silence breathe, tasting the tension it left behind.

She was struck. Minor wounds, no more. She lives, I think. The Platinum one carried her away."

Vorathos's nostrils flared, smoke whispering in slow coils, but she said nothing.

Stillness pressed down over the cavern.

Not Glaciera. Not Xalzorath. Not even Nocturna, whose shadows thickened against the stone.

They all knew.

They all heard the lie and the cold precision with which it was spoken.

The mysterious figure did not stir. They did not question. They didn't need to. Their silence pressed heavier than the molten rivers around them.

The crack came not from them, but from Zylron.

Smoke bled from his jaws as he stepped forward, every line of his body wound taut with restraint.

"For one as old as you," he rumbled, voice low as shifting stone, "you know the air above Lyra'el. You chose your path. You chose her."

Voraxia's head turned slowly. Her silver-white eyes locked onto his. No denial. No defense. Only silence, an acknowledgment sharper than any words.

"This was no accident," Zylron went on. "It was defiance. Against command."

The chamber pulsed. Glaciera shifted, frost cracking from her scales in brittle shards. Nocturna's shadows thickened, swallowing the floor in dark swells. Xalzorath's runes flared, then dulled, like a warning swallowed back.

The balance wavered.

Then the mysterious figure moved. Not in fury, though it licked beneath their silence, but with an icy precision that cracked the stone under each step. They advanced toward Voraxia, their voice drawn thin as glass about to break.

"Whether it was an accident," they said, "or a test of my leash... it will not happen again."

Voraxia did not bow. She stilled, wings coiling tight, violet fire flickering faintly at their edges.

The figure halted before her, shadows thickening around their form.

"You will come to your lair. We will speak privately. I must be certain you understand what is required of you."

Voraxia's eyes narrowed, violet fire licking faintly along her scales.

Then, slowly, deliberately, she bowed her head just enough to be called obedience.

"As you command."

Zylron exhaled sharply, smoke spilling from his jaws in a hot plume. He said nothing further. He didn't need to. His truth lingered in the cavern like molten stone cooling to ash.

The mysterious one turned away, shadows curling tighter around their form. The chamber's silence settled once more, neither peace nor trust. Balance. Fragile. Uneasy. A silence, the next breath could shatter.

Beneath the blackened rock, the flame still burned.

Voraxia and Vorathos moved together, wings folding close as they paced toward the upper tunnels. They passed Zylron without a word, yet both paused just long enough to glance back. Not an open challenge. Not an overt threat. Merely a look sharp, measuring, promising.

Zylron did not flinch. His crimson eyes burned with steady, unyielding certainty.

When the sisters vanished into shadow, the air loosened its grip. Glaciera released a slow breath, frost curling from her nostrils and dimming the molten glow. Nocturna drifted forward in silence, her shadows unfurling to brush the stone. Xalzorath coiled closer, runes pulsing in a low, steady rhythm like the heartbeat of the earth itself.

"You did not earn your temper for nothing," Xalzorath rumbled at last, his voice heavy with the weight of ancient years.

"At least," Nocturna whispered, soft as drifting smoke, "the message was received."

No one spoke further. One by one, they withdrew into the deep halls of Flameford, their vast forms swallowed by fire and shadow.

And yet, in the cavern's stillness, the air quivered with something unspoken—

An alliance formed not through trust or loyalty.

But through fear.

Far below, in the dark spiral of her lair, Voraxia landed in silence. The stone radiated the lingering warmth of past fires, but the air felt cooler now—taut, expectant.

The mysterious one stood at the center, still as carved obsidian, watching a thin stream of lava creep along the wall like a living scar.

Without turning, they spoke.

"Describe the Eladrin."

Voraxia stepped forward, her tone deliberate.

"She was red-haired. At first, I doubted—Eladrin rarely bear that coloring. But I watched her. The way she moved, the way the magic breathed around her."

Her head lifted slightly.

"It was her. The one you warned us of. So yes... I struck. I believed she was the one causing you trouble."

Silence stretched, heavy as stone.

Then the mysterious one turned, and a low laugh slipped from their throat—quiet, cold, edged with cruel amusement.

"That was Keisha," they said at last. Their veiled gaze gleamed. "The very one."

They began to pace, robes trailing over blackened stone, shadows curling behind them like a second cloak.

"And while I am not displeased to know she was injured..."

They stopped suddenly, their voice sharpened to a blade.

"You will remember your place."

Voraxia dipped her head—obedience sharpened by pride. "I understand."

Then, with a flicker of violet fire in her eyes, she added, low and deliberate:

"She was seriously injured. She may not rise quickly."

For the first time, the mysterious one let it slip.

A smile—thin, wicked, carved of hunger—curved across their face. It was not masked. It was meant to be seen.

Voraxia's gaze lingered, unreadable.

Vorathos entered a heartbeat later, coils sliding across the stone, abyssal blue eyes narrowing at the sight of that smile. Neither sister spoke of it. But both bowed their heads in silence—acknowledging, accepting, hiding their own thoughts.

The mysterious one turned without another word and vanished into the dark, their laughter echoing faintly against the stone as they went.

Vorathos's growl rumbled low, edged with sardonic humor, though her coils stayed wound tight.

"Well," she said at last, "that went better than expected."

Voraxia did not answer immediately. Firelight shimmered faintly along her scales. Then, softly—just loud enough for the lava to carry:

"Keisha was stronger than I thought."

Vorathos's wings flexed, smoke curling from her jaws. She glanced toward the tunnel where the mysterious one had disappeared, the shadows there still rippling faintly.

Voraxia's voice followed, low and measured, steel beneath silk.

"We need to watch Zylron. The red dragon's calm is a mask. Cracks are already forming."

Vorathos snorted. "He already is."

"Maybe," Voraxia murmured. "But we do nothing. Not to him. Not to Glaciera. Not to any of them."

Vorathos's eyes burned hotter. "Because of the mysterious one."

Voraxia's lips curved faintly, a glint of violet sheen along her fangs.

"Yes. Because if we cross them... we burn. And there is something in them, Vorathos, something we both know we cannot challenge."

Vorathos grumbled, coils loosening but not unwinding fully. At last, she inclined her head.

"Fine. For now."

Together, the sisters turned, their shadows stretching long across the lava-lit stone before the fire swallowed them whole.

When their echoes faded, the cavern fell silent.

The mysterious one lingered in the gloom a moment longer, then turned toward the black tower. Their steps were slow and deliberate, their robes whispering across the scorched stone. At the threshold, they paused.

The shadows along the walls stirred unbidden, restless as though the lair itself remembered. Dark tendrils writhed upward like smoke caught in a breath that did not belong to this world.

A laugh slipped from the figure, low and cold, edged with a predator's satisfaction. Their voice followed, soft as a secret not meant to be heard.

"Vuarus... perhaps, at last, the elf who slipped your sacrifice will not survive. It will not bring you back... but it will please me."

The shadows quivered in approval, their forms trembling against the stone. The figure's smile lingered as they stepped into the tower, and the obsidian closed around them.

Only silence and the echo of that laughter remained in the depths of Flameford.

Chapter 25

A Wound in the Wind

The morning sky over Goldmoor shimmered with early mist, but its peace felt brittle—like the land itself was holding its breath. On a wind-carved cliff, Kimras stood with wings folded tight, tail lashing in restless arcs. Memories pressed against him: Keisha bound in shadow's grip, the firestorm when he and Amara had torn her free. The same dread whispered through the air now, gnawing at his heart like teeth.

Below, at the edge of the Purplefire Woods, Amara rested on a moss-cloaked ridge. Her violet scales fractured the dawn into prisms of flame, but her gaze was fixed on Kimras. She felt it too, the shiver in the wind, the warning before the storm.

He descended beside her in a gust that rattled the trees.

"You're leaving," she said before he spoke.

Kimras dipped his head, golden mane catching the light. "I need you to watch over Goldmoor and the Purplefire. Keep the forests safe. And stay in contact with Ong."

Her violet eyes narrowed. "Where?"

His gaze never left the east. "Lyra'el. I cannot say why. Only that something is wrong with Keisha." His voice was quiet, but iron threaded through every word.

Silence pressed close, broken only by the whisper of wind in the trees.

Amara shifted her wings. "Do you want me to go to Crystal Vale? I could warn Ong."

"Yes," Kimras said, gentle but firm. "Tell him I have gone to Lyra'el. Nothing more. Until I know the truth, there is no need to sow fear."

She studied him, jaw tight, then inclined her head. "Very well. But be cautious. Whispers already stir that the Shadow and the Abyssal walk Vacari's skies again."

"I have heard," Kimras rumbled, a growl beneath his words. "It only confirms what I feel. Danger is nearer than we think."

Their silence was not emptiness, but trust tempered in fire, proven on battlefields where timing and faith meant survival. Amara lowered one claw to his shoulder. "Then fly fast."

Kimras bowed his head, molten eyes steady. "Guard the forests well."

With a thunderous sweep of wings, he rose into the mist, scales blazing until he became a streak of gold against the morning sky.

Amara watched him vanish, the purple blossoms trembling as wind rushed through their boughs like an unspoken vow. She turned west, unease pressing her toward Crystal Vale.

The crystalline towers blazed under the midday sun, their faceted walls scattering light in a thousand colors. Amara's landing struck harder than she intended, talons cracking crystal stone. From the palace steps, Ong broke into a run, boots ringing.

"Amara! What's wrong?"

She lowered her head, violet eyes aflame. "Kimras has gone to Lyra'el. He felt something amiss with Keisha; he could not name it, but he was certain."

Ong froze mid-step. Fear cracked through his mask of resolve. "Then I'm going too." The words came sharp, almost a challenge, though dread edged them. "She could be hurt right now. I won't stand here."

Amara barred his path with one great claw. "He asked me to tell you, but not to follow. He will see the truth himself before panic spreads."

"That's easy for him to say," Ong snapped, fists tightening. "She's my wife."

"Standing still is not the same as doing nothing," Amara said, calm but commanding. "Kimras knows what he does. If danger comes, you will feel it, and you will have your chance. But if you rush blind, you risk more than your own life."

His gaze faltered, storm held tight in his chest. "I should be there."

Footsteps echoed on crystal stone. Gailen appeared with King Manard at his side.

"Kimras would not ask for patience unless it were needful," Gailen said, steady though unease lingered in his eyes.

Manard's voice was grave, edged with sorrow. "She is in the care of dragons, Ong. She is not unprotected. Wait for word before you move."

Ong's fists remained clenched until his gaze met Amara's steadfast, unyielding, softened by memory. She lowered her head, her voice only for him.

"We have stood in fire before, you and I. The last time you charged without trust, it nearly cost us all. Do not let fear blind you now. Trust me to watch the skies for you."

His breath came rough. Slowly, his fists uncurled. "Fine," he muttered. "For now."

Amara's tone gentled. "Guard your strength. You may need it soon."

With a single sweep of her vast wings, she launched skyward, violet fire scattering through the mist as she vanished into the clouds.

Ong watched her go, the ache of distance heavy in his chest. At last, he turned toward the glade, where stone dragons towered in silent vigil.

Their carved wings stretched long shadows across him as he sank to the roots at their feet.

"They never failed their riders," he whispered. His hand closed on his hilt. "And neither will I fail Keisha ever again."

The wind stirred through the glade, whispering across stone wings like a vow. Far to the east, thunder rolled a reminder that silence in Vacari never lingered.

The outer gates of Lyra'el gleamed with wards and silver fire, steady against the morning sky. Then a vast shadow swept across the heavens.

Kimras.

He descended with a roar that split the air, golden wings blazing brighter than dawn. The stone trembled under his talons as he struck the terrace before the gates.

The Celestial guards stiffened, halberds lowering, eyes wide.

"Who is that?" one whispered.

"Should we summon the High Council?"

"No one lands at the threshold like that…"

Kimras' tail cracked thunder against the ground.

From a high balcony, Radiantus lifted his head, argent mane scattering brilliance. Recognition burned in his silver gaze.

"Kimras," he murmured. "And not in the mood to wait."

He vanished in a blaze of light, reappearing at the gates an instant later. Calm authority radiated from him, steadying the guards.

"Stand aside," Radiantus said. "This is Kimras, Noble Gold Dragon of Vacari. He has come for his rider."

At the name, murmurs rippled through the onlookers. A citizen at the wall whispered with certainty, "A bond between a noble dragon and their rider is not to be challenged, least of all by shadow."

The guards bowed low and stepped back, their faces filled with reverence.

Radiantus turned to his brother. "She lives. The healers work even now. The worst has been stemmed, but the wound is deep."

Molten fire lit Kimras' eyes, rage smoldering beneath his sorrow. He had sworn to shield her from every shadow. Yet she had bled while he was away.

"Take me to her," he rumbled, voice like a vow.

Radiantus inclined his shining head. "Come. We will speak more within."

Together, the ancients passed through the gates, filling the archway with gold and platinum light. The crystal doors closed behind them like a roll of thunder.

Above, the wards steadied once more, silver threads binding light across the sky. Yet the heavens seemed taut, as though they remembered the brush of shadowed wings.

Lyra'el still blazed with brilliance.

But only just.

Chapter 26
Shadows of Deceit

The skies above Lyra'el shimmered with quiet magic, but in the darker reaches of Vacari, shadows stirred with purpose, and silence no longer meant peace.

Rhys stood atop the obsidian balcony of the Umbral Hall, the city sprawled below like a maze of secrets. Far above, the surface sky was only a memory here; the air was cool, heavy, and touched with the faint scent of oil lamps and iron. His fingers traced the edge of a glass vial, empty now but recently filled with a slow-working poison that had thinned the leadership council one by one. No one had suspected.

Now, with new members in place—those who owed their positions to his whispered promises—only one obstacle remained.

Maedra.

The herbalist. The poison mistress. The one who had unknowingly taught him everything he needed to destroy her. He had not forgotten the way she once looked at him—first with pride, later with suspicion. Somewhere, buried deep, resentment smoldered. She had underestimated him. And he had waited.

Had she stayed in the shadows, he might have let her live. But she still held sway among the commoners, still walked the markets with respect from traders and outcasts alike. If anyone could name him as her student... if anyone looked too closely...

That could not happen.

He did not draw his blade. He drew whispers instead.

In Vacari, fear traveled faster than fact—and truth, once fractured, rarely healed. That was all he needed.

Soon, the Umbral Market hummed with quiet rumors:

"Maedra's been meeting someone from the surface."

"She's storing sealed letters; no one knows who they're for."

"She's been stockpiling herbs that enhance Eladrin strength... why would she need those?"

By the time the council heard them, belief had already taken root.

A pouch of gleaming Eladrin moonleaf appeared behind a loose stone in her stall.

A coded message, perfectly forged in her hand, slipped into her private ledger.

Vials unmarked, their contents carefully chosen, were buried in her garden with markings only the council would recognize as surface alchemy.

When the accusations came, the evidence was already in place.

"She's been conspiring with the Eladrin," one council member said. Torchlight wavered in the chamber, painting the walls in restless shadow.

"She's hidden herbs meant to strengthen Umbral warriors," another added. "She means to betray us all."

Rhys stood quietly near the back. He didn't need to speak. His satisfaction was not in gloating, but in knowing the trap had been set long before their voices rose.

Maedra was taken in the night. No trial. No public spectacle. Just silence, and a missing face in the morning.

But as they dragged her away, her pale eyes turned once, catching his and not pleading. Not afraid. Simply knowing. It was a look that struck deep, half accusation, half recognition. She knew what he had done. And even as she vanished into the dark, her silence pressed against him like a weight.

He smiled anyway. Bitter. Hollow. You taught me too well.

But he was not finished.

"If Maedra was capable of such betrayal," he murmured in the right ears, "who else knew?"

"I have always wondered about those who visited her often. We would be wise to watch them."

It spread like smoke under a closed door. Soon, a handful of Umbral Elves who had once supported her faced the same judgment. Evidence was convenient and irrefutable, tying them to quiet meetings, suspicious purchases, and discreet donations.

Some were exiled. Others were never seen again.

The fear Rhys had sown now grew without tending, and his control deepened.

By morning, he stood before the reshaped council. Poised. Calm. Ready to call the next vote.

The council chamber was lit in muted violet flame, the air heavy with the scent of burned resin. Darkstone banners hung above, motionless despite the faint stir of underground drafts.

One of the new members rose. "We must choose a single path forward. One voice. One leader."

"I nominate Rhys," another called.

A murmur of agreement followed. Another name was offered, but without conviction. The vote was quick. Unanimous.

Rhys lowered his head slightly, feigning humility. "You honor me more than I deserve," he said in a voice shaped for trust. It was a lie, of course.

This was not their will; it was Lyra's. He had worn the mask long enough for them to think it was theirs.

He stepped forward, letting his voice fill the chamber.

"Let us begin a new era, one where shadows no longer bow. Where the forgotten rise, and the world remembers why it feared the dark."

His tone sharpened, a blade hidden in velvet.

"It is time the Umbral Elves claimed their rightful place. No more hiding. No more silence. We will align with the Druchii, take their strength, their ruthlessness. Their enemies tremble at the sound of their name, and so shall ours."

He paced slowly, each step measured.

"For too long, we were bound by roots sunk too deep in caution. Those roots are gone."

The pause stretched until—

A slow clap broke it.

Another joined in.

Then another.

The sound swelled, echoing off stone walls until the chamber trembled with approval.

Rhys smiled, the expression a mask over calculation. He had not asked for power. He had removed everything that could deny it.

When the applause faded, he raised a hand. "I will not govern alone. I appoint six commanders who will carry my directives, oversee our operations, and speak my will."

Six Umbral Elves stepped forward—hardened, cunning, and loyal.

One bowed. "There was... an incident a few days past. A rumor of an Eladrin female near the outskirts. She was attacked and wounded."

Rhys's gaze sharpened a flicker of recognition, of unease—but smoothed to indifference. "Name?"

"Not yet. But we will find it."

Rhys nodded once. "See that you do."

He turned back to the council. "Begin issuing the new orders. Ready the outposts. Let the whispers spread again."

Without fanfare, he left the chamber, descending into the deeper halls where torchlight gave way to pure darkness. His new quarters awaited a chamber carved into obsidian, lined with silver-threaded maps and scrolls.

In silence, he dipped a quill and wrote a single message:

It is done.

He did not sign it. Did not seal it with wax.

As the ink dried, he sat back, letting the stillness coil around him. Maedra's knowing eyes still lingered in his memory, but he shoved them into shadow. Lyra would be pleased. That was what mattered.

Far above, in the bright skies of Lyra'el, alliances stirred, binding themselves in trust and hope.

Below, in the roots of the world, Rhys bound his council in silence and fear.

Two songs now rose across Vacari, one of light, one of shadow.

And only one would endure.

Chapter 27

Fractures in the Light

The halls of Lyra'el were hushed, their silence broken only by the measured tread of two cloaked figures.

Radiantus led Kimras through the inner sanctum of the Celestial enclave, footsteps echoing over marble veined with silver light. As they neared the chamber where Keisha lay, both dragons shed their true forms. Radiantus became a tall elf, hair streaked with argent, eyes luminous as starlight. Kimras chose a human guise, golden-haired, sapphire-eyed, his presence no less commanding for its smaller frame.

Within the healing chamber, the air shimmered with quiet enchantments. Crystalline walls pulsed with soft radiance, the stone itself humming with restorative power. On the bed, Keisha lay pale and still, her breath shallow but steady.

Valeon sat at her side, a vial of salve trembling in his hands. He had not opened it. Shoulders hunched, his gaze clung to her face as if sheer will might keep her tethered. When the door opened, he leapt to his feet, voice cracking.

"Are you the healers? She hasn't moved—her breathing's steady, but I think—"

Radiantus raised a hand, calm and commanding. "I am Radiantus, Platinum Dragon of Lyra'el."

Valeon froze, nearly dropping the vial. "Oh. Uh—sorry. I didn't recognize you."

Kimras ignored him. He crossed the chamber in three strides and knelt beside the bed, his hand trembling as he brushed a strand of fiery hair from Keisha's face. His jaw clenched; golden light flared beneath his mortal skin, threatening to break free.

"Voraxia and Vorathos injured her," Radiantus said quietly, steel threading his tone.

Kimras rose slowly, voice taut with fury. "Was it in battle?"

Radiantus's diamond-like silver eyes softened, though his expression stayed grave. "No. She was escorting Valeon on a Pegasus toward Lyra'el. They struck without provocation. It was deliberate. Calculated."

Kimras's hands curled into fists. His voice deepened into a growl too vast for the form he wore. "Then this is the work of the one in shadows, the same hand that whispers poison into dragons' ears. The same will that twisted Vuarus."

For a moment, silence pressed like stone. Valeon's breath caught, his eyes darting between them.

Kimras turned not in accusation, but in heavy realization. Keisha had taken the risk for someone else. For this.

The golden dragon's voice dropped into a rumble, thunder contained in human lungs.

"They will answer for this."

The chamber stilled, as if the very walls braced themselves against the fury gathering in his words.

Valeon lowered his gaze, voice breaking. "It was my fault. I should have stayed with her. She sent me ahead to the gate... but I should have gone back."

Memory slashed through him, Keisha's eyes, fierce even as blood streaked her lips, her voice commanding him to go. He had obeyed. And because he had, she had faced the storm alone. Guilt gnawed at him, raw and merciless.

Radiantus turned, his voice calm but confident. "No. You did the right thing. Your warning is the reason we arrived in time. Without it, she would already be lost."

Kimras nodded once, though his gaze never left Keisha. "He's right."

A long silence stretched. At last, Kimras looked thoroughly at Valeon. His expression was a mix of steel and sorrow, but his tone held unexpected steadiness. "Then tell me, Valeon, why did she not call for me to take you both?"

The words struck harder than any blow. For a heartbeat, even Kimras felt doubt gnaw at the edges of his resolve. She had always called for him when danger loomed. Always. Had she feared he would not come in time? Or feared he would not come at all?

Valeon's shoulders sagged. His throat worked, but only a whisper emerged. "Because... I was afraid. Afraid of flying on a dragon."

Kimras's hands tightened at his sides. He exhaled through his nose, air sharp with restrained fire. Slowly, he shook his head. "That will change. A Celestial dragon will teach you to ride not for war, but for survival. You will never be a dragonrider, Valeon. But the times we live in demand more than fear. Pegasus wings will not always be enough."

He did not say it aloud, but the vow burned behind his words: never again would Keisha be left to fight alone because of another's weakness.

Valeon opened his mouth, pride bristling, but then his gaze fell on Keisha. Pale. Still. Her breath shallow, her fingers limp where once they had gripped reins with defiance. Shame pricked his skin, hot and unrelenting. Whatever protest rose died on his tongue.

He nodded once. "Okay."

Radiantus inclined his head, quiet approval flickering in his silver gaze.

As they left the chamber, Kimras's voice dropped low. "Was there a place she could have landed, had she let the Pegasus go?"

Radiantus answered with measured calm. "Yes. A narrow ledge along the ridge. Treacherous, but survivable. She chose not to risk it for the creature's sake."

Kimras's jaw flexed. He saw it clearly in his mind: Keisha, even wounded, choosing to shield a beast rather than herself. Her heart always reaches outward, always carrying the weight of others. It was who she was. And what made her vulnerable.

"Typical of her," he muttered, half-pride, half-anguish. His eyes burned hotter, golden light beneath mortal skin straining to break free. "But those dark dragons..."

Radiantus did not answer, but the steel in his silence was enough.

Without another word, the two dragons strode from the chamber. Outside, noonday light blazed across the balcony. Their mortal guises dissolved, platinum and gold erupting into the sky, wings unfurling, scales blazing like suns brought to earth.

The city of Lyra'el shone around them, radiant and unbroken.

But the light they carried was edged with fire.

They moved along the crystalline pathway toward the inner spire when a pair of Umbral Elves, leaning near a garden wall, let their whispers carry.

"Good, it was an Eladrin that got hit. Maybe now Lyra'el will realize things are changing. Rhys won't be playing by their rules."

Kimras halted. His molten-gold eyes narrowed. Before either elf could flinch, his tail lashed out, knocking them to the ground.

They gasped, scrambling upright, faces pale with shame.

Radiantus stepped forward, voice low but edged with iron. "You will watch your words. One more whisper of that kind, and the Umbral Elves will find themselves banned from Lyra'el for eternity."

The threat hung in the air like thunder waiting to break.

Kimras loomed beside him, golden scales rippling with restrained fury. He did not roar for vengeance. He roared so they would understand what Keisha meant to him.

From deep within, his dragon's voice tore free a raw, resonant sound that shook the spires and sent flocks wheeling into the sky. Not an attack, but a vow. A declaration of war.

From a nearby balcony, a Celestial citizen leaned toward her companion, a faint, knowing smile on her lips.

"A bond between a noble dragon and their rider," she murmured, "is not something a dark dragon should ever test."

Her friend nodded gravely. "Especially not that one."

Radiantus placed a steadying claw on Kimras's shoulder and inclined his head toward the spire. "Come. There is something we must address. Now."

They followed the pathway winding toward the Grand Hall, which overlooked the endless sea. As they passed an open terrace, the horizon stretched wide before them.

Beyond the waves, shrouded in silver mist, an island rose like a phantom—its cliffs gleaming faintly in the midday light.

"That," Radiantus said, his gaze narrowing on the distant silhouette, "is Veyndralis. Few beyond the Celestial council know its name. Once, it was a sanctuary for dragons in the first wars. Since then, it has remained sealed by divine wards. It is not a place we speak of lightly... and rarer still is the need to stand upon it."

Kimras's eyes stayed fixed on the island. "Why show me now?"

Radiantus's expression did not shift. "Because the world is moving, Kimras. Whether this season or another, the day may come when Veyndralis matters again. And when it does, I would have you ready not caught unawares."

Kimras rumbled deep in his chest but said nothing more.

At the heart of the Grand Hall stood an ancient crystal obelisk, humming with restrained power. Its surface pulsed with light, ready to carry a message across every corner of the realm.

Radiantus stepped forward, pressing one claw against the conduit. Light flared within, spiraling upward in radiant threads. His voice carried with it, amplified and unyielding, echoing across Lyra'el and beyond.

"To all citizens of Lyra'el Eladrin, Fae, Druchii, Umbral, and beyond. Today, an Eladrin was struck down on sacred soil by dragons who defied our skies. And some among you dared to whisper that her suffering was a sign of change."

His tone hardened, ringing like a blade unsheathed. "Hear me well: there will be no uprising from within. There will be no tolerance for cruelty paraded as strength. Lyra'el stands for unity and balance. If the Umbral Elves or any among you believe Rhys's ambition will open these gates, they will instead find them sealed against them forever."

When his words faded, silence filled the chamber, broken only by the low thrum of the obelisk's light.

Radiantus lowered his claw and turned to Kimras, diamond-like silver eyes sharp. "Now... let us hope the rest of them are listening."

A vow burned unspoken in both of them: let the shadows test their resolve. They would see what dragons protected, and what dragons would never allow to fall.

In a narrow corridor overlooking the hall, hidden by a veil of shadow, Rhys stood listening. His lips curled into a sly smile.

"We will see, Radiantus," he whispered, voice low with satisfaction. "Even if you ban us, the dark has its ways."

One of his new commanders emerged from the gloom, bowing low. "My lord... I have confirmed the name of the Eladrin. It was Keisha."

Rhys's eyes gleamed like cold steel catching firelight. He gave a single sharp nod, then turned without a word, striding back into the depths of the Umbral Hall.

In his private chamber, lit only by rune-marked maps and shifting shadow, he summoned an enchanted scroll. With deliberate strokes, he wrote three words:

It is done.

He sealed the message and let it vanish into the waiting dark.

Far above, the light of Lyra'el burned brighter.

Far below, the roots of shadow twisted, carrying Rhys's words to the one who waited in silence.

Chapter 28
Threads of Defiance

In the heart of molten shadows,
whispers burn hotter than fire—and
truth is never the only thing being
forged.

In the twilight-drenched tower at the edge of Fel Thalor, Lyra stood before her scrying mirror, its surface rippling with blue flame. The connection flared, bringing Rhys's face into view—slightly distorted, but his false calm unmistakable.

Before he could speak, Lyra's voice cut through the static like a blade.

"Two messages, Rhys? Saying the same cursed thing? Do you think I forget that easily?"

Rhys flinched. He feared her power far more than he resented her command. Resistance was suicide, and he knew it.

"I—I only wanted to be sure you received it, Lady Lyra. The message was important."

Her eyes narrowed.

"Then say it once, clearly, and stop wasting my time. And if you ever send me the same self-satisfied words twice—especially something as trite as 'It is done'—I will carve them into your flesh so you remember not to."

His composure cracked. "Yes, of course." He cleared his throat. "There was... an incident. An Eladrin named Keisha has been injured. The attack came from a shadow dragon and an abyssal dragon near the outskirts of Lyra'el. And..."

He faltered.

Lyra's tone dropped to ice. "And what, Rhys?"

"Radiantus overheard some Umbral Elves speaking of it. They said it was good that an Eladrin was the one injured. He made a public declaration that if the Umbral Elves cause more trouble, they will be banished from Lyra'el entirely."

The name had already rooted itself in her mind.

Keisha.

Lyra's lips curved in a sharp, pleased smile. "Keisha," she murmured. "So, the gods place their hopes in you. How... predictable."

But as the rest of the report sank in, the smile vanished.

"You fool," she hissed. "You absolute fool."

Panic whispered beneath her fury. Chaos hinted at weakness, and weakness was the one thing she had never tolerated.

"Do you understand what you've allowed? I ordered influence. Quiet maneuvering. Not drunken-pirate gossip spilling into the streets."

Rhys winced. "I didn't tell them to—"

"Control them!" she snapped. "You were given the gift of leadership, not a license for chaos. If the Umbral Elves are cast out of Lyra'el now, every foothold I built for you will crumble, and I will personally flay you, Rhys. Skin. Bone. Soul. Do not tempt me."

He swallowed hard. "It won't happen again."

"Make sure it doesn't. And do not send me another double message unless you want it carved into your chest."

She turned as if to sever the connection but paused. Her gaze narrowed further.

"Have Keisha watched. If she begins to recover, you will tell me immediately. No delays."

The mirror went black.

Lyra's fingers twitched at her side, fury straining against her composure. The name still echoed, burning hotter with each heartbeat.

Keisha.

An Eladrin. A rival. A reminder of everything Lyra loathed. Her existence was insulting enough, but wounded, faltering? That, Lyra could savor.

Her lips curved again, slower this time, sharp as obsidian.

"Your magic will not outshine mine," she whispered into the waiting dark. "If fate does not finish you, I will."

The blue flames guttered and died, leaving only silence in the tower.

The Cost of Accord

Far to the south, beyond drifting sands and storm-wracked skies, Shadowhaven festered at the edge of the world like a wound that refused to close. The air was thick with brine, rot, and the tang of blood on rusted iron.

Qellaun strode into the heart of the pirate stronghold, the damp air clinging to his skin like oil. His silver eyes swept over the chaos—shanties clinging to blackened stone, banners sagging from harpoons, dragon bones lashed into crude gates.

He approached a cluster of pirates hunched around a smoky brazier. One a wiry man with a broken nose—rose, sneering.

"You look lost, elf."

"I'm looking for the one in charge," Qellaun replied evenly.

The pirate barked a laugh. "I'll take you. But fair warning, Maldrak hates elves."

Qellaun tilted his head, unimpressed. "And I'm not exactly fond of pirates."

Truth be told, he despised the errand and everyone who forced him to carry it. But his voice remained cool, almost amused.

The pirate chuckled again, jerking his thumb down the street. "This way. Let's see who hates who more."

They wound through streets littered with broken crates, sleeping dogs, and the occasional drunken brawl. The deeper they went, the more fortified the buildings became—until they reached a looming hall built from scavenged ship hulls, stretched dragonhide, and bleached bone.

The pirate slammed a fist against the heavy door. "You get one shot to speak. Don't waste it."

Inside, firelight guttered across hanging chains and mounted skulls. At the far end stood Maldrak, a broad-shouldered brute draped in sea-worn furs, his eyes sharp despite the drink on his breath.

"What do you want? I hate elves."

Qellaun didn't flinch. "As I told your man outside, I hate pirates. So, we're even. And believe me, if it were my choice, I would not be here. But the mysterious one commanded it."

Even as he spoke, the taste of borrowed authority soured in his mouth. He did not serve willingly, but power rarely came without compromise.

At the name, Maldrak's sneer faltered. He grunted, low and wary. "Stay out," he barked to his men. "I'll talk to this elf myself."

The door shut, sealing them in the chamber of bone and smoke. Qellaun delivered the order details veiled, but enough for Maldrak to understand.

The pirate lord chuckled grimly. "An alliance, then. Shadowhaven will profit. I'll agree." He waved to the guards. "Show him around. Then give him a place to rest. A private one."

That night, after being led through twisting lanes and stinking docks, Qellaun settled into a bare, salt-stained chamber. Alone at last, he summoned the connection.

The mysterious one's voice seeped through the shadows.

"Stay put for now."

Qellaun inclined his head. The link faded.

He exhaled, muttering into the stale air, "Stuck in Shadowhaven. Just what every elf dreams of: rotting sea air and pirate diplomacy."

He glanced toward the sealed window, waves battering the black cliffs beyond. There would be no escape until the voice allowed it.

So he sat in silence, brine and smoke clinging to him, wondering not for the first time whether this was strategy... or surrender.

Beneath the Flame

In the obsidian halls of Flameford, silence reigned, save for the crackle of ever-burning braziers. The mysterious one waited in a vaulted chamber lit by dragonfire, their shadow stretched long against ancient stone.

A shape moved in the doorway. Lyra entered, her cloak whispering over the floor like a blade across silk.

"Report," the mysterious one said, turning without greeting.

"Rhys has made a fool of himself again," Lyra replied coolly.

An eyebrow lifted.

"He sent two identical messages about Keisha being injured in an attack by a shadow dragon and an abyssal dragon outside Lyra'el. She's hurt, though we don't yet know the extent of the injury. Worse, his people couldn't keep quiet. Radiantus overheard their comments, and now the Umbral Elves stand one step from exile."

"What did you tell him?"

"I flayed him with words," she said without a flicker of shame. "Threatened worse if he lets things unravel further. He's terrified now—and knows they're being watched."

"Good. Keep him under control. He is yours to command now." The mysterious one's voice was iron wrapped in velvet, unmistakable authority, almost pleasant if one did not listen too closely. "If the Umbral Elves are exiled, find them a hidden place to regroup. I want them contained, not scattered."

"Understood." Yet beneath Lyra's calm answer, her thoughts were already calculating. Obedience was a currency she paid only so long as it served her.

"Qellaun is in Shadowhaven," the mysterious one continued. "The pirates have joined the alliance. He will remain there and monitor them."

A faint smirk curved her lips. "I'm sure he's thrilled."

"It wasn't a request. I need eyes in that den."

She inclined her head.

The mysterious one turned, their gaze drifting inward toward Afor. The desert ruins of Astoria whispered of forgotten arts, and rumors of Moon Seraphidians still haunting the sands had reached their ears. If true, they too could be bent to serve.

They paused mid-stride. "Lyra."

She returned within moments, her expression unreadable, though her patience thinned at the edges.

"The desert stronghold of Astoria," they said. "If its ties to dark magic remain, it may yet prove valuable. You will oversee the integration."

Her eyes narrowed. "You're sending me to Afor?"

"Yes. Afor lies within Vacari, still scarred by Vuarus's wrath and veiled by the Brass Dragons." Their tone was final. "You can monitor Rhys from anywhere. This is not a discussion."

She opened her mouth to protest, then closed it. Power had a way of reminding her who truly held the reins. One day, that balance would change.

A flick of their hand, and Lyra vanished from Flameford.

She reappeared on the outskirts of Astoria, sand already biting at her boots, the air dry and unyielding. Ruined towers jutted from the dunes like jagged teeth. Heat pressed against her skin in waves.

"I hate the desert," she muttered, cloak snapping in the wind as she strode toward the city's broken gates. If this failed, they would blame her.

Veiled Approval

Far below Flameford's upper halls, the molten heart of the caverns pulsed with heat. Voraxia and Vorathos lingered in the glow, their eyes half-lidded yet watchful.

The mysterious one entered, air shimmering as shadows curled tight to the stone. With a single gesture, the other dragons melted into the depths, leaving only the two sisters in the firelit chamber.

"You struck her," the veiled voice said, not a question, but a command, heavy as stone. "Tell me how."

Voraxia lowered her head, then raised it, violet sheen flickering across her scales. "She would not release the Pegasus. Even wounded, she clung to it as if it were her own blood. I dove. She took the strike instead. Had Radiantus and Aurelius not intervened, she would have fallen."

Vorathos rumbled, coils shifting in the heat. "Engaging them both was folly. We withdrew before their light cut deeper."

The mysterious one inclined their head, shadows rippling outward like ink in water. "You were right to retreat. That restraint has spared you for now. But there will be no boasts, no whispers. This wound must remain theirs to fear, not ours to claim."

Voraxia's silver-white eyes narrowed. "Zylron watches."

"As do the others," the voice replied, silk over steel. "Let them. They will find nothing but obedience... until I decide otherwise."

They turned as if to leave, then paused. For the first time in many ages, a smile slid across the shadowed veil, thin, cold, and almost pleased.

"Keisha bleeds," the mysterious one murmured, words curling like smoke. "How poetic. Vuarus fell because she slipped through that cursed ritual... and now, perhaps, fate begins to correct itself."

Voraxia and Vorathos exchanged a glance but held their silence. Wings folded tight, they lowered their heads in measured deference.

"Return to Lyra'el's skies," the figure commanded, voice once more composed. "Circle its borders. Watch. Report. Nothing more."

The sisters bowed and withdrew into the upper tunnels, shadows trailing them like storm clouds.

Left alone, the mysterious one lingered, the wicked curve of their smile widening as firelight licked the obsidian walls. The shadows stirred, restless, hungry for the thought coiling in their mind.

If Keisha does not rise again, the sisters may yet prove themselves worthy of more. Perhaps the others will bow when I grant them reign. And if not... they too will be broken.

A soft laugh echoed through the cavern, sharp as cracks in the earth. Then the shadows folded in, and the chamber was empty once more save for the hiss of molten rivers, and the promise of vengeance still to come.

Chapter 29
Wings of Worry

The skies above Ardinia blushed with first light as Aelina crossed the tranquil glade where the Pegasi dozed. Mist curled low, silvered by dawn, and dew jeweled the moss like fallen stars.

A sudden snort drew her eye. A white stallion pawed the earth, coat spotless—save for a streak of crimson along his flank.

Her heart lurched. Gentle hands pressed to his side, parting the shimmering hair. No wound. No swelling. The blood was not his.

A glimmer alit beside her a fairy, wings like moonlit glass.

"That one carried Keisha and the human boy to Lyra'el," she whispered.

Aelina stilled. "Keisha..."

She lifted her palm and breathed an old forest charm. Light gathered like silk, spun into a slender thread until it found Radiantus.

Aelina: I found blood on the Pegasus that Keisha rode. Tell me.

Radiantus: It was Keisha. Shadow and Abyssal struck near the outskirts. She lives. The healers tend her—and Kimras is here.

Relief loosened her shoulders; worry settled deeper. Thank you, she sent, letting the tether fade.

She turned from the glade in haste. Ardinia's crystalline paths sang underfoot, waterfalls laced green with silver. Keisha's laughter had once echoed here. Now she lay in a city of dragons because she had chosen to protect something smaller than herself.

"She always gives too much," Aelina murmured, hand to her heart.

Part of her reached for Ong in thought, but she stilled. If Kimras had come, Ong would hear soon enough—better from a dragon's mouth than a hurried message borne on fear.

She turned to the fairies, who were circling anxiously. "I'm going to the Emerald Woods. There's someone I need."

The fairies darted ahead in a jeweled stream. In the deeper forest, trunks rose tall, their leaves emerald laced with gold. Birdsong braided with riversong until the grove itself seemed to breathe.

Her arrival rippled the clearing. Fairies looped her in bright spirals. A water nymph crowned her braid with a flower. Aelina twirled once with them, laughing, then stilled. "I missed you," she said softly, "but I need help. Where is Kaelorn?"

"By the crystal grove," a fairy whispered solemnly. "Listening to the elder trees."

Sun fractured into prisms as Aelina stepped into the grove. At its heart stood Kaelorn, one hand against the bark of an ancient tree, eyes half-closed as though hearing the forest's pulse.

For a breath, memory blurred the present: Kaelorn at the Crystal Vale banquet, quiet under marble arches; later, the truth of him, half-Fae, half-human, belonging to two worlds yet resting in neither until the Emerald Woods claimed him.

He turned at her tread. Surprise softened into warmth.

"Aelina," he said, voice carrying quiet music. "It's good to see you."

"And you," she answered, wasting no time. "Keisha has been hurt in Lyra'el. She lives. Kimras is there. So are the Celestials. But shadow and abyss are moving, and I fear they'll need more than healers."

His brow furrowed. "She lives?"

"Yes. I spoke with Radiantus." Her gaze met his, steady. "Valeon is with her. He's begun herbal work—he'll need guidance. The dragons will aid where they can. Will you go? For Keisha. For him."

Kaelorn glanced to the staff leaning by the tree, a gift from fairies, nymphs... and Aelina. The runes glimmered faintly, as though listening.

"Then it is time I put that gift to use," he said, quiet but sure. He lifted the staff; its light steadied. "I'll go. For Keisha. For Valeon. And because you asked."

Aelina's breath eased. "Thank you."

"If shadow gathers beneath Lyra'el," Kaelorn said, "the light needs all its guardians."

They found Thalorian near the hill-grove roots speaking softly with Verdantia, the Emerald Dragon. Aelina's words required little more than a glance. Thalorian nodded once; Verdantia's eyes sharpened.

"I will watch the fairies while you are away," Thalorian said.

Verdantia lowered her head and summoned a young emerald, sleek, swift, bright-eyed. Her tone cut with protective weight. "Carry him to Lyra'el. Avoid shadowed routes. Do not engage. Drop him at the gates and return."

Kaelorn swung up with practiced ease, staff across his lap. The young dragon leapt, wings opening the sky.

By midday, white spires crowned the horizon. The emerald circled once, then descended to the terrace gate. Kaelorn dismounted, palm to scale in thanks.

Verdantia's will echoed: Return at once. With a sharp bank, the young dragon vanished into the clouds. She would risk none of her brood against abyss and shadow without cause.

Kaelorn turned toward the radiant gates of Lyra'el toward whatever truths, trials, and healings waited.

Chapter 30

Alliances in Motion

The high gates of Lyra'el rose before him, arched in white and lavender, entwined like ancient branches reaching for the sky. Runes shimmered faintly across their surface, a lattice of enchantments woven through centuries of devotion. Mist drifted low along the pathway, cool against Kaelorn's skin, veiling the forest beyond in a dreamlike silver glow.

He drew a steady breath, his keen Fae senses pricking at the layered magic that thrummed like a low chord in the air. Dust clung to his cloak, the rush of his journey still in his limbs, yet purpose lent him strength. Too swiftly, he had come perhaps unwisely, given Aelina's whispered warnings whispered before his departure.

A sudden pulse of light caught his eye.

On a stone rise just off the path stood a dragon. Not merely any dragon, this one gleamed like a fragment of the heavens. Silver-white scales shimmered as though they reflected stars unseen, each ridge traced with light. Half-furled wings arced behind him like living banners. His eyes, luminous white as moonfire, regarded the world with timeless calm.

Kaelorn slowed, breath catching, his gaze lifting in wary respect. He was no stranger to dragons, but few could stand before one without feeling the weight of such ancient power.

I should ask... perhaps he knows where Keisha is, he thought, gathering his voice.

He stepped forward and inclined his head.

"Good day to you," he said, tone measured, his natural lilt softened in deference. "Forgive the intrusion. I seek the Lady Keisha and a young man named Valeon. Might you know where to find them?"

The dragon tilted his head, luminous white eyes gleaming. His voice resonated with a melodic gravity, like distant bells tolling through mist. The sound thrummed in Kaelorn's bones and along the warded gates.

"You stand in the heart of Lyra'el, traveler. I know well those you seek."

Relief stirred in Kaelorn's chest. He managed a grateful smile, then faltered as the truth struck him with sudden weight. The very air seemed to bend around the dragon, answering his presence.

"Forgive me... but you are not simply any dragon, are you?" Kaelorn's voice thinned to a whisper. "You are... Aurelius?"

A glimmer of amusement lit the ancient dragon's gaze.

"I am."

Color rose to Kaelorn's cheeks. He bowed low, voice hushed. "Forgive my ignorance, great one. I meant no disrespect."

Aurelius's chest rumbled softly, laughter threaded with eternity. "There is no offense where none is meant. Stand tall, Luminara."

Relief steadied Kaelorn's breath. He straightened, though his pulse still raced.

"You will find Lady Keisha in the inner glade," Aurelius said. "The healers and council are gathered there. They will guide you further to young Valeon. But take heed, the Umbral Elves sow discord. Walk with care, and with watchful eyes."

Kaelorn inclined his head. "Your wisdom is well taken. My thanks, Aurelius. I shall tread carefully."

"Go in light," the dragon replied, his words a benediction that lingered in the mist like starlight.

With a final bow, Kaelorn turned, setting his steps along the silver-threaded path. The presence of the Celestial Dragon clung to him long after, a weight of grace and power at his back.

The forest closed around him, ancient trunks rising like pillars, their bark gleaming faintly with Lyra'el's eternal glow. Leaves whispered overhead, scattering motes of light that drifted down like falling stars.

Kaelorn moved swiftly, boots silent against moss-veined stone, his senses taut. Every shift of wind, every flicker of shadow pressed against his awareness.

A voice thin as a breath rose from the gloom to his right.

He slowed.

A second voice joined it. Cloaked in the deeper shade of the wood, he glimpsed them only in fragments: slender forms, dark robes, eyes gleaming faintly where sunlight dared not reach.

Umbral Elves.

He might have passed them by, melting into silence until one word rooted him in place.

Keisha.

At once, he slipped behind a broad-barked tree, cloak drawn close as he sank into the forest hush.

"...should've died, that Eladrin," one shadow muttered. "It would've sent a clearer message. Let the citizens of Lyra'el remember who holds the power now."

"Rhys won't tolerate hesitation," the other replied, voice laced with cold satisfaction. "They'll all learn. Things are already changing."

A pause—then, softer, more venomous:

"I'm glad he allied with the Druchii... and the mysterious one. With the three of them combined, even the dragons will bend. Or break."

Their footsteps faded, laughter trailing after them like a foul scent.

Kaelorn did not move for several breaths. His pulse thundered in his ears. Slowly, he stepped from the shelter of the tree, face pale in the dappled light. His fingers curled, then eased open again.

The Druchii. The mysterious figure. And Rhys.

He did not yet see the whole shape of their alliance, but the truth was enough. Keisha was marked. By proximity, so was Valeon.

Urgency tightened his steps as he pressed onward.

The trees parted, revealing the inner glade—a vast expanse bathed in golden light. Blossoms drifted from unseen boughs, their fragrance cool and sweet. A breeze wound through the leaves, carrying a melody faint as harp-strings.

At the center of the glade rose a structure of crystal and living wood, half temple, half grove, its arches spiraling upward like the ribs of some celestial being. The very ground thrummed with quiet strength, the air heavy with the pulse of ancient wards.

Kaelorn approached the threshold, where a healer in pale robes waited beneath the arching branches.

"I seek audience with Radiantus," Kaelorn said, bowing with measured grace. "There is news I carry, and it may bear weight upon the Council."

The healer inclined his head. "Radiantus will be summoned. In the meantime, enter the glade. Speak your name, your purpose, and you shall be received."

"Kaelorn of the Luminara, on request of Aelina," he replied, steadying his breath. "I have come to see Lady Keisha."

Crossing the threshold, ancient power folded around him like a mantle—cool, unyielding, as if the land itself judged his worth.

The sanctuary hummed with peace and reverence, or so its design promised. At the rear of the crystal hall, vines curled lazily along the arched beams, their leaves glowing as though they were drinking in the golden light above. A long wooden table stretched beneath them, scrolls scattered across its polished surface, neat Elven script glaring up like a silent adversary. A cluster of vials and powders had once been orderly; now they lay strewn like frost from a careless hand.

At the table sat Valeon. Ink smudged one cheek, his sleeves shoved high, his forearms dusted with chalk. He tapped a quill against parchment, frustration gathering in each stroke.

"By the blasted moons... I'll never master these cursed Elven scribbles. Might as well be reading dragon-scratch."

A willowy healer with laughing eyes chuckled softly.

"You do yourself no credit, Valeon. You've come a long way in a short span. Most would have set fire to the scrolls by now."

Valeon grunted, though a reluctant smile tugged at his mouth. "Aye, and I nearly did, yesterday. You were there."

The great door creaked open.

Kaelorn entered, movements fluid as moonlight, cloak trailing lightly across the floor. His gaze swept the hall before settling on the warded space where Valeon labored.

A familiar voice carried across the chamber, warm with humor.

"Still fighting the Elven script? You've come further than you had in Crystal Vale, my friend."

Valeon jerked upright in surprise, elbow striking a vial.

"Ah—curse it!"

A puff of pale-green powder burst across the scrolls. The nearest healer leapt back with a cry as the wards flared, humming brightly while they absorbed the reaction. A faint pop echoed, like a cork loosed from a bottle.

Blinking through the haze, Valeon brushed green dust from his hair. "Well. That went better than last time."

From beyond the wards, Kaelorn's laugh rippled like silver.

"You've a gift for the dramatic, though your poor table might disagree."

He stepped closer, offering the healers a nod before softening his tone.

"Aelina sent me," he said. "To see Keisha and to lend what aid I can. Whether with the Celestial Dragons or the healers, your training is not forgotten."

Valeon wiped his hands on the cloth, his grin crooked.

"Well, you've timed it well enough. Though I'll warn you—these dragons have sharper eyes for mistakes than any master I've ever known."

Kaelorn's mouth curved into a quick, easy smile. "As do some of us."

At the glade's center rose a structure of crystal and living wood, half temple, half grove, its arches spiraling skyward like the ribs of some celestial giant. The ground itself thrummed with quiet strength, the air heavy with the pulse of ancient wards.

A healer in pale silver robes waited at the threshold, her dark hair braided with ivy that glimmered faintly in the light. She carried the calm authority of one long accustomed to mending both flesh and spirit.

"Kaelorn of the Luminara?" she asked softly.

He inclined his head. "Aye."

"Come with me. I will take you to Lady Keisha. But I must caution you, do not be alarmed by what you see."

Kaelorn's gaze sharpened. "How fares she?"

The healer's expression softened, pride and sorrow mingling.

"She is stronger than most would be, given what she faced. The shadow and abyssal dragons left grievous wounds upon both body and spirit. Yet she did not falter. She fought not only for herself, but for the Pegasus she protected."

A faint, reverent smile curved her lips.

"Word of her courage has spread through Lyra'el. Many who once doubted her place now speak her name with respect."

Kaelorn's jaw tightened, though his voice held steady. "She is of rare spirit. I will not stay long. She needs rest."

"Good." The healer inclined her head and gestured toward a silken-draped archway. "Beyond here. Speak softly. Her strength returns, but slowly. Rest is her greatest need."

Kaelorn drew a quiet breath and stepped through. The silks whispered against his shoulders as if warning him to tread with care.

The hush within the chamber was almost tangible, sound itself subdued. Cool air drifted from the lattice windows, fragrant with moonflower and silverleaf—scents meant to soothe and steady. At the room's heart stood a low bed, not carved but grown, vines twined with crystal that pulsed faintly with the rhythm of life.

Upon it lay Keisha.

Even prepared, Kaelorn's heart clenched. Her skin, once luminous, was pale against the glow. Bandages bound her arms and side; bruises shadowed her cheek. Yet even in weariness, she radiated quiet strength. Her red hair, tousled but unbowed, spilled like flame across the pale linens.

Beside her rested a single silver feather, undoubtedly from the Pegasus she had shielded.

Kaelorn steadied himself and approached.

"Keisha," he murmured, voice warm with concern. "It is Kaelorn. May I sit with you a moment?"

Her eyes fluttered open. Pale green found him, weary yet unbroken. A faint smile curved her lips.

"Kaelorn... you came."

He drew a chair closer, lowering himself into it with gentle ease. "Aelina sent me. To see you, and to aid where I may, whether with the healers or the Celestial Dragons.

Her fingers shifted weakly on the coverlet. "They told me... of the shadow dragons. And the others..." Her gaze darkened. "I could not let them take her."

"And in doing so," Kaelorn said quietly, "you earned more than victory. You've won the respect of this realm. Already your courage is spoken of."

A breath escaped her—fragile, half pride, half exhaustion. "I only did what was right."

"That," Kaelorn replied with a faint, sorrow-tinged smile, "is why it matters most."

He rested his hand on the edge of the bed, close enough for her to feel his steadiness.

"Rest now. You have done more than enough. The dragons watch over you, and I will remain; however, I may serve."

Her eyes glistened with gratitude. "Thank you, Kaelorn..."

From the doorway came the healer's gentle call. "It is time to let her rest."

Kaelorn rose, bowing his head. "I will return when it is well to do so. Until then, may the stars guard you."

The silks whispered closed behind him. His face remained composed, but his eyes were shadowed with thought.

A figure leaned against a carved column, arms crossed, one brow arched.

"She was glad to see you," Valeon said quietly, straightening. His usual lilt lingered, but concern edged his voice. "She's tougher than any of us gave her credit for."

Kaelorn allowed a small smile. "She is indeed. But her road ahead will not be easy."

Valeon studied him, then narrowed his eyes. "You've got that look."

Kaelorn lifted a brow. "What look?"

"The look you wear when danger stirs. When you've overheard something."

Before Kaelorn could reply, a slender young healer approached, bowing.

"Master Kaelorn, Radiantus is ready to receive you. If you would come now, he awaits in the upper chamber."

Kaelorn inclined his head. "Of course." He cast a meaningful glance at Valeon. "Come. It may be wise for you to hear this as well."

Surprise flickered across Valeon's face, but curiosity quickly overtook it.

"Lead on, then."

Together they followed the healer along ascending stone paths and winding corridors lit by veins of crystal. With every step, the air grew cooler, heavier with ancient power, as though judgment itself gathered around them.

At last, they entered a vaulted chamber where starlight poured through a wide circular opening above, scattering brilliance across the crystalline walls. At the chamber's heart, Radiantus awaited—his platinum coils resting in regal repose, his eyes glowing with the clarity of dawn.

His voice rolled like resonant chimes through the vast space.

"Kaelorn. You are welcome here."

Both Kaelorn and Valeon bowed deeply.

"Radiantus," Kaelorn said, his tone grave, "I bring tidings that cannot wait. Upon my arrival in Lyra'el, I overheard two Umbral Elves speaking in the outer glades."

The dragon's silver gaze sharpened, light rippling across his scales. "Tell me what you heard."

Kaelorn's voice steadied, each word etched with memory.

"They spoke of Lady Keisha—saying she should have died, as a warning to the citizens. They claimed Rhys seeks to assert new power here, that an alliance is already in motion. With the Druchii... and with a third figure they named only as the mysterious one, already moving the pieces."

A rumble like distant thunder stirred in Radiantus's chest. His gaze narrowed, light flashing cold across the chamber.

"This alliance is troubling. And the identity of this mysterious one... more troubling still."

Valeon shifted uneasily. "They sounded confident. Too confident. If they've reached this deep—"

"Indeed," Radiantus said, his voice low and grave. "Their hand moves swiftly. We must move swifter still."

He turned his full gaze upon Kaelorn, each word carrying the weight of command.

"Your report comes in time. Remain close to the glade; your presence may be required again soon. I will speak with the Council and with the noble dragons. Lyra'el will not fall to shadow."

Kaelorn bowed low. "I stand ready to serve as does the rest of Vacari, should you call."

Valeon managed a crooked grin, though his eyes held earnest fire. "And I'll stand ready to do... whatever it is I'm good at."

A flicker of warmth touched Radiantus's ageless gaze.

"Even the smallest flame holds great power, Valeon. And we will need every spark."

As they descended the corridors once more, silence pressed heavier than before.

"He's not playing games anymore," Valeon murmured, falling in step beside Kaelorn. "You could feel it in the air."

Kaelorn's face remained solemn. "Nor should he. The line has been crossed. Soon, choice will be forced upon them."

They stepped into the lower glade, footsteps soft on crystal paths, though the storm gathering above weighed on them both.

At the heart of Lyra'el, a resonant tone rang out across the city. It was not a bell nor a horn but a deep pulse that throbbed through wood and stone. Elves halted where they stood, turning toward the circle at the roots of the Great Tree. For such a call could mean only one thing: one of the Ancients would speak.

By the time Radiantus descended, the circle was already ringed with hushed anticipation. Cloaked Umbral Elves stood among them, drawing wary stares yet refusing to bow.

Radiantus alighted with measured grace. His colossal form gleamed beneath shafts of silver light, wings folding with deliberate care. His eyes burned like crystalline fire.

When he spoke, his voice rippled through the glade like rolling thunder, calm, but implacable.

"Hear me now. This is your final warning."

The crowd stilled.

"Once before I said: any act of aggression, any attempt to undermine the balance of this realm, will not be tolerated."

His gaze swept across the Umbral Elves. Some held his eyes in defiance; others shifted under their weight.

"And now I hear whispers and threats against Lyra'el. Whispers of alliances forged in shadow. Know this: such treachery will not take root here."

The ground trembled faintly beneath his coils, as if the Great Tree itself resonated with his vow.

"This is the last time I will speak such words. The next transgression will bring no counsel, no parley. You will be removed, banished from Lyra'el, never to return."

Silver fire flared in his gaze, sealing the decree with the weight of ages.

"Choose well. There will be no second chance."

A long silence held the glade. Then Radiantus unfurled his wings and rose into the heavens, his ascent stirring a storm of golden light among the branches.

Only when the radiance faded did the crowd begin to murmur again. And though voices fell low, no one mistook the truth. From this moment forward, the Umbral Elves walked a razor's edge.

In the shadows beyond the circle, Rhys lingered beneath a twisted arch of stone, arms folded, eyes narrowed. He had heard every word of Radiantus's warning, sharp and final.

A long breath slipped between his teeth, low and bitter. "Damn it. Lyra will be furious. And she won't be wrong."

She would not take kindly to this turn, nor forgive that events were sliding beyond the balance he had worked to weave. But the path was already set.

He turned sharply and vanished into a hidden passage beneath the roots of the glade. The air grew damp and close, veins of black stone and silver moss winding through the tunnels. At their end lay the Umbral Elves' private hall, long abandoned by the elves of light, its twisted columns and vaulted roots now wholly claimed by shadow.

The chamber was stirring. Low voices fell silent as Rhys entered.

He wasted no words. His tone was clipped, resolute.

"It is time. Some of you will leave at once. Find Lyra, she is in Afor. Tell her what has happened. Ask her to secure a place for our people beyond Lyra'el. We will not wait to be driven out. We will choose where we stand."

The chosen swiftest and most loyal nodded, cloaks drawn close, blades hidden. One by one, they slipped into the dark.

Rhys's gaze followed until the chamber emptied, his silver eyes cold and unreadable. Then he turned to the others.

"The rest of you, tread carefully. Every step from this moment is watched. One mistake, and it is over. Do you understand?"

A low chorus of assent rose, some voices defiant, others heavy with resignation.

Without another word, Rhys departed, striding through twisting corridors until he reached the solitude of his chamber.

A single crystal burned faintly on the desk, casting shifting light across the stone walls. He seated himself, fingers steepled, thoughts coiling like shadows. Then, with deliberate precision, he drew parchment close.

In sharp, flowing script, he wrote:

Lyra, we must speak. Urgently. The time we feared has come.

He sealed the message, pressed it into the hand of a waiting runner, and sent it into the night.

Only then did he sink back into his chair, shadows curling around him like smoke, his mind already moving pieces across the darkening board.

Chapter 31
Wings of Shadow and Light

The skies above Lyra'el shimmered faintly beneath the waning moonlight. The protective wards pulsed over the treetops like a living veil, but the air carried an uneasy weight that even the roots of the oldest trees seemed to feel.

High above the forest spires, two vast shadows cut across the clouds.

Voraxia, the Shadow Dragon, moved with deliberate grace, her scales a shifting tapestry of midnight. Cold amusement burned in her eyes as she surveyed the warded skies.

"The Platinum fools grow bold," she hissed, her voice like silk dragged over stone. "Training riders beneath their gilded wings, as if that will save them."

Yet beneath the scorn coiled a thread of unease she dared not name. The memory of a light too fierce, too unnatural to ignore pressed against her mind like a thorn.

Beside her flew Vorathos, the Abyssal Dragon, her obsidian coils trailing tendrils of darkness that writhed and vanished into nothing. Her muffled voice rumbled like the depths themselves.

"Perhaps it is time they remembered whose skies these are."

On the cliffs below, younger kin shadow and abyssal alike waited in silence, wings folded tight, eyes gleaming with hunger.

Voraxia's smile cut like a blade.

"We test them first. And when the time is right, we will tear them down."

She angled her wings and glided toward the glowing wards, provocation made deliberate, unmistakable.

But she had been seen.

From the heart of the city, a blinding arc of silver light erupted skyward.

Radiantus.

The Platinum Dragon soared into the night, his wings vast, his body burning with dawnlight. Each beat sent ripples of radiance cascading through the dark, searing away the shadows. His eyes burned with unshaken resolve.

"Enough." His voice rolled like thunder through stone and sky alike. "You cross the line once again, Voraxia. You will not breach these skies."

Another surge of brilliance followed.

Aurelius rose in his Celestial form, gleaming like a living star. Behind him, more of their kin unfolded from the glade, platinum and silver wings weaving radiant patterns against the night.

Voraxia halted at the barrier's edge, her gaze narrowing as the hosts of light gathered.

"We only came to admire your... efforts," she purred, venom in the silk of her tone. "Surely you would not deny us a glimpse of your precious riders."

Radiantus's gaze hardened, his voice a low rumble that shook the wards themselves.

"Glance if you must, Voraxia, but hear me. Touch no rider of the noble dragons. Their lives are bound to ours by more than blood and breath.

To raise a claw or a shadow against them is to sign your own death-writ. Test that bond, and you will not survive the lesson."

Vorathos's growl followed, low and implacable.

"Or perhaps we came to remind them that war is never far from their fragile peace."

Radiantus spread his wings wider, his form blazing, unflinching.

"You will go no further."

Aurelius's voice rang out, bright and unbending.

"And if you choose to test our resolve, know this: we are ready."

The skies froze in a silence sharp as drawn steel. On the cliffs, the lesser dark dragons shifted uneasily, waiting for the signal.

Voraxia's gaze cut toward her sister. Fury coiled with something colder, but she managed only a thin, cruel smile.

"Shall we see how bright their resolve truly burns?"

With a shriek like rending night, she lunged.

The heavens split. Radiantus surged forward, silver fire wreathing him like a living shield. His claws struck hers with a crack that shook the forest below. Vorathos's roar followed, a torrent of black flame lashing outward, so cold it seemed to burn.

The blast caught Serathin, a young Platinum mid-turn. She screamed as the abyssal fire raked across her wings, smoke trailing as she spiraled toward the trees. At the last instant, she flared, battered and shuddered, her silver scales scorched black.

Vorathos's voice rumbled with grim satisfaction. "Down one already."

But then Aurelius moved.

He wheeled above the battlefield, starlight streaming from his wings, and loosed a pulse of pure Celestial fire. The radiance poured like a falling star reborn, cascading over the wounded dragon. Before the eyes, Serathin's blackened wings knit themselves whole, the glow of dawnlight spreading across her scales.

Voraxia faltered mid-beat, disbelief flaring before she masked it with rage.

"Impossible."

Vorathos's eyes narrowed. "They heal... faster than before. This was not so." A tremor of unease roughened her voice, and she hated it.

Light and shadow collided again, fire and void twisting in the night. The dragons of Lyra'el moved as one, a wall of radiant wings holding firm.

Aurelius's voice rang above the chaos, sharp and sonorous as a bell.

"You will not break us. You will never understand what binds us, but you will remember it."

Voraxia's mind raced. Some trick. Some new-born power...

"We are not ready," Vorathos growled, her coils shuddering. "Not yet."

Voraxia seethed, fury igniting her blood. She flung her wings wide, darkness boiling from her scales.

"Enough of this dance! Their light is no shield, I will tear it open myself!"

She dove at Radiantus, claws flashing, eyes locked not on him but on Aurelius.

Radiantus rose to meet her. Silver brilliance poured from his wings, his body a living wall of dawn. Their talons clashed with a thunder-crack that rattled the sky. Voraxia lashed with her tail, shadows gouging across his flank, but the Platinum did not yield.

Above them, Aurelius ascended higher, his glow intensifying until it blazed across the heavens.

Let her try.

From his throat burst a torrent of pure Celestial fire, searing and absolute. It tore the darkness apart like dawn splitting night. The beam struck, and Voraxia reeled back, her shriek piercing the stars—not from flame, but from the unbearable purity that seared her shadowed form.

"That light... it should not exist," she spat, fury twisted into disbelief. With a single beat of her vast wings, she wheeled away.

The lesser dark dragons wavered on the cliffs, caught between hunger and fear. At last, Voraxia's snarl cut through the night.

Not yet," Voraxia hissed. "But soon the Abyssal Dominion will rise again, and all your light will burn for nothing."

With a lash of their wings, she and Vorathos vanished into the storm clouds, their kin trailing after them in a ragged, hissing flock. Smoke and shadow scattered in their wake, leaving only silence and the bright thrum of the wards.

Radiantus hovered above the glade, his silver gaze hardening. The name lingered bitter on his tongue.

"The Abyssal Dominion..."

Aurelius descended beside him, his radiance dimming to a steady glow.

"They grow too bold or too desperate."

"Either way," Radiantus said, voice like a vow, "we must be ready. It will not be strength alone that turns the tide. It will be unity dragons, elves, riders, all who still stand for the light. Keisha bled to shield a single Pegasus. That choice was not a weakness; it was proof. And if we forget that..." His voice deepened, rumbling like distant stormclouds. "Then even our power will fail us. But if we remember—"

He wheeled higher, silver fire streaming from his wings until the night itself seemed to bow before his light.

"...then the Dominion will break before us."

The dragons of Lyra'el rose in his wake, their wings a storm of silver and flame. And though the shadows gathered beyond the horizon, the city beneath the Great Tree shone brighter still.

Chapter 32
The Summons

Crystal Vale shimmered beneath the morning sun, its spires of pale-blue stone glistening like frost-kissed glass. The air here always carried a subtle charge, as if magic had seeped into every root and vein of crystal.

On the high terrace of the palace, Ong stood in the training yard, blade in hand, his breath misting in the crisp air. His stance was steady, but his mind wandered.

Keisha.

Injured again. Too far away. And this time, no word yet of how deep the wounds might cut. Waiting was its own torment, each hour apart heavier than the last.

A ripple stirred the sky.

A vast shadow crossed the sun as wings of amethyst crystal caught the light, spiraling downward in graceful arcs.

Amara.

The practice blade slipped from Ong's hand, clattering to stone as he strode forward. He already knew why she had come. Her talons struck the terrace, the gust of her landing stirring his hair.

Her luminous eyes fixed on him.

"Ong," she rumbled, voice warm despite its depth. "I have been sent to bring you to Lyra'el. You are needed."

His jaw tightened. No further words were required.

"I will come."

From the palace steps, Prince Gailen appeared. Tension lined his face, though a faint smile flickered there.

"Go," he called. "I will follow as soon as I may. Keisha will need you."

Behind him came King Manard, his step steady though age bent his shoulders. He clasped Ong's arm firmly. The word son was still new upon his lips, but its weight carried like an anchor of belonging.

"You and Keisha... both take care, my son. The winds grow dark. But remember—this family stands with you. Always."

Ong bowed his head.

"I will remember."

Without delay, he climbed Amara's crystalline ridge, settling into the familiar place at her shoulders. Her wings unfurled with radiant strength, and with a single beat she bore him aloft. The spires of Crystal Vale fell swiftly away, the sky widening before them.

The flight was swift. Soon Lyra'el spread below, its vast glades and emerald canopies rolling like a living sea.

From a high balcony at the outer gate, Radiantus watched, his eyes narrowing as a familiar gleam caught the light.

"Amara," he murmured.

To the guards, his voice rang firm:

"Let her pass. She comes with one who is expected."

The silver gates opened, spilling light across the path as Amara descended toward the city's heart. Ong sat steady upon her back, his thoughts already racing to the moment he would see Keisha again. He remembered the last time she had fallen, her voice still calling his name, broken but unyielding.

The glades stirred as Amara swept in. Light rippled across her amethyst wings, casting violet fire in the morning sun, drawing wary awe from the sentries below. None barred her way; the word of Radiantus held.

The Platinum Dragon himself waited upon the central landing platform, his scales gleaming bright in the light. Around him, Celestial and Platinum kin lingered at a distance, the air still taut with the memory of battle.

Amara alighted with practiced ease, amethyst talons striking stone with ringing grace.

Radiantus inclined his head. His voice was steady, though warmth threaded through it.

"Amara, welcome. I would greet you under gentler skies, but I am grateful for your coming. Your counsel and your kin strengthen us more than you know."

The Amethyst Dragon lowered her head in greeting, humor glinting faintly in her gaze.

"Of course, you are glad to see me, Radiantus. Who would not?"

A short laugh escaped Ong as he dismounted, though his eyes already searched the pathways for Keisha.

But before Ong could move further, Radiantus lifted one great wing, a signal as commanding as it was silent. Ong froze, breath catching, his urgency clashing against the dragon's wordless command. His fists flexed at his sides, every instinct screaming for him to run, but he held, his jaw tight.

"Wait, Ong," Radiantus said, his voice heavy with command. "There are matters you must hear first—before you reach Keisha."

Ong's expression hardened.

"I have waited long enough. My wife lies wounded while we talk."

Another voice steadied the air, Kimras, stepping from among the gathered Council.

"You must hear this first, Ong, for her sake, and for yours. There are truths she is not yet ready to face. But you must be."

The tension between them hung taut as a bowstring. Then Ong gave a sharp nod.

"Very well. But speak swiftly."

Radiantus turned, wings sweeping outward toward the city square.

"Come. The Council gathers."

As they moved, Valeon and Kaelorn, lingering near a high terrace, exchanged a glance.

"Something's shifting," Valeon murmured.

"Aye," Kaelorn replied. "And not lightly."

They followed at a careful distance.

By the time they reached the square, a throng of elves, dragonkin, and allies had gathered—news of the skirmish and Ong's arrival spreading like wildfire through the crowd.

At the far edge, Aurelius circled once before alighting upon a stone outcropping, his gaze sharp and all-seeing. Umbral Elves lingered at the crowd's borders, cloaks heavy, their whispers curling like smoke. Aurelius's eyes narrowed. He caught the flicker of subtle movements listening, watching.

Radiantus stepped into the center, and even the restless hush gave way. His voice rang out like tempered steel.

"Enough."

The murmurs died at once. Even the Umbral Elves stilled.

"I have tolerated your presence here long enough," Radiantus declared. "Warnings were given. Promises were broken. Spies and whispers poison these halls even now."

His gaze locked upon the cloaked figures upon Rhys, who strode forward, hands twitching at his sides, his voice a brittle thread of defiance.

"You go too far, Radiantus. We have done nothing this day."

"Silence." The Platinum Dragon's voice cracked like a blade against stone.

"Either you take what remains of your place here and leave willingly, or you will be cast from these halls. The Umbral Elves are no longer welcome in Lyra'el. The time of patience is past."

From his perch, Aurelius's golden eyes flickered once, silent approval.

Rhys stiffened, jaw tight. His gaze swept the crowd, then returned to Radiantus, venom simmering in his voice.

"You will regret this."

Radiantus spread his wings, gaze burning cold. He took no pleasure in the decree, but peace demanded clarity and trust and could not endure rot.

"Perhaps. But not today. Today you will go, or you will be gone."

A silence rippled outward, heavy and final, marking the line at last drawn.

By morning's climb past the highest branches, the last of the Umbral Elves emerged from their quarters—packs hastily gathered, faces hidden beneath hoods. Above them, Celestial Dragons circled, wings shimmering like living banners in the pale sky.

At Radiantus's command, they descended. Great talons lifted crates, supplies, and even those who lingered too long in defiance. Too many had been lost when hesitation ruled before. He would not be late again.

No words were exchanged. None were needed.

Rhys stood among his people, fury burning in his eyes, but he did not speak. The line had been carved deep, and not even he dared cross it today.

As the Celestial Dragons bore the last of the Umbral Elves toward the horizon, Radiantus watched from the high terrace, his gaze unwavering until shadow faded from sight.

"They will be taken to Afor," he said quietly to those beside him. "And there they will remain. Its borders are sealed, and so too is their return."

The gathered guards and onlookers parted as Radiantus turned, his gaze settling upon Ong now standing with Kimras, Kaelorn, Valeon, and Aurelius.

"You have come at a time of change, Ong," Radiantus said gravely. "There was a skirmish two nights past. Voraxia and Vorathos tested our skies. We held them. No loss among the Platinum or Celestial kin."

He paused, the silver fire in his eyes dimming.

"But it was not the battle that concerns us most."

Aurelius's voice cut through, deliberate and resonant.

"Before they fled, Voraxia declared this: "The Abyssal Dominion has returned.""

A hush fell.

Valeon stiffened, eyes darting nervously, but Kaelorn was the first to find words, his tone low with unease.

"I have heard that name... but not its full weight. What did it bring upon Vacari?"

All eyes turned to Kimras. The Golden Dragon's silence pressed heavily, carrying centuries within it. At last, his wings folded, and his voice came deep and measured.

"You do not know, Kaelorn. Few people are alive now who truly do. The Dominion razed forests until groves stood blackened under their shadow. Rivers choked with ash. The skies darkened as Vuarus and his allies swept across the land. Even now, when the wind shifts, I still smell the char of the fallen groves."

His voice caught—not in weakness, but in the burden of memory.

Ong stepped forward, fists clenched, voice low and fierce.

"And it was here," he swept his gaze across the gathering, "that Vuarus and Phoenix Shadowwalker tried to sacrifice my wife to the abyss itself."

A ripple of shock moved through Valeon and Kaelorn, but they held their tongues.

"Had it not been for Kimras and Amara, we would have lost her."

His voice faltered, just for a breath, as the weight of that night pressed down. He still saw Keisha bound in chains, still heard her scream as the abyss closed in. Never again.

Amara's amethyst voice cut sharply through the stillness.

"What we want to know is this." Her gaze moved from Radiantus to Aurelius. "How has the Abyssal Dominion returned? Vuarus's power was destroyed. Talleoss the Silver Dragon ended him. And Ong slew Phoenix Shadowwalker. We saw it. It is not possible they lead this."

The square fell into silence.

At last, Aurelius spoke calmly, but edged with iron.

"Yes. Vuarus—Azeron—is dead. And Phoenix Shadowwalker as well." He let the words settle like stone.

"But who, or what, has taken up the name of the Abyssal Dominion... remains unknown."

Radiantus stirred, his gaze sweeping the assembly.

"One thing we do know," he said, his voice low but unyielding. "Whoever hides behind that veil is tied to them both. We do not yet know their full purpose save for a truth we cannot ignore."

His eyes darkened.

"Revenge."

A ripple coursed through the circle.

"Revenge against the noble dragons," he continued, "for what had been denied them."

Kimras turned, his golden gaze falling on Ong, his voice grave with certainty.

"And if they are tied to Vuarus and Phoenix... then Keisha is in danger."

Ong's fists tightened, knuckles white. For a heartbeat, he was not in Lyra'el but in that ruined grove again—Keisha's scream echoing, chains rattling, dark fire closing in. His voice came rough, laced with memory.

"Do they mean to sacrifice her again?"

Before Kimras could answer, Amara stepped forward, her amethyst voice like a shard of ice.

"No. Not this time."

Her gaze hardened, catching the morning light.

"They want her gone. For what she represents for what she survived. To them, that is a threat greater than death itself."

The silence that followed was heavy as stone.

At last, Ong gave a sharp nod, shoulders taut. His vow rose unyielding within him, silent and absolute: never again.

"Then I will stand by her side. Whatever comes."

Radiantus exhaled slowly, folding his wings.

"For now, return to your duties. We will prepare for what lies ahead."

He turned to Ong, his voice softening.

"Go. See your wife. She will need you now and you, her."

Ong nodded once, already moving toward the path that would take him to Keisha's side.

The gathering broke apart, shadows lingering among the ancient trees. Yet the unspoken truth weighed heavier than the air itself: the Abyssal Dominion had risen again, and vengeance walked with it.

Kaelorn lingered at the edge, the weight of Kimras's words pressing hard upon him. Forests razed. Rivers turned to ash. Skies drowned in shadow. He had seen the scars left in the Emerald Woods by lesser wars, how even fairies and nymphs trembled when darkness touched their groves.

If what Kimras spoke was true, if the Dominion had once blackened all of Vacari, then even the oldest wards of the Emerald Woods would not hold if it rose again. His gaze flicked skyward, toward the unseen borders of his home.

"I will not let them fall," he whispered, quiet but resolute. "Not the fairies. Not the forests."

The vow settled in his chest, bright and unyielding like a flame carried from starlight into shadow.

Chapter 33
Seeds of the Dominion

The sun burned white above Arcadia, pouring its blaze across towers of pale-blue stone cracked with age and shadowed by darker things. The air shimmered, heavy with heat—yet in the eastern wing of the palace, the temperature had fallen unnaturally. Frost clung to the corners of the once-opulent suite like lace spun from ice. Silken curtains sagged under a brittle crust. The floor beneath Lyra's bare feet was cool to the touch, a small comfort against the furnace-world outside. Her wards pulsed with threads of winter, each breath of frost pushing back the desert's fire.

She drew her black-silver cloak tighter across her shoulders, its enchantments whispering like distant bells, and allowed herself a flicker of satisfaction.

Arcadia, once proud, once free, now bent beneath her will. King Veydras had broken more swiftly than she anticipated, his council of scholars collapsing into fearful whispers. Guards no longer met her eyes. Servants moved like shades, silent and careful. The city was hers.

Molkrag, too, had yielded. The forge-complex of the Emberdeep Dwarves now groaned under a burden of molten corruption, its chimneys coughing black smoke into the scorched sky. Their defiance had lasted only moments before the shadow smothered it.

"One by one, they kneel," Lyra murmured, her lips curling.

Yet one prize still eluded her, the Moon Seraphidians. Elusive shades of silver and shadow, they haunted ruined wells and glades, surfacing only beneath the moon. Even her most cunning spies had missed them.

She was turning toward the door to renew the hunt when the chamber stirred. A sudden breath of frigid air glazed her wards with ice. A voice, low and edged with shadow, slipped through her mind:

"Rhys and the Umbral Elves are near Arcadia. See what they have achieved. Find a place for them within Afor. The Dominion's roots must spread further."

Lyra's smile vanished.

"Rhys," she hissed. "That incompetent fool."

She pressed her palm to the frozen door. Frost cracked as she shoved it wide, desert heat rushing in only to falter against her shimmering wards. "Let us see what blunders you bring me this time," she murmured, striding into the corridor. Her boots rang against stone, each step trailing a razor-edged chill.

In the front courtyard, beneath a fractured archway, a column of dark-cloaked figures emerged, moving swiftly and warily. At their head stood Rhys.

Lyra halted, eyes narrowing.

"Well," she drawled, arms folding, "the wind has finally carried you here, though far too slowly."

Her glare cut colder than the ice at her heels. The Umbral Elves shifted uneasily.

"I am told you bring word and ruin," she went on. "Let us hope it is more of the former this time."

Rhys straightened, forcing composure though unease flickered in his gaze. His stomach lurched as he opened his mouth.

"It was Radiantus," he said quickly. "He is unreasonable. We—"

A shadow lashed from Lyra's hand, coiling tight around his throat. His words broke into a strangled gasp, boots scraping stone as the darkness lifted him from the ground.

"Enough," Lyra snapped, her voice ringing like shattering glass. She tightened the coil until his vision swam, then released him. He crumpled to one knee, coughing. It was the first time he had stood in her presence—terror burned raw in his eyes.

"You should know better than to waste my time," she hissed. "Your people whispered in the wrong shadows, and now I must clean the stain of your failure."

She paced before them, frost cracking beneath her talons, each step leaving icy scars in the stone.

"You will not return to Lyra'el. You will remain here, in Afor. You will learn its heat, its hunger, its silence. Consider it your lesson."

Rhys bowed, throat raw. "As you command."

But when his head dipped, his silver eyes smoldered not only with fear, but with something darker.

"You will divide your forces," Lyra continued coldly. "Half to the Cradle of Echoes. Secure it. Its deep wells of power belong to the Dominion."

Murmurs rippled through the column. Rhys gestured sharply to Veyron and Selthra. Both stepped forward, cloaks whispering, and bowed low. At his signal, half their company wheeled away, vanishing toward the sunken cliffs in the east.

"The rest," Lyra said, "will take Driftpoint Haven. Strip its wreckage for our use. Find the truth of the Sable Leviathan, and bind it if it yet lives. I will not have my Dominion rooted in rot."

Rhys moved to follow, but her voice cracked like a whip. "Did I say you were going?"

He froze mid-step. "N–no, Lady Lyra."

"Then do not presume. Appoint others."

His jaw tightened. "Neydra. Kalthis."

The chosen commanders bowed sharply and led their warriors into the burning sands, shadows trailing them like smoke.

Lyra stepped closer, her own shadow stretching across Rhys. "As for you," her voice lowered, sharp with frost, "you will go to Oasis City. Make yourself indispensable to the Sultan. Win his favor. Worm your way into his court. Turn his banners toward the Dominion. When that is done, you will travel to the Cradle, to Driftpoint, to every holding that matters. Report to me without fail."

Rhys bowed deep, voice hoarse. "It will be done."

"Then why are you still here? Go."

He turned to leave, boots clattering, when her voice lashed out again. "Wait."

He froze, shoulders stiffening.

"I want something more," Lyra said, eyes narrowing. "You studied under Maedra. Did you learn what I commanded? The herbs. The poisons."

Rhys hesitated, then inclined his head. "I did. More than she intended me to know. Enough to carry her secrets away. Enough to wield them."

"And?" Lyra pressed. Her tone was sharp, merciless. "Did you bring them from Lyra'el?"

"Some," he admitted. "The rest are being gathered by one I left behind. They will follow."

Lyra's expression softened—not with kindness, but with cold satisfaction.

"Good. Afor's sands breed their own poisons. Learn them. Master them. I may require them sooner than you think."

Rhys bowed again, though his jaw was set like iron.

Only then did Lyra ask, her voice smooth as glass over ice, "And Keisha?"

He shifted, unease flickering once more. "When we were banished, she still lay in the infirmary. Alive. Wounded. Guarded."

A gleam of cruel delight sparked in Lyra's eyes before she masked it. "Then focus on your task. The herbs. The poisons. If she survives to leave Lyra'el... I will have other work for you."

Her words cut like frost across steel. "Now go."

Rhys dropped into a bow deeper than before, then turned and strode away, cloak snapping behind him. At the archway, he slowed, casting one last glance over his shoulder. His voice was a whisper, sharp with bitterness.

"She is beautiful... but too much heart will be the death of her."

The words dissolved into the heat as he vanished down the corridor, already bearing the weight of his new orders toward Oasis City.

Lyra lingered in the courtyard, a faint smirk curving her lips as the last of the Umbral company disappeared into the desert's glare.

"Soon enough," she murmured, "all of Afor will kneel. Piece by piece. Sector by sector."

Turning back toward her frost-laden chambers, she let the desert sun press against her wards until the air hissed in protest.

"If only conquest burned as hot as this wretched place," she whispered.

The door shut behind her with a crack of ice, leaving the palace silent beneath the blazing sky while, in its depths, the heart of Afor pulsed ever darker with the Dominion's claim.

Chapter 34

Dominion's Hand in Shadowhaven

The night in Shadowhaven was unusually still. Clouds rolled low and heavy, smothering the stars above the crooked sprawl of towers, alleys, and smoke-stained docks. To outsiders, the city might have seemed asleep, but shadows moved with purpose, and unease thrummed through the streets like a second heartbeat.

From the high chamber of Blackspire Keep, Qellaun stood at an arched window overlooking the pirate stronghold. Once chaotic, Shadowhaven now bore Maldrak's hand in every silenced brawl and every ship flying the Dominion's colors. Discipline had been hammered into disorder like a thin sheen of oil on water, gleaming but treacherous beneath the touch.

Qellaun knew better. Appearances were tools, never truths.

A cold flicker brushed his mind. The call. Familiar, sharp as frost. He straightened.

"I hear you."

The mysterious one's voice slid through the dark, silken as a blade drawn slowly from its sheath.

"Qellaun. The time has come to tighten our grip. Shadowhaven will be our harbor and our blade. You will command it."

His jaw tightened, though he masked it with a faint smile. "Maldrak has grown bold."

"Maldrak will remain the face they fear, but never the hand that holds the leash. That is yours. Should he forget this... remind him. A taste of your power. Enough to break arrogance, not usefulness."

The presence withdrew, leaving only the hiss of waves against the black cliffs.

Qellaun lingered at the window, bitterness curling in his mouth. "Let the city serve the Dominion," he murmured. "But it will serve through me."

His gaze hardened. Maldrak would learn his place.

Lyra. He worried for her more than he would ever admit. She was not the same girl he remembered—no longer content to advise from the edges, but now seizing power with ice-veined certainty. His loyalty to his sister remained unbroken, yet unease twisted beneath it, caught between the bond of blood and the shadowy ambitions that drew them ever deeper into a dangerous alliance.

Her rise in Afor had not surprised him. That she would carve dominion over forsaken sands with ruthless will was expected. What unsettled him was not her strength, but the one who commanded them both.

"Resurrect the Abyssal Dominion," they had said.

The name itself was a wound reopening. Vuarus. Phoenix Shadowwalker. Names bound to fire, ruin, and chains. Both had fallen, their power broken and their ambitions destroyed.

So who now dared weave their web beneath that banner? Who bound them all to a name steeped in blood and ashes?

A flicker of doubt clawed at Qellaun's chest, tightening like a vice. His jaw clenched. But ambition quickly overcame hesitation, as it always did.

One thing at a time.

And for now, there was Shadowhaven.

Qellaun smoothed the folds of his dark cloak, his eyes narrowing with resolve. "First the pirates," he murmured. "Then the rest."

His expression hardened. First, Maldrak would remember his place.

The command hall sat deep within the keep, a cavernous chamber where pirate captains and enforcers gathered to divide spoils. Two cutthroats flanked its iron-banded doors, blades half-drawn more for show than readiness.

One stepped forward, a cruel smirk splitting his scarred face. "No entry without Maldrak's word."

Qellaun's eyes slid to him, cold as obsidian.

"Then you've made the first mistake of your short life."

A crack of blue-black energy leapt from his hand. The guard convulsed, body seized in a net of shadow. Smoke and scorched leather stung the air. With a strangled cry, the man collapsed, writhing on the floor.

Qellaun stepped over him without pause and shoved the doors wide. They slammed into the stone walls with a thunderous clang.

At the far end, Maldrak rose sharply, fury carved into his face.

"I told them I do not want to speak with you."

Qellaun shut the door with deliberate calm, the bolt clicking into place.

"We will speak, Maldrak. And when we are done, you will understand who rules this city."

Maldrak's fists clenched. "This is my city. You think to walk in like some shadow-blessed tyrant and—"

The shadows moved. They coiled outward like living chains and snapped around his chest and limbs. With a crack, the pirate lord was hurled to the ground, stone fracturing beneath him. The weight of the binding pressed down until his breath came ragged.

Qellaun circled him slowly, eyes aglow with cold violet fire.

"You were told to be a figurehead. Useful. Visible. Feared, yes. But never the one who commands."

Maldrak strained against the bonds, veins standing in his neck. "I—"

"You serve," Qellaun cut him off, voice sharp as broken glass. "You obey. And you will remember this—"

A flick of his wrist, and pain surged through the bindings. Maldrak convulsed, a guttural cry tearing from his throat as scorched sweat rose acrid in the air.

"—with every breath you take from this day forward."

The shadows dissolved. Maldrak collapsed, trembling. Slowly, shame heavy on his shoulders, he lowered his head until his brow touched the stone.

Qellaun's lips curved faintly. He seated himself in the great chair at the head of the chamber, calm, deliberate, absolute.

"Good."

The summons spread quickly, carried on whispers sharper than knives. Within the hour, the command hall was crowded with pirate captains and lieutenants, the air stinking of brine, smoke, and unease. Every man and woman had heard something of what transpired, and none wished to test whether the rumors had spoken too kindly.

Maldrak stood at the fore, his usual roar forced into brittle authority. His pallor betrayed him.

"Listen close," he growled. Orders have changed. Cross them, and you'll regret it. First, the filth ends. The alleys, the docks, everything. Anyone caught looking the other way will answer to me."

His hand twitched at the scorched tunic clinging to his chest. None missed it.

"Second—the ships. I want them repaired, seaworthy, and ready. When the call comes, Shadowhaven will strike as fleet and fortress both."

Murmurs rippled, strangled quickly into silence.

"And third, the chamber above this hall belongs now to Lord Qellaun. Remember it."

Dozens of eyes shifted toward the silent figure seated in command. Qellaun had not spoken a word since the gathering began, yet his presence weighed on every soul like a blade across their throats.

The captains dispersed swiftly, muttering to themselves as they left.

By dawn, the whispers would spread: Maldrak gave the orders, but Qellaun ruled.

Alone once more, Qellaun climbed the stairs to the upper suite. The door stood ajar; the former occupant had fled without daring to linger.

The room reeked of stale ale and sea brine, a pirate's lair, crude and unworthy.

"No longer."

He raised a hand. Shadows unfurled, rippling outward, veining the walls with sigils of the Druchii. Crude furnishings shriveled to dust. In their place rose polished iron and dark wood, a throne-like chair settling beneath the arched window. The chamber shuddered once, then stilled, as though the keep itself acknowledged its new lord.

Qellaun crossed the room and seated himself with deliberate ease. Below, Shadowhaven stirred: pirates scouring streets, ships patched and armed, enforcers marching with new discipline. The rhythm of boots and steel echoed with the tide.

A thin smile touched his lips. He told himself it was for order, for the Dominion. But beneath the thought, ambition coiled sharp and selfish.

"Perhaps this time," he whispered, "the Dominion will not fail. Where others fell, we will rise not by fear alone, but by shadow sharpened into purpose."

He leaned back in his chair, Shadowhaven laboring below him, unaware that every step, every oath, every coin now moved to the will of the Dominion.

Chapter 35
The Dominion Awakens

The air in Flameford's underbelly was thick with ancient heat, the scent of scorched stone clinging to the hollow dark. The mysterious figure descended the winding stair cut into basalt, each step ringing faintly, the stone beneath their boots still warm—as though the mountain itself breathed. Torchlight sputtered in the suffocating air, throwing warped shadows that crawled across the volcanic walls like restless spirits.

At the stairs' end, the sanctum waited. Long abandoned, never forgotten. Obsidian walls loomed around them, etched with dragon shapes carved by claw and fire, their features eroded but still watching. At the far end yawned a black arch, nothing more now than a scar in the world, a hollow where once the gateway of the abyss had burned. It stood lifeless, yet the air around it still seemed to hum with memory.

The figure paused, pride coiling in their chest like smoke.

"I have brought it back," they murmured, voice low, too clear in the silence. The vow reverberated from the stone. "The Abyssal Dominion rises again. The people of Vacari will remember fear... and they will remember you."

Their hand tightened on the staff, voice sharpening.

"And Keisha..." A flicker of hate seared the name. "No light will shield her. I will see her fall."

The torches guttered. Shadows stretched unnaturally long, bending toward the dead archway. A phantom draft sliced through the furnace air cold enough to raise gooseflesh.

From the hollow came a hiss, faint as breath against glass.

"Good."

The figure froze, the cavern pressing inward with deafening silence. Was it real? Or only the echo of their own words, twisted by memory of what had once dwelled here?

With a sharp turn, they ascended again. The volcanic stair groaned as if remembering its old master. Heat closed around them like a cloak.

By the time they emerged onto the upper tier, night had fallen. The sky churned with torn clouds. Flameford's jagged walls caught the flash of distant lightning, their stone teeth lit in stark relief.

Voraxia descended first, wings folding with predator's grace, silver-white eyes glowing like embers. Her talons struck sparks, the rock beneath her frosting where shadow touched it. Moments later, Vorathos landed in a thunder of obsidian scales, ash spiraling from her wings as if the mountain itself bowed.

"They've returned," the figure murmured, stepping to the terrace's edge.

Voraxia lowered her horned head, her voice a hiss of contempt.

"We met resistance. The Celestials. Aurelius. Their light does not merely burn; it unravels shadow. And when they bleed..." Her gaze darkened. "They heal. Instantly."

Vorathos's tail cracked stone, her voice a low growl of reluctant awe.

"I tore one open, and the wound sealed before the blood touched the ground. No sorcery I know can do this. It is... wrong."

The figure inclined their hooded head, shadows shifting like smoke.

"That confirms it. The Celestials wield power not seen since the oldest days. Divine... or older still. They are a problem."

Voraxia's eyes narrowed. "A problem that could tip the scales if ignored."

"Indeed." The figure's voice was iron over stone. "But this remains between us. Do not seed doubt among the others. Strike where you can. Target the Celestials. Harass, divide. Do not meet them head-on. Not yet."

Vorathos's teeth bared in a delighted grin. "The Dominion's name alone unsettles them."

Voraxia's wings snapped wide, shadow curling from their edges. "Curb your hunger. Excitement blinds."

The figure's smirk lingered in their words. "Let her savor it. Fear feeds on chaos. And chaos is the herald of victory."

Later, the Cavern of Ash seethed with restless wings. Dragons crowded the ember-lit hollow, scales scraping stone, tails lashing sparks into the air. Shadows trembled across the walls, magnifying every motion until the chamber itself seemed alive.

Upon the dais, Voraxia and Vorathos stood like twin storms—midnight and abyss, shadow and flame.

The figure raised a gloved hand. Even the mountain's low rumble seemed to hush.

"The Abyssal Dominion," they intoned, smooth and unyielding, a chill draft threading through the heat.

The cavern groaned. Embers flared. Growls rippled through the gathering. Some dragons exhaled smoke in dark pride. Others shifted, uneasy, their eyes sharp with doubt.

The figure let silence stretch before sweeping their gaze across the host. At last, their lips curved in a thin smile.

"From this moment, Voraxia and Vorathos command you. They are the fang and the flame of the Dominion. Their words are my will. Defy them, and you defy me."

A ripple of unease spread through the host. Wings unfurled, claws scraped basalt.

Zylron's crimson gaze burned from the shadows, his voice a growl like stone splitting.

"That name died with them. Only those of us who bled remember it. So tell me, how do you know it?"

The figure's smile was cold as steel. "It does not matter how. Only that I do. And Vuarus would be pleased."

Glaciera's eyes gleamed like frozen steel. Frost crept over her talons, hissing in the furnace heat.

"You wield a dangerous name," she murmured.

"Dangerous," the figure agreed, shadows curling at their fingertips, "but true. The Dominion rises. Those who cling to doubt will be left behind."

Their voice fell to a blade's edge.

"Know this: it was by my will that Voraxia and Vorathos struck Keisha down. Should she live, she remains our target. Her death is overdue for the price of Vuarus's fall."

The words hung in the sulfur-thick air like ash.

Glaciera's smile sharpened, her fangs catching the molten glow.

"I froze her once. Fragile. Brittle... she shattered sweetly in my claws. This time, I'll finish it." Frost spidered outward, steam hissing as it struck molten seams.

Zylron's talons dug deep into basalt, sparks leaping from the pressure. His crimson eyes narrowed, fury banked but not quenched.

"Then let her be yours. But remember the first Dominion drowned in fire and blood. Names alone do not win wars. And shadows... always lie."

Nocturna and Xalzorath lingered in silence, their watchful eyes giving nothing away.

The figure lifted a hand. Shadows writhed upward, blotting out the ember-glow.

"Go. Spread fear. Break their unity. The Dominion rises."

The cavern erupted in thunder. Dragons launched skyward, wings beating storms into the night, their roars shaking the stone. Ash spiraled upward in their wake, carrying hunger, pride, and the first whispers of doubt into the dark.

When silence returned, the sanctum lay empty once more, save for molten rivers hissing through the rock and the lingering echo of a name reborn.

Yet not all eyes had turned away.

High in the shadows, Zylron lingered, crimson gaze fixed not on the sisters' triumph but on the one who had elevated them. For the briefest moment, he thought he saw the faintest curve of approval beneath the hood. Not the cold mask of command, but a trace of satisfaction.

His claws bit deeper into the basalt, fissures glowing with restrained fury.

Never for us, he thought, embers flaring in his throat. Never for me. We were bound, leashed, denied. But these two? They are granted freedom... indulgence.

Suspicion coiled tight within him, molten and corrosive. Perhaps the Dominion truly had risen anew. Or maybe it was only a shadow draped in old names, granting its chosen pets more leash than the rest.

Zylron's growl rumbled low, swallowed by the cavern's silence.

"Play your game, sisters. One day I'll see who truly holds the leash."

The crimson light in his eyes narrowed to slits as the last trace of the figure's presence dissolved into darkness.

Chapter 36

Echoes of a Shattered Name

The morning sun blazed across the crystal towers of Lyra'el, scattering rainbows through their facets and painting the white stone streets in shifting color. A cool breath of river air threaded through the walkways, carrying the faint chime of bells and the fragrance of flowering gardens.

Ong's boots struck hard against the polished stone as he strode through the city, dread pulsing with every beat of his heart. The beauty of the gleaming spires only deepened his ache, each corridor a reminder of the one he had not yet found.

He was searching for her.

Rounding the curve of the eastern courtyard, he nearly collided with two familiar figures.

"Ong!" Valeon exclaimed, a crooked grin tugging at his lips despite the near collision. His fingertips were smudged with ink, evidence of another sleepless night hunched over scrolls and salves. At his side, Kaelorn inclined his head, chestnut hair catching the light like strands of woven moonlight.

"I've been looking everywhere," Ong said, his voice taut with urgency.

Kaelorn's calm gaze softened. "We thought you might. Come, we'll take you to her. She is resting."

They moved swiftly through the crystalline walkways, the sun scattering prisms across their path. Valeon shifted the bundle of parchments under his arm, then glanced sideways at Ong.

"So, uh... this Abyssal Dominion everyone's whispering about, who were they? I've never even heard the name. But now every dragon and elf looks like they've seen a ghost."

Ong's jaw clenched, his stride unbroken. "A few years ago, they nearly destroyed everything. Forests burned to ash. Cities crumbled into ruin. Vuarus and Phoenix Shadowwalker led them in a coalition of shadow and madness. They tried to sacrifice Keisha to the Abyss itself." His voice dropped, rough with memory. "It took the Noble Dragons, the Sea God, and a miracle to stop them. I still see the fire on the horizon when I close my eyes."

Kaelorn's glade-fire gaze darkened, the calm around him broken by unease. "And now it returns..."

"Not with the same faces," Ong said, sharper now. "Phoenix and Vuarus are dead. I saw to one myself. But the name survives. Whoever dares claim it knows exactly what it means to those of us who lived through its shadow."

They turned into a quieter wing of the sanctuary, where moonblossoms spilled their fragrance into the cool air. Water whispered through carved channels in the walls, the sound gentle against the taut silence between them. Ahead, a chamber door stood slightly ajar, pale light spilling across the polished floor.

"She is inside," Kaelorn said quietly.

Valeon shifted the bundle of scrolls onto the bench outside the chamber, where vials and dried herbs already lay scattered. "We'll get back to work," he murmured. "These salves don't brew themselves... Don't blame me if she wakes smelling like roasted mint."

The faintest smile cracked through Ong's sternness. He gave a sharp nod of thanks, then pressed his palm to the door. It yielded at his touch, closing softly behind him as silence folded over the corridor once more.

The chamber glowed with gentle radiance, light filtering through sheer lavender curtains that stirred in the breeze. The air was cool and fragrant, moonblossoms drifting their sweetness upward from the garden below, threaded with the sharper bite of brewing salves. At the center lay Keisha upon a bed carved from living crystal, its facets humming with quiet, restorative magic. Her skin was pale against the soft linen wrappings, faint bruises blooming like stubborn shadows along her arms and cheek.

Ong's breath caught.

He crossed the chamber slowly, as though any sudden movement might shatter the fragile calm. Kneeling at her side, he reached for her hand. His calloused fingers brushed hers with the gentleness of a whisper, as if even touch itself might summon pain.

"I wasn't here," he whispered, the words raw with guilt. "I should've been. I should've known."

His voice broke. He bowed his head, fists tightening against his knees. "Always somewhere else, while you're out there fighting."

"You're here now."

The voice was soft, strained, but steady. His head snapped up. Her eyes had opened, lashes heavy with sleep, yet her smile, small and weary, warmed the cold knot in his chest.

"When did you get here?" she murmured, a flicker of teasing in her rasping voice. "Shouldn't you be in Crystal Vale, arguing with your brother?"

He gave her a look equal parts scolding and relief. "With you like this? I'm not leaving."

She let out a tired laugh and let her eyes half-close again. "It's not that bad."

His gaze sharpened, though his tone gentled as he leaned closer. "Keisha... what did you do to draw the eyes of those dragons?"

Her lips curved faintly. "Nothing. Just keeping a Pegasus safe. Didn't like the way they circled."

Ong sank into the chair beside her bed, disbelief flickering in his eyes. "You faced two of the darkest dragons alive... for a horse."

Keisha's shoulders lifted in a fragile shrug. "He's a very special horse."

Silence settled over them, soft as a blanket. Beyond the lattice windows, birdsong carried on the morning air, twining with the steady murmur of Lyra'el's streets. Ong never let go of her hand, and she never once tried to pull away.

Keisha studied him closely. Though Ong sat at her side with quiet care, tension coiled through every line of him, the hard set of his jaw, the relentless rhythm of his thumb brushing over her hand as if trying to soothe himself as much as her. A memory haunted his eyes: her body limp in that frozen cell long ago, skin turned blue with frost, breath fading. The knot in his chest only drew tighter.

"You're not telling me everything," she whispered. Her fingers tightened weakly around his, her gaze steady, unyielding.

He froze. For a heartbeat, the curtains only whispered in the breeze, secrets rustling in the silence. At last, he exhaled, rough with reluctance.

"You always did know when I was holding back."

"Then tell me."

Ong leaned forward, elbows braced to his knees, eyes fixed on the floor as though it might lend him courage. "There was a skirmish beyond Lyra'el. Radiantus and Aurelius led the defense—Platinum and Celestial dragons driving back a host of shadow and abyssal kin."

Keisha's brow furrowed. "More of them?"

"Yes." His voice was taut, edged with something darker. "But that wasn't the worst. Voraxia spoke a name we thought buried forever."

He lifted his head, gaze locking with hers, haunted and unflinching.

"She said the Abyssal Dominion has returned."

The words fell heavy between them, rippling through the chamber like stones sinking into deep water. Even the curtains were still, the hush pressing close.

Keisha's breath caught. Her lips parted, voice barely above a whisper. "...That name should not exist anymore."

Ong nodded grimly. "Exactly. Vuarus and Phoenix died with it on their tongues. It should have ended with them." His grip on her hand hardened, fierce with an unspoken vow. "But someone has claimed it anew. And this time, they don't mean to capture you, Keisha. No chains. No ritual. No bargaining. They want you gone."

Her eyes did not waver. She absorbed the words like stone enduring flame, pain already familiar. Slowly, she drew in a breath, her voice steady despite the strain.

"Oh. So that's all."

Ong blinked, incredulous. "Keisha—"

Her hand tightened over his, gentle but firm, grounding him before his temper could flare. "Listen. I've been marked for death before. Phoenix tried to sacrifice me. Vuarus sent his shadows to tear me apart. I survived chains, frost, and flame. Kimras carried me from that chamber. Amara shook the skies for me. And I'm still here."

His gaze lingered on the bandages swathing her ribs, the bruises shadowing her skin. He shook his head, voice rough with the weight of fear he could not hide. "And still look at you. Broken. Hurt. Do you really believe this is only about a Pegasus?"

Her smile faded into something sharper, steadier. "No. I know better. I only hoped you wouldn't see it so soon." She lifted one trembling hand, brushing a lock of hair from his brow, her touch soft despite the heaviness of her words. "But it doesn't matter. Things will be as they must. And this time, I am not alone."

Ong lowered his gaze, the memory clawing at him again, her body limp in that frozen cell, skin turned blue with Glaciera's frost, breath so shallow he feared it would never return. The knot in his chest tightened until it hurt to breathe.

She must have seen it in his eyes, for her voice softened, though her words carried steel. "You remember the first time? When they broke me. It worked only because I believed I didn't matter. That no one would come."

Her pale green eyes burned with quiet fire, unwavering despite her exhaustion. "But I know better now. I have you. Kimras. My father. Half the realm. I'm not that girl in the freezing cell anymore, Ong."

A reluctant smile tugged at his lips, trembling at the edges. "That's true. You're more dangerous now."

She smirked faintly, her voice still hoarse. "And harder to kill."

He leaned closer, pressing his lips to her forehead with aching tenderness, his vow spilling raw into the hush between them.

"They may come again. But they'll find me there with you. I will not let them take you, not now, not ever."

She rested her head against his shoulder, her breath mingling with his. For a fleeting moment, the world grew still. No shadows. No whispers of the Dominion. Only the rhythm of two hearts, steady and intertwined, holding fast against the storm.

Yet beyond the lattice windows, the wards of Lyra'el pulsed with silver light, straining against the weight of the gathering dark.

A soft knock broke the stillness.

"Come in," Keisha called.

The door eased open. Kaelorn stepped inside first, chestunut hair slightly mussed, a trace of exasperation in his expression as if he had been fending off questions all morning. Valeon trailed close behind, curiosity burning in his eyes despite Kaelorn's muttered warning.

"Don't ask," Kaelorn hissed under his breath. "Just don't—"

Valeon ignored him, folding his arms across his chest. "Sorry, I know this isn't the time, but... why aren't you worried, Keisha? The Abyssal Dominion just hearing the name makes my skin crawl. And after what happened last time."

Kaelorn groaned, pinching the bridge of his nose. "By the stars..."

Ong looked to Keisha. She met his gaze and gave the faintest nod, granting permission.

Ong's chest rose and fell once before he spoke, voice low and taut. "The last time the Abyssal Dominion rose, it nearly destroyed Vacari. Cities burned. Groves turned to ash. And Keisha..." His jaw locked before he forced the words out. "She was their chosen sacrifice. They meant to give her to the Abyss."

Kaelorn's eyes widened. Valeon blanched.

"That's what she meant by the first time?" Valeon asked, his voice thin.

Keisha's smile was faint and wry. "Not exactly a vacation."

"Kimras and Amara saved her," Ong said firmly. "And I reached her just in time. But what she endured..." His voice faltered, shadows stirring in his eyes.

Keisha caught his hand, steadying him as much as herself. "That's why I'm not afraid," she said softly. Fire flickered in her pale green gaze. "Because I already survived their worst. They tried to erase me. I'm still here. Still standing."

Valeon blinked, at a rare loss for words. "Okay. Yeah... wow."

Kaelorn inclined his head, voice low with quiet respect. "Then they made a mistake letting you live."

Keisha's smirk sharpened. "They tend to."

Valeon opened his mouth again, but Kaelorn clamped a hand on his shoulder before he could speak. "That's enough. Back to work."

"But—"

"Nope," Kaelorn muttered, dragging him firmly toward the door.

Valeon sighed with exaggerated drama but allowed himself to be herded out. The door clicked shut behind them, leaving the chamber steeped once more in lavender light and silence.

Silence reclaimed the room.

Yet unease coiled in Keisha's chest, cold and insistent. She didn't speak it aloud; she didn't want to, but one name haunted the edges of her thoughts.

Glaciera.

The others had broken her body, threatened her life. But only the Ice Dragon had nearly shattered her spirit. She remembered the breath locking in her lungs, the silence sharper than any scream, the way her very soul had seemed to crack beneath the weight of that endless frost. That chill had never fully left her bones. And if any of them came again, she knew who it would be.

Beside her, Ong still held her hand, his thumb brushing gently across the band of cloth at her wrist. In that steady, grounding motion lay an unspoken vow that he would never let her fall alone again. His eyes burned with fire, but her faint smile steadied him.

"They'll regret coming after you," he whispered, low and fierce.

Her lashes lowered, exhaustion pulling at her, but her voice remained soft, threaded with iron. She leaned back against the pillow, lips curving into a spark of defiance.

"Let them try," she murmured. "They did once. And now they'll learn how great a mistake that was."

Chapter 37

Echoes of the Abyss

The stained-glass windows of Crystal Vale's eastern tower caught the late afternoon light, scattering fractured rainbows across the marble floor. King Manard stood motionless at their center, hands clasped behind his back, eyes fixed on the skies beyond the crystal spires.

On the surface, peace shimmered. Yet beneath it, tension coiled in his shoulders, an old ache stirring as if his body remembered what his mind tried to deny.

Behind him, on the carved desk, lay a sealed message stamped with Lyra'el's crest. He had not broken the wax. He didn't need to. One name had been enough.

Abyssal Dominion.

His breath slowed, heavy with memory.

It hadn't been decades since that name scarred Vacari. Barely a handful of years, and still the wounds lingered. He remembered how close the realm had come to ruin. He remembered Keisha, shattered and scarred, yet risen from the abyss stronger than before. Of all who had suffered under that shadow, hers had been the deepest wound... and the fiercest recovery.

Keisha.

He saw her as she had been after Phoenix and Vuarus had broken her spirit, the fire in her eyes reduced to ash. She had clawed her way back, fiercer and wiser, but no one crossed that darkness unchanged.

And now the Dominion's name had returned.

The founders were gone, yet someone else had seized their mantle. A new master. The same nightmare.

Manard exhaled, gaze lingering on the horizon where Lyra'el glimmered in the distance. Ong was there now—his son. The word was still new on his tongue, yet the bond between them had rooted as though it had always been. And where Ong stood, Keisha was at his side.

Keisha. Not only was Vacari's champion, not only the girl who had endured the abyssal fire, but she was family now. His daughter. The thought filled him with pride... and with a weight heavier than any crown. He had nearly lost her once. He could still see her broken in the aftermath, still hear Ong's furious vow as he fought to protect her. To lose her again, after all they had endured.

It would break more than one heart.

The Dominion was no longer only a threat to the realm. It was a threat to his blood.

He turned from the window at last. Two people needed to hear this: Prince Gailen, his son, who had not been in Crystal Vale during the Dominion's first rise, and Thalorian, the Moon Elf, whose loyalty and quiet strength Manard had come to respect. They deserved to know what stirred.

He moved to the writing table, drew out a sheet of pale parchment, and dipped his quill.

To Prince Gailen, and to Thalorian of the Moon Elves. Come to the palace at once. There is a matter of grave importance I must share with you both. The name "Abyssal Dominion" has resurfaced, and you must understand what it means.

He sealed the message with the royal crest and handed it to a swift-winged courier. As the messenger's footsteps faded down the corridor, Manard rested one hand against the cool glass of the window, eyes on the far horizon.

This time, he vowed, the past would not be allowed to blindside the future.

The sound of boots on polished stone echoed through the upper halls of Crystal Vale's palace. A pair of Elven guards swung open the great doors as Prince Gailen and Thalorian stepped inside—both silent, both carrying an edge of alertness that needed no words.

King Manard awaited them just beyond the threshold. The lines around his eyes were deeper than usual, carved by a concern he no longer bothered to hide.

Gailen's brow knit. "Father? What's happened?"

"Walk with me," Manard said, his voice clipped. "There is a chamber we will use."

He turned at once, leading them down the gilded corridor. High-arched windows spilled fractured light across statues of kings long gone, their marble faces watching in solemn silence. The three moved in measured step, their hush heavier than the echo of their boots. Gailen glanced at Thalorian, but the Moon Elf's face revealed nothing. Only the taut set of his stride betrayed the tension he carried.

They entered the private council chamber. The doors closed behind them with a muted thud. No guards. No courtiers. Only the three of them, and the weight of what had brought them there.

Manard turned, hands clasped behind his back. His gaze lingered on the carved table at the chamber's heart, as though the words he carried were stone too heavy to lift. At last, he spoke.

"Tell me, have either of you heard the name Abyssal Dominion spoken of late?"

Thalorian inclined his head. "Whispers," he admitted. "I was uncertain of their meaning. But Verdantia... she knew. When the words were spoken, her eyes changed. I had not thought to see fear in her."

Manard gave a slow, grim nod.

Gailen shifted where he stood, unease threading his voice. "I've heard it too. Some of the older citizens fall silent when it's mentioned, as if it drags up memories best left buried." He hesitated, then added quietly, "Aurelia grew... unsettled when she heard it. But it's only a name, isn't it? Dark, yes, but nothing more now."

Manard's hands pressed flat against the carved table, shoulders squaring as his voice cut through the chamber like tempered steel.

"No, Gailen. It was never just a name."

The air seemed to thicken with his words. His gaze moved between them, heavy with memory.

"The Abyssal Dominion was no banner to rally behind. It was Vuarus and Phoenix Shadowwalker's vision of conquest. They nearly unmade Vacari beneath its shadow. Forests burned. Cities fell. Magic itself was twisted into weapons. The scars of that time remain, whether we speak of them or not."

Silence followed, deep and unbroken. Gailen's breath caught. Even Thalorian's calm expression faltered, his jade-fire gaze darkening as the weight of the words pressed down on them.

But Manard's voice only grew heavier.

"The worst of it came when they captured Keisha."

Gailen's brows snapped together. His voice was tight. "Captured?"

"For six long months," Manard said, each word dropping like a stone, "she was held in the abyss they carved beneath New Flameford." His jaw clenched, as if bracing against the taste of ash. "Day by day, piece by piece, they broke her down. Her spirit was shattered, her light nearly extinguished. Every breath she drew was its own battle."

Thalorian did not move, yet horror flickered across his eyes, horror tempered by a dawning respect.

"Ong never yielded," Manard went on. "Not for a single heartbeat. He hunted through ruins, followed whispers across the realm, carrying despair but never surrendering to it. And at last, when they found her... Kimras and Amara descended. Called by more than rumor." His voice lowered, reverent. "Called by destiny itself."

He drew a long, steadying breath, grief roughening its edges.

"If not for them, she would have been lost, sacrificed to the Abyss."

The words struck like stones cast into still water, ripples of silence spreading through the chamber. Manard stepped back from the table, clasping his hands behind him. Gratitude pressed close, as vivid as the sight burned into his memory: golden and amethyst talons lifting Keisha from the darkness, her body broken but her life still clinging to her.

Too close. Far too close.

At last, Thalorian's voice broke the silence, calm but honed like a drawn blade.

"Why? Why torment her so? What purpose could such cruelty serve?"

Manard lifted his gaze, steady and grim. "It was never cruelty for its own sake. Not to Vuarus."

Gailen shifted uneasily, frowning. Thalorian's eyes narrowed, though his stance remained composed, tension visible in the way his hands curled behind his back.

Manard turned toward the fire, though its flames offered little warmth. "From the beginning, Vuarus sought her. He let Phoenix believe it was vengeance that breaking her would break Ong, would shatter the Eladrin's faith. But the truth was darker still."

He paused, the silence deepening, then spoke with quiet finality.

"Vuarus craved her spirit, her elemental bond, her tie to the forests of Vacari. He believed that if he broke her and offered her to the Abyss, he could consume her essence and seize the divinity he desired. Every lash, every wound, every torment she endured... was preparation for his ritual."

Manard's tone softened, reverence threading through it.

"Kimras pulled her back from that edge. He carried her himself, his talons cradling her as if she were both flame and glass. It was more than rescue. It was devotion. It was defiance."

He let the silence breathe, the truth settling over them like ash.

"Vuarus and Phoenix fell in the end. Talleoss struck Vuarus from the skies, and Ong's blade pierced Phoenix before the shadows could claim him. Their Dominion burned to ash."

The chamber went still. Gailen bowed his head, his face solemn. When he raised his eyes again, confusion was gone—replaced by gravity.

"I understand now," he said softly. "It was never just a name. It's what my sister endured, what Ong fought against. A scar that never fully healed."

Thalorian's jade-fire gaze remained on Manard, his voice calm but edged with steel.

"A scar that remembers. And one that warns."

Gailen turned to his father, something firm taking root behind his eyes. His voice carried no hesitation.

"Then I'm going to Lyra'el. Ong is my brother, my stepbrother, yes, but more than that, he's family."

A flicker of pride stirred in him, mingled with quiet astonishment. The words felt right, like truth long known but only now spoken. For the first time, he sensed the fragile beginnings of a sense of belonging.

"I won't let him face this alone."

Manard's sternness eased, pride breaking through the worry etched into his features.

Thalorian's hand rested lightly on the hilt of his blade. He inclined his head.

"Then I ride as well. If the rumors are true, shadows stirring, abyssal dragons waking, Vacari will need more than courage. It will need unity."

Silence passed between the three of them, not empty, but full, weighted with understanding.

At last, Manard gave a small, tired smile.

"Then go. With my blessing. May your blades stay sharp, and your dragons swifter still."

Gailen stepped forward, gripping his father's forearm. "We'll bring back word. And if it comes to battle…"

"You will not be alone," Manard finished, his voice firm.

Without another word, Gailen and Thalorian turned and strode from the chamber, their footsteps ringing with new resolve.

Outside, the dragons were already restless. A low hum rippled through the courtyard wings, twitching, tails lashing as if instinct itself warned of what was coming. Even the banners tugged hard against their poles, caught in a shifting wind heavy with fate.

Aurelia waited for Gailen, crystalline wings scattering prisms across the marble, each feathered plate gleaming like shards of living glass. Verdantia lowered her great emerald head for Thalorian, eyes deep as ancient groves, her breath carrying the scent of green earth even here in Crystal Vale.

Gailen buckled the last clasp of his armor with steady hands. Beside him, Thalorian checked his blade and lifted his gaze toward the horizon, jade-fire eyes hard as moonlit steel.

The two shared a final nod, an unspoken unity forged in shared purpose.

They mounted in unison.

With a thunder of wings and a rush of wind, Aurelia and Verdantia surged skyward, their riders lifted into the radiant air. The courtyard trembled beneath their ascent as Crystal Vale looked on, watching two figures blaze eastward toward Lyra'el, where shadows gathered, and where not only Keisha, but all who loved her, would soon be tested against the darkness once more.

Chapter 38

Riders of Flame and Starlight

The skies above Lyra'el darkened not with storm clouds, but with wings. Each beat thundered like war drums, rattling the crystal watchtowers and shaking blossoms loose from the high forest spires. A roar so vast it seemed to split the heavens rolled across the land, quaking even the deep-rooted sentinels.

Shadow and Abyssal dragons swept across the horizon, cruelly majestic, cloaked in roiling darkness. Their flight blotted out the morning light, and their cries split the air like jagged steel.

Voraxia's form rippled through the sky like a living shadow, her silver-white eyes locked on the distant glow of the Celestial sanctuary. Beside her, Vorathos surged with eager hunger, her scales glimmering like liquid void. Behind them came their kin, twisted cousins of the darker realms, bent on tearing down the radiant dragons who dared to defy the Dominion.

"They're here," Kimras growled from a rocky overlook, golden scales igniting with the first light of dawn. His tail lashed once, claws gouging stone as his eyes fixed on the oncoming storm. Resolve burned in him like molten fire. Voraxia would not have Lyra'el. "And they brought company."

"Then so have we," Amara answered, her voice like amethyst struck into melody. Her amethyst eyes narrowed, wings unfurling in radiant arcs of violet light.

Ong tightened his grip on the saddle between her shoulders, his drag-onlance gleaming like silver fire. A flicker of unease churned in his chest—not fear, but the heavy weight of what was coming. He drew a long breath, hardening it into resolve. "Let's give them a proper wel-come."

From their flanks, armored riders wheeled into formation, mounted on gleaming dragons of light. Each bore sigils of resistance, their spears and blades shimmering with elemental enchantments that sparked against the dawn.

Below, in the sacred groves, Kaelorn felt the tremor of the clash rising. His hand brushed the hilt at his side, his voice low. "They're going to try to take out the Celestials."

Valeon glanced up from the wards he was reinforcing, chalk and ink smudged across his hands. A crooked grin tugged his lips. "Then they're going to find out we're not as fragile as we used to be."

Above, the first cries of battle split the heavens.

Vorathos dove with murderous glee, a streak of void slicing through the light, only to be met midair by a Platinum dragon. Its rider launched a sun-forged spear into her shoulder, and the shriek she gave shattered branches far below. Smoke spiraled off her scales, but the Platinum circled again, pressing the attack.

Kimras roared and surged forward, colliding with an obsidian brute whose claws screeched across his golden hide without piercing it. Their impact shook the skies like colliding storms.

Ong leaned low as Amara wheeled through shadowflame, her violet fire arcing back in ribbons that split the dark haze. Below him, Voraxia darted between combatants, not seeking battle but prey. Her gaze slithered past Platinum, past Gold, seeking something no, someone.

"She's hunting the Celestials," Ong muttered, eyes narrowing. "Or worse, Keisha."

Amara's voice rippled through his mind, low and protective. Then we end this before she gets the chance.

And with a surge of wings and fury, they dove deeper into the fray.

Far below, the winds of Lyra'el shifted not in temperature, but in something older. The resonance of war, of bonds forged and tested, swept through the trees.

Keisha stirred, her heart pounding not in fear but in recognition. The bond flared—a rush of Ong's determination, Amara's strength, Kimras's fury. It was the same blazing current she had felt the day they escaped the ruins together. She thought it was only the soulbond to Ong, but another chord struck—the Celestials' presence. The heavens above were no longer still.

Clutching the frame of the arched doorway, she stepped barefoot into the courtyard, cool stone meeting her skin.

"Keisha!" Kaelorn's voice rang as he rushed toward her, Valeon close behind, flask in hand and panic in his eyes. "You shouldn't be out here, you're still recovering."

"I know," she said quietly, eyes fixed on the burning skies. "But I felt it."

The air vibrated with dragonfire and warding sigils. Shadows scythed across the sun, and her aura stirred in response.

"I can't ride Kimras yet," she admitted, steady despite the pain tugging at her ribs. "But I will not hide. My magic may not scorch skies, but it protects. It heals. And I will use it to make sure Ong, Kimras, and the others come back."

Kaelorn faltered, wanting to argue but unable to deny the light in her gaze.

Valeon gave a low whistle, his smirk edged with admiration. "Remind me never to doubt the queen of silver and storms."

Keisha moved forward, pressing her hand over her heart. Silver radiance rose from her skin, her Eladrin aura flaring like a shimmering wind that made the wards Valeon carved glow brighter.

Above the emerald canopy, the skies erupted. Celestial brilliance clashed with abyssal shadow, color and darkness colliding in thunderous waves.

Voraxia twisted midair, obsidian wings slicing through sunlight, only to stagger as Amara's psionic wave cracked the heavens like a thunderclap. Invisible force rippled through the battlefield, dragons staggering in its wake.

Vorathos snarled, circling wide, abyssal runes glowing faintly across her scales. "You dare throw mindfire at us, jewel-spawned pretender?"

Amara's eyes blazed like starlit amethysts. "I do more than dare." Her voice rolled calmly and anciently. "You are not the first to threaten Lyra'el. And you will not be the last we bury."

Below her, Ong raised his dragonlance, his voice carried on the wind. "If you're looking for Keisha, my wife, she's not here. But I am. And you'll leave the Celestial dragons alone. You're not welcome here, Voraxia."

Voraxia's laughter rolled like storm clouds. She coiled in midair, wings veiling the sky. "Bold words... for a human clinging to a borrowed perch. But no matter. We'll raze your skies all the same."

A crystalline resonance hummed through the battlefield, vibrating in bone and stone alike. Amara's voice rang across minds and air alike: "He is no passenger. He is my dragonrider—and you will learn what that bond means."

Voraxia sneered. "Not welcome? Oh, Ong... I wasn't asking." Her eyes gleamed with cruel intent. "And as for your little Eladrin, I've drawn her blood before. Next time, she won't rise again."

Rage surged through Ong, his grip whitening around the lance. Keisha's bloodied form, Pegasus circling helplessly, the memory of his absence, they all struck him like barbs. His bond with her flared, hot and fierce, braided through with Amara's power.

Before he could respond, a roar like molten sunfire shattered the sky.

Kimras descended in a blaze, golden flame pouring like dawn itself unleashed. His voice boomed across the heavens, scorching shadow with sheer radiance:

"Do not threaten my dragonrider!"

Voraxia shrieked, banking hard, her wings seared by light that was more than fire—it was morning given form.

Above them, Aurelius hovered, wings spread wide, his gaze a steady blaze of white fire. His voice rang across the battlefield like a tolling bell, calm yet unyielding.

"You were warned, Voraxia. No hand will rise against the riders of the Noble Dragons. To strike at them is to bind yourself to your own ruin."

Vorathos's snarl rumbled through the clouds. "Stern words, Celestial. Let us see how long your light can hold."

But even as she spoke, her wings pulled taut, hesitation coiling in her movements.

The shadow host circled once, casting long silhouettes that scarred the forest. Then, with a final glare, they vanished into the darkening sky.

Silence pressed in after the storm. Not a victory, not a defeat. The breath before the next strike.

"They'll be back," Ong murmured, lowering his lance only slightly.

"And we'll be ready," Amara answered, her tone a vow.

From the courtyard, Keisha stood with bow in hand, her aura fading but her eyes unyielding. Her spine straightened, a storm rising in her chest.

Next time, she vowed silently, I will not stand still.

And in the shadows left behind, the storm had already stirred.

Chapter 39

The Calm After Fury

The shimmer of battle still clung to the skies, fading like the after-glow of a dying flame. Ash drifted on the breeze, carrying the tang of smoke, while dragons wheeled overhead, Celestial and Platinum alike, wingbeats echoing across Lyra'el's crystal towers. Though the skirmish was won, tension still pressed heavy over the city.

Kimras was the first to spot her.

"There," he rumbled, tilting his golden head toward the overlook.

Ong followed his gaze. By the scorched stone where flames had licked the sky only moments ago, Keisha stood. Her red hair stirred in the wind, catching glimmers of light like embers that refused to fade. She held herself steady, but the strain showed in her shoulders.

Ong's jaw clenched, a sharp breath escaping between his teeth. "She shouldn't be out here. Not like this." The memory of her crumpled body in the Pegasi fields flashed in his mind. He hadn't reached her in time then. He would not allow history to repeat itself.

Amara gave a long, slow exhale as she glided downward, wings folding. "That girl," she sighed, "is about to be fussed at."

Kimras's snort rumbled like a rockslide. "You think?"

The three descended toward the city, wind curling around their wings. The battlefield below lay hushed, scorched but still.

Ong dismounted before Amara's talons had even settled. His boots struck the stone with purpose, eyes locked on Keisha. Kimras landed beside him, golden scales gleaming, looming like a sentinel carved of molten sunlight.

The silence between them wasn't empty. It was the silence before storms.

Keisha turned as they approached. Despite her pallor, she managed to smile and lifted a hand in greeting.

They descended upon her at once.

"You shouldn't be here," Ong snapped, voice tight with worry.

"You are not healed—what were you thinking?" Kimras growled, his thunder shaking the air.

Keisha blinked, caught between the two of them, her smile faltering into bemused disbelief. Affection flickered beneath her exasperation, though, because every sharp word was born of care.

Amara landed gracefully, her amethyst wings scattering light, and lowered her head. Her eyes glimmered with restrained laughter. "One at a time, perhaps?"

The pause lasted only a heartbeat, then, as though answering a signal, Ong and Kimras launched back in—alternating now like a well-practiced duet.

"You were supposed to be resting."

"You could have been hurt again."

"What if someone saw you?"

"You're not riding yet!"

Keisha folded her arms, sighing. Part of her wanted to laugh outright, but another part felt warmed by the noise and the sheer force of their protectiveness.

High above, Radiantus and Aurelius hovered near the spires, their deep, rumbling laughter rolling across the city like distant thunder.

Kimras's golden eye fixed on her. "Take her back," he commanded, his tail lashing. "And this time, set guards to keep her in her chamber until the Celestials themselves say she is fit to leave."

Ong was already striding forward. Before Keisha could protest, he scooped her into his arms.

"Put me down!" she yelped, squirming. But the reluctant grin tugging at her lips betrayed the affection beneath her outrage.

He carried her through Lyra'el's crystalline halls, ignoring her protests. At her chamber, he pushed the door open with his shoulder and set her gently but firmly back on the bed.

"Stay. Here."

Before she could argue again, he turned and called for the guards. Two Elven sentinels appeared within moments, taking their posts at the door.

Keisha crossed her arms and muttered, "Ridiculous. Absolutely ridiculous." But warmth threaded through the annoyance, wrapping around her like a shield she hadn't known she needed.

A golden eye appeared at the window. Kimras's draconic chuckle rumbled. "We heard that."

Keisha scowled at the window. "Not fair."

From the hall, Ong's voice joined the growl. "Do you want me to summon Lord Karrenen to keep you in place?"

Her eyes widened. "You wouldn't dare."

"Try me," he answered, perfectly calm.

Before she could reply, another voice filled the chamber, calm, resonant, impossible to ignore.

"You two don't need to trouble yourselves. I am already here."

Keisha stiffened. Lord Karrenen materialized in the doorway, robes shimmering with crystalline light. His presence stilled the very air. His gaze swept over her, then turned to Ong and Kimras.

"I heard she was injured," he said evenly. "And what has she done now?"

Keisha flushed and looked away. "You didn't need to come, Father. I'm fine."

"She refuses to stay put," Kimras rumbled, unrepentant.

Karrenen's eyes narrowed slightly as he approached the bed. "Keisha..."

She groaned and flopped back against the pillows. "Fine! I surrender! You all win!"

At the doorway, Valeon and Kaelorn, who had wandered in during the commotion, burst into laughter.

Keisha pouted, sinking deeper into the blankets. "It's not fair. How can I win against all of you?"

As if rehearsed, the entire room answered in perfect unison:

"You can't."

Laughter rolled through the chamber, warm as sunlight breaking through storm clouds.

Keisha huffed, but the corners of her mouth betrayed her. Compared to the silence of her old wounds, this noisy, bossy storm of family was the best kind of chaos. Ong with his scowls, Kimras with his roars, her father with his quiet disapproval overbearing, yes, but all of it born of love.

She wouldn't trade them for anything.

Still, as she pulled the blanket up to her chin, she muttered, "Doesn't mean they're not bossy."

A muffled chuckle drifted through the door. Every one of them had heard her.

Chapter 40
The Skies of Lyra'el

The skies above Lyra'el shimmered like a dream spun from starlight. Silver and gold rippled across the clouds, waves of brilliance drifting slowly through an endless blue. The very air hummed, carrying the resonance of the realm's eternal song.

Prince Gailen could only stare.

"By the gods," he whispered, the words stolen by the wind before they ever touched the ground.

Beneath him, Aurelia glided with effortless grace, crystalline wings scattering rainbows that danced across the air. A low hum rose from her throat, pure and clear, like glass singing in the sun.

Beside them, Verdantia carved through the heavens, her emerald wings gleaming like living blades. Thalorian sat tall against the wind, his jade-fire gaze sharp though it never lingered. Too much beauty. Too much wonder.

"I have seen enchanted groves and the floating city of my kin," he said at last, voice carrying softly. "But this... this is like flying inside a prayer."

"It's more than that," Gailen replied, his tone tightening. "It's a sanctuary. And even sanctuaries bleed, Thalorian."

The words brought back memories. He saw Crystal Vale again the day Aurelia's wing tore midflight, silver light pouring from the wound like shattered stars. He had felt every pulse of her pain burn through his own body, a torment shared. Yet she had flown on, roaring her defiance into the storm. That was the day he had learned how deep their bond truly ran and how fragile even the brightest refuge became when shadow struck.

The wonder faded from Thalorian's gaze, replaced by grim understanding. "You mean the attacks."

Gailen nodded, his eyes scanning the radiant plains below. Perfect on the surface, yet tense, bracing against a storm unseen. "I've heard the whispers. Shadow dragons. Abyssal kin at the borders. This isn't the Lyra'el I dreamed of as a child."

"Radiantus and Aurelius have held firm," Thalorian said, his palm resting against Verdantia's neck. The great emerald dragon rumbled low, a sound like thunder rolling through the heavens. "Light and crystal stand together. Every strike of shadow has been broken."

"Even so," Gailen murmured, steel flashing in his voice, "the name Abyssal Dominion should have died with its master."

Thalorian's jaw tightened, his voice edged with warning. "The world does not forget evil, even when it sleeps. The question is who has woken it and why now."

Gailen's answer came after a long silence, his gaze never leaving the radiant spires ahead.

"I need to find Ong. He was here when the shadows came. If anyone knows how deep this runs, it's him. And Keisha..." His voice caught. "By the gods, after everything she endured, to hear that name again..."

Aurelia's wings shifted, and the air itself seemed to sing with her, every feather shimmering like sunlight on water.

"She is stronger than they know," Aurelia whispered. "But even the strongest hearts ache in silence."

Thalorian's eyes flicked toward Gailen, sharp with unspoken meaning. "Do you think he has told her yet?"

Gailen swallowed hard. "I don't know. But if he hasn't... he will. And when he does." His gaze fixed on the glowing gates ahead, gleaming like a promise and a warning. "I'll be there."

The dragons banked together, their wings cutting arcs of light across the sky. The closer they drew to Lyra'el, the heavier the air became—not with heat or shadow, but with purpose. The sanctuary gleamed like a star in the morning, bracing itself for what was to come.

And within those shining walls waited Ong, along with truths too long buried. Truths that could shatter not only Lyra'el's fragile refuge... but the bonds that held them all together.

Just as the radiant spires of Lyra'el broke through the clouds, gleaming like the bones of the stars themselves, the sky shuddered.

A ripple.

A fracture.

Starlight bent, as though the heavens themselves recoiled.

Gailen's head snapped upward. "Above!"

The answer was a shriek high, hollow, ancient.

Voraxia burst from the rift, her onyx scales devouring the light until she became a wound in the sky. Wings of smoke unfurled like a shroud as she plummeted, jaws wide in predatory fury.

A second roar followed, deeper and resonant enough to rattle the marrow in their bones.

Vorathos tore through the clouds behind her, a storm of abyssal hunger. Crimson mist bled from the spines along her back, poisoning the air as she spiraled downward, claws gleaming like razors, eyes burning with hate.

"Break formation!" Thalorian's command cracked across the wind.

Verdantia wheeled sharply left, emerald wings flaring as she drew in a breath that rumbled like an oncoming tempest. A heartbeat later, she loosed it in a thunderous roar that split the air like shattering wood.

Gailen stayed tight to Aurelia's back, his hand flying to the Crystalbow. The weapon bloomed into his grasp, its prismed arc gleaming with starlight, the string humming beneath his fingers. "Not today," he growled, drawing it taut.

Voraxia shrieked, diving hard. Gailen loosed. The arrow screamed through the heavens, striking her wing joint in a burst of searing brilliance. The Shadow Dragon howled, twisting, but she did not fall.

"She's fast," he muttered through clenched teeth.

"Then strike faster," Thalorian replied, his jaw set like stone. Verdantia rolled beneath a torrent of abyssal flame, green fire flashing along her scales as Thalorian drove the Arborblade through the dark.

Another spray of black fire raked across the sky. Aurelia surged upward, her wings flaring wide. Light exploded from her body in a radiant shield that wrapped Gailen in a cocoon of silver brilliance.

For a heartbeat, the heavens froze, shadow and light clashing in midair, sparks raining down like meteors. And in that breathless instant, Gailen felt it: the sharp echo of memory. The day in Crystal Vale when Aurelia's wing had torn, spilling light like broken stars. The terror of nearly losing her.

His pulse hammered. History could not be allowed to repeat itself.

Far below, Kimras lifted his golden head from the cliffs of Lyra'el. His ancient eyes narrowed on the shadowed wings blotting out the sky. Even the air seemed to shrink from them. His roar split the heavens, shaking the crystal peaks.

"Radiantus!" Kimras bellowed. "They've returned!"

From the highest spire came an answering note deeper than thunder, ringing like a thousand blades struck against an anvil of flame.

Radiantus, the Platinum Dragon, surged skyward. His vast platinum wings unfurled like war banners, each scale burning with divine fire. His roar poured through the clouds like a hymn that made the shadows recoil.

Kimras rose to meet him, gold and platinum cutting across the heavens together, twin titans, guardians reborn.

"Hold them," Radiantus thundered, his voice resounding like a thousand bells. "We fly."

The sky erupted.

Aurelia and Verdantia spiraled as one, crystal and emerald weaving a barrier of light and leaf. Gailen and Thalorian held fast on their backs, weapons flashing, outnumbered, but unbroken.

"Gailen!" Thalorian's voice carried over the storm as Verdantia banked hard from Vorathos's snapping jaws.

"I see her!" Gailen called.

He drew the Crystalbow. Light coalesced into a taut, glowing string, pulsing with his heartbeat. He pulled not with muscle alone, but with every fragment of will he possessed.

Light. Radiance. Revelation.

The arrow flared into being, no longer a mere shard but a burning spear of sunfire. He loosed. The air cracked.

The shot slammed into Voraxia's chest. Her onyx scales split, shadow peeling from her body in molten ribbons. She screamed, staggering back, the night itself unraveling around her.

Verdantia dove like a falling star, wings folding tight. Thalorian's Arborblade swept in a blazing emerald arc, its light burning away the venom streaming from Vorathos's maw.

Verdantia's growl rumbled like the deep roots of the earth. "They will regret waking the wilds."

Above the radiant gates, gold, platinum, crystal, and emerald flared against shadow and abyss. The battle had truly begun, and Lyra'el itself trembled on the edge of ruin.

Radiantus loomed above, his voice rolling like thunder.

"When will you learn," he bellowed, "that Lyra'el is forbidden to your kind? To raise tooth or flame against a bonded rider of the Noble Dragons is to sign your own death."

Voraxia hissed, her onyx form faltering under his presence, but Vorathos only pressed closer, tail lashing like iron.

Then the air itself split.

A third dragon burst from the rift, wings violet and aflame with amethyst light. Amara.

Ong stood upon her back, the dragonlance raised, its gleaming tip catching the firelight like a spear of judgment.

He said nothing. He didn't need to.

The weight of his presence and Amara's might was enough.

Voraxia wavered. Hemmed in by crystal, emerald, gold, and platinum, she bared her fangs in furious defiance. Shadows bled from her wings like ink unraveling in water.

"We will return," she hissed.

"And we will be waiting," Amara answered, her voice vast and deliberate, resonant with unshaken resolve.

The black rift folded inward, swallowing shadow and abyss. In a rush of smoke, they were gone.

Silence fell.

Aurelia exhaled, crystalline wings flaring once before folding in. "Too close," she murmured.

Kimras growled low, his golden eyes still fixed on the empty sky. "Far too close."

Radiantus's gaze swept across the survivors before settling on Ong. His voice carried like tempered steel.

"Well timed."

Ong lowered the dragonlance and stroked Amara's neck. She rumbled a satisfied chuff, dipping her head toward Gailen in brief acknowledgment.

"She said the skies didn't feel right," Ong said at last, his tone quiet but edged with certainty. "We followed her instincts."

Above, the spires of Lyra'el blazed once more as light bled back into the heavens. The realm's eternal song rose again, fragile but unbroken.

And yet none of them truly relaxed.

Not yet.

Because shadows that flee do not vanish.

They wait.

Chapter 41

The Storm on the Horizon

The shadows of Flameford never slept. Beneath the smoldering sky and the jagged ruins of what had once been Phoenix's stronghold, something ancient stirred.

Voraxia landed first, her onyx wings folding with a hiss of displaced air. The ground beneath her blackened claws cracked, embers sparking where her tail coiled.

Vorathos followed, descending with a guttural growl, her spined form wreathed in the remnants of the crimson mist that still clung to her from battle. The air thickened with dread as the two dark dragons came to rest at the foot of the obsidian tower.

From within, a voice spoke. No greetings. No warmth.

"Enter."

The great doors groaned open at the command of unseen forces. Shadow flowed like liquid through the cracks, curling around their feet as they moved forward. Inside, the chamber was vast and dark, lit only by the faint pulse of runes carved into black stone.

A figure sat upon a throne wrought from twisted steel and scorched bone. Cloaked in darkness, they radiated quiet power. The air vibrated subtly with it, a presence that needed no name, only obedience.

Voraxia bowed her head, wings folding tightly. "The skies of Lyra'el were contested. Radiantus and Kimras joined the defense. Aurelia and Verdantia fought beside their riders."

Vorathos added, voice rough as a landslide. "The Amethyst came too. With Ong upon her back. We were driven back."

A pause.

The figure steepled their fingers, considering the words.

"So. The ancient ones stir. The realms unite. And still, Lyra'el breathes."

Neither dragon dared respond.

"We have lingered too long," the figure said softly. "The time for skirmishes is over."

The room fell colder.

"You will gather every shadow dragon. Every Abyssal beast that yet draws breath. You will take them to Lyra'el."

The runes shivered, their glow deepening to a hungry red. Vorathos's tail twitched, restrained violence coiling in her muscles. Even Voraxia's wings shuddered, bracing against the weight of what had just been declared.

"You will bring them to Lyra'el," the figure continued, voice rising with an echo that rang like a funeral bell, "and you will not return until the Celestial realm is ash."

Voraxia lifted her head, silver-white eyes glittering with cruel hunger. "And the riders?"

The figure's presence pressed down like a storm.

"None shall remain. And the Eladrin girl Keisha, you will see to her yourself. No chains. No bargaining. Her death will break more than walls."

The words fell into the chamber, heavy as doom. Shadows trembled across the obsidian carvings.

Vorathos's abyssal blue gaze narrowed, her voice a low growl. "You would risk the wrath of Radiantus? He has spoken threaten the noble riders, and we sign our own death."

The figure stilled. For a heartbeat, silence gripped the cavern. Then the shadows around the throne writhed violently, flaring like a storm of living smoke. The figure's voice tore through the chamber, no longer silken but raw, searing, unrestrained:

"Do not dare speak to me of his warnings!"

The obsidian walls groaned. The blood-red runes flared brighter, the air pressing heavy until even the twin sisters bowed low beneath its crushing weight. Voraxia hissed, wings trembling; Vorathos lowered her head, fury flickering beneath her unease.

Then, as swiftly as it came, the fury ebbed. The shadows coiled back around the throne, pulsing like a heartbeat. The figure's voice returned to its cold, deliberate calm.

"He will protect them. He always does. That is his weakness. And it will be his undoing."

Voraxia's lips curled into a predatory smile. "Then the skies will burn."

Vorathos's growl rumbled deep in her chest, reluctant but bound by command. "It will be done."

The figure rose slightly, their form a ripple of shadow against the burning runes, impossible and undeniable.

"Go. Prepare the end."

The cavern thundered with wings. Ash spiraled from the ground as the dragons launched skyward, their departure shaking the stone and scattering sparks into the smoldering air.

When silence at last returned, the figure remained unmoving on the throne. The chamber breathed around them, shadows curling like smoke across scorched stone.

A single thought lingered, dark as the abyss itself:

Radiantus has returned. Our time is short.

The storm had reached its heart.

And Lyra'el would burn.

Chapter 42

Shields of the Sky

Meanwhile, in Lyra'el, the light was beginning to return.

Before Ong could lead Prince Gailen to Keisha, a familiar voice cut through the quiet hum of magic.

"Don't you dare act like I should still be in bed," Keisha said as she stepped from the healing pavilion, posture steady despite the faint bruises that traced her skin.

Ong spun, eyes wide. "Keisha! What are you doing up? You should be resting—" Relief washed over his face, sweeping away the edge of worry. For a breath, he looked ready to scold her—yet pride and protectiveness tangled in his expression, neither winning.

Keisha's lips curved in a faint smile, her chin lifting. "I have rested," she said firmly. "And I'm fine."

Before Ong could argue, a calm, resonant voice drifted down from above.

Aurelius, the Celestial Dragon, descended in a sweeping arc, his vast wings shimmering with inner starlight. He touched the terrace with impossible grace, eyes glowing as they fixed on Ong.

"She is healed," Aurelius said, his voice deep and gentle. "The bruises will fade. The wounds are closed. Her spirit is intact and strong."

Ong's arms stayed folded, but a reluctant nod betrayed the weight sliding from his chest. His stance remained taut, protectiveness coiled in every muscle.

Keisha inclined her head. "Thank you."

Aurelius's crystalline chuckle rippled like glass struck by light. "It is not thanks I seek, child. Only peace restored to the wounded."

Gailen's gaze lingered. For a moment, he hesitated, torn between silence and truth. Then Keisha met his eyes, unflinching.

"I know the Dominion name has been reborn," she said, voice firm as steel. "But they will find that things have changed. And they will be stopped just as before."

A quiet fire burned in her words, daring the shadows to return. Ong drew her close, one hand steady at her back, a gesture at once protective and grounding.

From the archway to the inner sanctum, Lord Karrenen emerged, robes still sparking with enchantment.

"Radiantus requests everyone's presence," he said, tone heavy with urgency. "A gathering in the central sanctum. All riders and dragons. Now."

Ong inclined his head. Gailen stepped to Keisha's side, the air taut with unspoken truths, and together they followed.

Verdantia and Aurelia landed in tandem, wings folding with practiced grace as their luminous eyes swept the skies. The silence that followed was brittle, fragile as glass beneath a storm's weight. Yet both dragons held their heads high, unyielding as they moved toward the heart of Lyra'el.

Behind them, the celestial realm itself seemed to brace.

The central sanctum shimmered with quiet tension. Crystal platforms pulsed beneath the gathering of riders, dragons, and elders. At the chamber's center stood Radiantus, his vast platinum form aglow with restrained power. The hush deepened as dragons furled their wings and riders straightened instinctively, drawn upright by the gravity of his presence. He needed no words to command reverence; his being steadied the room.

"Hear me," Radiantus said, his voice rumbling with the weight of ages. "Another attack is imminent. The last was not their strength, but their measure. They will return."

The chamber stilled, as if Lyra'el itself had paused to listen.

"This will not be a skirmish," Radiantus continued, diamond-like silver eyes gleaming like molten steel. "They will come to destroy Lyra'el. To end us."

Dragons shifted uneasily, wings brushing. Riders exchanged tense glances, fingers tightening on staves and hilts.

Then Aurelius stepped forward, crystalline wings folding like sheets of light. "If any wish to leave, now is the time. The Celestial Dragons will carry you to Crystal Vale, where you will be safe until the battle ends."

At his word, radiant dragons moved to the fore, wings stretching in solemn readiness.

But no one moved.

An elder elf, with spun silver hair and molten gold eyes, stepped out. Her voice rang clear, unwavering. "We will not leave. If you fight, we will fight. Lyra'el's halls will not fall unguarded."

A murmur swelled, agreement spreading like wildfire.

Radiantus inclined his head, the faintest echo of pride in his thunderous presence. "Then let it be known: Lyra'el does not stand alone."

Dragons unfurled their wings in a silent salute, the chamber brightening with crystal shimmer and flame. Riders stood tall beside them, resolve anchoring them like iron in stone.

War was coming.

But so was unity.

From the crowd, a young woman with braids of gold stepped forward, gaze steady as she approached Radiantus. She bowed low, then lifted her chin to meet his diamond-like silver eyes.

"Will you want me as your dragon rider for this battle?" Tahlira's voice carried, clear and strong.

Radiantus tilted his massive head, scales bathing her in silver fire. "It could be dangerous."

Tahlira's chin lifted higher. "It is always dangerous for dragon riders."

Kimras shifted, the golden dragon's gaze brushing Keisha before returning to Radiantus. "She speaks the truth."

Radiantus gave a solemn nod. "Then gather the others. Tell the Platinum riders to prepare."

Aurelius stepped forward, luminous wings folding, presence suffused with quiet divinity. "While dragon riders are indeed valuable, the Celestial Dragons will forgo them in this battle. We must fly unbound, free to heal and to guard without endangering those we carry."

Lord Karrenen inclined his head, fingers steepled. "So, it must be. The Celestial Dragons hold the light itself within their veins. To hinder that is to weaken us all."

A murmur swept the chamber, solemn but resolute, as roles sharpened into clarity. Each dragon and rider accepted their place in the defense of Lyra'el.

Radiantus turned, gaze lingering on Kimras, Amara, Verdantia, and Aurelius in turn, diamond-like silver eyes heavy with unspoken questions. But before he could voice them, Kimras stepped forward.

"Do not ask, Radiantus," the Ancient Golden Dragon declared, voice ringing firm. "We, with our dragon riders, will fight. This battle is not only for Lyra'el. It is for all of Vacari."

Agreement rippled through the noble dragons. Wings shifted, scales glinting as if ready for fire and storm alike.

Ong leaned toward Keisha, his voice low and taut. "Would it do me any good to tell you not to ride Kimras into battle?"

Keisha's smile was calm, unshaken. "No. You know my magic will be needed."

Prince Gailen gave a short laugh, glancing between them. "Seems your wife is just as stubborn as you are, Ong."

Ong's dry look was answer enough. You are not helping.

From the edge of the sanctum, an elder stepped forward, voice steady with purpose.

"Platinum Dragon riders, follow me. It is time you received a gift long kept hidden."

Curiosity flickered, but they obeyed. The elder led them into a narrow corridor veined with starlit crystal. At its end loomed a vaulted door etched with ancient runes. He laid his hand upon the seal. A pulse of light rippled outward, and the stone parted with a sigh.

Inside, resting on velvet pedestals, shimmered shields of inner radiance.

"These," the elder said, lifting his hand, "are the Lightforged Shields crafted centuries ago for those sworn to defend the Celestial Realm."

One rider stepped forward, awe in their voice. "What do they do?"

"They form a barrier around rider and dragon alike," the elder replied. "They reflect dark magic, strengthen defenses, and resonate with the purity of your intent. Treat them with honor."

One by one, the riders approached, reverent hands lifting the radiant relics. Light cascaded across the chamber walls as shields gleamed like captured starlight.

But when Tahlira stepped forward, the elder paused. Upon the final pedestal rested a shield unlike the rest, its surface veined with silver light, sigils carved deeper, the metal faintly alive.

"This one," the elder said softly, "was forged at Radiantus's command, long ago. It was meant for the rider who would stand beside him when

Vacari's need was greatest. It will answer only to one bound to him by oath and spirit."

Radiantus lowered his head, diamond-like silver eyes steady upon Tahlira. "Take it."

Her fingers closed around the grip, and the runes blazed to life. Silver fire leapt across its surface, resonating with Radiantus's glow until dragon and relic pulsed in unison.

A hush fell. Even the air seemed to bow to the weight of the moment.

Tahlira lifted the shield high, its light wrapping her in Radiantus's strength. "I will not fail you."

Radiantus's reply rumbled through the chamber, deep as the earth and vast as the stars. "Nor will I."

Lord Karrenen appeared again, enchantments shimmering across his robes. His voice was low but certain. "Kaelorn has offered to join the civilians, aiding the barrier around Lyra'el's mountains and towers. Valeon will remain here, assisting the medics."

Kaelorn's eyes swept the gathering one last time. "Good luck to you all. Stay sharp, stay safe."

Valeon stepped forward hesitantly, voice little more than a whisper. "Do you think I can do this?"

A medic smiled, firm but kind. "You've learned much, Valeon. Your training may not be complete, but you are ready."

Uncertainty flickered, shadowing his eyes.

Ong stepped to his side, resting a steady hand on his shoulder. "You've come a long way from being a puppet to that stranger, to a man who knows where he belongs."

Valeon's expression softened with gratitude. "Thank you, Ong." He turned, shoulders squared with new resolve and followed the medics toward the supply pavilion.

Lord Karrenen moved to Keisha, drawing her into a brief, warm embrace. For a heartbeat, she stilled, the weight of his words pressing into her chest.

"My daughter."

The phrase sank deeper than any magic, steadying her even as it left an ache.

His voice dropped into the lilting cadence of Elven, meant for her alone.

"Belethiel, yáre enethiel."

(Be careful, my daughter.)

Then softer still, words like a secret long carried:

"Nin úva telanth ilthi... náni uin nar ilthi náren sira."

(I could not bear to lose you... not as I lost your mother.)

Keisha froze. The Elven flowed through her like music she had always known, its meaning cutting deeper than any blade. *He loved my mother.* The thought thundered in her chest, reverberating with the storm that gathered at Lyra'el's gates.

The Celestial elders fell in beside Karrenen, footsteps ringing against crystal floors as they moved toward the barrier.

All around, the city stirred. Dragons took their stations, wings spreading in gleaming ranks. Enchanters wove fresh wards across the outer rings. Armor clattered, blades sang free, and the hum of magic deepened into a rising chord.

Together, Lyra'el marched toward preparation for war and whatever dawn might follow.

Above, the stars still burned.

But soon, they would be put to the test.

Chapter 43
The Sky Holds Its Breath

In Lyra'el, silence clung to the city like a breath held too long, stretched taut and trembling. The crystal towers shimmered in the pale light of dawn, scattering shards of brilliance across the valley below. The beauty of the suspended bridges, their lattice of silver threads catching the sunrise, belied the storm gathering just beyond the horizon. The wind that wound between spires carried no birdsong, only a low, expectant hush, as if the city itself had gone still in anticipation.

Across the dragon terraces, riders stood beside their bonded companions, armor polished to a cold gleam. The Platinum dragons were already in formation, their massive wings half-unfurled, eyes reflecting the silver wards that shimmered faintly at the city's edge. Each dragon radiated power, their Lightforged Shields interlacing in a lattice of brilliance, while the Elders and enchanters chanted in steady cadence. Their voices braided with the city's eternal hum, weaving light into a dome that wrapped Lyra'el like a gleaming fortress in the sky.

Within the healing sanctum, the air was taut with purpose. Medics darted between rows of prepared cots, arms laden with linen rolls, crystal vials, and bundles of herbs. Alchemists stirred luminous draughts in glass vessels that pulsed like captive stars, while apprentices whispered spells of mending under their breath. Every movement carried urgency, but not panic. They knew what was coming; they had been preparing for this day their whole lives.

On the eastern flank, Prince Gailen stood tall in his gleaming armor, hand resting on Aurelia's ridged neck. The Crystalbow lay strapped across his back, its string vibrating faintly, resonant with her breath as though the weapon had already chosen the battle's rhythm. Aurelia's crystalline scales caught the sun, scattering radiant shards of light into the darkening sky.

"You'll likely need to break their shadows when they come," Aurelia murmured, her voice like wind-chimes stirred by a distant breeze. "Blinding light may be our best chance to shatter their formations."

Gailen's jaw tightened. His heart pounded in time with the bow's glow, but his eyes never wavered from the horizon. "Then I'll be ready."

On the western edge, Thalorian's silhouette cut a proud figure astride Verdantia. The Arborblade was already drawn, its emerald edge humming with a song older than the city itself, a resonance that seemed to draw strength from the roots of the mountains below. Verdantia's great wings flexed, shaking frost from their golden-green feathers.

"If they seek to breach the wards from the ground," Verdantia rumbled, her voice like leaves whispering in a storm, "then here, amid the trees of the Singing Forest, we will break them. Let their darkness falter against the wild."

"We will not yield," Thalorian vowed, raising the Arborblade. His words were not loud, yet they rang clear through the bond he shared with his dragon, carried to the hearts of those who stood beside them.

High above, Kimras carved a steady path through the heavens, his vast golden wings cutting through the dimming sky. Morning light rolled down his scales like rivers of fire, each beat of his wings reverberating with ancient power. On his back, Keisha sat poised, her red hair whipped by the wind, her hands glowing faintly with gathering magic. Her green eyes fixed on the horizon, where shadows gathered like a wound in the sky. She spoke no words, but her silence burned with iron resolve.

Amara swept alongside them, her amethyst wings casting arcs of violet fire as they caught the dawn. Ong leaned low against her neck, the dragonlance strapped to his back gleaming with deadly promise. His eyes scanned the rolling clouds with the keen focus of a man who had fought, bled, and chosen to belong to this place. Amara's tail flicked in irritation, her voice ringing sharp in the minds of those near her. "The air stinks of their corruption already. My head aches from it. Disgusting."

Between the noble dragons soared the Celestial beings, radiant, riderless, their vast wings spanning the sky like banners of living light. They circled above the city as though forming a second, higher firmament, their silver brilliance rippling in harmony with Lyra'el's wards below.

On the highest spire, Kaelorn stood at the nexus of magic, robes aflame with woven light. His arms rose, palms outstretched, as streams of silver fire bled from the stones into the air. His voice thundered through the linkstones, unwavering and sure: "Hold your positions. Watch for any fracture points. If you see even the faintest flicker, speak it."

From the sanctum balconies, the citizens pressed together, their faces pale but unbroken, lips moving in silent prayers to gods who might no longer listen. No one fled. None looked away. They knew if Lyra'el fell, there would be no refuge left.

Then, the wind died.

The dawn dimmed.

A crawling tide of blackness crept across the horizon, coiling and seething with venomous intent. The air itself shuddered. The first notes of battle struck like a drumbeat in the bones.

From the south, the shadows split wide.

Voraxia tore through the veil, her wings unfurling like serrated scythes of smoke, her onyx scales glimmering with corrupted light. Her jagged smile gleamed as she dove, a predator savoring the kill before the strike.

To the east, the horizon bled crimson. Vorathos surged upward, vast and terrible, her body wreathed in burning mist. Each beat of her wings smeared fire across the sky, a herald of ruin.

Behind them, an onyx host poured forth dark dragons by the dozen, their wings blotting out the light, their maws spilling flame blacker than night. The storm had come for Lyra'el.

The crystal city shone like a beacon against the encroaching dark, silver wards blazing at full strength. Every soul knew it then: this day, the sky itself would decide their fate.

Voraxia's gaze swept the battlefield until it locked on Keisha astride Kimras. Her jagged lips twisted into a sneer, her eyes alight with cruel delight.

"You're back for another beating, elf?"

Keisha's laugh rang out, fierce and unshaken, her green eyes blazing like emerald fire. "Voraxia, you're still full of hot air."

Kimras answered before she could say more. His roar cracked like golden thunder, rolling across the heavens, making the silver bridges of Lyra'el shiver as though they might splinter apart under the force. Light shimmered in waves from his scales, each pulse a declaration of defiance.

On the eastern horizon, Vorathos's abyssal gaze was fixed upon Amara and Ong. Smoke and flame curled from her spined maw as her voice ground out like boulders breaking beneath a volcanic tide. "Oh, you two again. I thought you'd learned your lesson."

Amara's wings snapped wide, their vast span searing the sky with violet flame. Sparks bled across her scales in jagged arcs as her mind-voice cut cold and amethyst-sharp through the storm. "Yes, but spare me your blunders. I forgot how much I despised the last dark dragon who whined. I've no wish for another headache."

Ong let out a short, rough laugh, a sound like steel grating on stone. He leaned low against her neck, his hand brushing her scales with easy familiarity. "Still got that sting, Amara."

Above them, the heavens writhed. Light and shadow slammed together in turbulent waves, the sky itself shuddering as though caught in the throes of some vast and merciless storm. The dance had begun.

Radiantus surged forward, his vast wings unfurling like banners of living silver. Tahlira rose proud upon his back, her hair streaming behind her as though it, too, had caught the dawn. With a single sweep, Radiantus turned the morning air into a gale, his voice thundering across the heavens, ancient power woven into every syllable.

"This is the only warning you will receive. Leave Lyra'el now or face certain defeat. You will not breach these skies."

Voraxia's hiss unfurled like poisoned silk, sliding across the battlefield. "We will not leave. It is you who will fall, Platinum fool."

Vorathos answered with a roar that split the air. Abyssal fire coiled along his spine, dripping molten streams that scarred the sky itself. "Abyssal flight engage the Platinum and Radiantus. Drown their shine in the deep."

Then Aurelius descended.

The Celestial Dragon carved a vast arc across the heavens, trailing a river of starlight that burned brighter than dawn. His voice carried not as thunder but as a calm, resonant, unshakable prayer.

"You underestimate the light, Shadow Queen. It will not yield to darkness. Light was not given to bow. It was given to endure."

The words struck the defenders like a benediction, echoing through the linkstones and into every heart that stood upon Lyra'el's terraces.

At his vow, the horizon tore apart.

The dark host erupted, a torrent of wings and fire. Dozens of shadowed dragons surged forward, their roars ripping the sky, their maws vomiting flame blacker than night. The air quaked with their descent.

The first collision came like the crash of worlds silver and gold colliding with smoke and abyssal fire. The storm broke in an explosion of light and shadow that painted the heavens in ruin and radiance.

Meanwhile, at the barrier's pinnacle, Kaelorn stood rooted at the nexus of the weave. His staff blazed with caged brilliance, streams of power flooding from the crystalline heart beneath the city into his veins. His arms trembled as he chanted, ancient words burning across the air in a tongue older than memory. Silver fire laced itself into the trembling dome, flaring bright once more.

From the eastern quarter came a shout through the linkstones: "Kaelorn! The ward falters! The weave is tearing!"

Kaelorn spun, robes snapping in the wind as he sprinted across the crystalline platform. Ahead, a section of the barrier wavered like a dying star, its threads unraveling into sparks. He slammed the butt of his staff down, and light flared outward in a torrent, knitting the strands together. The dome shone steady again, but the effort drove him to his knees. Sweat traced molten lines down his brow as he clutched the staff in both hands.

A watcher above the sanctum exhaled shakily. "It's holding again!"

The relief shattered in an instant. A massive shadow dragon slammed into the barrier, claws screeching against the silver weave. Sparks cascaded like meteors, the sound a shriek that pierced bone.

One of the Platinum dragons hurtled forward in a flash of steel and fire, its rider lowering his spear as they struck the beast with a crash that lit the sky. The shadow recoiled, wings flailing as it tumbled back into the maelstrom.

Kaelorn's knuckles whitened on his staff. His chest heaved, each breath ragged, every word of power scraped raw from his throat. "I do not know," he whispered into the storm, the confession meant for no ears but his own, "how long we can keep this up."

High above, Voraxia's fury boiled over. With a guttural snarl, she tore from her quarry and wheeled through the turbulent air, her colossal wings leaving a wake of roiling smoke. Her shadow streamed behind her like a living curse, staining the light as she arrowed toward Radiantus and Tahlira.

But Keisha's eyes narrowed, emerald fire sparking in their depths. She leaned low against Kimras, her voice a fierce whisper along their bond. The Ancient Golden Dragon responded instantly, banking hard into the path of the Shadowed Empress. His wings cleaved the storm winds, and his throat kindled with molten radiance. Then he opened his jaws and poured forth a torrent of searing gold — a sunburst unleashed across the sky. The blaze struck Voraxia head-on, swallowing her in fire that cracked the very air and lit the silver bridges below in molten reflection.

The Shadow Dragon reeled, shrieking as golden flame scalded her onyx scales. For a heartbeat, her form wavered, shadows peeling back, exposing a glimpse of something vulnerable beneath the corruption.

Through that breach surged Aurelia, crystalline wings flashing with razor light. Gailen rose in his saddle, the Crystalbow thrumming in his grip, its pulse synchronized with his heartbeat and Aurelia's. He drew back the bowstring, light condensing into a single blazing arrow, pure and unbroken. Every shred of his will poured into that radiant point.

"Now!" Aurelia's cry rang like a thousand glass bells.

The arrow flew. It struck Voraxia's shoulder with a shattering crack. Light exploded outward in a storm of crystalline shards, each fragment bursting into a sunflare that burned across her flank. Voraxia screamed, whipping her massive tail in fury. The strike missed Aurelia by a breath, but the force ripped the air apart, hurling glittering fragments of broken shadow and crystal into the wind.

Aurelia did not falter. With a roar like chimes turned to war-horns, she unfurled her wings in full and loosed a volley of radiant shards. They cut through the storm's darkness, embedding deep into Voraxia's hide, each strike igniting a flare of searing light. The heavens themselves trembled with the collision of brilliance against the void, devotion against malice, as the actual battle for Lyra'el roared into being.

Radiantus veered left, a sweep of his vast wings scattering silver fire across the sky. He surged into the path of three descending dark dragons, intercepting their charge toward the sanctum's ridge. His talons tore through shadowed flesh, rending one beast from the air, its scream dissolving into a trail of black flame.

—and then Vorathos struck.

She descended like a mountain of living abyss, her colossal wings dragging nightfall behind them. Crimson mist bled from her ridges; abyssal fire coiled in her throat. Her roar hammered the heavens, as if the sky itself were stone shattering under her fury.

Radiantus rose to meet her, his platinum form a blazing star against her darkness. His chest burned with celestial fire, and in one devastating exhalation, he loosed a beam of silver radiance. It met Vorathos's torrent of crimson flame in midair. The collision tore the heavens open. Light and shadow smashed together in a blinding detonation, shredding the clouds into ribbons. Shockwaves rippled across the valley, shuddering through every tower of Lyra'el.

Vorathos circled, smoke streaming from her fanged maw. Her voice was a growl of contempt. "You shine so brightly, Platinum. Let us see how long your light endures when I blot out the heavens."

Tahlira raised the Lightforged Shield, its surface blazing with sacred script that shimmered like molten emerald. When she lifted it high, the runes flared in unison with Radiantus's blazing scales, their powers intertwining, amplifying one another until light itself seemed to take form. The shield expanded into a radiant dome that wrapped around dragon and rider, a living fortress of faith and fire. Vorathos's abyssal fire struck like a tidal wave, crimson flame and shadow slamming against the barrier. The dome blazed brighter, searing the darkness until it fractured, splintered into sparks, and dissolved into nothing. More than a shield, it was a vow made visible, and an unbreakable bond forged between Radiantus and his rider.

Radiantus's eyes blazed, silver fire pouring from their depths. "Try. And fail." His roar boomed across the battlefield, deep and unyielding, echoing like war drums across the crystal peaks.

"You will not face me alone," he thundered. "Vacari stands with me."

Through the bond, his call ignited hearts. From every quarter of the sky, the noble dragons answered, their voices rising in a chorus of defiance. Golden, emerald, amethyst, and silver tones layered together, a storm of song that shook the heavens and made the city's crystal towers sing in resonance with their roar.

From below, the heavens split with twin streams of emerald and violet fire. Verdantia and Amara surged upward together, flanking the abyssal behemoth in a storm of color and flame. On Verdantia's back, Thalorian held the Arborblade aloft, its emerald edge pulsing with the wrath of the wild. Opposite him, Ong rose in the saddle, the dragonlance gleaming like a shard of vengeance across his back as Amara's wings painted the sky in violet fire. Between them, Keisha pressed her glowing hands to Kimras's golden scales, weaving threads of protective magic into a barrier that shimmered like living glass around them all.

Vorathos wheeled above, her vast shadow blotting the horizon. With a guttural bellow, she hurled herself forward in a second strike. Her maw yawned wide, abyssal fire coiling into a spiral of crimson death that promised to consume everything it touched.

Ong rose to meet it. Braced against Amara's neck, he lifted the dragonlance. His cry rang out, harsh and unyielding, like steel grinding across stone. He hurled the weapon with all his strength. The lance blazed as it flew, a streak of violet and silver that buried itself beneath Vorathos's armored shoulder. The weapon sank deep, piercing the abyssal flesh.

The Shadow Dragon's shriek tore across the sky, raw pain laced with fury. Black ichor rained down, sizzling like acid where it splashed against Lyra'el's glowing wards.

Verdantia seized the moment. With a resonant bellow, her emerald wings folded, and she plummeted in a lethal dive. Thalorian's arm swept the Arborblade in a perfect arc. Its radiant edge sang as it sliced through a writhing tendril of shadow spilling from Vorathos's wound. The cut ignited with green fire, a wave of living light bursting outward and slamming into the dark dragon's chest. The impact forced Vorathos back, her massive wings thrashing as she fought for balance amid the shredded clouds.

The defenders roared their defiance, voices carried on the wind. For the first time, the Abyssal Dragon faltered.

Across the battlefield, Aurelius rose with his Celestial kin. Vast silver wings cut the darkened sky, each beat scattering cascades of starlight. Together, the Celestials formed a living constellation, arcs of brilliance weaving radiant shields as they crashed into the onyx swarm head-on.

High above, Voraxia wheeled, her wings stretched with terrible grace, smoke coiling from her form like banners of war. The air itself chilled as her presence spread. Her voice ripped through the storm, venomous and triumphant. "Let me show you the Black Sun!"

From her chest, darkness erupted. A vortex spiraled outward, swelling into a sphere of writhing shadow that devoured the light. The heavens dimmed. Stars winked out, as though swallowed whole. The world sank beneath an endless eclipse. Even Lyra'el's crystalline hum faltered, muffled beneath the suffocating shroud.

But Aurelius did not bend. His massive form burned with inner radiance, scales flowing like molten silver. He soared higher, cutting into the darkness, his voice steady as a hymn. "Let the skies remember their light."

His chest blazed, and with a thunderous exhale, he released a pulse of pure celestial fire. A spear of brilliance lanced upward, striking the roiling heart of the Black Sun.

Light met shadow.

The collision detonated with apocalyptic fury. Silver radiance tangled with crimson flame, shredding the swirling shroud into ribbons of smoke. Fissures of brilliance cracked through the false night, tearing holes where daylight poured through in burning shafts. Each rupture revealed terrified faces on Lyra'el's terraces, momentarily bathed in silver glow.

Still Voraxia pressed forward, her silhouette a vast maw of hunger and hate. Her wings hammered against the radiant gale, shadow colliding with starfire. The Black Sun writhed and clawed at the sky.

And still Aurelius burned brighter.

Below, Gailen staggered beneath the weight of that clash. The oppressive dark clawed at his spirit, dragging at his breath, smothering his courage. Yet the Crystalbow pulsed steadily in his hands, its rhythm echoing Aurelia's song. Her presence surged through their bond, fierce and unyielding, lending him her strength.

Together, he thought. Always together.

He whispered through clenched teeth, "Let them see."

The bow answered. Radiance bloomed between his fingers, an arrow of pure intent drawn from the marrow of his will. He loosed, and the shot became a spear of sunfire, tearing through the dark.

It struck the heart of the Black Sun.

For a heartbeat, the void held, seething. Then the spear fractured, erupting into a storm of light. Shards of brilliance cascaded outward in blinding waves, ripping through the coiling shadows. The Black Sun buckled, fractured, and burst. The suffocating night ripped apart, light shattering through in radiant torrents.

The abyssal host shrieked as the storm consumed them. Dark dragons reeled, their wings buckling, as their forms tumbled through the air in chaos. Whole ranks scattered, blinded by radiance searing through their shadow-veins.

With a crystalline cry, Aurelia folded her wings and dove, streaking like a falling star. The Celestial Dragons plunged with her, a storm of silver and light carving a radiant path straight through the broken darkness.

Voraxia shrieked in fury, twisting against the unraveling eclipse. Her power bled away, the Black Sun collapsing in shreds of smoke and dying sparks. Her hateful gaze locked on Gailen.

High above, Aurelius met his eyes, white fire burning deep within his gaze. His voice carried over the battlefield, a sonorous hymn that rang louder than the storm itself. "Well struck, Prince. The stars themselves bear witness."

Meanwhile, Vorathos wheeled back toward Radiantus, rage boiling in every thunderous beat of her vast wings. The jagged wound beneath her shoulder still poured black fire, dripping like molten tar, yet she drove herself onward with reckless ferocity. Abyssal magic seethed from her talons in storm-born ribbons of crimson and shadow. Her roar was a cataclysm, mountains collapsing in sound, the sky itself quaking with her fury.

But Radiantus was waiting.

The Platinum Dragon flared his wings wide, silver brilliance cascading like waterfalls of light. His gaze burned steady, fixed upon her descent. Tahlira's cry rang fiercely at his back, a clarion call that sharpened his resolve.

"This ends now."

Radiantus's chest ignited, molten light surging to his throat. He exhaled, unleashing a column of celestial fire that tore the heavens apart. The beam was pure wrath and purity entwined, and it did not blaze alone. From across the chaos, Aurelius wheeled in midair, his own radiance building until the sky itself seemed to hold its breath. He joined his light to Radiantus's, and the twin torrents fused into a single, devastating spear of starlit fury.

The heavens ignited.

The combined strike hammered into Vorathos's onrushing darkness, tearing her abyssal fire apart thread by thread. Shadow writhed and shredded under the assault. Silver fire and starlight carved across her vast chest, across wings black as midnight, peeling away scale and sinew until streams of sizzling ichor rained onto the glowing dome below.

Vorathos screamed, her voice a storm of rage and anguish that echoed across the mountains. She faltered mid-dive, twisting violently as the light forced her back, driving her upward and away. Clouds split beneath her thrashing wings, the sky itself scarred by her retreat.

On the terraces below, the people cried out—not with terror, but in awe. Faces upturned, they watched their champions blaze against the abyss, the firmament itself aflame with silver, emerald, violet, and gold.

The Dragons of Vacari roared as one, the sound a hymn of defiance. Their wings flashed in radiant arcs, a living tapestry unfurling across the storm-wracked sky.

And as Voraxia writhed within the sundered light of Aurelia's storm, Vorathos gathered herself once more. With a bone-shaking bellow, she hurled her massive form toward Aurelius. Hurricanes whipped from her wings, darkness streaming from her scales in choking rivers that painted the dawn like ink spilled across parchment. Her eyes glared with venomous resolve, fixed on the Celestial's burning form.

However, the Platinum Dragons were already in motion.

In flawless unison, they surged into her path, rider and dragon fused by will and bond. Their Lightforged Shields burst into radiant life, domes overlapping until they became a wall of living brilliance. Steel flashed as riders raised their blades, their battle cries weaving with the thunder of wings and the roars of dragons.

Vorathos slammed into them with the force of a falling mountain. Her claws raked across the shields, casting a storm of sparks. Crimson fire boiled from her jaws, pouring against the radiant barrier. Yet the domes held. Each impact flared brighter, as if the courage of the riders themselves fueled the ancient sigils carved into the shields.

Aurelius soared above, his vast wings sweeping forward. Silver radiance cascaded down like a second dawn, bathing the defenders in divine fire. His calm presence steadied the line, and where despair had lurked, resolve burned brighter.

Above them all, the clash of steel, light, fang, and shadow rolled through the skies like a war symphony.

Lyra'el's defenders did not break.

They did not falter.

They became the wall.

Verdantia and Amara carved through the storm, their wings cleaving the choking black mists that coiled across the battlefield. Emerald fire streamed from Verdantia's pinions in sweeping arcs, while Amara's amethyst blaze tore through the gloom like a rain of falling stars. Their flight carved radiant scars into the darkness, a defiance written in flame.

On Verdantia's back, Thalorian rose tall and unshaken, the Arborblade glowing a fierce green in his grip, its edge thrumming with the pulse of the living wild. Across from him, Ong crouched low on Amara's neck, dragonlance poised, his stance braced against the storm, eyes blazing with resolve.

Vorathos lunged to meet them. Her abyssal wings drove her downward with savage force, claws stretched wide, void fire boiling between her fangs. The air itself buckled beneath the fury of her descent, the sky folding inward as though it were being dragged into her wake.

Ong's voice rang out, raw and fierce, carrying across the storm like steel tearing stone. He rose and hurled the dragonlance. The weapon cut through the dark like a bolt of lightning, slamming beneath Vorathos's front leg and embedding deep in her flesh.

The impact was thunder: steel split scale and sinew. Black ichor burst forth in a scorching torrent, hissing as it rained across the shimmering dome below.

Vorathos roared, a sound so vast it rattled the crystal towers of Lyra'el and shook the mountains themselves. Her massive wings faltered, the rhythm of her dive shattered into chaos.

Thalorian was already moving. The Arborblade swept out in a radiant arc, its emerald edge blazing with primal fury. Verdantia's roar merged with the song of the blade, a harmony that became a tide of green fire. The stroke ripped through the abyssal shadows trailing from Vorathos's wound, shredding them into burning fragments that fell like smoldering leaves.

The blast struck home. Vorathos staggered, her colossal chest lit with emerald fire, the corruption on her scales peeled away in sizzling streams of black smoke. She reeled with a howl that split the storm, driven backward through the writhing dark.

Above, the skies of Lyra'el convulsed with colliding forces. Silver radiance and abyssal shadow clashed in vast, whirling currents, tearing the heavens into a maelstrom of flame, light, and void. Yet through the chaos, the defenders of Vacari held their formation. Wings gleamed like radiant banners. Blades flashed. Roars of defiance wove through the storm, each cry a vow.

They would not yield. Not now. Not ever.

High above, Voraxia and Vorathos circled, their once-regal forms battered and scarred. Smoke trailed from Vorathos's wound, crimson mist swirling with her fury. Where they had counted on numbers and terror, they now saw ruin. Their dark flight reeled in disarray. Shadow dragons shrieked as radiant arrows pierced them, as emerald fire and violet flame tore their wings to tatters. Abyssal beasts spiraled toward the horizon, black ichor raining in their wake.

The noble dragons of Vacari held the skies. Their united roars rolled like earthquakes through the crystal city, their radiant scales blazing as though the heavens themselves had descended to shield Lyra'el.

Voraxia's eyes burned with venom, her malice pouring out in waves so hot it warped the air. She lashed her tail again and again, every stroke carving scars of darkness across the broken dawn.

Beside her, Vorathos hovered, chest still bleeding radiant wounds that smoked and hissed in the air. Her abyssal eyes burned cold, sharper than her sister's fire, calculating and cruel. She was already measuring not only the clash before her, but the war yet to come.

The two dark titans drifted side by side, wings shuddering as they looked down upon the ruin of their scattered host. Shadowed dragons reeled through the air, some plummeting in flaming spirals, others limping back into the yawning black rift. What had descended as an unstoppable tide now looked ragged and broken.

"We are not winning this," Voraxia growled, her voice a serrated edge of fury.

Vorathos bared her fangs, abyssal fire curling at the corners of her mouth. Rage burned hot in her chest, but calculation pressed colder still. At last, she dipped her massive head in a single, reluctant nod. "Retreat."

Yet even as she spoke the word, her gaze cut toward the east. Her burning eyes locked on Keisha astride Kimras, hatred coiling within them, sharp and merciless. "Next time," she hissed, every syllable steeped in venom, "I will not leave without her. She will be taken one way or another."

Radiantus hovered in answer, his platinum scales ablaze with silver fire. His voice thundered like a vow carved into the bones of the world itself. "You will not touch her. Not while any of us yet draw breath."

Kimras surged forward at his side, golden radiance igniting in his chest. With a roar that split the firmament, he loosed a jet of searing flame. The torrent arced outward, not at Voraxia or Vorathos, but around Keisha. Fire and light coiled into a radiant halo, a blazing barrier that wrapped his rider in untouchable brilliance.

"She is under my protection," Kimras roared, golden light spilling from his jaws in a storm of defiance. "Any who threaten her will answer to me."

Amara swept up beside him, violet fire shimmering across her scales, her wings cutting the darkness with ruthless grace. Her mental voice rang sharp as steel. "Let them come. I would welcome the chance to remind them what happens when they dare to target one of ours."

Ong rose tall upon her back, dragonlance gleaming in the fractured light. His voice rang like iron driven into stone. "You already failed once. You won't get another chance."

Voraxia's vast wings beat the storm into submission as she turned away. Her snarl dripped venom, a final roar splitting the heavens. "This is not over, Radiantus! We will return!"

From the battlefield's shattered heart, Radiantus ascended, his platinum wings unfurling into the dawn. His body blazed like a second sunrise, a vision of unyielding light. His thunderous vow rolled across Lyra'el: "And we will be waiting. We will drive you from Vacari, for you do not belong here."

Aurelius drew alongside, his vast silver wings scattering the last tatters of shadow. His eyes burned with steady fire, his voice a solemn hymn that rang like a temple bell through the broken skies. "Isp dout pliso nomeno: sjachi shilta ti houpe malrak. Wer visupra geou confn ekess light—and svadrav coi tiric, mobi geou qe thric refuge, tangis persvek wer drasonameko."

(Tell your master this: shadows cannot hide forever. The truth will come to light, and when it does, there will be no refuge, even in the abyss.)

The Draconic challenge reverberated through the air like a tolling star-bell, its echoes lingering even as the storm itself unraveled. Vorathos's colossal wings shivered, and Voraxia's hiss rose in furious denial. Yet neither dared remain.

With a final, echoing shriek, the dark sisters wheeled and vanished into the gaping rift, their broken host scattering after them like ash on the wind.

For a long, breathless moment, silence reigned. The storm had passed.

Lyra'el still trembled, its crystal towers veined with scars of fire and shadow. The air reeked of smoke and char, but the silver dome still held, burning like a promise against the sky. The city had endured.

Radiantus hovered, his vast form haloed in fading brilliance, the weight of his vow lingering in the air. Aurelius glided at his side, silent but watchful, eyes like white moons fixed on the horizon where the rift had closed.

All across the terraces, the people exhaled, their prayers dissolving into sobs and shouts of relief. Yet beneath the chorus of voices, beneath the thunder of retreating wings, Aurelius's words lingered in every heart:

The enemy would return.

And this time, their master's face would not remain hidden.

Radiantus turned at last, his immense wings catching the first true light of dawn. His voice rolled firm and clear, a beacon across the sky. "Return home to Lyra'el."

The war-horns were silent now, their echoes fading into the wounded morning. Yet the spirit of unity still burned—bright, unbroken, defiant. One by one, the defenders wheeled back toward the crystal terraces. The Platinum Dragons drew inward, their shields dimming as their riders lowered them at last. Verdantia and Thalorian descended in a spiral of emerald flame, while Amara and Ong cut through the thinning smoke, violet fire trailing in their wake. High above, Kimras and Keisha lingered a moment longer, golden flame still curling protectively around her like a living vow.

Together, they turned toward the radiant spires of the celestial city. Their wings beat as one, a tide of light returning to Lyra'el battered, scarred, yet unbroken.

Silence fell once more across the realm. But this was not the fragile hush of dawn. It was the silence after a storm, heavy with the breath of the weary, the echo of dragon wings, and the fragile, rising promise of hope.

For now, the battle was ended.

But in every heart, a truth burned bright: it was only the beginning.

Chapter 44
Whispers in the Shadows

Voraxia and Vorathos returned to Flameford beneath the shroud of night. Their vast wings beat the air in ragged strokes, slowed by blood and scarred by the fury of battle. The ruined fortress rose from the mountainside like a crown of jagged teeth, its blackened spires clawing upward into the darkness, shrouded by the eternal fog that draped the land like a funeral veil.

From the fortress's hollow heart, the mysterious figure stirred. They rose from a throne of carved obsidian, their steps unhurried as they glided through the labyrinth of ruined corridors. Shadows bent close, curling about their form like obedient serpents, eager to whisper of the dragons' return. They did not need to see it; they had already felt the sting of defeat echo through the void.

Voraxia landed first. Her claws scraped sparks from the fractured stone, her vast wings folding with a sound like tearing storms. Rivers of faint silver light marred the onyx sheen of her scales, the lingering scar where Gailen's crystal arrow had struck. His name seared her mind like a thorn she could not dislodge. One arrow, one insolent mortal with a dragon at his back, and shame burned hotter than fire in her veins.

Behind her, Vorathos descended. Slower, heavier. Black ichor trailed in smoking rivulets from the wound beneath her front leg, the sear of the dragonlance's magic refusing to fade. She hit the ground with such force the mountain shuddered, her wings folding raggedly as she steadied herself with a guttural snarl.

The figure awaited them, cloaked in shadow, unmoved by the restless wind that prowled the broken hall. Their voice was low, measured, and colder than the stone walls around them. "You are injured. Explain."

Voraxia's breath came sharp, a hiss like steel drawn across bone. "We underestimated them. The elf Keisha is not only alive, but healed. She rode into battle upon Kimras, and her magic burned brighter than before."

The shadows coiling around the figure writhed, dark flame licking up the cavern walls, but still the hooded presence gave no reply.

Vorathos lowered her massive head, her growl rumbling like avalanches in the deep. "It was not just Kimras. We faced Aurelia, the Crystal Dragon. Verdantia, the Emerald. Amara, the Amethyst. None of this was foretold. Their strength was... considerable."

The cavern fell into silence, stretched so taut it seemed ready to shatter. Then, through the choking darkness, another voice stirred, not born of a dragon's throat or stone, but riding on unseen currents of light.

Calm. Radiant. Unyielding.

"Shadows cannot hide forever. The truth will come to light. And when it does, there will be no refuge, even in the abyss."

Aurelius's vow still lingered, echoing across realms. The figure's hooded head lifted, eyes flaring like coals stoked to sudden flame. For the first time, the shadows themselves shivered, recoiling as if scorched.

A growl rolled from the figure's chest, low at first, then swelling until it rattled the cavern stones. "You were meant to destroy Lyra'el. Not return broken and full of excuses."

Voraxia did not bow. She reared her head, hatred seeping from every word. "You called us from the Void, yes—but you withheld the truth. These noble dragons are not as they were. The Celestial's power makes them more than wing and flame."

Vorathos's voice was ground low and jagged, thick with pain. "And their bonds... the elf, and the human with the lance. It is not natural. It should not be possible. Yet together, they were more than we could break."

The figure's eyes flared brighter, burning with a silence that weighed heavier than their words. It was not the retreat that unsettled them most, but the echo of Aurelius's warning gnawing at the edges of the dark.

At last, the shadows stilled. The figure's voice came soft and deadly, a whisper that carried like a command. "Enough. Go to the Cavern of Ash. The time has come for a change that will touch every dark dragon."

The air thickened, and the shadows themselves pulsed with the promise of what was to come.

Voraxia turned, claws screeching against the cracked stone as she lumbered toward the jagged path that tunneled into the mountain's heart. Anticipation burned in her gaze, sharp and venomous. Vorathos followed, limping, her colossal frame dragging shadows with every step. Yet before she entered the passage, she cast one last look back, not with loyalty, but with the smoldering suspicion of a predator gauging its master.

The mysterious figure did not move. They stood in the cavern's center, half-swallowed by living shadow, their cloak untouched by the restless wind that prowled the ruined halls. Eyes glowed like embers in the dark, their silence heavier than stone.

And in that silence, Aurelius's vow lingered still as a spark of light that would not die.

Soon, the shadows would no longer be enough.

Soon, the master's face would be revealed.

The Cavern of Ash swallowed them whole. Its vast hollow chamber yawned from the mountain's heart, its jagged black walls veined with molten fire that bled like open wounds. Every sound echoed the scrape of claws across basalt, the hiss of shadowflame fading, the slow drip of burning stone into pools of smoking ash.

Already, the host had gathered. Shadow and Abyssal dragons coiled among the crags and ledges, their wings tattered, their maws still steaming. The air was thick with the copper sting of blood and the reek of charred stone.

From his perch upon a shattered ridge of volcanic rock, Zylron stirred, his colossal bulk shifting with a grinding groan. Heat shimmered from his crimson scales, staining the cavern in waves of scarlet light. His crimson eyes narrowed, and a rumble of cruel amusement rolled from his chest.

"Oh, how the mighty return," he growled, his voice rough with mockery. "I thought you two were beyond defeat."

Voraxia's snarl cracked like a whip across the chamber, her claws gouging furrows in the stone. Her tattered wings twitched, her onyx scales shivering with fury. She snapped her gaze toward Zylron, venom blazing, her chest swelling as though ready to loose either a retort—or a killing blast.

Before the words could fall from her tongue, the shadows stirred.

The cavern darkened. Black fire along the walls dimmed, recoiling into deeper currents. From the heart of the hollow stepped the mysterious figure, the gloom folding around them like a living mantle. They did not stride, they drifted, their presence heavier than the mountain's weight.

Silence fell like a guillotine. Zylron's laughter choked into stillness. The vast wings of Abyssal and Shadow dragons stiffened, their fury smothered beneath the crushing gravity of that presence. Shadows bowed. Even the air seemed to withhold its breath.

No one spoke. Not even Zylron.

The figure halted at the center of the cavern. Their voice emerged slowly and deliberately, each word dropping like a stone into the silence. "I have been in contact with two more who will join the Dominion, one master of illusions and deceit, the other of thunderous precision, once sworn to the light. Their arrival will shift the balance once more."

From the deeper dark, Nocturna stirred. Her obsidian scales gleamed with a mirror-dark sheen, fractured light sliding across her form like shards of night. Her tail lashed once, a whisper of contempt sharpening her voice. "Who are they?"

"The Mirage Dragon," the figure intoned. "And the Topaz Dragon."

A ripple of unease coursed through the chamber. Vorathos tilted her massive head, voice rasping with disbelief. "Topaz? That is a gem dragon. I thought they bent knee only to the light."

Nocturna's eyes flared like twin void-lanterns. Her head snapped toward the wounded sisters, shadows bristling off her scales in silent accusation. "So am I. Yet not all gem dragons are bound to light. Unlike you, my sisters, I have already left my mark. Aurelia still carries the wound I gave her. You," her voice dripped scorn, "did not even touch Radiantus or his Celestial kin."

Voraxia's wings flared violently, her snarl echoing off the cavern's scorched walls. For a breath, the Cavern of Ash quaked with the threat of civil war, the air vibrating with the promise of unleashed wrath.

Then Glaciera exhaled from her frozen perch, a plume of frost spilling across the heat-hazed air, hissing against molten stone. Her words fell sharp as breaking ice. "Thundria, the Topaz Dragon, once bent the knee to Vuarus and Phoenix. Do you not remember her screams when Aurelia cast her down in the battle for Vacari?"

The reminder rang like a crack through silence. The cavern quieted, every shadowed gaze turning back toward the cloaked figure at its center.

They inclined their hooded head, the hush deepening until even the molten drip seemed to still. Shadows coiled tighter, pulsing as though the void itself awaited judgment.

From his perch of broken basalt, Zylron shattered the silence with a contemptuous snort. Sparks spat from his nostrils, scattering across the ash-strewn floor like falling stars. The cavern rumbled faintly with the weight of his voice. "Where are they to dwell? Flameford can scarcely contain those of us already bound here."

The figure did not flinch. Cloaked in living darkness, they lifted one hand, and the shadows drew tighter, curling around their form as though to shield them from even the question. "That has been accounted for. Your kin will remain in their own domains. Only the Ancients shall linger in Flameford—and only when summoned for council."

Satisfaction gleamed in Zylron's crimson eyes. He arched his neck, exhaling a plume of smoke that rolled along the ceiling in waves of scarlet haze. "Good. I have longed for the volcanic peaks of Fel Thalor. They remember my name in fire."

Across the cavern, Glaciera shifted upon her frozen spire. Frost whispered from her scales, veiling her in ghostly mist. She lifted her head with slow, regal grace, her voice a blade of glacial steel. "Then my kin shall return to the snowbound reaches of Friornak. The frozen spires have waited long enough." Her breath curled into spirals of white, hissing as it kissed the molten stone.

Voraxia let her ragged wings ripple in disdain. "Retreating already, to your precious peaks? That place has always felt like another world."

Glaciera did not spare her a glance. A shard of ice dropped from her jaws, striking the black stone floor and fracturing in a sharp, crystalline crack. "It is no other world," she said, her voice ringing with frozen finality. "Friornak is Vacari's own veil of frost, endless, living, eternal. Unlike your abyss, where shadow stagnates and even ruin rots in silence."

The words fell like winter's weight. Frost spread in jagged veins across the cavern walls, and the air plunged to a biting chill. A ripple of unease moved through the shadowed host, wings folding tighter, dark fire guttering low as the cold gnawed at the stone.

The mysterious figure's voice cut through the silence at last, resonant and iron-bound. "When you are called, you will come. There will be no hesitation. No delay. The age of waiting is ended."

One by one, the dark dragons lowered their heads, the scrape of scale on stone echoing like chains drawn taut. Pride gave way to submission beneath the crushing presence at the cavern's heart. Only Nocturna held her gaze steady. Not in defiance, but in thought, her mirror-dark eyes glinting with secrets she chose not to share. She would watch. And she would remember.

The figure stepped forward, shadows curling higher, their presence pressing against every stone. Their voice rang sharper now, slicing through the cavern's air. "Keisha lives. And her magic burns stronger than before."

Glaciera's head rose, frost steaming from her jaws. Her eyes glimmered with cruel satisfaction, her tone edged in crystalline pride. "Then perhaps I am the one to end her. I nearly froze the elf to death once. If anyone knows how to finish her, it is I."

Vorathos's snarl cut through the chamber, venom dripping from every syllable as she prowled a step closer. "You had your chance and failed. You think your ice alone can break her bond with the Golden One?"

Above, Zylron shifted, crimson eyes flashing. His tail lashed against the stone, sparks scattering like meteors. A mocking laugh coiled in his throat, ready to twist Glaciera's boast into another barb against the sisters—

But the mysterious figure's word struck first.

"Enough."

The command split the cavern like a blade. Shadows erupted from every crevice, writhing up the jagged walls, spilling across the floor in a living tide. They coiled around colossal limbs and talons, cold and merciless, strangling even the dragons' roars into silence.

In that crushing stillness, the Dominion bent its neck beneath the master's will.

"This is not about pride," the figure intoned, their voice a thunderous whisper. "It is about elimination. Keisha lives, and that is a failure borne by all of you. If she appears again, she is to be destroyed. I care not who claims the kill."

A tense silence followed. Zylron's tail froze mid-swing, molten sparks dying on the stone. Glaciera's breath hissed between bared fangs, frost spiraling from her nostrils in restrained fury. Even Nocturna's obsidian eyes narrowed, unreadable yet intent. The rivalries that had filled the cavern only moments before dissolved like smoke, replaced by something darker.

A grim unity settled across the chamber. Heavy as falling ash, suffocating as the shadows that pressed in from every wall, it wrapped the gathered host in a single, terrible purpose. A low chorus of growls rumbled through the hollow, not defiance, but assent. The sound shook the cavern like a vow carved into stone.

The figure's gaze swept the assembly, their words cold and precise. "Lyra moves in Afor, extending the Dominion's reach among the desert kingdoms. Qellaun binds the pirates of Shadowhaven to our cause. The net tightens."

A ripple passed through the gathered dragons, wings shifting uneasily, but none dared voice dissent.

"From this night forward, we strike in shadows," the figure declared. "Skirmishes across Vacari. Let them scatter their strength, chasing ghosts.

Let Kimras, Aurelia, and their allies bleed themselves thin. When the next true battle comes, they will stand divided, and we will break them."

They lifted a hand toward the jagged arch of the cavern. At once, the shadows surged upward, writhing like a vast, living tide.

"Go. Be ready. The next tide rises soon."

One by one, the dark dragons withdrew into the black, their colossal forms swallowed by the abyssal dark. No mocking laughter followed them. No proud defiance lingered.

For the first time since their return, the dark dragons bowed not to pride, but to purpose.

From the heart of Flameford, a single will coiled around them all—

The mysterious figure remained as the last wing vanished into the abyssal dark. The cavern was empty, but for the whisper of shadows, and still they lingered, their eyes burning like coals beneath the hoods. For a moment, silence reigned.

Then the figure turned sharply and strode toward the tower that speared upward from the ruined fortress. Each step echoed like a tolling bell, the shadows surging in agitation around them. At the base of the obsidian stair, they halted, head thrown back, and their voice erupted in a scream that split the dark. The sound was not command this time, but fury raw, unbound, a tempest of wrath that shook loose shards of stone from the cavern walls.

"Keisha yet lives!" the figure roared into the shadows, their voice rising until it broke into a jagged cry. The words reverberated through the abyss, searing with venom. "She defies us, still she dares to endure!" The cloak of darkness lashed out, striking the ground, clawing at the air like a wounded beast. "No matter the cost, no matter who else falls, that elf will die. Even if the Dominion itself must burn, she will fall!"

The oath was not spoken to the dragons, for they had already departed. It was hurled into the abyss, into the waiting silence of the rift. And the abyss answered.

From the void came a whisper, vast and terrible, echoing like fire beneath the sea.

"You will see that she does."

The figure stilled, shadows tightening about them like armor. A slow smile curved beneath the hood, jagged and cold.

"So be it," they murmured, their voice dripping with malice. "The age of light ends. The Dominion shall rise anew."

Outside, the mountain shuddered, and the Cavern of Ash groaned like a living thing. Darkness swelled, rolling outward in a tide that clawed across the horizon. The realm of Vacari lay beneath its spreading shadow, unaware that the true master of the Dominion had spoken and their war had only just begun.

Chapter 45

For Now, It Is Enough

High atop one of Lyra'el's crystalline watchtowers, Kaelorn stood with his staff braced against the carved railing, his gaze fixed on the horizon where night still clung to the sky. His robes stirred in the fading wind as he tracked the last vestiges of shadow retreating into the distance. Far beyond the mountain ridges, Voraxia and Vorathos, bloodied and furious, vanished at last into the dark.

A long breath escaped him, weighted with both weariness and fragile relief. "They are leaving..." he murmured, his voice scarcely louder than the whisper of the dawn breeze.

His hand pressed against the rune-stone embedded in the tower's edge. The ward flared faintly beneath his touch, then resonated with his command. "Lower the shield. The dragons return. The battle is won for now."

Across the mountaintops, a hush swept outward, followed by the deep, resonant hum of the wards unwinding. The dome of silver light encircling Lyra'el quivered, then dissolved. Its translucent threads unraveled into the brightening sky, a final pulse of magic rippling outward like a sigh that washed the valley in light.

The air hung thick with the acrid tang of scorched shadow, but beneath it breathed the sweet, tentative promise of morning.

From the terraces below, horns rang out not the blaring alarm of battle, but the swelling chorus of victory. Relief rippled through the city. Doors opened. Voices rose. The people of Lyra'el emerged from towers and sanctums, from healing halls and fortified caverns. The city exhaled as one.

And then, gilded by the first golden light of dawn, the noble dragons descended. They swept down in radiant arcs, vast wings kindled by dawnfire, their gleaming forms spiraling toward the crystal terraces.

Cheers erupted, echoing against the mountainsides. The sound mingled with cries of joy and the ragged sobs of relief.

Kimras landed first, his golden scales streaked with soot, ember-glow lingering across his chest. Keisha sat steadily astride him, her green eyes searching the crowd not for celebration, but for the measure of loss. Behind them came Amara with Ong, violet fire dimmed yet steady in her wings.

Verdantia descended in a rush of emerald flame, Thalorian poised tall upon her back, the Arborblade glinting faintly at his side. Aurelia followed, crystalline light scattering in her wake, Prince Gailen astride her with the Crystalbow glowing faintly upon his shoulder. Last came Radiantus, gleaming and unbowed, with Tahlira seated firmly behind the silver ridges of his mane.

The moment talons struck sanctum stone, the people surged forward. Applause thundered. Healers rushed in, bowing low before tending to scorched scales and battered wings. Children darted through the crowd, laughter carrying on the morning air as they pressed flowers into outstretched talons. One elven child placed a bloom in Radiantus's claw.

The Platinum Dragon bent low, eyes gleaming with warmth that softened even the hardened sanctum.

From the watchtower, Kaelorn descended. His staff hummed softly, the runes whispering as ash and starlight twined on the breeze. Gratitude swelled in his chest, but unease shadowed it. Even the wards seemed to murmur of what lingered beyond, of peace fragile as spun glass.

One by one, the riders dismounted. Ong reached for Keisha, drawing her into an embrace. She leaned into him, her smile was weary but resolute. Gailen extended his hand to Thalorian, who clasped it firmly, a soldier's nod passing between them.

For this moment, it was enough.

They had held the line. Darkness had been driven back.

But above, the noble dragons raised their gazes to the horizon. Their eyes reflected no triumph, only the weight of knowing. Between their riders, silent glances passed—acknowledgment of the same truth.

This was not the end.

Only a pause.

Only a breath.

And for today, that breath would be honored.

As the first waves of celebration ebbed into softer murmurs and grateful embraces, Prince Gailen and Thalorian stepped aside from the gathering. Their boots struck quiet notes against the polished crystal floor of Lyra'el's inner sanctum, muted beneath the faint hum of magic still clinging to the air.

Nearby, Radiantus conversed with one of the elders, his vast silvered form radiant in the dawn. As the two riders approached, the Platinum Dragon turned, his gaze steady and grave.

Thalorian bowed his head in respect, his green cloak still charred along its edges. "Radiantus. The battle may be done, but we both feel the call of our realms."

Gailen stood at his side, his voice calm but unwavering. "Crystal Vale and the Emerald Woods cannot remain unguarded. The dark dragons may have retreated, but their reach is not ended."

Radiantus regarded them with solemn eyes, dawnlight glinting across his ridged scales. "You are right. Vacari remains a battlefield, even in silence. Thank you for your valor for fighting with honor. Keep your lands vigilant. We will send word if the Dominion stirs again."

"We'll be ready," Thalorian vowed.

"As will I," Gailen added, his hand brushing the Crystalbow at his shoulder, as though renewing a silent oath with its touch.

The two parted from Radiantus and made their final rounds, weaving through the quiet corridors toward the sanctum's edge. There, Kaelorn stood with Valeon, the younger man balancing crates of potions and salves while speaking to a medic about supplies.

Kaelorn glanced up as Thalorian neared. "Heading back to the Emerald Woods?"

Thalorian inclined his head. "Now that the skies are clear. The roots of the forest already stir."

A thoughtful smile tugged at Kaelorn's lips. "Then... may I join you? I must return to Luminara. The fairies must hear of what transpired. And there are matters of light magic awaiting me."

"You are always welcome," Thalorian said warmly, clasping his shoulder. "We depart within the hour."

Kaelorn turned to Valeon, his tone softening. He offered a small, affectionate bow. "Keep your eyes sharp and try not to burn through the potions this time."

Valeon snorted, lifting a hand in mock salute. "Just don't let the fairies weave leaves in your hair again."

Kaelorn's chuckle followed him as he fell into step with Thalorian down the central passage. Outside, Verdantia waited, emerald wings lifting into the morning breeze. Dawnlight shimmered along her scales as she spread them wide; the earth beneath her claws hummed in recognition, the forest calling to the forest.

In moments, she bore them aloft. Their flight arced high, gilded in gold, before angling toward the distant canopy of the Emerald Woods, the living heart of Vacari.

The wind carried them swiftly, their shadows sliding across mountain and cloud alike. Yet beneath the rush of air lingered the memory of darkness, a reminder etched in every beat of wing: though their skies were clear, the Dominion's storm was far from ended.

Gailen lingered behind, his gaze still anchored to the horizon. His departure would come soon—but not yet.

He walked through the softened light of Lyra'el's courtyard, where celebration had dwindled into quiet farewells. There, he found Ong and Keisha beside Kimras. The golden Ancient rested with wings half-folded, his eyes half-lidded yet vigilant, molten depths never straying far from his rider.

"I wanted to speak with you before I left," Gailen said as he approached, his voice low but steady. "With the Dominion name rising again... I know that must weigh heavily on you both."

Keisha's gaze flicked toward Ong, then back to Gailen. She stepped forward, her eyes calm yet unyielding. "The name is something I hoped never to hear again. But it no longer frightens me. They did their worst years ago. And in doing so, they taught me something they never intended."

Her chin lifted, her voice clear. "That I was never truly alone."

Ong's arm slipped around her shoulders, drawing her close. His expression remained guarded, but the warmth of the gesture spoke louder than words.

For a moment, Gailen's breath caught. Then he spoke softly, almost reverently. "You're my sister, Keisha. And they will never break that."

Her eyes softened, a quiet smile curving her lips. She gave him a slight nod and leaned into Ong's embrace, her head resting lightly against his shoulder.

Resolve sharpened in Gailen's eyes. "Then it's clear they've underestimated the wrong people."

He drew a steady breath. "I must return to Crystal Vale. The dragons there already sense the power shift. I need to be sure they remain safe."

Ong clasped his shoulder firmly. "Tell our father I'm well. And if you need anything... call."

"I will," Gailen replied with a faint smile. His gaze shifted toward Valeon, who stood beneath a crystal arch, arms full of supplies being stowed away.

"Leaving so soon?" Valeon asked as he stepped forward.

"Time to return home," Gailen answered.

Without a word, Valeon reached into his satchel and pressed a small silver vial into Gailen's hand.

Gailen raised a brow. "A farewell gift?"

"A potion I brewed," Valeon said, his mouth quirking. "Don't worry—you won't turn into a fairy."

A chuckle escaped Gailen. "A pity. I hear they have better fortune in battle."

Valeon smirked, though his tone softened. "Perhaps. But Lyra'el needs healers. For now, I'll remain. Besides... when I come to Crystal Vale, it will be on a dragon's back. Traveling the skies is safer these days."

This time, Gailen's laughter came freer, the weight in his chest easing. "You've changed."

"So have we all," Valeon answered quietly.

With a final nod, Gailen turned toward Aurelia waiting at the sanctum's edge. Her crystalline hide shimmered with living light as she extended one vast wing in invitation.

He mounted the Crystalbow resting against his back. Before she leapt skyward, he glanced once more at those gathered below: Ong and Keisha side by side, Valeon beneath the archway, and Kimras watching with steady, molten eyes.

Then Aurelia sprang aloft, wings carving through the morning mist. Sunlight fractured across her crystalline scales as she bore them upward, carrying Gailen homeward toward Crystal Vale, and the battles yet to come.

Kimras stretched his vast wings in a slow, deliberate sweep, golden light rippling across their ember-streaked span. His gaze lowered to Keisha, warm and unwavering. "We'll return to Goldmoor for now. Amara will take wing for Purplefire Woods. But the two of you..." His voice softened, rumbling with quiet care. "Should return home to E'vahona for a time. Rest. And perhaps check on Pumpkin. I suspect she will not be pleased to have been left behind again."

Keisha laughed, the sound breaking through the weight that had pressed on her chest since the battle. A memory surfaced. Pumpkin perched indignantly atop the crystal roof of E'vahona, tail lashing, eyes narrowed in feline accusation, the last time they dared to leave her behind.

"You're probably right."

She stepped forward, arms encircling Kimras's neck. Her cheek pressed against his warm scales, the steady hum of his golden fire vibrating beneath her palms. For a heartbeat, neither spoke. They didn't need to. He had felt her pain in the fight, the sharp echo of her wound lancing through his chest, and she knew he still carried that fear within him. Their silence was not emptiness, but communion, a bond stronger than oath or vow.

"See you soon, my friend," she whispered, her voice tender, more promise than parting.

Kimras rumbled deep in his chest, a resonance of reassurance and farewell. His golden eyes lingered on her, fierce with the same unyielding protectiveness that had once driven him to roar into Voraxia's face: Do not threaten my dragonrider.

Beside him, Amara curved her sleek amethyst neck toward Ong, violet eyes alight with sly amusement. "Stay out of trouble," she teased, her voice smooth as silk, "and try to keep your feet on the ground for once. Though I suspect even gravity has surrendered to you."

Ong smirked, shaking his head. "No promises."

"Mm." Amara's purr rolled like distant thunder. "Keisha, do keep him alive. He grows reckless when he believes no one is watching."

Ong gave a low chuckle, not bothering to deny it.

With a final shared nod, the two noble dragons unfurled their wings. Sunlight caught on amethyst and gold as they rose together, climbing high into the brightening sky. Their roars rang out once, not as a challenge, but as a farewell before they veered apart: one toward Goldmoor, the other toward Purplefire Woods. Their part in this battle was fulfilled.

In their absence, silence draped itself once more across Lyra'el, a fragile peace settling over the crystal city like morning mist.

Lord Karrenen approached, his robes whispering against the crystal floor. He paused, expression shadowed by thought, as though weighing his words before letting them fall.

"One thing before we go," he said at last, his tone carrying quiet urgency. His gaze lifted to Radiantus. "The Sylvan Elves of the Ivory Moonbeams sent word that Qellaun passed through their woods not long ago. They could not mark his destination, but his presence that far north... it bears watching."

A ripple of unease stirred among those who heard the name.

Radiantus's diamond-like silver eyes narrowed, dawnlight striking them like tempered steel. His voice remained calm, but iron threaded every syllable. "He travels with caution, but not without purpose. I will have our scouts remain vigilant. If he moves again... I will know."

The words lingered sharp as drawn blades before silence reclaimed the sanctum.

Lord Karrenen gave a slight nod, his thoughts already shifting toward the next duty. Yet before he turned away, his hand slipped into the folds of his cloak.

From the shadows of the fabric, a narrow, curious face emerged.

A fox, its fur pale copper streaked with ember-tones, shimmering faintly as though sparks danced beneath its pelt. Golden eyes blinked up with calm audacity, unafraid even beneath the looming presence of dragons.

"One more thing," Karrenen said, stepping toward Valeon. He carefully set the creature into the young man's arms. "You've earned a measure of mischief. And perhaps... companionship."

Valeon froze, uncertain, staring down at the warm bundle curling against his chest. The fox nosed at the strap of his satchel, its tail brushing lazily along his side as if it had already claimed the place as its own.

"This isn't tradition," Valeon said flatly. Yet even as the words left him, his fingers tightened protectively around the animal, the instinct undeniable. Beneath his sarcasm stirred something quieter, an ember of comfort he had not expected.

Karrenen raised a brow, dry amusement flickering in his gaze. "It is now."

Keisha laughed, her eyes alight. "A fox? Really?"

Ong folded his arms, his voice as steady as stone. "We've had panthers, wolves, and hawks. Why not a fox? It suits him."

The fox licked Valeon's thumb, then gave a decisive thump of its tail against his ribs—as though sealing the claim.

"I'm not naming you," Valeon muttered.

Thump.

Keisha grinned, delighted. "Oh, you will."

Ong smirked, his voice dry with certainty. "And when you do, we'll all pretend to be surprised."

Valeon scowled, though the faintest twitch of a smile betrayed him.

Karrenen turned last to Ong and Keisha, his robes rippling faintly with the fading hum of protective wards. His gaze lingered on them, measuring not only their strength but the weariness etched beneath it.

"Are you ready to return?" he asked softly.

They nodded in unison.

Karrenen lifted his staff. Light whispered into being, threads unfurling like silver leaves caught in an unseen breeze. In the span of a heartbeat, the sanctum of Lyra'el dissolved into radiance—then gave way to the tranquil embrace of E'vahona.

Home.

The air was gentler here, cool and fragrant with the scent of blossoms. The murmur of hidden streams threaded through the underbrush, and shafts of sunlight dappled the crystal paths, dancing across the ground in shifting beams. Birds sang faintly from the canopy, and branches swayed as though bowing in greeting.

Ong exhaled slowly, his hand brushing against Keisha's. She leaned into him, her steps easing as her gaze softened at the sight of their sanctuary rising between the trees.

For now, the fighting has ended. The shadows had been pushed back but not destroyed. Darkness still stirred beyond the horizon, plotting in silence.

Yet here, within this breath of peace, Ong and Keisha stood side by side, not bound by battle, but by belonging.

For this fleeting moment, there was rest.

And they would hold to it.

Before the storm returned.

Radiantus stood at the terrace's edge, his vast form outlined against the golden glow of morning. Below, Lyra'el breathed in fragile peace. The cheers had dwindled to murmurs, healers moved with quiet urgency, and families clung to one another amidst the softened hum of recovery. Yet beyond the horizon, the air remained heavy, thick with storms not yet broken.

Tahlira approached with measured steps, her armor scuffed and streaked from battle. Her stance held firm, though her eyes betrayed hesitation. She lingered at his side, uncertain what words the great Platinum would speak.

Radiantus lowered his head until his silver gaze met hers. His voice rumbled deep, carrying both warmth and gravity. "You fought bravely, Tahlira. You did well as my rider."

Her shoulders straightened, pride flickering in her weary eyes. But his gaze sharpened, tempered steel beneath the praise. "The truth is... You need more training. All of you do. This battle was but the beginning. The next will demand more than valor alone."

Tahlira swallowed, her pride steadied by the weight of his warning. She bowed her head, one hand brushing against his gleaming scales. "I'll train. I'll rise to whatever you ask. I remembered what you told me when the shadows closed in: you said to hold fast. I did. And I will again."

A low rumble of approval rolled from his chest. Radiantus extended one vast wing, curving it around her like a vow. "Then we are bound—not only by circumstance, but by choice."

Her eyes lifted, steady now. "Then I am yours. Until the end."

As she turned to adjust the saddle, her hand brushed something she had not noticed before. Tucked into the leather straps was a length of ribbon, woven in deep amethyst purple. She drew it out slowly, realization dawning.

Keisha's gift.

Tahlira's breath caught. Her fingers curled gently around the ribbon as if it were more fragile than glass. With careful hands, she tied it into her braid, the amethyst gleam catching the light of dawn.

Radiantus's gaze softened, pride warming his tone. "A rider's welcome," he murmured. "You are no longer alone, Tahlira. You stand among them now."

And for the first time, she allowed herself a smile unshadowed by doubt, simple, bright, and wholly her own.

Radiantus's gaze lingered on the amethyst ribbon glinting in her braid, pride warming the silver of his eyes. Then his attention shifted toward the courtyard below, where Valeon stood with the copper fox curled stubbornly in his arms.

"There is one more matter," Radiantus rumbled, his tone dipping into dry amusement. "I have yet to introduce you properly to another of Lyra'el's defenders. Do you remember the one I spoke of—the young man who tends to blow things up even without a weapon in hand?"

Tahlira blinked, then followed his gaze downward. Valeon was attempting to coax the fox into his satchel, only for the creature to wriggle free and thump its tail against his ribs in triumph. Her lips quirked despite herself.

"That... would be him?" she asked carefully.

Radiantus's chest vibrated with a low chuckle. "Indeed. Valeon. He has grown since the last time we spoke of him. Perhaps not in restraint, but in heart. And it is time you met him."

He lowered his wing, signaling her to follow. Together, they descended toward the courtyard where Valeon wrestled with the fox's stubborn antics. The creature wriggled in his arms, thumping his tail against his ribs in decisive victory as Valeon muttered under his breath.

Radiantus's voice carried a thread of dry amusement. "Tahlira, this is Valeon, alchemist, healer, and, on occasion, a walking explosion. Valeon, this is Tahlira, my chosen rider."

Valeon glanced up, cheeks flushing faintly as the fox shifted in his grasp. "Walking explosion? That's generous." Still, he inclined his head with polite respect. "An honor."

Tahlira straightened, her braid gleaming with Keisha's ribbon. "The honor is mine. Any who stands with Lyra'el earns my respect."

The fox gave another decisive thump of its tail, as though seconding the introduction. For a moment, laughter softened the weight of battle, binding rider, dragon, and ally in a fragile yet growing unity.

Radiantus turned outward once more, his vast wings shifting as his gaze swept across the crystalline towers and shining walkways of Lyra'el. The city glimmered in dawn's embrace, but its radiance felt fragile—like a flame cupped against the wind.

Across the sanctum, Aurelius stood tall, starlight shimmering faintly along his argent scales. For a long moment, silence bridged the distance between them. Their eyes met silver and celestial, and in that exchange lay more than acknowledgment.

It was a vow.

A vow that the shadows would not remain hidden forever.

That the Dominion's master, cloaked and nameless, would be revealed.

That truth would blaze where deception reigned.

Both dragons inclined their heads, the gesture heavy with unity and unspoken strategy.

This was not peace.

This was preparation.

And when the darkness rose again, Lyra'el would not stand alone.

They would rise together.

Epilogue
A Queen's Purr

The air in E'vahona was warm with the scent of wildflowers and distant rain. Evening draped the trees in a silver glow, each leaf shimmering as though the forest itself welcomed its guardians home.

Keisha stepped onto the elevated crystal bridge, its surface gleaming like diamonds suspended above the forest floor. Light fractured beneath her feet as Ong walked at her side. She had barely drawn a second breath of peace when a low growl rolled from the shadows near their cottage.

"I told you she'd be waiting," Ong muttered.

From an arching limb above, two green eyes appeared fiery, unblinking.

Pumpkin, the black panther who had once defied dragons, emerged from the shadows. She radiated an offended majesty, her sleek form coiled in silent accusation. Muscles rippled beneath her midnight fur, her tail lashing once in judgment. She did not pounce. She did not purr. She turned, sat, and very deliberately faced away from them.

"Pumpkin..." Keisha stepped closer, voice soft, uncertain.

The tail flicked. Once. Twice.

"She's ignoring you," Ong observed dryly. "That's worse than roaring."

"I know." Keisha sighed, her shoulders slumping. "She's very dramatic."

"She's your companion," Ong reminded her.

Keisha arched a brow. "Our companion. You say that every time she steals your side of the fire."

"Traitor," Ong grunted.

Smiling faintly, Keisha knelt and unbuckled the pouch at her belt. She drew out a small bundle wrapped in silk and held it forward. "I brought you something from Lyra'el. Enchanted deer jerky. Blessed in the light."

Pumpkin's ears twitched. Slowly, with regal disdain, she turned her head. A pause. A flick of her tail. Then she padded down from the limb, moving with silent grace. With theatrical reluctance, she accepted the jerky, crunching it once before pressing her great head against Keisha's shoulder. A low, rumbling purr vibrated through her chest, a mix of forgiveness and reproach.

Keisha buried her face in the familiar fur, her eyes closing. "I missed you, too."

Pumpkin's green gaze slid toward Ong, offering him a pointed, almost smug glance before she settled firmly between them, curling her tail like a warding line.

Ong exhaled in defeat. "We've been replaced."

Keisha laughed, the sound soft but genuine. "No. We've been forgiven. For now."

As the first stars bloomed above the forest canopy, the three of them sat together on the glowing path before their home guardian, healer, and the black-furred shadow who would never again be left behind.

Ong lifted his gaze to the heavens, then down the winding path that vanished into the trees. His voice was quiet, but sure.

"Peace never lasts long. But that won't stop us from savoring it."

Far beyond the tranquil glade, in the hidden reaches where the Dominion's grip still lingered, the darkness stirred anew, waiting for its hour to strike.

DRAGONS OF VACARI

Battlecraft of Vacari
Celestial Convergence Edition

Battlecraft of Vacari

A record of the legendary weapons, gear, and craftsmanship that shaped the Dragon Wars and the rise of the alliance.

Note: A full expanded archive with detailed histories and craftsmanship notes is available on the author's official website.

Characters of Vacari

Key Figures

- Keisha (Eladrin) – Courageous adventurer with elemental magic, skilled in archery, bonded with Kimras, the Gold Dragon.

- Lord Karrenen (Eladrin) – Master of magic with unmatched arcane command.

- Thalorian (Moon Elf) – Skilled warrior and rider of Verdantia, deeply connected to nature.

- Kaelorn (Luminara) – Leader dedicated to harmony within the Emerald Woods.

- Qellaun Dreadcrusher (Druchii) – Fearsome warrior, once in service to Phoenix and Vuarus.

- Lyra Dreadcrusher (Druchii) – Cunning sorceress, formerly allied with Phoenix and Vuarus.

- Ong Swifthammer (Human) – Loyal warrior, married to Keisha, bonded with Amara, the Amethyst Dragon.

- King Manard (Human) – King of Crystal Vale.

- Gailen (Human) – Prince of Crystal Vale, bonded with Aurelia, the Crystal Dragon.

- King Alex (Human) – Noble ruler of Goldmoor.

- Queen Jeanne (Human) – Queen of Goldmoor.

- Tahlira (Human) – Rider of Radiantus, the Platinum Dragon.

- Valeon (Human) – Young man seeking his place in Vacari.

- Rhys (Umbral Elf) – Shadow mage of the Umbral Order, motives concealed.

- Maldrak – Exiled ruler of Shadowhaven, under Dominion's sway.

Noble Dragons

- Kimras (Gold Dragon) – Regal leader of wisdom and benevolence.

- Aurelia (Crystal Dragon) – Ethereal, bearer of ancient knowledge.

- Verdantia (Emerald Dragon) – Guardian tied to nature's vitality.

- Amara (Amethyst Dragon) – Spiritual and powerful.

- Radiantus (Platinum Dragon) – Brilliant, embodying radiant power.

- Aurelius (Celestial Dragon) – Ancient dragon of mercy and light.

Dark Dragons

- Zylron (Red Dragon) – Treacherous, embodying fire's fury.

- Glaciera (White Dragon) – Ruthless, embodiment of winter's cruelty.

- Xalzorath (Black Dragon) – Cunning and merciless.

- Nocturna (Obsidian Dragon) – Cold and unbreakable.

- Voraxia (Shadow Dragon) – Shadowed Empress of darkness.

- Vorathos (Abyssal Dragon) – Abyss-born terror.

Divine and Significant Beings

- Aeliana – Guardian of Ardinia.

- Lysander – God of the Sea.

- Kadona – Goddess of Light, Protector of the Eladrin.

- Mysterious Person – Enigmatic power within the dark divine realm.

Companions

- Pumpkin (Panther) – Mischievous and loyal to Keisha.

- Casper (Cougar) – Protector of Queen Jeanne.

- Thump (Fox) – Valeon's companion, a gift from Lord Karrenen.

Dragon Rider Academies

Following the first alliance victories, dragon rider training expanded from individual mentorships to formal academies across Vacari. These institutions teach the core skills all riders require—flight coordination, aerial recovery, mounted combat, and bond strengthening—while also offering specialized instruction for unique weapons or advanced techniques.

Some methods, such as Standing Combat, are taught only to riders whose gear or fighting style demands it. As the alliance continues to innovate, new weapons and tactics, such as the Lightforged Shields, are integrated into the academies' training programs.

DRAGONS OF ACARI

Eladrin Physiology & Traits

Eladrin Ocular Luminescence:

Eladrin possess eyes that reflect the strength and balance of their life-essence. In times of illness, poisoning, magical disruption, or grave injury, the natural brilliance of their eye color fades — sometimes to a pale or washed-out hue. As vitality and essence are restored, the true color returns, often shining brighter in moments of heightened emotion or awakened power.

Dragons of Vacari

Eyes of Vacari: Unique Colors & Meanings

A record of the distinctive eye colors among the people and dragons of Vacari, acknowledging their heritage, magic, or other unique traits.

• Thalorian — Jade-Fire eyes; a rare emerald brilliance with inner flame, reflecting his fierce connection to nature and the living energy of the forest.

• Kaelorn — Glade-Fire eyes; a vibrant hue of green kindled with golden sparks, echoing the life and light of Vacari's sacred glades.

• Nocturna (Dragon) — Silver eyes streaked with violet; an uncommon fusion of wisdom and shadow magic, hinting at deep, ancient powers and a storm of internal conflict.

• Radiantus (Dragon) — Diamond-Silver eyes; a radiant gleam like cut crystal catching the sun, embodying purity, healing light, and the unyielding clarity of celestial grace.

• Aurelius (Celestial Dragon) — Luminous White eyes; a serene radiance, aglow with timeless wisdom and celestial harmony, reflecting the guiding light of the heavens.

• Voraxia (Shadow Dragon) — Silver-White eyes; a spectral gleam that pierces the dark, embodying veiled power and the cold silence of shadow.

• Vorathos (Abyssal Dragon) — Abyssal-Blue eyes; a haunting glow, fathomless as the void, echoing ancient depths and the consuming hunger of the abyss.

Dragons of Vacari

Forged Gear & Equipment

A chronicle of exceptional craftsmanship, forged to endure the trials of war and the bond between rider and dragon.

Bonded Dragon Rider Armor — Crafted of reinforced, enchanted leather and woven with stardust enchantments by the fairies of Vacari. This armor not only protects but deepens the bond between rider and dragon, shifting its hue to reflect the dragon's colors. It is form-fitting, seamlessly adapting to the rider's body for agility in battle. Each piece bears ancient engravings telling the tales of past warriors, etched with reverence. Gloves crafted to match, finely enchanted for both protection and flexibility. *Note: This armor is not a skirt. It is built for real combat.*

Eladrin Dragon Saddles — Masterworks of Eladrin artistry, these saddles are forged from high-quality, supple materials and woven with magical runes to secure the rider through even the most evasive aerial maneuvers. They enhance the bond between rider and dragon, infusing comfort and control into long flights and battles alike.

Lightforged Shields (Platinum Riders) — Hidden within Lyra'el for centuries, these radiant shields were revealed only when the Celestial Realm itself faced imminent peril. Forged of celestial alloys veined with starlight, they resonate with the purity of intent, creating a barrier that extends around both rider and dragon. In battle, they reflect and weaken dark magic, strengthening the unity of those who wield them. Though each shield adapts to the rider it bonds with, they all share the same unyielding purpose: to stand as Vacari's last defense when light is most endangered.

Dragons of Vacari

Herbal Origins Index

This document lists the primary regions across the realms and bordering worlds where notable herbs can be found.

Afor (Veiled Desert Realm within Vacari)

Afor lies beyond the Emberwoods, hidden beneath sands and sealed pathways. Its scorching winds and forgotten paths harbor potent, volatile herbs—used by survivors, smugglers, and shadow-walkers alike.

• Scorchroot Bulb – A pungent, fire-veined root used in tonics to boost stamina and prevent dehydration.

• Dustpetal Bloom – Pale golden flowers that ease fever and cleanse mild toxins when steeped into tea.

• Cindermoss – Grows under rocks in volcanic sand. Used in burn salves and heat warding charms.

• Ashthorn Needle – A sharp, wiry herb that causes swelling and painful numbness if ingested raw; sometimes weaponized in darts.

• Serpentblight Resin – A thick, sticky sap from desert thorns. Ingested in small doses, it causes violent cramps and hallucinations. Used by assassins and desert smugglers.

Cerulean Expanse

The water-drenched region of tide kingdoms and oceanic mysteries. Herbs here thrive in salt spray, moonlit shores, and abyssal trenches.

• Mistral Coralbud – A soft blue-pink bloom found on drifting reef roots. When dried and steeped, it soothes internal swelling and is used to treat lung infections caused by water inhalation.

• Tidefern Silk – A silver-green aquatic frond used in dream elixirs and scrying rituals. When smoked or brewed under a full moon, it enhances divination but may cause dizziness on land.

• Abyssfruit Pearl – A translucent, sea-plum fruit that forms in deep pressure trenches. Extremely rare. Eating the flesh strengthens one's magical wards, but too much induces temporary deafness and pressure hallucinations.

• Brineleaf Cluster – Thick, oily leaves with a bitter edge. Used in poultices for sea-creature venom or wounds from jagged coral. Smells like kelp and blood.

• Sirenshade Algae – A bluish-black algae that clings to wrecks. When consumed in teas, it suppresses the voice and weakens magical projection—used by underwater assassins and silence-casters.

• Glimmerkelp – A softly glowing seaweed strand. In daylight it's inert, but under starlight or moonlight, it radiates calm and can be brewed to reduce magical burnout or emotional spikes.

Emberwoods

• Coalshade Vine – A smoky-black creeper that releases choking fumes when burned. Inhaling them causes dizziness and disorientation.

• Feverthorn – A bramble with searing sap. Even light contact causes skin to burn and itch for hours.

• Embermint Leaf – A fiery red herb used in warming tonics. Stimulates blood flow and combats chill.

• Smokeflare Bud – When steeped, its vapor soothes the lungs and aids in breath recovery after smoke inhalation.

• Pyrewine Berry – A rare fruit used in enchanted elixirs. When properly distilled, it can temporarily enhance magical potency or emotional clarity—depending on intent

Emerald Woods

• Lifesap Bloom – A vibrant green flower that grows near healing springs. Its nectar is used in regeneration elixirs and calming balms.

• Verdant Lace – A soft-fronded herb known for its magical balancing effect. Often brewed by Moon Elves to stabilize volatile spells.

• Thorncurl Spindle – A beautiful, spiral herb with fine red thorns. Causes intense itching and confusion if touched bare-handed.

• Greenmire Pollen – Carried on the wind, it causes sleepiness and dreamlike disassociation when inhaled in large doses.

• Everdew Pearlcap – A round, pale mushroom with glittering spots. Considered sacred, it's used in vision quests and divine communion rituals.

Etharyon (Mystic Forest Realm within Vacari)

Veiled in mists and bound by ancient magic, Etharyon lies nestled near the southern coast. Time and memory bend among its enchanted groves, and the flora reflects this strange stillness.

• Starleaf Bloom – A radiant blue flower that enhances mental clarity and is used in spells requiring focus.

• Aethergrass – A shimmering reed that grows near leyline pools, amplifies light-based magic when steeped.

• Silvertuft Vine – Used in healing salves; known to rapidly close shallow wounds.

• Moonlace Root – Crushed and added to tea, calms anxiety and stabilizes magical surges.

• Thornless Celain – A culinary herb with soothing properties, commonly used in restorative broths.

• Duskleaf Fern – Mistaken for Moonlace Root; causes magical dulling and trance-like sleep.

• Frostpetal Bind – A delicate white flower from enchanted springs. Improper brewing leads to emotional detachment and memory fog.

Fel Thalor

• Blackthorn Coil – A parasitic vine with needle-like leaves. When brewed, it causes paranoia, rapid heartbeat, and hallucinations.

• Gravemoss – A lichen found near ancient ruins. Ingesting it dulls the senses and disrupts dream magic.

• Ashlure Root – Powdered and inhaled, it induces false memories and confusion. Used in manipulation rituals.

• Bleeding Shroud Fungus – Emits a red mist when crushed. Prolonged exposure causes coughing fits and magical instability.

• Dusksage – A rare silvery herb that, when properly distilled, soothes nightmares and can be used in protective charms.

• Verdant Hollowcap – A soft green mushroom that calms nerves and is used in truth-serum blends when paired with moonlace.

Friornak (Frostbound Northern Realm of Vacari)

Hidden in Vacari's upper reaches, Friornak's eternal snows and frozen caverns yield herbs of preservation, numbness, and mystical defense against the cold.

• Frostveil Bloom – A delicate blue flower that grows beneath ice-crusted stone. When steeped, it calms nerves and numbs pain. Used in winter survival brews and deep meditation.

• Shiverthorn – A jagged white herb with needle-like leaves. Contact with skin causes numbness and stiffness. Sometimes used in frost-forging rituals or cruel punishment tinctures.

• Icelace Moss – Thin, silver moss that drapes from frostbitten trees. When burned with incense, it slows the heart and mimics death. Used in escape rituals or burial rites.

• Wintersap Root – A thick, pale root that stores warmth. When chewed, it boosts stamina and slows the effects of hypothermia.

• Snowgloom Cap – A dome-shaped fungus that only grows in ice caves. Emits spores that dull emotion and memory. Brewed into forgetfulness draughts.

Ivory Moonbeams

• Dreamwillow Bark – Ground into powder and added to teas. Enhances meditation and dreamwalking rituals. Used by Sylvan seers.

• Mistfern Veil – A rare trailing fern that amplifies healing when burned in moonlight. Used in purification rites.

• Duskgloom Thorn – Barbed plant that releases a vapor causing vertigo and nausea. Exposure is dangerous in closed spaces.

• Twilight Creep – A creeping vine with tiny flowers that induces sluggishness and delayed reaction time when touched or brewed.

• Whispersting Pod – Emits a numbing pollen. Inhaled in large amounts, it disrupts memory and silences internal magical flow.

Lyra'el (Celestial Realm)

• Veinroot Briar – Resembles dark basil. In low doses, it causes joint stiffness and tremors. Dangerous for mages and warriors.

• Glassvine Thorn – Translucent petals that slow blood flow and cause blurred vision. Subtle and disorienting.

• Whispermoss – Found near still ponds. Numbs focus and short-term memory, making concentration difficult.

• Moonblister Pod – Crushed into broths, it causes weakness and fatigue over time.

• Hollowshade Bloom – A fragrant bloom that weakens magical auras and disrupts spellwork without killing.

• Thistledawn Petal – Lovely in tea. Adds floral sweetness. Very gentle. Heals minor inflammation, too.

• Glowmint – Cool, soothing. Mix it into wine or cider and it sharpens the taste.

• Ironfern Root – Earthy. Crushed into pastes or broths. Makes thin meals taste rich.

• Sunberry Leaf – Sharp, tangy. Use sparingly. Balances meats or strong oils. Resembles dark basil. In low doses, it causes joint stiffness and tremors. Dangerous for mages and warriors.

Purple Fire Woods

• Blazeblossom – A vibrant crimson flower that blooms under intense heat. Used in energizing tonics and fire resistance brews.

• Flaregrass – Thin, golden blades that shimmer with residual heat. Used in forging rites and warming salves.

• Cinderpetal Balm – A soft orange flower that produces a soothing oil for burns and inflammation.

• Ignistalk Mold – A fungus that grows near smoldering roots. Inhalation of its spores causes intense coughing and temporary vision blur.

• Singeweed – A small, ash-colored herb that burns the throat when consumed. Causes dryness and disorientation in even small doses.

Sacred Grove (E'vahona)

• Lunaria Bloom – A shimmering petal used in moon rituals and calming potions. Enhances clarity and emotional balance.

• Heartroot Vine – Brewed into teas for heart healing and emotional grounding; often used by the Eladrin in rites of restoration.

• Silverdew Moss – Grows on ancient stones. Used in salves for magical burns or overstressed channels.

• Wyrdfern – A rare fern with spiritual properties; heightens sensitivity to divine presence and truth-speaking.

• Gloamshade Berry – Small, dark berries with a sweet taste. In large doses, they can slow the heart rate and dull magical senses.

• Twilight Fangleaf – A lovely lilac leaf that causes vivid hallucinations and confusion when smoked or brewed.

Shadowhaven — Alchemy, Smuggling, and the Unregulated Trade "Not all herbs are grown. Some are... acquired."

Black Market Blends of Shadowhaven (Codex Add-on)

In Shadowhaven, nothing grows—but everything can be bought, brewed, or stolen. The herbs here aren't listed in any archive. They're whispered about in dark corners, traded in iron flasks, and tested on rivals.

• Siren's Poison – A deep blue extract distilled from stolen Coralunan kelp and smokeleaf. Causes vivid hallucinations and temporary infatuation with the nearest voice. Used by pirates for interrogations... or seduction.

• Wakevine Spoor – A powdered stimulant mixed with ground bone ash and duskleaf. Keeps users awake for three days—at the cost of crashing into vivid nightmares and nerve tremors.

• Tideburn Draught – A volatile tonic made from fermented sea-bramble and stormroot shavings. Said to numb all pain and stoke berserker rage. Illegal in most ports.

• Moonblind Ink – A diluted blend used in tattoos and binding contracts. Glows under moonlight but causes paranoia and blurred memory over time. Origin unknown—possibly Etharyon-tainted.

• Gutterroot Balm – A greasy salve scraped from alley molds and burnt herbs. Stops bleeding, but leaves a permanent discoloration and sometimes... extra sensitivity to shadow magic.

Twilight Grove

• Nightcoil Stem – A slick, dark vine that seeps paralytic oils when split. Even brief exposure can numb limbs for hours.

• Emberblight Spore – A fungus that glows faintly orange. Inhalation causes burning lungs and fevered hallucinations.

• Shivershade Root – A chilled, fibrous root that induces involuntary tremors when brewed incorrectly.

• Moonveil Nectar – A soft-scented flower whose nectar soothes emotional distress and helps restore mental clarity.

• Gleamsprig – A twilight-pale herb that heightens magical sensitivity and sharpens vision in the dark.

City-Based Exceptions

While many regions are represented in the Herbal Origins Index, cities like Crystal Vale and Goldmoor are not included. These are located within the world of Vacari, and their herbal practices rely on surrounding forests like the Emerald Woods and Purple Fire Woods. Herbalists here focus on refinement, enchantment, and ritual preparation rather than direct harvesting.

Fel Thalor Exception

Though part of Vacari, Fel Thalor possesses a unique volcanic and abyssal terrain, distinct from other fire-aligned regions like the Emberwoods. The herbs found here are shaped by corruption, ancient ruins, or unstable magic, and are therefore included despite its proximity to the gateway to Afor.

DRAGONS OF ACARI

Legendary Weapons

Crystalbow (Gailen) — A relic forged in ages past, imbued with the essence of the first Crystal Dragon. It channels the bond between rider and dragon, manifesting in arrows of living crystal that respond to Gailen's will and Aurelia's presence. In battle, it can momentarily draw upon the power of nearby allied dragons, amplifying its might.

Arborblade (Thalorian) — A blade of emerald light, forged by the Moon Elves and pulsing with a living heartbeat. The Arborblade is both spear and shield, a weapon of balance, drawing upon the natural world and Thalorian's intent to defend life and land alike.

Dragonlance (Ong) — Crafted by Lord Karrenen, the strongest mage of the Eladrin, and blessed by Kadona herself. Ong's personal lance carries enchantments tied to Amara's amethyst energy, creating a powerful link between rider and dragon, and carrying the legacy of unity between Eladrin and Goldmoor.

Eladrin Longbow of Serena (Now Keisha's) — Gifted by Lord Karrenen to Serena, a master archer of the Eladrin. Passed to Keisha, whose rare nature magic awakens the longbow's latent potential, turning it into a living extension of her will and elemental power.

Radiantus's Shield (Talhira) — Forged in secret at the Celestial Dragon's command, this Lightforged relic is unlike any other. Veined with silver fire and alive with his essence, it resonates only with Talhira, chosen to stand at his side in Vacari's darkest hour. When raised, its runes blaze in unison with Radiantus's scales, amplifying his light and binding their strength as one. More than a shield, it is a testament of trust—an unbreakable bond between dragon and rider.

DRAGONS OF ACARI

Locations of Vacari

A categorized index of the known cities, realms, and wild domains of Vacari and its neighboring lands. Some lie open beneath the sun, others remain veiled by enchantment or shadow, and all carry legacies that shape the balance of the world. Expanded histories and travelogues are available on the author's website.

Cities & Realms

Crystal Vale — The shimmering jewel of Vacari, famed for crystalline towers and the union of Ong and Keisha.

Etharyon — Realm of the Moon Elves and dwarves, where forested valleys meet mountain strongholds along the Shimmering Beach. Once thought distant, its halls now open to allies of Vacari, gleaming with moonlit stone and the glow of hidden forges.

Fel Thalor — The Druchii's dark city, scarred by blood rites and abyssal corruption.

Flameford (Old Flameford) — Once Phoenix Shadowwalker's city; now home to dragon lairs and shadowed ruins.

Goldmoor — Vacari's shining capital, blending elven grace with human craftsmanship.

Shadowhaven — Maldrak's haven of exile, a pirate and outlaw city shrouded in twilight.

Forest Realms

Emberwoods — A fiery forest near volcanic lands, tangled in dragon-pixie illusions around Fel Thalor.

Emerald Woods — A verdant passage to Crystal Vale, site of Ong and Keisha's engagement.

Ivory Moonbeams — Mystical home of the Sylvan Elves, glowing beneath moonlight.

Purplefire Woods — Enchanted forest of violet hues, site of Ong and Keisha's wedding.

Twilight Glade — The liminal forest between Ivory Moonbeams and Shadowhaven.

Waters & Coastal Realms

Cerulean Expanse — Vast ocean bordering Vacari, home to secrets and merfolk kingdoms.

Coraluna — Majestic underwater merfolk kingdom ruled by King Oceanous.

Luminaqua — Underwater city of the Aquanar Elves, glowing with coral architecture.

Shimmering Coast — Sunlit shoreline where landfolk and merfolk meet.

Regions & Wilds

Vast landscapes untamed by crown or council, where the land itself can be as perilous as the creatures who claim it.

Firornak — The Frozen Wastes, a land of endless ice and jagged peaks. Caverns echo with the cries of Glaciera, Sanguis, and Nyxathor, their dominion etched into frost and shadow. Few who cross its blizzards return, for the land itself is as merciless as the dragons who dwell there.

Fel Thalor Wastes — Volcanic lands scarred by eruptions, lairs of Zylron and Pyothos.

DRAGONS OF ACARI

Specialized Aerial Techniques

Standing Combat Techniques A rare but vital skill among Vacari's dragonriders, standing combat allows a rider to fight upright on their dragon's back during flight. This is essential for weapons requiring full reach
and leverage, such as the Dragonlance (Ong) and Arborblade (Thalorian). Training begins with balance drills at hover, then advances to
maneuver adaptation and weapon integration.

Not all riders use this technique—some skills and weapons, such as
Keisha's magic and longbow, are best performed from a seated stance. In
these cases, training instead focuses on precision, magical control, and
aerial recovery in the event of a fall.

Due to the risks—loss of harness security, extreme balance demands,
and physical strain—standing combat is used only by the most experi-
enced riders, and only when the battle demands it.

Aerial Recovery All Vacari dragonriders are trained in emergency aerial
recovery, regardless of combat style. This skill prepares riders to survive
an unplanned fall—whether from enemy attack, sudden turbulence, or
evasive maneuvers gone wrong.

Training covers controlled freefall positioning, minimizing spin, protecting vital areas, and timing for magical or dragon-assisted intercep-

tion. Riders learn to maintain mental composure in open sky, as panic is often more dangerous than the fall itself.

Keisha's calm during her fall from Kimras in battle—turning what could have been fatal into a recoverable descent—remains a key example taught in rider academies. In such moments, trust between dragon and rider is paramount, with the dragon adjusting flight and positioning to make the catch.

Teaser

Enchantment of E'vahona

Far beyond the crystal paths of E'vahona and the cloud-kissed towers of Lyra'el, a new shadow stirred.

High above the emerald canopy of the Emberwoods, the sky shimmered not with the gentle warmth of dawn, but with fractured brilliance, bending and breaking as though the heavens themselves had become a mirage. Ixalia, the Mirage Dragon, drifted through the clouds like living glass, her vast translucent wings scattering shards of prismatic light across the night. To gaze upon her was to question sight itself, as though the world could no longer decide where it ended and illusion began.

She slowed above a labyrinth sprawling across the threshold of Fel Thalor, a maze of thorned hedges and spiraled glyphs that pulsed faintly with ancient enchantment. From above, its winding paths shifted and re-formed, folding in on themselves as if the land were alive and breathing.

"A maze..." Ixalia's voice was like crystal splintering, soft yet cutting, carried on a wind that was not there. "Ancient magic. Curious."

Her words scarcely stirred the night. Yet something below heard.

A small winged figure, wreathed in the shimmering glamour of the woodland folk, froze at the sound. The pixie's wings blurred with panic as it darted deeper into the branches, heart pounding with dread it could not name. Raelithar must be told.

Above, Ixalia hovered, her opalescent body bending the starlight into impossible shapes. She lingered, watching, violet eyes unreadable, her presence a riddle wrapped in brilliance.

The labyrinth pulsed again. This time, a tendril of shadow seeped outward through its runes, curling into the night like a beckoning hand.

Ixalia's eyes narrowed, facets flashing with secret fire.

"The barrier weakens," she whispered, voice thin as mist. "And something within remembers the world beyond."

The wind shifted not with weather, but with warning.

Ixalia's wings beat once, scattering a rain of false light.

"Too soon," she murmured, like glass breaking. "But not unprepared."

She melted into the clouds, leaving only a fading shimmer.

And in her absence, silence settled over the Emberwoods, heavy with foreboding.

DRAGONS OF ACARI

Acknowledgements

Jean McEvoy

To my wonderful mother—your red pen and unwavering belief in me will never be forgotten. Thank you for always standing by me.

Caroline Otto

To my best friend from high school, Caroline, thank you for taking the time to read the rough drafts.   Thank you for also being there for me during high school and believing in me now. Her friendship has meant a lot to me. She is more of like a sister.

Steven Thomas

To my dear friend, Steven, who took the time to read early drafts of the chapters. Your friendship and feedback mean the world to me.

Special Acknowledgements to the Fur Babies (whose names are used in the book

Pumpkin

I rescued my little black panther over five years ago, and her playful spirit became the inspiration for Pumpkin in this book.

DRAGONS OF ACARI

About the author

T.A. McEvoy grew up in heels and high fantasy, despite being told girls weren't supposed to love dragons, elves, or galaxies far, far away. She never saw a reason to stop.

Though she avoids camping (unless it involves a bed, a shower, and zero bugs), she's drawn to darker tales of quiet strength, broken heroes, and healing that matters as much as vengeance. In her world of *Vacari*, forests mourn, dragons remember, and love comes in many forms—none of them asking you to change to be worthy.

She writes for readers who never quite fit in, who carry their softness like armor, and who crave fantasy with both heart and teeth.

Her dragons love deeply, but not always romantically.

They are guardians.

And sometimes, they are the only ones who truly understand.

Thank you for reading *Celestial Convergence*.

If you enjoyed the book, I would be immensely grateful if you could take a moment to leave a review where you purchased it. Your feedback is invaluable and helps other readers discover the world of *Vacari*.

— *T.A. McEvoy*

Dragons of Vacari

Also, by T.A. McEvoy

The Elves of Vacari Series:

The Wicked Published 11-01-2023

Shadows Unveiled- Published 12-05-2023.

Vacari's Resurgence: Healing Bonds 04-12-2024

Dragons of Vacari Series:

Rise of the Ancients 12-02-2024

Shadows of Betrayal 04-21-2025

Celestial Convergence 10-20-2025

Enchantment of E'vahona (Coming Soon)

The print editions of my books are produced through Lulu, whose print quality is second to none. For the best experience — and to explore more about each book and series — please visit:

https://www.tamcevoy.com